Wicked Revenge

Heather Beal

A Dark Twisted Fairytale

Book 1

Book Cover by Heather Beal and Runa Nelson
ISBN: 9798879156003
First edition 2024

Table Of Contents

Acknowledgements

To my Editor:
Runa Nelson

The laughs we have shared editing will forever be one of my favorite things about this book. "My balls are his face" will forever be etched in my memories. Tash, from the bottom of my heart, thank you for the HOURS we spent on video calls, all the forms, lists, team management, formatting, and ALL of the hidden little funnies we've found together. I love you and appreciate everything you've done to help me make this book the very best it can be. You're a fucking ROCKSTAR!

Allie & Korinna & NaToysha

Thank you for being my honorary editors and being the last set of eyes on my work. Allie-baby, I know how much you loved 'bloody cherry'. Korinna, only you can appreciate the 'growling' men in this book. NaToysha, you were my comma queen. Y'all are going to be my good fucking girls in book 2, right?

To my very long list of ALPHAS, BETAS, and ARC Readers:

Most of y'all took a chance on a first-time author before you even knew a single thing about this book. I will forever be grateful for the time, energy, and faith you've put into this secret project and in me.

PA's:

Runa N. Nelson, Madison Watson, Kelsey Ford, Savannah Jones, Taielar DeZotell, Amber Rabe, Erin Alford, Kaitlyn Denny

You ladies stepped up when I was just starting this journey and volunteered to help me in whatever way I needed, even when I told you I didn't know what the fuck I was doing. We fucked around and figured it out though! Thank y'all. Words can't express what our daily video calls mean to me. I don't know how I managed to bring together a group of introverted, antisocial ladies, but here we are. I love each of you so much. Thank you for helping me 'people' again, even if it's just on video calls.

Good Girls Book Club:

My Good Girls, thank y'all for following me on this journey and accepting me for who I am. I'm not 'too much' in your eyes. You don't judge me for appreciating masked tattooed stalkers with big 'schlongs'! I'll drive to therapy this week, ladies. Y'all bring the snacks!

My Husband:

Daddy, thank you for supporting me in everything I do. You haven't once complained about how time-consuming this project has been, or the hours I spend on calls with my Good Girls. You've just picked up every bit of the slack, cooking dinner, doing homework with the kids, etc… so I didn't have to stop what I was doing. That means the world to me.

I love you, Daddy. Always and Forever.

Authors Note

This is Book One of a Duet, and it's the first story in a series of interconnected, twisted fairytales. These books are 18+, spicy, very dark, and NOT for the faint of heart. **Proceed with caution. Don't bother wearing any panties!**

Puppy Pads are REQUIRED!

TROPES:

Dark & Twisted Fairytale
Blood Kink
Daddy Kink
Dark Romance
Mask Kink
Primal Kink
Why Choose?

TRIGGERS:

Anxiety
Blood/Gore
Bondage and Restraints
Descriptive Torture
Dominate/Submissive
Drugging
Filicide
Forced Sodomy (Not by MMCs)
Found Family
Gang/Criminal Activities
Hunting
Kidnapping
Knife Play
Mentions of drug use
and addiction
Mentions of Grief, Loss, and Death
Mutilation

Murder
Obsessive
OTT
Possessive
PTSD & Flashbacks
Violence
Rape (In detail, NOT BY MMCs)
Self-Harm
Serial Killer
Sexually open minded MMCs
Somnophilia
Spanking
Stalking
Suicide (Parental)
Switch
Sword Crossing (Within the harem)
Trauma

Dedication

To my mother…

You raised me to chase my wildest dreams. I bet you didn't think it would include masked men with a daddy kink, but here we are...

You were my best friend and my biggest fan. You told me I would write a book one day-- I just hate that you're not here to see it now.

If you're watching me from above, just pretend you didn't read The Playroom scene.

Tonya Nicole Simpson
August 4th, 1969 - February 14th, 2023

You thought you could escape me, Little Wolf?
You bled so beautifully for me the first time,
When I catch you, I will enjoy breaking you all over again.

Your mouth will beg me to stop.
Pleading with me for a reprieve that will never come.
Your tears of despair tasting like desperation on my tongue.
Your blood dripping down my thighs.
Painting the floors of your concrete cage once more.

You can't run forever.
You are mine.
Mine to use.
To break.
To bleed.
I own every inch of your goddamn soul.

Prologue

Red.

Warm blood slicks every inch of my naked skin. The rich, coppery scent invades my senses as red-hot rage floods my mind. I'm trapped here again, inside the familiar nightmare that assaults me when I am feeling out of control.

Blood pools around my bruised knees, flowing freely from the dead man's mutilated body next to me on the cold stone floor, from his gaping throat to his severed cock that now lies at his feet.

Crimson-soaked concrete walls are staring back once more, the splatter making pretty patterns against the grey stone.

Rocking back and forth with my gaze fixed on the wall, I welcome the numbness. After years of captivity, retreating into my mind is how I survive. That and…

No, no, no! Please, God no!

Shoving down the devastation that threatens to drown me, a crack in the doorway draws my attention. I use the bed to leverage myself up off the floor, my feet sliding in the slippery mess I made. That heavy steel door is always shut, locked, and guarded.

After all the years spent being his captive, I thought I knew torment. Abuse. Pain. Hopelessness.

But nothing could have prepared me for the fresh hell he unleashed on me tonight.

I make my way through the destroyed cell, looking around at the carnage that remains. Blood coats almost every surface. In the far-right corner lies the remnants of a small wooden desk. It was a gift from the Monster when he caught me drawing on the concrete floor in my own blood.

It smashed to pieces when I threw it against the stone wall. My artwork is now shredded, the ruined papers scattered around the entire space, painting a blood-soaked portrait of the trauma I've endured in the cell.

"How fitting," I mutter, trekking through the chaos.

Splinters of wood dig into the soles of my feet, but I don't feel the pain as I mindlessly drag myself to the metal door.

Not only did this dumb fuck forget to check his weapons at the door, but he didn't even shut it. The rage that flowed through me when the Monster left must have been distracting to him. That was a mistake this man won't get a chance to make again.

He threw me to the hard floor, pieces of the broken desk cutting into the scarred flesh along my back as he overpowered me. His heavy thighs straddled one of mine, and his meaty hand wrapped around my throat.

I could feel his blade digging into my leg as he struggled to control my thrashing body. I hit and scratched him like a feral animal trying to free myself.

He used his body weight to pin me in place, spreading me open. Fighting only turned him on more. Without another thought, his disgusting dick ripped into me, the force enough to steal the breath from my lungs.

Not again. Never again!

That was the last thing I remember. When I came back to myself, I was rocking on the floor next to this guard's mutilated body. *I killed him...*

Looking back at his bloody corpse and severed cock, I smile sadistically. The emotions feel foreign to me, but I don't question it. Instead, I welcome the darkness in.

The blood drips down my mangled back, and my whole body aches with each movement, but that is nothing new to me. My scars are proof that I'll heal, but he'll never touch me again— never be able to give me new scars.

None of them will.

The Monster stole everything from me, but tonight, he took the one thing that was tethering me to this miserable life. I will end him. I'll bring him to his knees, as I burn his whole kingdom to the ground, and when I do...

I will rise from the ashes as the *Queen.*

My bloody handprints smear across the door as I use every ounce of my strength to open it enough to fit my small figure through. Peeking back through the crack, I look into the corner of the room one last time.

I'm so sorry. I am so fucking sorry.

Chapter 1

The nightmare dissipates and my consciousness slowly slips back in. The sheets stick to my sweat-soaked body as I stretch, shivering as I try to shove the terrible memories down.

Rubbing my hand over my tear-soaked face, I lock everything in my mental box, and pull myself out of bed. Two years have passed since that night, but it still creeps in when I least expect it.

Fuck.

I don't have to analyze this nightmare. I've come to terms with this one over the years. Now? It just pisses me off and fuels my need for revenge. I won't lie… sometimes they still get to me. This particular nightmare doesn't anymore. It reminds me of the power I took back that day.

However, it's the memories from *before* this one– those are still haunting me, like the monster in the dark. They follow me around, reminding me of everything I survived, everything I lost, just waiting for their moment to strike out and swallow me whole. The memories of my entire world before it was taken away from me.

Nope. Not going there today.

Today is too important. I've been training for two years for this day. The day I go back home.

Shadow Forest.

When I escaped, I found sanctuary in White Harbor. A complete stranger took pity on a broken and bruised girl. She gave me a home and a job within her organization, trained me, and gave me a purpose.

Revenge.

Padding across the plush carpet, I grab the clothes I laid out last night off the dresser and head into the bathroom. I can't take everything, just what will fit in my riding bag. I don't need much anyway. The rest I will figure out once I get home.

Home.

My heart aches in my chest at the memories of what I left behind when I ran, and everything I lost. I've spent the better part of these past two years healing– and by healing, I mean shoving my trauma and pain so far down inside me that it might never resurface. Avoidance and redirection have worked so far. Every time a memory threatens to undo me, I go hunting. It helps keep my anxiety at bay.

Once I'm showered and dressed, I sling my bag over my shoulder. I slip out of my room and tiptoe down the hall, trying not to wake anyone. We said our goodbyes last night before bed. I knew how hard it would be to leave if they saw me off.

But of course, I find my friends– *my saviors*– standing in the kitchen, waiting for me.

"You didn't think we would let you slip out of here without seeing you off, did you, Red?" Tears well in my eyes as they surround me.

Snow embraces me in a tight hug first, her three Huntsmen a step behind, bear-hugging and lifting us off the ground.

"I did, actually," my breathless response comes after they set us down, and I can breathe again.

"We're family, Red. Of course, we want to see you off. Are you sure you don't want us to come with you? You don't have to face this alone," Snow says, rubbing her hands up and down my arms, the comforting motion barely felt through my leather jacket sleeves.

"I know. But I have to do this for myself." My voice is strong, but inside, my head is screaming to take her offer. She has been my rock for two years, and I don't want to let her go now. But I need to do this on my own.

She nods her head in understanding, and I know she's remembering when she faced the demons of her past. "I understand that. It wasn't easy letting these guys help me when I needed it. I wanted to do it on my own, too."

She chose a different route than me. She showed mercy when I thought it warranted revenge. I understand her reasoning, but that's not the path I am on. I want my revenge staining my hands red. She's a better person than me though. Our pasts are not the same. She's been through some bad shit too, but our trauma is different.

"Promise me you will call us if you find yourself in trouble," one of her huntsmen asks me as he hands me a shiny new phone. "This is untraceable. Our numbers are already programmed in it. Use it if you need us. Don't you dare get yourself killed, Red."

"I promise," I reply to him as he pulls me in for another hug.

I'm going to miss these guys so much. They have seen me at my worst and helped me put my broken pieces back together. We make our way out the side door to the garage, flipping on the lights to illuminate the massive room. My ride sits the furthest back, next to the entry door.

My tears threaten to spill over while we say our final goodbyes, and I try my best not to let them fall. Today is the day I've been training for. I mount my bike and grab my helmet hanging on the handle.

"I'm going to miss you guys and this place. I'll check in when I can. I promise," I whisper, tucking my flaming red curls inside the helmet before shoving it on my head and popping up the visor.

"You'll always have a home here. Stay safe," Snow says with tears in her eyes as her huntsmen surround her for support. I nod back, not trusting my voice not to break.

This is why I wanted to slip out this morning. I knew it would be so hard to leave my safe haven and my friends this morning. I close the visor back down, concealing the tears that stream down my face.

The last thing I hear before the engine of my bike purrs to life is, "Give 'em hell, Red."

Chapter 2

It's a full day's ride to Shadow Forest from White Harbor. I left early this morning because I wanted to arrive under the cover of night when the town would be asleep. I'm slightly regretting that decision now. I can't find my damn cottage.

I bought it online with a local realtor, and I've only seen pictures. I need the seclusion that this property offers, but I've been driving up and down the road for over an hour trying to find the unmarked entry.

"Fucking hell," I mutter, turning around once more. My ass is numb, and my back aches from riding so long. I should have stopped to stretch my legs more on my way here, but I didn't want to waste any time. Now I'm paying for that negligence.

I want nothing more than to find my new home, shower off the sweat and dust, and crawl into bed. I don't want to do laundry on top of everything else, but at the same time, now I have the freedom to do it if I want.

The power and water have been on for a few days, I'm sure it'll need some cleaning as well since the realtor said it's been vacant for quite a while, but that will have to wait until tomorrow. Later today? Fuck, I don't even know anymore. I'm so exhausted. At least it's furnished, so I have a bed to fall into.

Just as I'm about to give up and find a tree to sleep under tonight, I finally see it. A little trail is hidden behind some thick green brush. There is no mailbox or marker, but this has to be it.

Slowing to a near stop, I navigate my bike through the small opening, carefully trying not to scratch the matte black paint. My headlights cut through the darkness, illuminating a long path. I can't see the house from here, but hopefully, this is it and not someone's private property I'm about to pull into.

The trail is smooth enough, though, from the overgrowth of the forest, I can tell it's actually wider than it appears in its current state. I'll have to take some time to clean this up.

I think I'll leave the entrance as it is. I don't want people noticing a freshly cleared path and coming to investigate.

Up ahead, I can see the trail widens into a yard. My lights briefly reflect off the river running to the left and behind the house before the path curves slightly to the right, revealing a dark cottage.

The porch light is on, at least the realtor was kind enough to turn it on for me. The darkness of the forest prevents me from seeing much detail of the cottage house, but I see enough to know I've finally made it.

There is a shed around back that will be perfect for concealing my bike, but I don't bother with it tonight. I can barely dismount her and walk up the small stoney path to the porch. There is a mailbox on the side of the house next to the door, which is where the realtor said he put the keys. Digging around inside it, I pull them out, quickly unlocking the door and shoving it open.

As soon as I'm inside, I quickly find and claim the first bedroom I see. I don't bother checking out the rest of the house tonight, I'll have a better look tomorrow. My lead-filled legs barely hold me up as I crawl into the bed that smells clean and looks freshly made.

At this point, I'm so fucking exhausted I wouldn't even care if it smells like musty ass. Normally I'd freak out and bleach everything first, but I don't have the mental fortitude to keep my eyes open anymore.

My mind runs with a list of everything I need to do— settling in the house, fixing up the property, and starting phase one of the plan. Honestly, it can all wait until morning.

My body barely has time to get comfortable between the sheets before I'm fast asleep.

***

It's been two weeks since arriving back in Shadow Forest. My cottage, isolated among the dense foliage of the forest, doesn't feel like home, but I also haven't spent much time here past the first week.

I miss my friends in White Harbor. This place is lonely and feels foreign to me. I wish I could stay at Gram's house, but it's not safe.

Grimm River runs through these woods, and my cottage is tucked in beside it. The entire river travels through several towns, including White Harbor. I can see glimpses of the rushing water through the trees, the large stones making small waterfalls as the river flows through.

It felt like I had a piece of home when I was living with Aspen. This cottage has been abandoned for years, but I'm glad I found one secluded that sits beside this river when I returned back to Shadow Forest.

Ronan helped me buy this place online, transferring the money electronically, using a fake name and account so it wouldn't be traced back to me.

I might not know everything that goes on in this town now, but I know the Monster would recognize my name if he looked into it. He owns this town and a newcomer who comes in and buys a house in full, he would definitely look into who it was.

All he'll find now is a shell company that bought a small piece of land in his territory. He won't come looking if he doesn't suspect anyone living out here. At least, that is the hope.

The first thing that stood out to me when looking at purchasing a place back here, other than the secluded location, was the intricate designs on the exterior.

It's charming, almost enchanting, to look at with its matte black paint and intricate beige designs. The steep roof curves high into the trees, with a smaller steeped window on the left side.

The bold, but delicate designs form an arch over the glass front door, even the windows have scrolling patterns decorating them. The craftsmanship and curved woodwork alone must have cost a fortune. I wondered who lived here before and why they abandoned it years ago. When I had Ronan look into the property, it was owned by a company called S. Corp, with no previous owners mentioned.

My body is slightly achy as I roll around and stretch out in this bed. A bit of warmth would be nice right now. It's still dark out so the smoke should be concealed.

Focusing on relighting the fire in my room, I begin sweeping up the ashes, before dumping them into the bucket sitting beside the fireplace to empty outside later. Laying the new logs in the bottom, I add the kindling on top and swipe the matches from the mantel above.

The warm fire crackles and pops as it flickers to life, creating an orange glow emanating around me, the smokey pinewood scent drifting to me as I enter the shower and adjust the water to scalding hot.

Between the steam from my shower and the fire heating my little room, my body begins to relax. The water runs in tiny rivers down my heavy breasts to my smooth pussy. I allow myself to revel in the kill I made last night. He was the third Kingsmen to die at my blade since I've been back.

Just thinking about the red that coated my dagger when I made him smile at me one last time sends a jolt of excitement through me.

Granted, it was a crimson smile that I carved into his throat. I find it fucking ironic that this limp dick motherfucker got off on my screams when he was raping me, and now it's me getting off on how beautifully he screamed for me.

Fuck. My pussy pulses at the memory. I run my hand down my breast and pull at my nipples before finally giving in to the need surging through my body and finding my swollen little clit.

An orgasm before breakfast? Yes, please.

The dark images fill my mind– my latest prey bleeding out from his gaping throat. His severed cock stuffed into his mouth with my mark on his chest. My orgasm rushes to its peak before I can even get started.

My other hand moves lower, circling my entrance before plunging two fingers into myself quickly. My needy cunt clenches around my fingers and the release makes my knees weak. I lean against the shower wall to steady myself, panting hard. My head is light and fuzzy as I come down from the high.

Fucking hell.

Only a few seconds pass before the familiar emotions of shame and guilt start to seep into my mind. They steal the high of my orgasm and leave me feeling like something is wrong with me.

Fundamentally, I know something is broken deep inside of me when killing someone turns me on. I know that. Still, I can't find any fucks to give about it. They did this to me. They broke me beyond repair. I make no apologies for how I chose to rebuild myself from the broken pieces I was left with.

I shove the unwelcome feelings down in the same place where I keep the nightmares of the past, they're a problem for future me. I'll deal with the guilt over my dark desires after I get my revenge. It's not like I can act on them right now.

I can't explain my desires. Just that something inside of me is broken, and sometimes, it consumes me. I'm not normal anymore. *I am the hunter.* I stalk my prey, taunt them, and kill them. I get off on it. I don't think men are ever going to be a part of my future, sexually or otherwise. I wouldn't know how to feel safe with a man in that way. This is just how it's going to be.

***

Mark number four stands with his back to the dumpster behind the Twisted Tavern.

The blonde on her knees cries out as he wraps his hand around her long curls and thrusts into her throat like a madman.

This fucker.

I'd love to slash his throat just before he releases into hers but now is not the time. I have to stick to the plan.

Besides, from what I can tell, this poor girl came out back with him on her own. I doubt she knew what she was getting into, and I highly doubt she will be back for seconds.

So for now, I just watch and wait.

If he wasn't so blinded by his need to get his cock sucked, he might have noticed my presence, hiding in the shadows of this narrow alley. My black hood conceals me though, and my fiery red locks are tucked inside. I don't want them to be seen yet. The unnatural red tone is highly memorable.

I want him to feel as if his every move is being watched. To wonder what is coming for him. It won't be long until every time he opens his eyes, he'll feel mine burrowing beneath his wretched skin.

This part is easy, but it's also time-consuming. Learning the routine of my prey is something that helps me later on, but in moments like this, it annoys me. I never wanted to see his cock again until I detached it from his body, much less when he is using it to exert his power and control over another victim.

I remember being in her position. I remember everything each of the Kingsmen ever did to me. I used it to create my list and determine the order of their deaths, deciding to start with the ones who hurt me least. The worst of them will see the deaths of those before them and know theirs are coming.

Snow and her Huntsmen taught me the art of stalking your prey and fueling their fear before you take their lives. I met Aspen Snow when I first escaped Shadow Forest two years ago.

I didn't know where I was going, but when I stumbled upon her sanctuary in White Harbor, she took one look at my bruised and battered body, riddled with scars, inside and out, and took me in. Snow and her men helped me heal and grieve. When I was ready, she helped me become the hunter.

It wasn't easy, trusting her men at first. The only men I had ever been exposed to were the ones who hurt me daily for three years. I moved through their sanctuary like a timid little mouse at first. My grief was all-consuming, and it took a lot of time and reassurance for me to be comfortable in their presence.

Jasper was the first one to break me out of my shell. He made my first dagger and gave it to me to protect myself. When I was comfortable enough, I asked him to show me how to use it. He taught me all the different creative ways to kill a man. That was the very beginning of my training.

Over time, Ronan taught me how to be confident in myself and stop being a victim. He said if I continued to feel sorry for myself and cower away from potential danger, I would never be able to get my revenge.

He's a big guy, with broad shoulders and bulging muscles. I was terrified of him at first. He worked with me to build my confidence around men who could hurt me, who would use my tiny size to their advantage to overpower me. The day I finally took his big ass down to the mat is a day I will never forget.

Dax was the one to teach me how to go unnoticed. He taught me the art of the hunt, stalking my prey and drawing out their fear before going in for the kill. He also gave me Nightshade, my bike. It is matte black with red accents. He said it had to have my signature red on it, without it standing out too much of course. He taught me to move through a city like a shadow on her.

My heart aches as I remember those first few months with the Huntsman and Aspen. They became my family in every way possible. The *only* family I have left now. They offered to come with me when I came back, but their people needed them there.

The world doesn't just stop being cruel. People suffer every single day like I did. At the hands of men like the Monster. The work Aspen and her men are doing is too important to delay. I promised I would let them know if I needed them, and I will, but I don't think I'll need to.

The Kingsmen will get what's coming to them soon enough. They will pay for their crimes in blood, by my hand, but they will fear for their lives first. They won't see me until I want them to, and I will be the last thing they ever see.

I drag my mind out of the past and back to the man when I hear a slap ring out, quickly followed by a yelp. He is still jackhammering his disgusting, half-soft cock down the blonde's throat. I know he can't get off unless he hurts her. The sick bastard needs to hear her beg him to stop, to claw at him. He needs her to fight. It doesn't take long for him to slap her face enough for her to give him exactly what he wants.

He snatches her head back and slaps her face one more time before grabbing onto his cock and spraying his release all over her face. He drops her to the cold hard ground with a look of disgust on his face as he stuffs his cock back into his pants. I know what's coming next. I guess he hasn't changed at all.

He grabs her by the hair, brings her tear and come-soaked face to his, and spits. It takes everything in me to remain where I am, hidden in the shadows.

"Look at you. You're nothing but a disgusting whore, begging for scraps of attention." His cruel tone is so familiar to me as he sneers at the girl on her knees, spitting in her face again, "Go get yourself cleaned up so the next Kingsman to put you on your knees can at least pretend you're worthy of their time."

He drops his grip on her hair, and she scrambles to her feet and runs down the dark alley, right past me. She couldn't see me even if she was looking right at me, her tear-soaked face passing by me in a blur.

I wait until she disappears before looking back at the Kingsman. He leans against the wall of the tavern, smoking a cigarette with his eyes closed.

He has no idea that the peace of mind he has right now will be his last. He'll feel nothing but fear until I decide his time is up.

He pushes off of the wall before heading back inside Twisted, the door closing behind him. I don't follow. I make my way back towards the road leading out of town. By tomorrow morning, he'll know he's living on borrowed time, and his time is about to run out.

Chapter 3

There is beauty in hunting a predator and making them your prey.

Stalking them until they look over their shoulders for a change. Making them fear their own shadow before they even know who you are.

This world will be a better place with a few less Kingsmen, violating and defiling innocents like it's their goddamn right.

Wicked men like them always think they are the predators, not someone else's prey.

This morning, I made my way to town on Nightshade. I parked her in the shadows of the forest and hid her behind the dense foliage, then walked the short distance into the town square.

Lunchtime around the square means heavy foot traffic, and I don't want to draw attention to myself yet. I stick to the shadows, watching and observing my fourth mark. It seems it's business as usual for him, as though I didn't slaughter three of his Kingsmen in the last few weeks.

I've been here a few hours now, following him around town, watching as he asserts his power to the business owners around town. It seems his role is to collect payments from the locals in exchange for the Kingsmen's protection.

It's a crock of shit.

They only need protection *from* him. Maybe they don't see that now, or they don't think there is another way, but they will soon.

I will show them what it means to be protected. Aspen showed me with her actions what it means to protect your people and the community. I might have been locked away for three years and in hiding for two, but these are my people.

I still remember my best friend Ella and her parents who own the Twisted Tavern. Mr. Henry sold me fresh fruit and homemade jams from his little stand in the town square.

Beatrice and her sons from the hardware store helped Grams and I fix things around the cottage because they knew we didn't have any help.

Jenna, the art teacher at the school, would come over and bring me extra supplies and would take me into the woods to show me how to capture living nature on paper.

So many good people in this town, and they are all under the control of the fucking Monster.

I guess I was just a naive little girl, because before I was taken, I didn't see the danger lurking in Shadow Forest until it was too late.

Grams always told me to carry a weapon on me, but I wish she would have warned me better and explained what was happening in our town. If I knew, I think I could have saved her. I would never have been taken, and I wouldn't be standing in the shadows, watching my mark beat Mr. Henry for not paying his protection debt.

Fighting against the urge to end this wicked motherfucker before his time, I close my eyes for just a few seconds and exhale silently. Just a little more time and it will be over for him. I have to be smart about this. Striking too soon will only lead me back to captivity.

I will *never* go back there.

Tears sting my eyes when I open them back up to see Mr. Henry starting to gather his destroyed fruit from the street with blood dripping down his face.

He was just beaten in broad daylight in the town square, and no one batted an eye or stepped in. I look around at the people on the sidewalks, their gazes cast down while the Kingsman walks past them into Twisted.

They are terrified of him.

That is going to end.

Several people rush over now that the Kingsman is no longer out here, helping Mr. Henry salvage his fruit stand. Beatrice's oldest son comes over and checks his injuries as I make my way into the alley beside the old tavern.

I guess it's time to see my best friend for the first time in five years. She probably won't recognize me, but at least I can check up on her for now.

***

The inside of Twisted Tavern is just as I remember it.

The delicious aroma of baked bread and decadent stew is enough to make my stomach grumble with the subtle reminder that just an apple for breakfast was probably not a good choice. Even if it is my favorite food. I need to get some groceries for the cottage before I starve to death.

The dim lighting works in my favor as I keep to the shadows in the dark hallway leading out to the dining hall. Ella's father, being obsessed with all things noble and knightly, made the place scream 'medieval tavern'.

Not wanting to be noticed by anyone, I slide into the corner booth in the back. Luckily, it's lunchtime, so everyone is paying attention to their meals and hushed conversations.

My seat can't be seen from the main room, but I can see my mark. He sits with his back to me, talking loudly to two other Kingsmen.

Their presence clearly makes everyone in here uncomfortable, but they don't have a fuck to give about it. Luckily, their raised voices work in my favor. Apart from the food, I'm here to gather information.

They speak loudly, with confidence and certainty in thinking no one will stand against them.

I recognize each of these men. I have no idea what their names are; they never told me, so I made up my own.

The one sitting across from my mark– I named him *Whimper Will*. He would hold me down on my stomach, lay on top of me, and just fucking whimper in my ear and pet my hair like he really thought he was showing me affection.

Weird fuck.

The bile rises in my throat just thinking about him calling me his *little girl*. I hope to God he doesn't have a daughter. Sick bastard. I will enjoy every second of his torment regardless but if I learn he has a child, I will peel the skin from his cock with my blade like a goddamn peach.

Sitting right next to him–*Creepy Chris*. He was mostly harmless but still creepy as fuck. He would come into my room while I slept. He never touched me, but I would wake up to him jerking his cock over me, spraying his come on my face. He never spoke, just covered my face in his come and walked back out the door to stand guard.

Creepy motherfucker.

I watch as my childhood friend makes her way over to their table, and I barely contain an audible gasp. Ella is fucking gorgeous.

Her long blonde hair is French braided down the middle of her back, the end of it brushing against her ass as she walks. She wears a full leather outfit consisting of black pants and a matching strapless corset that's cinched up tight, pushing up her breasts and showing off her tiny waist and hips.

A full sleeve of tattoos are on display down her right arm, and I can see more peeking out of her top on her hips and back. She even has a tattoo wrapping around her throat, though she is too far away for me to make out the details… roses, maybe?

She swings her hips wide with attitude as she strolls right next to my mark and slaps him in the back of the head.

Holy fucking shit.

At least someone in this fucking place isn't scared of these men.

"I already told you, if you keep disturbing my customers, I'm going to put my fucking foot so far up your ass you'll taste my goddamn nail polish. Keep it down!" She says with more venom and confidence than I thought she possessed.

"Ella, you know we are just having a good time. Join us, princess," my mark says as he grabs her waist and drags her to his lap.

Before I can even blink once, she has him by the hair and a knife at his throat.

"Don't start with me, shit stain. I'm feeling extra stabby at the moment, and I'd hate to accidentally slit your fucking throat. What would my mother say if I stained her freshly polished floor with your blood?" Ella replies with a bored and unbothered tone.

She slams his face into the wood table top and walks to the next set of customers. Keeping her back to them, she doesn't even bother to spare them another glance as they get up from the table to leave.

"Tip your waitress," she yells at them while clearing the plates from her other customer's table.

Holy fuck.

The balls on her are unbelievable. It makes me wonder why they listen to her. What happened in the last five years that makes her untouchable?

I want to ask her, but I won't. Not yet.

Ella is different than she was before. She is no longer the pretty teenage princess who never spoke an unkind word. She is now a woman with more balls than every man in this place.

Even still, she doesn't need to be dragged into this right now. It's clear she can hold her own, but I am cautious because I don't know how she is associated with them. I think it's best if I leave before she sees me.

Before I can slide my ass from the booth, she starts walking in my direction. Fuck. Maybe she won't see me here in the shadows.

That wishful thinking is dissolved quickly as she saunters right up to my table.

"What can I get for you?" Ella continues looking down at her notepad, without seeing me.

I might as well eat since slipping back out is no longer an option. I am starving.

"I'll just have the Twisted Special," I say, keeping my head down and my eyes hidden beneath my black hood.

She gasps and drops her notepad and pen to the ground.

Her reaction has my head snapping up and when she locks on my eyes, I nearly burst into tears.

She remembers me.

"Rae," she whispers in a shocked tone, and tears immediately fill her eyes.

"Ella." My own tears build at the emotion behind our childhood nicknames as I hold my finger to my lips.

I don't want anyone else to notice me. She immediately understands, looks around, and grabs my hand, pulling me from the booth down the dark hallway, and into the office at the end.

I don't even have time to look around before she crushes me in a squeezing hug.

"I thought you were dead, Rae. You just vanished. When they found Grams in her cottage, we assumed you were dead too. Where the fuck have you been?" Her words are rushed as she sobs.

"El, calm down. I'm okay. Also, I can't breathe," I say to her with very little breath left in my lungs from her crushing hug, "I haven't seen you in five years, Ella. Let me look at you." I grab her arms to push her back enough to see her tear-streaked face, "I've missed you so damn much."

I pull her over to a couch across from the room and take both of her hands in mine. I don't know if I can tell her everything right now. Even though seeing her has cracked my black heart open, I don't know what she is to him or his men. I have to protect myself.

"Ella, why did those Kingsmen listen to you? Why didn't they punish you for threatening them?" I look into her eyes when I ask to see the truth her lips might not say.

Please don't be involved with them.

A smirk forms on her face that reminds me of the badass who just put my mark in his place out in the dining hall. "Twisted is protected by the Shadows."

That is not what I was expecting.

"Who are the Shadows?"

"No one knows, not really. We only know that once their protection has been established, no one goes against it, not even the Kingsmen," she says, sighing as she pulls her legs onto the couch under her before continuing.

"Last year, after my father died, the Kingsmen came in and tried to re-offer us protection for a price. I'm not stupid. I know the deal my father made for them before he knew that the only protection we needed was *from* them.

"My mother was still so stricken with grief over my father, to the point she couldn't function, let alone run the tavern. So it's up to me to run and take care of Twisted now. I promise you that I will protect it till my dying breath.

"The Kingsmen thought they would drag me out in the street to set an example of me when I told them to fuck all the way off. They didn't even get in the first swing before they were laid out on the ground and tied up. Three men wearing solid black were standing there. They said they were the Shadows, and that I was protected by them, and Twisted by extension. Since then, the Kingsmen won't touch me. If they do anything I can't handle on my own, all I have to do is call the Shadows.

"I might have gotten a little cocky in there today, but I don't take kindly to disrupting my business. It's just me now. My mother hasn't been able to come back here since this was Dad's place. So I can't have the Kingsmen scaring off my paying customers," She explains while I sit here and take in all the information she just dumped on me.

"Wow, they sound too good to be true, Ella."

"I know, but that's what happened. Now, enough about me, I need to know what the fuck happened to you." She squeezes my hands tightly in hers.

"I will tell you everything, but not here. Can you meet me after you close at my cottage?"

"Are you staying in Grams's old cottage?"

"No, I bought a place," I get up and walk over to the desk to grab a pen and paper. I am still wary of anyone finding out where I am staying, but this is my best friend. I know I can trust her. I draw her out some directions she should be able to understand and fold it in half. "Make sure you are not followed," I instruct as she stands.

I tuck the paper in her apron pocket before crushing her back into my chest in a hug that hopefully shows her how happy I am to see her again. I release her after a few moments and make my way to the door, before looking back at her frozen in place with tears in her eyes.

"Ella, I promise, I will be there when you come," I try to reassure her fears. The last time I left her here, I disappeared. I get it, she doesn't think she will see me again. "Bring some food with you, I am fucking starving." I smile at her to break the tension before walking out the door.

She doesn't follow me.

It's for the best. It was hard enough to walk away from her now that I've gotten her back. I will see her again. No one is taking me this time. I am the one doing the taking now, and I've got to stick to the plan.

Today wasn't a complete waste. My childhood friend might have made me, but she also gave me some vital information, even if I have more questions. I need to find out more about these Shadows.

Who are they?

Why do the Kingsmen fear them?

But first, my fourth mark needs to learn of his place on my list.

Making my way back out of the alley, I follow the cobblestone path to his house. He will be the fourth Kingsmen to receive my special little calling card, and by tomorrow, he will know exactly what that means.

Chapter 4

As a child, I walked these streets into town and back, exploring the woods as I went. Shadow Forest reminds me of the fairy tales my Grams would read to me.

The darkness that I've experienced now taints my memories like a curse, but it doesn't take away from the beauty of the town.

The sun is starting its descent for the day, washing the sky in deep purples and pink hues. The streets are bare right now, only a few stragglers here and there as I take the path away from my mark's house near the town square that leads to the main road.

Most of the houses around town have that similar whimsical feel that my Grams had. My cottage is similar, even if it appears to have been completely renovated. It has a modern vibe while still having the same feel as hers– but also a certain darkness to it.

It really matches my soul.

I've noticed a few newer builds, and I'm sure there are more deep throughout the forest for the loners like me.

Taking in the houses as I walk down the cobbled path, my boots crunching on the loose stones, I notice there are no children playing in the yards. It's late enough in the day that children are no longer in school, so where are they?

Do they not feel safe here? Knowing the darkness that I endured at the hands of the Monster and his men, I'd imagine that to be the case.

It won't be like this much longer.

I long to see the children of this town exploring the forest, playing in their own yards, walking freely in and out of town like I did growing up. It wasn't always like this.

The years have not been kind to Shadow Forest, and the darkness that shrouds this town can all be traced back to *him*.

The path that leads me to my bike is just up ahead, but I stop and look back into town. The people of this town deserve to live happy, free lives.

They shouldn't have to live in a constant state of fear, wondering who, or what, will come out of the woodwork to torment them into submission. The people deserve to feel the love, joy, and peace that once flowed like a river through the town.

Turning to the hidden path, I take in the forest surrounding the town. I spent so much of my time exploring these woods as a child, my Grams worried I'd decide to move out here and live my days in the trees. This was my happy place.

The smell of the sap as it drips from the tall pines and the fallen logs scattered throughout, make a perfect spot to sit and rest after a long walk, or to sit and draw. I'd spend hours lost in my sketchbook out here.

I need to learn everything I can about how this town runs now. The last time I walked these streets freely, I was a naive child who couldn't see past my own childish ideals. Seeing what I've seen, enduring what I have, I refuse to watch everything become a tumultuous disaster.

When I escaped, I didn't look back, until now.

Hopefully, when Ella comes over tonight, she can give me the intel I need.

The spot where I park Nightshade comes into view. I'm glad this hidden path is even enough that riding her out here isn't too dangerous. She isn't really meant for off-road, but I'll make do until I can freely drive in and out of town. Uncovering my bike, I smile to myself.

When Dax gave her to me, I was so intimidated. My confidence in myself was so low. Learning to master this bike gave it back to me. I became a completely different person when I let go of the fear holding me back. Riding her makes me feel *free*.

After I pull away the dense green brush covering her, I put my helmet on and roll her out into the pathway. Mounting her, I revel in the rush I feel. There is nothing else that compares to the feeling.

The smooth rumble of the engine vibrates between my thighs, sending that familiar thrill through my veins and washing over me like a comforting breeze.

The ride is kind of long, about five miles out of town, but it suits my needs. This far into the woods, I don't have to worry about the small roar she gives when I take off down the path to my new cottage.

It's quieter than most bikes; Dax modified it for me to keep me concealed while I'm hunting.

The sun has set a little deeper by the time my cottage comes into view, the tree's thinning only slightly around it, but still it's surrounded on all three sides by the forest, with the rocky river bank on the left side.

The ambiance of it looks like someone took a fairytale cottage straight out of a storybook and dumped it in the middle of the forest.

After pulling around to the shed and locking my bike up, I grab enough firewood from beside the shed to keep warm tonight before making my way inside the house. I'll have to chop some more soon.

Winter isn't here yet, but the nights still get pretty cold here in the fall.

***

The warmth of the fire from my room has trickled throughout my small cottage as I sit at the table in the kitchen, looking over my files on the town's criminal organization.

It's getting close to two in the morning; Ella should be closing up Twisted pretty soon.

I've decided that even though I don't know her now, she was my best friend for eighteen years, and I need an ally in this town if I'm going to tear the corruption out from the root. I trust her, and I can't really explain where I've been all these years without telling her everything that happened and what I'm doing here now.

The food I bought for the cabin when I came here has dwindled down to almost nothing. I had another apple when I got home and heated a lone can of soup from the bare panty. Grocery shopping has to happen soon.

Delivery isn't an option, and shopping in town where someone might recognize me isn't either. Maybe I can ask Ella to bring some tomorrow. I can't exactly haul a lot of groceries on my bike anyway.

The roar of an engine coming down my driveway catches my attention. I blow the candles out on the table, plunging the house into darkness, and move to the window to take a peek.

One headlight tells me it's a bike, the rider gets close enough for the moonlight to reveal to me it's an opalescent white. It's a similar model to mine, but louder, and lacking the amount of modifications.

I grab my dagger from my thigh holster and ease to the front door. The darkness allows me to slip outside without being seen, just as the bike comes to a stop in front of the cottage.

I keep my back along the wall, my black hoodie and pants helping to conceal me in the darkness, as the driver dismounts and removes their helmet.

The long blonde braid that falls down her shoulder has me breathing a loud sigh of relief, and causing her to startle and drop her helmet as I emerge from the shadows, putting my dagger back in place.

"Fucking hell, Rae, I almost pissed myself!" Ella yells as she clutches her braid and tries to calm her racing heart. "What the fuck were you planning on doing, girl, stabbing me?"

"I didn't know it was you," I respond calmly, ignoring the stabbing remark she made. I don't want her to fear me. "Come on in, I hope you brought some food because I'm fucking starving out here." I turn around and head back inside to relight the candles on the table.

She stands there for a moment just staring at me, before reaching down to grab her helmet and securing it to her bike, then following me inside, and shutting the door behind her. She leans against it, her hand to her heart as she looks around.

She is still just as gorgeous as she was earlier, but now she wears a white leather jacket over her corset top. Her knee-high lace-up black boots and leather pants are still the same.

She takes a moment to gaze around the cottage, the interior following the color scheme of the exterior, with matte black on the smooth walls, and beige and gold patterns accenting the stunning woodwork and craftsmanship.

The kitchen cabinets and drawers are black wood with beige scrolling painted on the doors with shiny gold knobs, with the appliances in all black. The countertops are solid chunks of butcher's block stained black with gold accents on the edges and corners with the small kitchen table and chairs following the same theme.

"Holy fuck, this place is insane. It's like a fucking fairytale threw-up in here. All you need is your witch's broom in the corner and a cauldron bubbling over a fire," she chuckles as she places her backpack on the kitchen counter and unzips it.

She pulls out containers of the delicious stew I smelled earlier at Twisted and a paper bag full of baked bread and places them on the stained wood.

My stomach gives an appreciative grumble when the aroma of hearty goodness hits my nose. She starts rummaging through my cabinets and drawers, looking for bowls and spoons.

She must see that my kitchen is damn near empty, of even items needed to actually eat with because she looks at me with sympathy and more questions in her eyes.

"Rae, why is there nothing here? When was the last time you ate?"

"I ate earlier, I just ran out of my supplies today," I walk in the foyer by the front door and pulling out two plastic spoons from my own backpack. Thank God I still have them from my journey from White Harbor. "These will work for now. I think we have to eat from the containers though," I say, feeling a little embarrassed with myself.

"Well, don't you worry, I'll fix this shit first thing tomorrow morning," she states with her familiar sass that I miss so much. She grabs the containers, I grab the bread, and we make our way to the candle-lit table.

"It's just… I can't be spotted in town, and while I can somewhat stick to the shadows and avoid being seen here and there, actually going into a store and shopping, the risk is too high."

"The risk is too high for what?" She asks with confusion. "Raena LeRoux, what the fuck is going on? I think it's time you tell me where the fuck you've been and what the fuck is going on. Now."

Emotion fills her voice. I can hear the fear and heartbreak, but also a hint of protectiveness. I know I can trust her with this.

"Have a seat. I'll tell you everything, just let me eat first."

Chapter 5

Ella let me eat until I was so stuffed I thought I might burst. She packed the food away and stuck it in the refrigerator before pulling out a bottle of wine from her backpack and following me to my room.

We sit cross-legged on a fuzzy blanket with pillows from my bed in front of the fire, passing the wine bottle back and forth.

After ensuring my emotions are locked up tight and stuffed down in the "do not touch" part of my soul, I start at the beginning. The day I was taken.

"Do you remember the last day I saw you? It was my 18th birthday, and I came into town for Grams to get apples for her famous Apple Crisp. It was my favorite. I stopped by Twisted and you gave me two sandwiches for Grams and I, promising to come over later to celebrate with us."

She nods along with me, tears already pooling in her eyes. I can't look at her, fearing my own will well up too. So I stare into the orange glow of the flames, focusing on them as I continue.

"When I approached the house, I knew something was wrong. The front door was wide open, and the whole house was dark. I rushed inside, needing to find Grams and make sure she was okay. I found her in her bed. Oh God, El… there was so much blood. I tried shaking her, screaming for her to wake up… then someone grabbed me from behind and covered my mouth with a rag soaked in chemicals or something. I never even fucking saw them.

"The last thing I did see before the darkness took me was Grams… her throat had been cut. She must have been taking a nap when they came in." Ella grabs my hand but doesn't say anything, and I keep my gaze on the flames. "When I woke up, I was in a concrete room. There was a bed in one corner, and a toilet and sink in another. I was cold and alone, just thrown onto the stone floor, still covered in Gram's blood. I beat on the metal door until my hands were bloody, yelling and screaming to be let out, but no one came for what felt like days."

"Oh my God, Rae," she whispers, squeezing my hand and making me lock my eyes with her. That was a mistake. The emotions I've kept stuffed down come rushing at me all at once. She pulls me into her arms and rubs her hands down my hooded head. I'm oblivious of it still being on, since I've spent so much time in it. "What happened next? Who was it? Who took you?" She questions me gently like I'm a frightened child.

I pull back and look into her tear-filled eyes, gripping her forearms to prepare her for what she is about to learn.

"It was the 'Monster'… Kingston Wolfe."

"What the fuck?" Her face scrunches up into confusion and rage. "Why would he do that? What is his motive? I mean, I know he's a fucking cuntwaffleous gang leader, but he fucking kidnapped you? Why the fuck did he kill Grams? Did you get those answers? I'm shocked– confused… I'm so sorry, Rae."

It's a lot to process all at once, so I wait patiently and let her get all of her questions out. I need a minute to myself after speaking on the trauma I've buried beneath layers of locks inside my mind. I take a steading breath before speaking again.

"I don't know. Ella... I don't know why he kidnapped me or why he killed Grams. But the things he did to me and what he let his men do, what he stole from me– I'm going to kill him. I'm going to dismantle his entire operation, piece by piece. The Kingsmen will fall until the streets run red, and he is the only one left standing over his corrupt kingdom. Then, and only then, will I take his life. It will be a slow and painful death. After everything he's done, he doesn't deserve the courtesy of a quick death. "

"Sign me the fuck up! Let's kill King," she spits out, her rage slightly overshadowed by her newfound determination.

She has always been protective of those she loves, but this is too dangerous. I can't lose her; I just got her back. I would never forgive myself if she got caught in the crossfire of my war against King.

"El, no. You can help me by giving me information, but I won't have you hurt in this. This is my battle, and I can't ask you to get involved like that."

"Bitch, if you don't shut the fuck up, I'm going to slap you. I'm going to help you, and you damn well *will* accept it. You've been gone for five years. But don't forget, I can take you any day, even in a princess dress and plastic high heels." She isn't wrong, and from what I saw in Twisted today, she can take care of herself just like I can. "Also, let me remind you, I'm protected by the Shadows. The Kingsmen know not to mess with me." She pulls me up and snatches the empty wine bottle from the floor. "We need more wine, and you need to fill me in on everything that's happened since you left, and what the plan is now."

"Come on, let me show you what I have on King so far, and you can tell me more about these elusive shadow angels you have protecting you."

"They're called Shadows, not angels," she says, rolling her eyes at me as we take a seat back at the table. I spread the files out in front of us. "Angels definitely don't get my panties wet like these masked men do."

"Ella!"

I swat at her, but I'm smiling ear to ear for the first time since coming back here.

"What can I say, masked men on motorcycles with bad boy vibes and a hero complex just do something to my kitty, I make no apologies," she just smirks at me in reply.

***

Ella ended up staying with me all night. We laid in my bed while she caught me up on everything I've missed.

I told her a little about my stay with Aspen in White Harbor. A lot can happen in five years.

Apparently, during the three years I was held captive, the Kingsmen grew bolder, and things got worse in this town.

Before everything happened, I remember Grams telling me to be careful, but I don't think she ever truly knew how dangerous the Monster– King– and his men were.

They were well-known around town back then. People looked at them as saviors, protectors even, not a gang of dangerous criminals. No one ever suspected they were capable of murdering an old woman and kidnapping her granddaughter.

Turns out, everyone in Shadow Forest thought my mother had something to do with it. I guess they assumed she murdered her own mother and took me with her because no one has seen her since I was taken.

My mother was never really in my life growing up anyway, but I am curious as to where she is now. Why did she disappear at the same time I did? She's had a problem with drugs since before she got pregnant with me.

Grams was the one who raised me since I was born. When my mother came around, it was to get money for drugs or she needed a place to stay for a night or two, and then she was gone again.

She barely acknowledged I existed, but Grams more than made up for the love lost there. She was more like an older rebellious sister than a mom to me.

Ella and I fell asleep sometime early this morning, as the sun was beginning to rise and peak through my curtains. Judging by the light shining through, I'd say it's about noon.

I've been lying here staring at the ceiling for a while now, thinking about everything I didn't tell Ella last night. She knows I went through severe trauma in captivity and a little about my time spent in White Harbor. I just couldn't bring myself to relive every detail. I will tell her eventually, but I haven't told my story since I met Aspen.

I've spent the last two years shoving it down and focusing all of my energy on training and preparing for my revenge. If I open up that locked box of memories, I am terrified I'll find myself spiraling into a deep, dark hole of depression again.

I can't afford to lose focus now. Not when I am so close to bringing King down for good.

Deciding that I can't lay here any longer, I ease out of bed, careful not to wake Ella. She doesn't have to be at work until later this afternoon, so I'll let her sleep a while longer.

Quietly making my way to my bathroom, I carefully shut the door and stand in front of the mirror above the sink. My emerald green eyes and messy hair stare back at me.

When we were dressing for bed last night, Ella had a fit when I finally untucked my fiery red curls from my hood. The last time she saw me, my hair was naturally blonde, almost white. The unruly locks reach my waist, sticking up in every direction from my sleep.

Twisting them into a high bun on top of my head, I make my way to the shower, adjusting the water to nearly boiling hot, and slipping out of my nightshirt and shorts.

I stopped looking at my body a long time ago. My scars are a road map that remind me daily of the hell I endured. I survived, and that's what really matters, but I can't help feeling damaged. I used to dream of meeting a man, falling in love, and giving myself to him. Now, I don't think anyone could ever want me like that.

No, I'm destined to be alone. I'll have my friends, like Snow and Ella, and I'll reconnect with the people I once knew. But at the end of the day, I'll come home to an empty house, and that's okay. King stole my innocence and turned me into something much worse than even he could imagine. For the things I have done and am about to do, I deserve to be alone.

Stepping into scalding hot water, I close my eyes, allowing the heat of the water to consume me and my negative thoughts. I won't allow myself to wallow in self-pity about the future that was stolen from me.

I will never get back what I lost, or live a life most would consider normal, but I've made my peace with that. I'll spend the rest of my life protecting those who are like I once was, naive to the dangers lurking in the shadows, so they can live happily ever after.

That is enough for me.

***

Standing in my kitchen, I hear Ella finally roll out of bed. Literally. She hit the floor with a loud "umph" before groaning out, "What the fucking hell?"

I chuckle from my spot at the stove, reheating the stew she brought over last night. I see her emerge from my room, her blonde braid is sleep rumpled, with strands of hair falling loose from their confines, and the t-shirt and shorts she borrowed from me are twisted around her body.

That girl sleeps like the dead.

"Morning, Cinderella," I say, smirking at her childhood nickname I gave her when she couldn't come to play with me because she was stuck inside helping her family at Twisted most days. "Though with the way you sleep, maybe Sleeping Beauty is more accurate."

"Good morning, Rae, though it isn't morning anymore, is it?"

She looks out the window at the bright sun. She runs her hands up her face and into her hair, smoothing out her braid, before looking back at me and smiling, "Ya know, the red suits you better than the blonde. I love it! Maybe I'll dye mine. I think I need a change too."

"Oh, yes please. I'll help you. It will be just like old times– playing dress-up and doing each other's hair."

Memories of our friendship over the years flash through my mind. Ella has been my best friend for as long as I can remember. Before I was taken, I can't remember a single childhood memory she wasn't present for.

We were inseparable. We had plans after high school– even if we didn't know exactly what we wanted out of life. We were going to go to college and figure it out together.

I'd love nothing more than to get back to living a carefree life with my best friend. Maybe that starts with helping her change her hair.

"Ooooh, what about pink? With undercut sides? It would match the whole badass biker-bitch vibe you've got going on now," I suggest, pouring the warm stew back into the containers and take them to the table so we can eat.

"Maybe," she responds with her hand on her chin like she is really thinking about it. "So, I've got to run soon so I can check on Mom before going in to work, but I will have some groceries delivered to Twisted today. I can slip away later with Dad's truck and bring them out."

"Thank you, El." The gratitude I feel makes my voice crack, and I clear my throat. "I have to head out too, so we can ride out together."

"You gonna ride bitch with me, Rae?" She smirks at me.

"Oh no, you'll see." I return the smirk back to her. "You better eat fast."

We scarf down our stew and get dressed. She puts yesterday's outfit back on since it's all she has here, and I dress in my usual all-black attire– leather leggings, tank top, hoodie, and knee-high boots similar to hers.

I grab my black leather jacket from the hook by the door and slip it on. Ella slips on her white one before we make our way outside and around to the shed.

When I unlock the shed and roll Nightshade out from the shadows, the sound of Ella's squeal makes a flock of birds in the trees flee.

"Oh. My. Fucking. God. Are you fucking serious right now? This is fucking perfect!" Her excitement over our shared interest has me smiling.

I love riding alone, but I do miss riding with other people. Once everything is settled here in Shadow Forest, maybe Ella and I will be able to ride together somewhere other than just down my driveway.

"This is Nightshade," I introduce her, pushing my bike around to the front next to hers. "Does yours have a name?"

"I call him Gus." She shrugs while smiling and pats her seat before mounting the bike.

We slip our helmets on and take off down the driveway, speeding ahead of each other before falling back, and doing it again and again.

We make it to my hideaway spot quicker than I normally do alone and slow to a stop together. Ella pops her visor up and kills her engine, I can see her grinning ear to ear.

"I'll go on foot from here for now," I tell her, easing Nightshade in place and covering her with the brush. "Thank you for coming over. I've missed you, El."

"Bitch don't make me cry, I've missed you so much. This is just the beginning. I'm going to help you take him down– including his men. We're going to free this town and everyone in it from their cruelty. This is going to work, Rae, I just know it."

"It will. I won't stop until one of us is dead," I assure her as determination sets in and I tuck my curls into my hood once more. I grab her forearm and stare into her eyes. "I can do this."

"*We* can do this," she insists, gripping my arm back and squeezing tight.

"Th-thank you, El," I nod back at her, trying to steady my voice as it breaks amidst the emotion swirling inside me.

I'm so grateful she's with me. I've missed her so fucking much.

"Are you sure you don't want a ride into town? I know the walk isn't far, but you don't have to walk if you don't want to."

"No, I want to walk. I need some time to decompress," I tell her honestly. I know she gets it. Even if it's been years since we've seen each other, she knows me better than I know myself.

She smiles and gives me a nod. She flips her visor back down before restarting her engine and continuing her journey back into town.

After I've got Nightshade covered, I take off down the driveway. This forest has always relaxed me. After spilling everything last night, I need time to shove everything back down in its personal lock-box.

Reining in the trauma after opening up for the first time in years is hard. I've kept them buried for so long, I don't even know how to function with the gaping wounds I'm left with.

But I don't have a choice.

I have to shove this shit down until nothing but The Hunter remains.

Chapter 6

"Maddox, if I wake up to your nasty ass balls stuck to my leather couch one more time, I'm going to cut them off and shove them up your ass," Royal yells from the living room.

I slowly make my way downstairs, rubbing my hands down my face. This is already going to be a fucked up day, I just know it.

I find Royal standing over Maddox, who is smiling up at him, still half asleep with no clothes, no blanket, nothing. His morning wood stands proudly, the piercings reflecting off the sunlight streaming in from the full glass wall of our home.

"You know you like looking at my cock every morning, Royal, just admit it. You want it bad," Maddox teases back, grabbing his dick and rolling off the couch. He takes off running up the stairs as Royal charges at him to beat his ass. Maddox cackles his psychotic laugh, slamming and locking his bedroom door.

I hear the shower turn on, and Royal walks back down. "I'm going to kill him one day, Alek." He sighs as he makes his way to the kitchen and sets his cup under the coffee maker.

"No, you won't. You love his crazy ass," I say smugly. It's been like this since we all got placed into the same group home fifteen years ago. Even though he is only a year older, Royal has always acted like the parent, and Maddox is forever the unruly child who gets into everything. Me? I'm the calm, level-headed one who gets to referee them.

Making my way to the coffee maker, I grab a cup and wait for the black life force to drip into it. Royal makes his way to the couch, looking at it in disgust before sitting on the opposite end, coffee in one hand, his phone in the other, looking at it with more irritation than Maddox can cause.

"What's wrong?" I ask, feeling dread pooling in my stomach.

"Something's going on." His face sets into that familiar scowl that I know means it has to do with King. "He's called for an emergency meeting at the warehouse, nine o'clock tonight."

"Fuck, that's the last thing I want to do tonight," I sigh, sitting on the other end of the couch. I place my coffee on the end table and pull my own phone from the pocket of my sweats, checking to see if an update miraculously showed up this morning.

Royal sighs heavily, mocking me, when I shake my head. Both of us know we will be at this fucked up meeting. We are stuck being his puppets until we find our sister, Emma. King is a sick bastard. We once thought he was our savior, back when he took us all out of foster care and made us officially brothers, if only in name.

He adopted us when Maddox and I were 15, Royal was 16. King took in three hot-headed, fucked up boys who were just trying to survive together, adopted us, and gave us the most powerful name in Shadow Forest. We thought he shit gold bricks and could do no wrong.

We were so wrong. It didn't take long until we realized we were recruited for his organization. King had no heirs, and he needed someone to pass his legacy down to. I didn't know it at the time, but when he initially approached Royal, who was getting into trouble with the Kingsmen, he only agreed to the adoption on the condition that Maddox and I were adopted too.

"What's going on?" Maddox asks, walking back into the room and running the towel over his jet-black hair. He has it shaved into a short fade on the sides, with the top sitting a few inches longer. It always looks like he spends hours on end pulling on it.

Of course, since the towel in his hand is the only towel he has, he's still butt-ass naked when he plops down between us on the couch.

"Fucking hell, Maddie! Put some goddamn clothes on!" Royal snaps at him, getting up and storming down to the basement where our training gym is set up.

"What crawled up his ass this morning?" Maddox asks me, tilting his head.

"King."

Just that one name is enough to wipe the playful smirk right off his face. His eyes darken from his normal grey-blue to almost black in seconds. "Fuck," he mutters, standing up and pacing the room.

"Yeah, that's what I said. Go get dressed and meet us in the basement. King called a meeting." I slap the back of his head as I walk past him to the basement door.

Maddox is the most unhinged of us all. We have to manage his moods so he doesn't get himself, or us, killed before we can find our sister. He is likely to go rogue if we don't keep him in check. He's fucked up, but we all are. There's not a person on Earth who wouldn't be messed up after living the lives we have.

Even before foster care, our lives were not rainbows and unicorns. The things we survived left us with a darkness that can only be sated by blood. We aren't monsters though. Every kill we make is for the greater good. We only target evil, and Kingston Wolfe– is at the top of that list. Unfortunately, we have to play it smart if we want to find Emma and bring her home.

Emma showed up a few years ago. Kingston brought her home one day and introduced her to us as our sister. He said her mother was a junkie who OD'ed and she had no one else. By this time, we already knew King was an evil bastard.

The abuse we endured living in his home over the years was proof of that. We were already planning our move out of his mansion, but there was no way we were leaving her in his care. So we stayed to watch over her.

After a year, we made our move. We packed up while he was away. Jewels, the nanny, grabbed all of Emma's things and was supposed to meet us. She never showed up at our place. When we arrived back at the mansion, we found Jewels on the floor in the living room, her throat slit, and King sitting in his leather chair, sipping his whiskey. Emma was gone.

He was furious, but he said if we stayed in line and continued our roles in his family and organization, no harm would come to Emma. We've been searching for her since. We created an organization of our own.

They call us the *Shadows.*

We've recruited our own men, to not only search for Em, but to help us protect the innocents in Shadow Forest. However, wherever King has her, we've had no luck finding her.

***

Half of the basement functions as a training facility, while the other half is where we track down Em and plan for our targets. As I come down the stairs, I hear Royal wailing on the punching bag. He struggles the most out of all of us because he is the oldest, the leader. He thinks he has to shoulder the burden all on his own.

"Hey man." I put my hand on his shoulder, trying to bring his attention to me, but it just startles him out of his self-destructive trance.

Even though I have a good 100 lbs of muscle on him, he can put me on my ass if he wants to. I'm laid out on the mat with his hand on my throat before I can even register the "hmph" that leaves my lungs.

"Fuck, Alek. I'm sorry," he says, shaking his head and letting me breathe. He falls to his ass and hangs his head between his knees.

"Look man, this isn't just your fight. You don't have to protect us anymore. You've got to let us take the burden off your back brother. Everything isn't all on you. We've got you."

I sit next to him, grabbing the back of his neck and squeezing. He looks up at me and nods. While it wasn't a complete agreement, I'll take it for now.

Maddox walks in as we sit there on the mats and try to process the fresh hell we'll be walking into tonight. I have no idea why he would call an emergency meeting. I doubt it has anything to do with the Shadows. We've been too careful in keeping our identities a secret. Even the people we recruit have never seen our faces.

Maddox sits across from us, crisscrossing his legs like a child, and fidgeting with his blade, unable to stay still for even a second.

"Do we know what he wants?" He asks, drawing a line down his arm with his blade, not deep enough to hurt, but enough to have red beads of blood pooling on the cut. He has always been obsessed with blood. He started cutting not long after we moved in with Kingston. He doesn't cut to hurt himself. He cuts because he likes to see the blood. It calms him.

"No, the message just said emergency meeting at nine," Royal responds, watching the blood beads forming. "Stop that! One day you're going to really hurt yourself."

"I like pain, remember?" Maddox winks at him.

"Okay, enough. We don't have an update on Em, so we go to this meeting and pretend to be his little lap dogs, like always. Maybe we'll luck out and get some intel on where he's keeping her," I remind them. They will bicker all day if I don't bring the focus back to the problem at hand.

"I still say you let me skin him alive, peel his skin off in layers until he is a bloody lump of exposed muscle. Ooooh, *or*, let me roast him with the torch, only stopping when he passes out, and starting again when he wakes. Or…" he says, rubbing his chin like he is thinking of every possible way to take out King that would have the biggest impact.

"No! You know the deal. We can't make our move yet, not until we get Em back," Royal says, even though we all already know this.

"Fine, but if I accidentally kill one of his men at the meeting, just know, I tripped and my blade slipped," Maddox responds, pulling himself up and walking towards the stairs. "I'm going to get some coffee, and then we can see where we are with our men and Em's location. If the men we have can't find her, we might need to find more or call in other help."

He isn't wrong. We might have to recruit more Shadows who have different skills that could aid in finding her. I heard about a group up north in White Harbor that is notorious for hunting and tracking people, but they were too dangerous to get involved with. We might need to take the risk and see if they can help us.

Royal and I make our way to the table and investigation board we have along the back wall. The trail is all but ice-cold now. We haven't had a solid lead in months. *Somethings gotta give.* The longer she is away, the greater the chance of Kingston doing something to hurt her, especially if he finds out what we are doing behind his back.

Chapter 7

The warehouse we meet at is located on the outskirts of town, sitting off in the forest woods and down a long driveway. You would miss it from the main road unless you are looking for it, but that's what makes it the perfect place for the Kingsmen. It is used for everything from packaging to torturing, and sometimes holding emergency meetings.

I pull the blacked-out SUV into the warehouse parking lot, and we sit for a minute since we are early. Our bikes are for Shadow business only. I drove us here in our standard-issued Kingsman vehicle. It's bulletproof, built to withstand just about anything, and the last thing we need is someone to see us on our bikes and blow our covers.

The drive over was quiet, each of us mentally preparing for the shit show this meeting will be. It always is with King. He can never just tell us what he wants over the phone. He has to call us in, making a spectacle of his prized ponies. I don't understand his reasons for keeping us around. He is just a cruel man who preys on the weakness of those he claims to be helping.

Sitting here now in silence, I have a moment to just breathe. The burden to protect my family from Kingston weighs heavy on me. I have spent my entire life taking care of others- my brothers since we met in the system, but before that, I had to take care of my drug-addict mother and my baby sister.

They both died when I was eight. I thought my mother's house was bad, but the foster home they sent me to was worse. The only good thing to come out of it was Maddox and Alek. They are my brothers in all the ways that count, even if we don't share the same blood.

Now, our little sister is missing. Just the thought of King doing to her what he's done to me, what I've witnessed him do to others, sickens me. Bile rises in my throat.

I'd like to say she's safe because she's still so young, but with King being here in Shadow Forest, I have no idea who is taking care of her. Is she safe? Hurt? Does she even remember us? I shove my thoughts and impending nausea down as I see the first vehicle since we arrived pull up to the warehouse doors.

"Remember, don't let him get in your head. The more he talks, the greater chance he will slip up and give us something new to go on," I remind my brothers as we climb out and start making our way into the warehouse.

This place is isolated and secluded from the rest of the town. Only the Kingsmen come here. The warehouse is an old factory shell that King bought and had gutted to house his inventory, drugs, and weapons. There are a couple of underground bunkers out in the woods nearby, but those have been off-limits to the boys and me since we came to live with King.

The bunkers are guarded around-the-clock by at least one guard, with video surveillance and motion sensors. We haven't been able to get close enough to tell what the hell is going on there. I suspect some sort of human trafficking, but I haven't been able to prove it yet.

As we make our way inside the heavy metal door, I see King standing with two of his trusted Kingsmen talking in hushed tones. One looks so panicked and on edge, I'm worried he might piss his pants where he stands. The other looks his usual cocky self. *Fucking Jackson.* When they spot us walking in, King raises his hand to silence them. Interesting.

"Sons," King announces, an evil smile spreads across his face. He knows how much I loathe him. I hate when he calls me 'son'. "Thank you for coming, we have a situation that requires your… expertise."

I nod my head, barely containing the rage that boils beneath my skin. "And what situation might that be, *sir?*" I spit back at him, trying and failing to rein in my hatred for this man.

"Oh, you'll see. Let's wait until everyone is here, you know I hate to repeat myself," he quips back calmly, his devilish smile never leaving his face as we make our way to the table that sits in the middle of the open room.

King sits at one end, I sit to his right, with Alek next to me. Maddox takes the seat on the other side of him. I hate this. I hate being forced to sit here at this table like his obedient 'heir'.

More Kingsmen begin to arrive, all of them putting me on edge with their panicked looks and manic expressions. I make eye contact with Alek and he mouths, "What the fuck?"

King is still smiling sadistically when I look over at him. He isn't looking at me though. He's looking down at his hand, holding something, under the table. I can't see what it is, but the bile is back and rising to my throat. Something doesn't feel right.

"Well, let's get straight to the point gentleman," King says.

He slaps down what was in his hand in front of me on the table, making me sit up and pay attention now. It's a card.

"We have ourselves a hunter in town."

Picking up the card to examine it, the first thing I notice is the matte-black finish and a blood-red "X" embossed on one side. Flipping it over, it looks similar to a normal playing card. It's a king card, no suit or face, just solid matte black and red, like the front.

"What the fuck is this, King?" I ask, passing the card to Alek and Maddox to look at.

"That, *son*, is a hunter's calling card," he says with malice in his tone. "Look around this table, do you notice anything off?"

I look at each member that sits around the table, and now that I'm paying more attention, I see three empty seats scattered throughout. This meeting was mandatory for all upper level Kingsmen, so where the fuck are they?

"Where are O'Connell, Jones, and Stevens?" I gesture to the empty chairs they usually occupy.

"Over the last couple of weeks, we've been targeted by a hunter. We found their bodies, along with cards like the one you're looking at. They are killing off my men one by one. Stevens was first, then Jones. By the time we found O'Connell last night, another card had been delivered to another member. Jackson found it lying on his bed when he got home," he explains as he lays down photographs of each member in front of me as he says their names.

Their bodies have been mutilated– their throats slit clean across. But that's not all. Their dicks have been severed and stuffed into their mouths.

"So, they mark their kill before actually killing them. How long between the first card and their death?" Alek asks, laying the card back down in front of me.

"A few days," King responds, looking back at the card with a puzzled look. "That's where you come in. I want you to track this hunter and bring them to me. Do *not* kill them. They are mine. Do you understand me?"

"Yes, Sir," we spit in unison, the hatred seeping into our tones, and it doesn't go unnoticed.

"You know what's at stake boys. Do not fuck this up. Find me the hunter and deliver them to me before they kill again. I won't tolerate anything else." The look in his eyes tells me exactly what's at stake if we don't deliver on this.

Fuck.

"We'll get it done." He walks behind me, squeezing my shoulders roughly. It takes everything inside of me to keep myself seated. "Sir," I grit through clenched teeth.

"See that you do, *son.*" He leans down to whisper in my ear so no one else hears. "I'd hate to see something bad happen to little Emma if you disappoint me again." Straightening his suit jacket and buttoning it up as he stands, he adds, "I want you all to be on guard, watch your backs. You're dismissed."

As everyone pushes their chairs back and begins filing out of the room, I grab Jackson by his arm, keeping him from leaving.. I *really* can't stand this slimy bastard.

"If we are going to find the hunter, the obvious answer is to follow their mark. Go on about your day as usual. We'll be watching. Do not fucking contact us, do not look for us. We don't want to tip the hunter off. Got it?"

"Got it, *son.*" Jackson spits as he jerks his arm from my grasp, jealousy dripping off his tongue before he heads out the door.

It's not news to me that the other Kingsmen hate us. They all want King's attention so badly, and they hate that he chose an heir outside of the organization instead of recruiting from within. He storms out of the warehouse, the door vibrating off the metal wall when he slings it open.

"You'd think he'd be a little more grateful that we have to save his ass. I vote we let the hunter take him out, one less for us," Maddox mutters as we make our way back to the SUV.

If only it were that simple.

Alek looks at me once we are inside, a silent question in his eyes. He wants to know what King said to me when he whispered in my ear. I nod at him. "He threatened Em if we fail, didn't he?"

I might be the leader of our group, but he has the biggest heart. Emma stole his heart the moment she came into our lives. I know he would die for her without a thought. We all would. His protectiveness of our family rivals mine, and that's saying something.

"We won't fail," I tell them both, looking into each of their eyes, before putting the SUV in drive and heading back to our house to grab our gear. It's time to start a hunt of our own.

This time, the hunter becomes the prey.

Chapter 8

Over the last three days, I've stalked my mark, Jackson, learning his actual name only yesterday when one of the other Kingsmen called it out.

I never picked a nickname for this one.

Nothing seemed to fit, and I never really wanted to think about him. He was cruel and got his rocks off by brutalizing me. He wasn't the worst of the men who guarded me, but he was bad enough.

When he was on guard duty, he'd slip into my room and put me on my knees. He'd slap me repeatedly and force his half-soft dick down my throat. On days it seemed like slapping wasn't enough for him, he would take his knife to my skin.

He got off on beating me until he had to hold me up by my hair to finish on my face. My body would be so limp that he would rip out chunks of my blonde curls.

I can see nothing has changed. He's still the same limp dick asshole who gets off on hurting people, but that is not the most disgusting thing I've witnessed over the last three days.

No, the most disgusting part is watching him visit his elderly mother, hugging her and kissing her cheek as he comes and goes. She must not know her son is a disgusting rapist.

They say a mother's love is blind.

It almost makes me blind with rage because he can still visit his mother, while they killed my Grams. I can never visit her or feel the comfort of her warm embrace.

They stole that from me, and if I was a lesser person, I would take that away from him before I kill him, but I'm not. I don't kill innocents like they do.

I watch from the shadows as he leaves his mother's home for the third day in a row. I have to wonder if he is visiting her so much because he knows his time is up.

He gets in the driver seat of his blue truck that sits in her driveway, backing out and heading back towards town. I follow at a distance. Staying true to his routine for the last few days, he heads to King's mansion which sits in the forest on the other side of town.

Pulling the truck off into the woods, I get out and walk ahead on foot to a safe spot. This would be easier if I could do this on my bike. Ella's dad's old truck sticks out like a sore thumb, but she let me borrow it so I wouldn't be recognized.

I watch as he pulls up to the security box that sits beside the large iron gate. He rolls his window down and says something to the two guards who walk out. Their heads snap up immediately, and they sweep the area with their gaze, looking for something.

Me. They are looking for me. Good.

He can feel me following him, but they will never see me, just as he hasn't any of the times he's whipped around looking for me. They must be satisfied that no one followed him. One of them radios in while the other walks back into the box. A second later, the gate slides open, allowing Jackson to pull through it.

He will be here for a few hours at least, if the past few nights are any indication. He is scared and doesn't want to be alone.

I need him to be alone. His time is up.

My feet move silently through the forest edge as I walk back to the truck. I've got one stop to make before I go hide out in his house and wait for him to return.

Tonight, I take from him what they should have taken from me.

***

The drive back to town is quiet, the radio silent, the sky darkening with pinks and purples as the sun sinks down beyond the trees. I try to mentally prepare myself for what is going to happen tonight.

Not the killing part. Killing is easy for me now. I'm preparing myself to be face to face with one of the Kingsmen again, to be outside of the shadows that allow me to watch but stay safe.

This mental preparation is a new step in my routine– one I didn't know I needed until I came face to face with my first mark here in Shadow Forest. I didn't have this issue when I was hunting for Aspen, but those marks had never hurt me like these men have.

I can lie and say I'm fine until I am blue in the face, but the trauma still haunts me. I still wake up screaming at night. I still look over my shoulder, thinking someone is watching me.

I've had this feeling since I escaped, but I think the closer I get to my goal, the more my fears try to manifest against me. I've been feeling eyes on me for a few days.

Checking my mirrors for the tenth time since I left my hideout by the mansion, I take a deep breath, holding it before slowly releasing it.

"There is no one there bitch, get a grip," I tell myself, needing an extra pep talk before I get into town.

"Listen to your gut, Red," Dax's voice filters through my mind, causing an internal war between instinct and reality, and panic starts to flood my body.

Deciding to play it safe, I drive around aimlessly for a while. When it becomes clear that my mind is just playing tricks on me, and no one is actually following me, I pull behind the now dark parking lot behind Twisted.

Shutting the engine off, I allow myself a moment to breathe, resting my forehead against the steering wheel. Feeling like this reminds me of my time on the run, constantly looking over my shoulder for King to find me, and I hate it. I need to squash this feeling now before I spiral into a panic that gets me killed.

Readying myself and blowing out a large breath, I open the old truck door and climb out. A gust of chilled wind blows through the alley, causing the debris to rustle along the cobblestones. The air has shifted, a storm must be moving in tonight. Hurrying into the back door, I run straight into a rock hard body, and almost lose my footing in the dark hallway.

A pair of steel arms lock on to my hips, pulling me upright and pushing my back against the wall, caging me in as the back door slams shut.

We're dressed similarly, with all black clothes and hoods shrouding our faces from view, but that doesn't stop me from feeling his stare bore into the depths of my soul. My breath catches in my lungs when he lifts one hand from my hip and runs his gloved thumb across my ruby red lips, undoubtedly smearing my lipstick.

In the dark shadows of this hallway, I barely make out his head tilting to the side, almost studying me. I just stand there, staring at this dark figure as he stares back at me, neither of us finding words to speak aloud as desire like I've never felt courses through my body and makes my knees weak.

A small whimper escapes my lips when he lowers his hand from my mouth to rest it across my throat, not squeezing, but possessively holding. He leans his face close enough that I'm hit with the scent of fresh pine wood, smoke, and a hint of men's cologne.

Fuck he smells delicious.

He rubs his nose down my hooded neck and back up, inhaling deeply.

Did he just fucking sniff me?

I open my mouth to say something; I'm not quite sure what. Suddenly, Ella's voice rings out from just beyond the hall and pulls me out of whatever the fuck this is. My head snaps to the end of the hall and in the next second, his heavy body is no longer pressed against me. I spin around in a circle, but he's gone, vanished into thin air as the backdoor slams shut once more.

What the fuck just happened?

Ella comes into view, she reaches beyond me to flip on the overhead light I didn't know was there, the concern showing on her face now that I can see. "What happened, Rae? You look like you've seen a ghost."

"Ummm, I think I just met a Shadow."

Chapter 9

What the fuck?

My heart pounds a million miles an hour in my chest, my breath coming out rapidly and choppy as I stumble my way out of the dark alley to my bike. I've never felt that, whatever that was, in my entire life. It was like I was under a siren's spell.

Her sweet scent like cherry apple pie, and her plump lips, red like fresh spilled blood. *Fuck, her lips.* That was the only thing I could see in the dark hallway, but that was enough to draw me in.

I need to know her.

I look down at my gloved hand and I can see her lipstick across my thumb. Bringing it to my mouth, I lick it off as if it were her blood. My cock could already cut glass, and it twitches in the confines of my pants at the thought of making her bleed so beautifully for me.

Fuck.

I shake my head to clear the fog of her siren spell from my mind as I mount my bike, knock the kickstand back, and take off towards our home in the forest. Too much is on the line for me to be unfocused right now.

I only came to Twisted tonight because Royal and Alek have been following Jackson around the past few days. I've been focused on looking at any newcomers in town, new lease agreements, or purchases in the last month that could lead us to this hunter.

Royal called in to have me check Twisted for Ella's father's truck. She drives it sometimes when her bike isn't an option, but it's been spotted at several locations near where Jackson is, but she isn't with it, so I came to find out why.

Turns out, she's letting one of her old girlfriends who is back in town borrow it since she doesn't have a car, and she's trying to find a place to stay and a job.

I wonder if Cherry is her friend?

No, it doesn't matter right now. I can't think about that when Em's life is on the line. I'll have to revisit Ella and find out once things settle down. There was just something about her that called to me in a way that I've never experienced before.

Pulling down our long drive, I hit the button I installed on my bike to open the gate. You can't see the house from the gate, the trees are thick on both sides lining our driveway. Our house sits deep in the forest, its black wood frame and solid glass walls giving it a more modern vibe than most of the houses in Shadow Forest.

We picked this piece of land to build our home because it's on the opposite side of town as King's mansion. We wanted to be as far away from him as we could possibly be when we were finally able to get out of his house.

We've been buying up properties all around town right under his nose for years. Soon enough, we will own more than him and make taking his kingdom that much easier. He won't see us coming this time.

We just have to find Em first.

I can't wait for the day I get to gut him and pull his intestines out through his asshole. He is an evil bastard, and the things even my demented mind can come up with to take him out are too merciful.

The garage door is open when I reach it, Royal and Alek stand propped against the black SUV sitting inside it next to their bikes. Pulling in next to them, I shut the engine off and kick the stand, but stay seated.

I heave a heavy sigh, opening my helmet visor. "Twisted was a bust. Ella's girlfriend is using her dad's truck to find a job and house hunt." Even though I can guess the answer based on their pissed off expressions, I ask anyway, "Any luck?"

"Nope," Royal responds, rubbing his tattooed hands down his face, a gesture he does when he is frustrated. "Whoever it is, they are good at being invisible. We've been chasing our own asses for three days."

"Then let's just skip this chasing bullshit and go to where we know they are going to be tonight. It's the fourth day. If they stick to their pattern, they're going to come to his house tonight to kill him. We will be waiting in the shadows instead." I'm starting to get excited, bouncing on my seat and grinning like a deranged little kid.

"Let's go then. We've got eyes on Jackson. He is hiding out at King's place like a scared little bitch, so that works in our favor," Alek says as he pushes off the side of the SUV and treks over to his own bike.

Before he can mount it, Royal stops him, "Wait." He grabs Alek's arm before he can get on the bike. "What if this is all one big trap? What if King made this whole thing up to draw us out as Shadows and take us out?"

"He makes a good point," I say, clearly shocking the shit out of both of them. "But, I am done living in fear of King. If that's the case, we can just kill them all. We will find Em, one way or another. They can all die right now."

"He's right, Royal," Alek chimes in. Now it's my turn to look shocked, my jaw dropping open and my eyes bugging out comically as I stare at him. He steps over to me, pulling out of Royal's hold, and puts his finger under my chin, snapping it closed. A cocky smirk tilts at the corners of his mouth. "Close your mouth Maddie, unless you need me to stuff it for you." His deep dominating tone has my cock jerking in my pants again.

Fucking hell, he is such a cock tease.

"Knock it off," Royal grumbles, walking over to us from beside Alek's bike, and crossing his arms. "I know he is right, but I don't want to lose either of you, I can't..." He trails off, his voice thick with emotion. I'm not used to this from him. He is always so serious, and that's because he thinks he has to be. If he only would realize that he isn't in this by himself and he doesn't have to protect us anymore. "Why don't I go alone? I'll check it out, and if-"

"No!" Alek and I yell in unison, cutting off his martyr speech before it gets out of hand.

"We do this together, Royal." Alek grips the back of his neck and brings their foreheads together before continuing. "Brothers bound in blood." Royal takes a deep breath in, closing his eyes and gripping Alek's neck back and squeezing. "You aren't alone in this, and it is not your job to protect us anymore. We are equals now, a team. We won't let you martyr yourself to save us any more than you would let us do that for you. Now, shut the fuck up, and get on your bike. We need to be there before they show up," Alek says, slapping the back of his head playfully and shoving him off before stalking his big burly ass over to his own beast of a bike, mounting it with ease.

Each of us pulls our black masks in place, a full head cover with only a small strip open for our eyes, then put our helmets on to completely black us out. They don't call us Shadows for nothing.

From our solid matte-black bikes to our head-to-toe blacked-out gear, seeing us is nearly impossible unless we want to be seen. They can't even hear us coming unless we are right on top of them with the modifications we had done to our bikes.

Backing out of the garage and taking off toward the gate, I can't help but feel like Royal is on to something. It feels like we're missing something major here, something doesn't line up. He is either sending us into a trap, or this hunter is a fucking master?

If the latter is the case, maybe we should be asking ourselves why we're hunting a hunter who's set on killing our enemy when we could be helping them.

You know, the enemy of my enemy, and all that shit.

Chapter 10

The forest thins out the closer we get to town. Jackson lives as close to town as he can without being right inside it. We take the shadow trails that lead all the way around town to avoid being seen— trails me and my brothers made ourselves over the years, so we could watch over the people without King finding us.

The trail is smooth from our years of use, usually making the trip around easy for us to navigate on our bikes. That may not be the case coming out because a storm is moving in that will likely make our trail a soggy marsh. The sparse raindrops are already dotting the visor on my helmet.

Pulling to a stop near the backside of Jackson's property, I kick the stand out and dismount. My brothers both do the same as we remove our helmets.

Looking around, I notice small boot tracks leading from the trail going in the direction of his house. They are tiny, I'd almost say like an older kid or teenager. Must be some kid up to no good sneaking around.

I point it out to my brothers silently, both of them nodding back, and we move in formation through the trees and come to the backside of his house.

"Maddox, take the front, I'll take the back. Alek, sweep the perimeter," I whisper, and they nod back silently, before skirting along the side of the house in either direction.

Walking as quietly as possible, I take the stairs up the back deck and kneel before the door, grabbing my kit from my pocket to work the lock. I'm inside the pitch black kitchen within seconds. You'd think a motherfucker as slimy as him would have a better lock.

Within minutes, we've swept through the house and there is no one here. We stand in the living room facing the front door, like our mysterious hunter will just walk right in and announce themselves.

"Now we just wait," I say finally, making my way through the dark area and sitting on the long leather couch. Maddox and Alek find seats as well, still concealed in the shadows, so whoever enters won't see us until we are ready for them to.

We sit in the dark room, watching both the front and back doors from our seats, when a shadow moves across the floor from the tiny amount of light streaming into the window. Looking around the room, I lock eyes with Maddox. He eases out of his seat and skirts quietly along the wall, disappearing down the dark hallway.

Alek and I don't move or make a sound. Within a minute, the sound of glass breaking and Maddox's bellowing has us both on our feet, running to investigate. We find him leaning out the back bedroom window. When he turns around he is holding his side and sliding to the floor with a debauched smile across his face.

"She fucking stabbed me," he says, grinning like an idiot.

"She?"

"Yep. She took off through the trail. Go."

"Alek, take care of him," I demand as I jump through the busted window and take off after her into the woods.

I don't know what the fuck is going on. Why was there a girl in his house? I see a figure dart past the trees up ahead, and I charge toward the forest.

Fuck, she's fast. But chasing is my game, and I always catch my prey.

Chapter 11

My boots splash in the puddles on the forest floor, the rain coming down in heavy sheets as I run from the man chasing me. My socks are already wet from walking all the way here, and it doesn't help the chill I feel now.

When I arrived at Jackson's house, I wasn't expecting to be charged by what I am assuming is one of the Shadows. I know Ella says they protect the people of this town, but if they are associated with King, I have every reason to run.

I will never go back there.

I stabbed the one who tried to tackle me to the floor. I had climbed through a window in what I assumed was a spare bedroom. Just as I started my sweep of the other rooms to make sure no one was here, a shadowed figure rammed me into the window.

It was more reflex than anything to reach for my dagger, and I wonder if the man I stabbed was the same shadow from Twisted. I can't worry about that right now though, because a different one is chasing me through the woods and I need to find a place to hide to wait him out.

I have never been chased like this before, by a masked man who might want to kill me. Adrenaline, and maybe even desire, flood my body as my feet pound against the wet ground. I know there is something wrong with me when a small part of me wants to let this man catch me.

I can now see what Ella meant about the Shadows making her panties wet.

What the fuck is wrong with me? I chastise myself and try to rein in my thoughts .

My cottage isn't far. I can hear the rushing waters of Grimm River to my left, but I refuse to be as stupid as my traitorous pussy would like me to be and lead these men to my home. I'm counting on the fact that I know this forest better than them, and I can only hope they give up their search.

Coming to the familiar cliff on the edge of the river, I climb down into one of my old hideouts. I remember it being along the water from when I explored this forest as a child. I use the exposed roots to hold onto so I don't fall onto the rocks below.

No one would ever know this tree has a hollow spot within its roots. Flood waters washed it out many years ago, but it can't be seen unless someone is looking up from below.

Tucking myself safely inside the makeshift shelter, I try to catch my staggered breath. Only a few moments later, I hear the sound of boots pounding against the forest floor and my adrenaline spikes. I hold my breath until they pass and I can no longer hear them. I will wait here all night if I have to, because there is no way I'm going back to the hell I escaped.

***

The forest is silent for a long while, the only sound to be heard is the water rushing over the rocks below me. My body is crashing from the adrenaline rush, my weakened state allowing my mind to play tricks on me. My breath comes out in strangled gasps as panic seizes me and I am plunged into a waking nightmare.

My bruised stomach digs into the cold stone floor with each thrust, a heavy weight pinning me down. My arms are bound behind my back so tightly, my shoulders feel like they might dislocate from the pressure.

There's something in my mouth making me gag, and the canvas bag over my head is wet from his earlier torture session. The combination threatens to suffocate me. I scream into the gag, saliva choking me and making the sound come out gurgled. The pain is so excruciating, that I let my mind go somewhere else.

On days King visits me, I want to die so I don't have to endure this torture any longer. He's a depraved monster that would try to find a way to fuck me in the afterlife. Just so my soul would never be able to find peace.

He was angry when he showed up today, and that is never good for me. I don't know what he wants from me, but whatever it is, he isn't getting it so he takes it out on my body. King thrives on seeing the bruises and gets off on the way his men desecrate my skin.

I don't know how long I've actually been locked in this room, since Grams was murdered in her bed and I was stolen from our home. My only concept of time outside these four walls is a visit from an elderly man about once a month. He has visited me ten times since I've been here. I think he is a doctor or something.

He never speaks to me directly and I am blindfolded by a guard before he comes in. He just tends to any wounds I have gently, and sticks me with a needle in the crease of my arm, drawing blood, I think. I don't understand why, but the next visit I get from King after the old man visits, he is always angry.

The doctor came yesterday.

I don't know how to keep going. A scream rips from my throat and I choke on it behind my gag. My mind withdraws from the safespace I created to block out the pain and brings me back into the moment.

He plunges his cock into my ass so hard I feel my insides rip, and I know I'm going to be bleeding from there again. This is normal when he comes to visit me. All I know now is pain and blood.

"You're a worthless whore," he grits out as he takes a fist full of the wet canvas bag, and my long blonde curls and yanks my head back to bring his face closer.

His other hand comes to the front of my face, gripping my jaw tightly through the bag and turning my head to him as far as it will go.

"You have one thing I need, and you can't even give me that. This is your punishment, and you're going to take everything I give you. You will give me what I want like the little slut you are," he grinds out. His brutal thrusts punctuate the last few words.

I hear him spit on me before I feel the warm saliva slithering down my ass cheek and mixing with the blood. I want to curl up and die. The lewd sound of his cock plopping free of my ass fills the room seconds before he plunges quickly into my pussy and empties himself there.

One more piece of my soul dies as he pulls out of me, flipping me over and gently rubbing his hand over my hair through the bag.

"Yes, Little Wolf, you're going to give me what I want, aren't you?"

***

My body aches, and it feels like I'm floating. Pain radiates from my head. My mind drifts in and out of consciousness mixing the present with the past in a way that makes it hard to tell if I am dreaming or awake.

I think I hear voices whispering around me, but it feels like my head is inside a drum and it might explode at any moment. I don't know where I am, but parts of my body are cocooned in warmth while other parts feel painfully cold. My eyes are so heavy I can't open them.

Despite the pain and confusion, I feel safe. It's something that should surprise me, but I don't have the willpower to focus on that feeling right now. My mind is starting to black out on me, losing the battle with consciousness fast. The last thing I hear before my mind goes dark is "Cherry," and that only adds to my confusion.

MADDOX

Chapter 12

The pain in my side barely registers as Alek helps me to my feet. It's a deep cut that will need stitches for sure, but pain is something I welcome.

I can feel the warm, sticky blood soaking through my clothes as he helps me out of the bedroom and back into the living room, forcing me to lie down on the couch.

"Just stay here, you crazy fucker, while I hunt down a kit," he demands before walking away to do just that.

I grunt as I sit up, because yes, I am a crazy fucker. I don't need to be coddled. Getting to my feet, I stumble my ass over to the built-in bar and swipe a bottle from the top. It's too dark to tell what it is, but I really don't give a fuck as long as it burns on the way down.

When Alek comes back in, he finds me across the room with a bottle to my lips mid-pull. He walks over and snatches it from my hand. "What the fuck did I say?"

"Sorry, Daddy," I pout, winking at him on my way back to the couch. I don't miss the way he clenches his perfectly chiseled jaw at my antics.

Oh, he liked that. I fucking knew it!

I like to think of myself as a sexually open-minded person. I'm attracted to people based on their personalities, not what's between their thighs. I won't deny I'm attracted to both Royal and Alek, brothers or not. If that makes me a fucked up person, I never claimed to be anything else. I've never openly acted on the attraction, or outright told them, but they know me well enough to know the door is open should they feel the same.

"Could you just listen for once in your goddamn life, Maddie? You're going to make it worse. Let me take care of you."

Fuck. The daddy vibes are just dripping off of him tonight, but I don't push him anymore. I've got something else on my mind, or rather someone, and she is the reason he has to take care of me at all.

My Bloody Cherry.

The moment I saw her tiny little figure in the dark room, I knew it was the same girl from Twisted that sirened me in the hallway. I tried to take her down, but the little shadow surprised the shit out of me, pulling a blade on me so fast that I didn't see it coming.

My cock is still rock hard from her little magic trick, and thinking about it again has my cock twitching inside my pants. My piercings throb with need at the idea of making *her* bleed next time. I bet she tastes as sweet as she smells.

My raging boner doesn't go unnoticed by Alek either since his arm is pressed against me as he stitches up my wound. "Fucking hell, Maddie, put the sword away. Now is not the time."

"Don't worry, Daddy. This big one isn't for you." I wink at him and again I swear to fucking God he blushes a little. "I met her earlier, the girl who did this."

"What the fuck? Who is she?" His face is a mask of confusion and curiosity.

"Man, I don't have a fucking clue. She literally ran into me on my way out of Twisted, and it was..." I trail off, not really sure how to express what happened in that hall. "I can't explain it. I just need to figure out who she is, and what the fuck she was doing in Jackson's house."

"Maddie," he starts, sighing as he finishes my stitches. He starts wiping the fresh blood that has leaked from them with an alcohol swab before sticking a gauze bandage over it. I know what he is going to say before the words come out of his mouth. "We need to stay focused on getting Em back for now. We can't bring anyone into this fucked up world we live in. You know what he did to Em's nanny."

"You don't think I fucking know that," I scoff, pushing him back and standing. I grab the bottle he took away and abandoned on the floor. "I fucking know that. You just don't understand. Fuck. I don't even fucking understand it. I can't control this, whatever this is!"

Pacing the floor, my thoughts racing, I bring the bottle to my lips and take a giant gulp.

He grips my shoulders, spinning me around and forcing me to stop my manic pacing with a firm grip on my neck. "Stop before you rip your stitches, asshole. I understand. Trust me, I do. We will figure this out. I promise you."

I give him a sharp nod because my manic thoughts are still racing, and I don't know what to say to him.

"We need to go help Royal. You good?" He asks, nodding towards my wound.

"Let's go then." I take another long pull from the bottle before walking to the door. I know now is not the time to be involving someone else in our bullshit, but I have to see her again.

***

The forest is soggy under our boots as we trudge through the trees in the direction Royal headed. We stay quiet, moving as slowly and silently as possible, listening for any signs of them. The rain is still pouring down, soaking our clothes and making this trek a cold, wet mess.

My wound isn't bothering me though; The alcohol eased the pain and helped to calm me down. Hopefully, it'll last long enough to get through this fucked up night.

We come to the edge of a cliff that the river runs under. We're walking the path next to it when a high-pitched scream rings out through the forest. It's close enough to hear but still off in the distance, and it makes every hair on my body stand on end. It's her; I fucking know it in my soul.

I lock eyes with Alek before we both break out into a run, heading in the direction it came from, which sounds like it's straight ahead of us.

We run for what seems like forever but can only be a few minutes before I hear Royal's panicked voice up ahead.

"It's okay, I'm not going to hurt you. I need you to breathe for me, I'm coming down to get you. It's okay, I promise."

I push myself even harder, adrenaline and liquor fueling my body, and when I see Royal go over the edge of the cliff, I swear my heart stops beating in my chest. I dive for the edge, my knees hitting the soft mud as I lean over.

It's not a huge drop, but the large boulders in this area are dangerous. I let out a sigh of relief when I spot Royal hanging from the roots of a tree that must have washed out.

"What the fuck are you doing?" I yell. Alek's hand is on my back gripping my hoodie, so I don't slide down. Royal is climbing down the cliff by the roots before he turns and dives into the water.

My relief is short lived when I see what made Royal do something so stupid, and my heart stops for a second time. Cherry is down at the bottom, her body has floated a little way downstream, and is half on the rocky shore, half in the water.

"Nooooooo!" I scream, lunging forward to get to her only to be yanked back by my jacket. "I swear to fucking God, if you don't let me go!" Spit flies from my mouth while I try to scramble away from Alek.

"He has her. You've got a fucking stab wound on your side. Let Royal get her." He pulls me back into his chest as he sits on the wet ground. Alek growls in my ear as he bear-hugs me from behind so I can't get free. The fight takes a minute to leave my panicked body. He loosens his grip when I relax into his hold a bit, but he doesn't let me go.

"She's alive, I need some help getting her up," Royal calls up to us.

"I'm going to let you go now, are you good?" Alek asks me. I nod at him, crawling forward to lean over the edge once more. "It's too high here to bring her up," he calls down to Royal, who now has her cradled against his chest. "Keep walking in that direction, and the cliff will even out a little way downstream. We'll meet you there."

We both take off in the direction we just came from, the rain finally easing up a little. The cliff's edge begins to decline, and I keep my eyes on Royal holding my girl. My girl. That statement should scare me, but it doesn't. I haven't even seen her face and I'm laying claim on her, and I don't give a fuck. That's my girl, even if she doesn't know it yet.

Royal climbs the rocky shore to meet us, and I get the first glimpse at her.

"Cherry," I say, cupping her cheek in my hand and looking at my mystery girl.

Fuck. She is gorgeous.

Her hood has come off, revealing long fiery red curls that are currently dangling over his arm and run almost to his knees. A quick look at her stunning face has my knees weak, but the blood that coats her face pulls me out of my thoughts.

"She fell into the water and the current pulled her in. She hit her head on the rocks then washed up on the shore. I don't think it's too bad, but she is unconscious. We need to get Doc," Royal tells us before I can say anything. Alek pulls his phone out of his pocket, undoubtedly to text Doc to meet us. "Do you know her?" Royal questions me, clearly knowing something is up.

"Kinda. I'll fill you in later. Did she fall, or did she jump?" Worry fills my stomach as we walk as quickly as we can without jostling her around too much.

"I don't really know what happened for sure. I couldn't find her, and then when I was on my way back through, I heard her screaming bloody murder. She was hiding in the roots of that old tree on the cliff's edge. I called out to her, but it was like she was panicking and couldn't hear me. She was thrashing around and crying out, then she was falling into the water." He looks down at her as we walk, and I see something I've never seen before on his face.

I can't quite pin down the emotion he is showing, but it seems to me like my little siren enchanted him too. I don't know what it is about this girl, but whatever it is, I know I can't stay away from her.

"Doc will meet us at Twisted. I texted Ella to pick us up at Jackson's house. We can get the bikes tomorrow," Alek blurts, interrupting my thoughts as he shoves his phone back into his soaked pocket.

"Are you sure we need to involve Ella in this?" Royal asks. "She doesn't know who we are."

"I don't think we have much of a choice unless you want to try to move her on the bikes. Ella is closest and stands with the Shadows. We will figure out the rest later, just keep your masks on," Alek demands as we walk down the hill onto Jackson's property.

Honestly, I didn't even remember it was on my face until now. It had become like a second skin to me.

Ella lives with her mother a few houses over, and when we make it around the house, she is waiting in her Dad's truck that now sits on the curb.

When she sees us, she jumps out of the truck, running the short distance, panic on her face and tears in her eyes. "Rae, fuck!" She comes to a halt in front of Royal. "What the fuck happened?"

"Wait, you know her?" I ask.

"Yes, this is my friend that I told you was using my truck today." Her voice breaks as she runs her hand gently down my girl's hair, her hand coming back bloody. "Fuck, what happened? She was fine a few hours ago when she left Twisted. Did King do this to her?" Her tone changes from broken to pissed off as her questions come out, and the last one causes me to pause.

"Listen, El, we gotta get her to Doc. She fell into the river and hit her head, and she hasn't woken up since. We'll explain everything later, let's just get her some help," Alek takes over, always the level-headed one of us.

I'm still over here reeling at the mention of King's name where my girl is concerned. We all know who and what King is, but the way she said it sounded like there was a history there.

That is something I will be finding out, right after I make sure she is okay.

Chapter 13

"Get her in the truck where it's warm," Ella barks, jumping into action.

She opens the passenger side door for me before closing us in. Coming around to the driver's side, she slams the door shut while Maddox and Alek jump into the bed, and we take off towards Twisted.

"I know the Shadows have protected me this last year, but if Raena isn't okay…" she trails off, wiping her tears in a rage, trying to be brave. She's scared for her friend, I get it.

"Ella, we are going to take care of her," I promise her as I look down at the sleeping angel in my arms. I know I'm promising it to both of them.

"She's been through enough. I just got her back. I can't lose her again," Ella rambles.

It makes me wonder what this girl has been through.

It doesn't make any sense– the feelings I am having for this girl I don't know. I *do* know, without question, that I'll kill anyone who tries to harm her. I don't give a fuck if it doesn't make sense. It's just a feeling I can't explain.

I've had similar feelings three times in my entire life: when I met Alek, when I met Maddox, and when I met Emma– my brothers and sister. I didn't question it then, and I won't question it now.

Looking down at her, I hold her tighter to my chest and push the curls that have fallen onto her face back. "You said her name is Raena?"

"Yes. Raena LeRoux. She grew up here before…" she trails off again, a look of panic flashing across her face before she schools it. But I saw it. "She just moved back into town."

I have more questions, but we're pulling in behind Twisted into the alley. Doc is waiting at the backdoor, so those questions will have to wait.

When we stop next to him, Doc opens the passenger door for me to slide out with her. Ella runs to unlock the door while Maddox and Alek jump out of the truck bed to stand beside me.

"Thank you for coming, Doc. I know it's late," Alek says, shaking the old man's hand.

He is the only doctor in Shadow Forest, and he is paid well for his discretion, both by the Shadows and King. He knows how to keep his mouth shut, and he is always on call for us. He doesn't know who we are though, so on the rare occasion we need him, Ella lets us use the basement here. With it being underground, it keeps people from just walking in, and it keeps the sound controlled.

As Ella opens the door, I look up from Raena to see the doctor has stopped and is looking at her with confusion, maybe even a hint of panic, but when he sees me looking at him, he shakes his head. "Let's get her downstairs so I can take a look, and you can tell me what happened to her."

"Do you know her?" I blurt out, confused at his reaction to her.

"I don't think so. She does look familiar to me, but I can't place her. Maybe I saw her as a child?" He sounds confused as he questions his memory.

Ella did say she lived here, so it's likely she saw him before she moved away. I get a nagging feeling in my gut, but I brush it off for now. Getting her medical care is top priority, the rest we can figure out later.

We move through the back door- Ella turns and opens another door with her key before heading down first. We follow closely behind her to the basement. This space is nothing more than a main concrete room and a smaller storage room off to the side. Ella let us set up the smaller room as a makeshift examination room, with a table in the middle, and a supply cabinet with a sink on the opposite side.

Doc motions for me to lay her on the table as he sets his bag on the end and starts pulling out what he needs. "Ella, I need as many warm blankets as you can gather to warm her up," he tells her, and she nods before quickly leaving the room.

My brothers come to stand on either side of me as I gently lay her down on the table. But I can't seem to let her go completely, so I grab her ice cold hand and wrap one of my large hands around it.

It seems Maddox has the same feeling, needing to be close and touching her because he puts his hand over mine, slightly squeezing them together and tracing circles over our skin mindlessly as he stares at her face.

Alek doesn't really seem to know what to do, so he puts his hand on my shoulder, lightly squeezing it, connecting the four of us in a way that just feels right.

Before I can think too much about that, Doc finishes getting his shit together to take a look at her. Ella walks back into the room, carrying an armload of blankets and sits them at her feet.

"Tell me what happened," Doc orders, using his light to check her pupils before feeling her head to check the wound.

"She fell off a cliff into Grimm River, about an eight to ten foot drop. She landed in the water, but the current took her, and she hit her head on the rocks before I got to her. She hasn't woken up since I pulled her out," I answer.

"Okay. I need you boys to step out while I take a look. I have to cut her out of these wet clothes and get her warm." He grabs the scissors he laid out a few moments ago, pausing for us to leave the room. Maddox's grip tightens around mine as my jaw clenches.

"Yeah, that's not happening, Doc," Maddox says, but Ella speaks up.

"Listen, I won't even pretend to know what the fuck is happening right now, and I won't tell you anything about her without her permission, but what I can tell you is this. What Rae has been through, what she survived… If she wakes up with three big-ass masked men standing over her naked body, she might freak the fuck out. I'll stay with her and come get you when she is covered."

Her words make my stomach drop, and my heart thrashes painfully against my ribs. My jaw aches at how tightly it's clenched, and my blood boils with unexplainable rage.

What the fuck happened to her?

My brothers and I would never violate a woman, but it's hard to let her go. They seem to notice my hesitation, and Maddox gently takes my hand in his, cradling her hand that's in mine with his free one before easing it onto the bed. Alek grips my shoulders and guides us all from the room. Maddox keeps my hand in his, squeezing gently before closing the door behind him.

All three of us stand just outside the door, watching and waiting. Maddox is practically vibrating in place, needing to get back inside that room just as much as I do. I can't even begin to try to understand what the fuck is going on right now, and I can see Alek studying the both of us out of the corner of my eye.

This is insane.

We don't even know her, but I know we would kill whoever hurt her. Maddox is on the same wavelength as me when he speaks. "I will gut them inside out for laying a finger on her."

Alek is quiet, but he is nodding in agreement with Maddox— it's clear he feels something for the girl lying on the table in there, but he has always been the level-headed, calm one out of all of us. I have a feeling that this little red-headed angel is gonna turn *him* inside out, too.

Maybe that is exactly what we need.

We stand there for a little while longer, the anxiety amping up to get back inside the room when Ella steps out and closes the door.

Maddox and I rush forward, but she puts her hands up to stop us.

"Before you go back in, I want to say this. I don't know who you really are, but that is my best friend on that table. She has been through hell. I didn't even know how much until I just saw her, so keep that in mind," she says.

Before she can continue, a high-pitched scream rips from the room. I hear a crash forcing my legs to move on their own as I dart past her, barging in.

What I find has me seeing *red.*

Raena is curled into a ball in the corner of the room by the sink in nothing but her underwear. Doc is holding his hands up above her like he is trying to approach her. I shove him out of the way and scoop her trembling body into my arms.

Her eyes are squeezed tightly shut as she softly cries against my chest, her hand immediately clenching my shirt into her fist. I move to stand up, and she whimpers and holds tighter, like she's scared I'm going to let her go.

That will never happen, Angel.

Sliding to my ass and sitting back against the wall, I lift my eyes from her tear-soaked face to see Alek pinning Doc to the wall by his throat, rage burning in his eyes. Maddox grabs a blanket from the bed, covering us both before slowly turning back to Doc.

"What the fuck did you do to her?" Maddox says in a slow, psychotic tone, his head tilting to the side just adds to it.

"N-Nothing, she woke up when I was trying to hear her heart rhythm, and I told her I was going to take a listen and she just p-panicked," he stumbles out the words around Alek's tight grip on his throat.

Ella pushes forward, kneeling in front of me, gently placing her hand on Raena's cheek. "Rae, it's me, it's El. You're safe. Can you open your eyes?" She asks in a soothing tone, one like you would speak to a child in. All eyes are on my Angel as she slightly shakes her head no, keeping her eyes tightly shut. "Okay. That's okay, Rae. The doctor was just checking you out. You had an accident. Do you remember what happened?" Ella continues to stroke her cheek softly as I gently rub her back, and we get another *no*.

"H-he, he…" She cries harder as she tries to speak, and her angelic voice hits me right in the chest.

My arms tighten around her, holding her closer against me. Finally coming back down from her panic and realizing there is a strange man holding her, she finally lifts her head. I am greeted with the most stunning, emerald green eyes. My breath catches in my lungs when she finally locks those eyes on mine.

She doesn't know me, but she doesn't panic like I feared she would. She just stares into my soul as I stare back into hers.

And I know, without a shadow of a doubt, *she is mine.*

Chapter 14

The aqua blue eyes staring into mine through the black mask should terrify me.

Instead, I feel like they're burrowing their way deep into my soul, never to be removed, and I've never felt safer in my entire life. It doesn't make sense, but I can blame it on my throbbing head later, I guess. His arms are cradling me as he sits on the floor, and I have this overwhelming urge to see the rest of his face.

So, I do what any mentally unstable and possibly concussed girl would do when she is being held like this by a masked stranger, I lift my hand to his neck and try to push the mask up.

He immediately stops me, grabbing my wrist in his strong hand and bringing it to where his mouth is, kissing the inside of it through the thin material. My breath catches in my lungs as I finally hear his voice clearly.

It comes out gravelly when he says, "Not yet," against my wrist, before he places my hand back on his chest and runs his hand through my hair. I wince at the pain that shoots from my head when he touches a particularly tender spot, and I am gifted with his deep, low voice once more, "Will you let Doc take a look, Angel?"

Angel?

Why does that make my heartbeat so fast in my chest? It takes me a moment to realize what he said before it. Panic seeps back in, and I grip his jacket tightly with my fist again. My fearful gaze finds my best friend crouching down beside me, and the masked man goes rigid beneath me.

"I… I remember h-his voice," I whisper to her, locking eyes with her, silently pleading with her to understand what I mean.

I can't talk about it right now. The memories of what happened tonight start coming back to me, and I can't make myself relive that panic right now. I take a few deep breaths into this stranger's chest, smells of fresh rain, forest dirt, and a hint of cologne hitting my nose. His scent calms my breathing in a way I don't understand, but I'm too exhausted to question it.

"He was there… before?" Ella asks calmly, her tone is nothing short of murderous. I nod my head and I hear her stand and move away. "Get him out of here!" She says angrily, causing me to finally look around the room.

I see two more masked men, all in black from head to toe. One is holding an older man by his throat against the wall, and the other is pacing the floor. When their eyes lock on mine, my breath catches again at the intensity of their stares.

"Wait… what's going on? I haven't done anything," the old man shouts, and he must be looking at me because I hear a deep growl come from across the small room.

A deep voice grits out, "Don't fucking look at her."

I can now hear the doctor being forcefully removed from the room.

"Tie him up in the main room out there," Ella says before crouching down beside me again. I peek my eyes open at her, and she looks at me, not with pity but with compassion and love. "He's gone, Rae. Can I take a look at you now?"

I nod my head. The man holding me shifts me slightly to stand, his muscles flexing around my body, trying not to hurt me as he moves me to the table I rolled off when the doctor's voice caused me to freak out. When he lays me on the table, my clutch on him tightens, my need to keep him near confusing me.

"I'm sorry," I whisper, embarrassed at myself for how I'm reacting to these strangers. His hand gently pushes my hair back that has fallen in my face, then cups my cheek.

"Don't worry, I'm not going anywhere." He straightens up when I release his shirt, grabbing my hand in both of his and squeezing.

The loss of his body heat makes me shiver, and I realize I'm only in my bra and panties. My cheeks flame- I'm sure they match my fiery curls right now, and I close my eyes and use my hands to cover my body quickly. Immediately, I feel the warmth of a blanket covering me.

Sighing heavily in relief, I open one eye to see the masked man staring at the blanket like he can see through it. My body is a road map of marks and scars across my skin, a daily reminder of my time in hell.

I expect to see disgust on his face, but all I see is red-hot rage vibrating off him in waves. A small whimper escapes me, and I go to pull my hand out of his grasp, embarrassment and confusion flooding me once again, but he holds tight.

Leaning down, his blue eyes have darkened with unhinged rage bubbling in them, bringing one hand to my chin where his thumb gently rubs. He stares into my soul again before speaking. "Who hurt you? Give me a name."

I am stunned into silence, my mouth opening and closing with no words coming out. His rage isn't directed at me. It's directed at the person who put these scars on me. I can't answer him.

This reminds me that I don't even know who this person is. As much as I want to trust this feeling of safety I feel right now, I also don't know who I *can* trust and where their loyalties lie.

It takes tremendous effort, but I manage to pull my gaze from his gorgeous eyes and look over at my best friend, who is watching our interaction. I can tell by the look on her face she's as confused as I feel, but since I already know how she feels about these Shadows, I see the hint of a smile she is hiding.

She sees the pleading look on my face immediately, and I force the breath out of my lungs in relief when she speaks. "Why don't we check you out? You still don't remember anything?"

"It's coming back in waves. I remember falling into the river. I think I hit my head, it hurts here." I reach my free hand up to touch that aching spot, and my hand comes away bloody. Before she can say anything else, one of the other masked men returns, the big one who held the doctor against the wall.

"I have some medical experience. Is it okay with you if I take a look?" He asks me directly in that deep growly voice that does something funny to my insides. His honey golden eyes never leave mine as he comes to stand beside Ella.

I stare back at him, unsure what it is about these men that seem to put me at ease, I nod at him. Ella steps aside, allowing him to come closer, and I take a moment to really look at him.

He's big. He has broad shoulders and massive arms, his muscles straining against his solid black hoodie. Black gloves cover his huge hands.

I wonder what it would be like to feel them bare against my skin?

My thoughts surprise me, and I feel heat creeping up my cheeks again.

He has a pair of latex gloves in his hand, his eyes staying locked on mine for a few moments before he removes his black riding gloves and snaps the others on. He gently probes my head. I wince when he gets to the tender area that is still oozing blood.

There is a light attached to the table that he bends and brings closer to my head to help him see. "It's not too bad. I can see if Doc has some wound glue in his bag and close it to stop the bleeding."

His eyes come back to mine, and I nod my head, letting him know he can proceed. He moves to the end of the bed, bending down to rummage through Doc's bag that must have crashed to the floor when I panicked.

When he comes back, he takes my hand in his, making the smooth glove warm against my cold skin, his honey eyes connecting with mine again.

"This is going to hurt, Baby Girl. I'm sorry."

My stomach does little flips at him calling me Baby Girl with his deep, growling voice. I don't know what it is about these men and their little nicknames that are doing something weird to me, but I am not usually easily flustered.

I've cut off the cocks of grown ass men before I kill them, for fucks sake. What the actual fuck is happening to me right now? These men are bringing out a side of me I didn't even know existed.

With the internal reminder that I'm a badass who has lived through hell and walked through the flames to survival, I put on my bravest face for this big bear of a man.

"I'm no stranger to pain. Go ahead, I can take it." Turning my head forward, I close my eyes, taking a deep breath to prepare myself and he growls. He actually fucking growls at me. Again!

I feel his other gloved hand gently lift my chin and turn my face back to him. "Look at me, Baby Girl."

His tone is commanding and even deeper than before, causing my insides to flutter, and my thighs clench on their own. My heavy eyelids flutter open at his command, and the intensity in his eyes steals the breath from my lungs.

"I don't know who hurt you, but my hands will never cause you that kind of pain." His words make my eyes fill with tears in an instant. They spill over my lashes and run down my cheek. He brings his thumb up to wipe them away. "I'm going to get started. When the pain is too much, I want you to squeeze my brother's hand as hard as you can, he can take it." He winks at me before nodding to his brother, who has been silent for a while.

I look up at the man whose black gloved hands are cocooning mine, his blue eyes watching me. They are now creased in the corners, making me think he's smiling behind the mask. I wish I could see his face, all of their faces really.

"You okay, Angel?" He asks, leaning down slightly and bringing one hand up to brush my hair back out of my face again.

I smile up at him, nodding my head before taking a deep breath and keeping my eyes on his blue ones. "I'm ready."

He holds my head steady as his brother begins.

The cold sting of the alcohol makes my body tense for a second as he cleans the blood from my forehead with care. Then I feel him pinching the wound together before applying the glue. The pain is bad, not unbearable, but I still tense up and squeeze his brother's hand tightly.

"You're doing so good. I'm almost done," he praises before softly blowing on the glue, so it dries quicker.

His breath, fanning my face in waves, smells slightly of mint, making me think he pulled his mask up at least enough to uncover his mouth. I slowly turn my head towards him, finding that I was right. His stubble beard and plump lips are uncovered, revealing a sharp, chiseled jawline, and a tattoo that goes up his neck that peeks out of his hoodie.

I bet the rest of this man is gorgeous. I want to see the rest of him. I want to see all of them.

His eyes meet mine and the smirk that tilts the corner of his mouth as he blows his breath on my face threatens to undo me.

"All done." He straightens up, pulling his mask back down and removing the gloves, revealing more tattoos on his hands. "The glue is dry to the touch, but you'll need to wait a few hours before getting it wet." He starts to clean up the supplies and moves back to the bag at the end of the table.

"Thank you." My voice is raspy, and I'm so thirsty. I look at my best friend who is not even trying to hide her shit-eating grin now. "Can I have some water?"

"Yes! I'll run upstairs and grab it. Some clothes for you, too," Ella says, her smile fades into a seriousness when she continues. "Are you going to be okay alone with them for a few minutes?" I know what she is asking. Am I going to freak out again?

"I'll be fine, El. I'm sorry for freaking out and scaring you."

She comes to my side and hugs me. "You have nothing to be sorry for. I'll be right back. Then we'll figure out what to do next."

She steps back and looks at the two brothers intensely, both of them giving her a nod before she walks out of the room and shuts the door.

The silence that follows her departure isn't awkward. It's comfortable. My eyes dart back and forth between the two men. Both of them stare at me, studying me like they are trying to figure me out.

Good luck with that.

100

ALEK

Chapter 15

This is definitely *not* how I envisioned tonight going.

We were supposed to take the hunter down to keep Emma safe, buying us more time to find her. I never would have guessed our lives would be turned upside down in a matter of hours.

I know what I told Maddox earlier tonight, after I stitched the stab wound this little vixen gave him. I guess he was right, I didn't understand. I can't explain this feeling in my chest. All I know is I want to wrap her in my arms and protect her.

I've never been particularly bloodthirsty like Maddox or Royal, but an unbridled rage rushed through my body when we came running into the room to find her cowering in the corner. I saw the scars. I decided instantly that I would bleed out whoever put those marks on her.

After a few minutes of just watching each other in silence, Ella returns and helps her into the clothes she brought down for her. I get another look at her body, unashamed at how my eyes take in her tiny figure. As beautiful as this woman is, this is not sexual, right now. No,

I'm mentally cataloging every mark, scar, and blemish that has caused her pain.

I have so many questions that need to be answered, but I don't want to overwhelm her. I wait until she is dressed and sipping on the water Ella handed her, before I pick the one that needs to be handled immediately. He is currently tied up outside this room with Maddox.

"Will you tell us what happened with Doc? Did he hurt you?" I try to keep the rage out of my voice when I ask, but it's exceptionally hard. I don't want to send her into another panic.

I watch her face, waiting for her to answer. I can see the mental walls go up as her expression changes, and she retreats back into herself.

She pulls her legging-clad knees up to her chest, her bare feet flat on the exam table. I step towards her, and she flinches. She fucking flinches! I feel my heart squeeze inside my chest when she drops her head down and covers her face with her hands. I look at Ella and my brother, a silent plea because I am about 10 seconds away from ripping Doc's head from his body and delivering it to her as a gift.

Ella steps towards her, gently pulling her hands down so she can look at her face. "You don't have to tell me details. Just tell me this. Is he on the list?" Her question has my eyes snapping up to Royals as he does the same.

"What list?" We say in unison.

"It doesn't matter," Ella retorts, her tone telling us to shut the fuck up and let Raena speak. "Is he, Rae?" She presses, and Raena slowly shakes her head no.

I think we all sigh with relief before the little vixen finally finds her voice. "But I don't think we can let him go either." She must see the confusion on all of our faces. "Listen, I appreciate you saving me and all your help, but I don't know who to trust. It's not safe for me here. There are people who can't know I am back and if the doctor recognized me…" she trails off, squeezing her knees tighter with her arms before dropping her head again. "I don't know what to do," she whispers.

I understand where she's coming from. She has clearly been through some traumatic shit, and somebody's responsible. She doesn't know anything about us. I realize that if we want her to trust us with her secrets, we're going to have to do the same.

I look over at Royal, his eyes find mine, and I can tell by the look that he knows it too. He gives me a slight nod, and we both slowly move in beside her on either side of the table. Ella looks between us both.

"Can we trust you, Ella?" I ask, already knowing the answer but needing to ask it anyway. She nods at me before moving to stand at the foot of the table. This is a risk, but I just have this gut feeling that this is a risk worth taking.

I drop to my knees beside her, Royal doing the same on the other side.

"Baby Girl, look at me."

She lifts her head from her knees and looks between us cautiously before her eyes land on mine and stay there. Her breathing is starting to even out the longer she looks down at me, like our closeness calms her down.

I reach up and pull my mask off, showing her my full face for the first time. Her eyes widen comically as she drinks in my features, swallowing hard.

"I'm Alek, and this is my brother, Royal." I nod my head at him and she looks in his direction. He removes his mask as well.

"Hey, Angel," he says, grabbing her hand and bringing it to his lips for a gentle kiss.

"Our other brother, Maddox, is the one you stabbed tonight," I say, giving her a little smirk. "You met him briefly at Twisted before that, I think." She nods her head and blushes, and I have to wonder if it's because she is embarrassed that she stabbed him or whatever went down when they met before.

"Holy. Fucking. Shit." Ella says, and I look at her. She stumbles back a second before steadying herself on the table with both hands. "You're the Shadows, I don't understand. You're Kingsmen."

Her words cause Raena to tense and try to pull her hands from us. I give her a gentle squeeze to let her know it's okay as Royal says, "Not by choice."

"It's a long story, but all you need to know is that we became the Shadows to protect people like you and places like Twisted from King's corruption until we can take him out," I explain, feeling Raena relax once more, her eyes studying my face as if to see if I'm lying. Her reaction makes me think that King is involved in whatever she went through.

"Okay, but why are you waiting? Why not just kill King now?" Ella asks.

"We can't. Not yet. He took our sister," I say and Raena's entire body freezes, and the look on her face tells me she knows exactly what happens to girls in King's care.

"W-we…. We have to get her back. NOW." Her voice starts off as a broken whisper before turning into molten rage as she speaks.

She swings her legs over the side to stand, but I'm still kneeling there. I place my hands on her waist, caging her in and stopping her from standing. She moved so fast that she was swaying with dizziness, even seated.

"Easy there, baby. You have a head injury. Listen, we know she is in danger, but he has her hidden, and we haven't been able to find her yet. There is nothing we can do tonight. I need you to take a couple deep breaths for me so you don't pass out."

Her breathing is coming out in panicked pants. She listens to me though, breathing in and out a couple of controlled breaths until she can open her eyes. The tears that pool along her bottom lashes spill over and down her flushed cheeks. Bringing my hands to her face, I swipe away her tears.

"It was King, wasn't it? He's the one who hurt you?" I ask, because even though I know it in the depths of my soul, I need to hear it from her.

She searches my face for a few moments, like she is trying to decide if she can trust me now that I've opened up to her. Whatever she's looking for, she must find it because she takes another deep breath in and out before nodding her head and letting out a strangled sob that shakes her entire body.

I know she's fragile right now, on edge from everything that has happened tonight and whatever hell King put her through is fresh on her mind, but I can't stop myself. I wrap her legs around my waist and pull her into my chest, turning us around and walking out the door.

"I'm taking her home."

I don't know where her home is, but for tonight, she is coming home with us. I need her to be okay, and there is no way in hell I'm letting her out of my sight right now. I can feel Ella and Royal following close behind me.

Maddox is out in the main room with Doc tied to a chair, a blindfold over his eyes, his mouth stuffed with something, and taped shut. When he sees me with Raena in my arms, he darts forward to meet me on my way to the stairs.

"Keep your eyes shut. Don't open them until I tell you to," I whisper into her hair, and I know she heard me because she presses her face deeper into my neck and nods. "Good girl." I rub her back gently as I stop by the stairs, as far away from Doc as I can, and turn to face Maddox.

106

"Is she okay?" He whispers, his tone is serious and concerned, despite the manic look in his eyes. It seems that whatever information he got out of Doc has him halfway to losing his shit, too.

"She will be. We're taking her home. Grab his stuff and put him in the truck," I instruct. He nods while staring at Raena. His eyes finally move to mine, silently asking if I've got her, and it's my turn to nod at him.

He runs back to the room to gather Doc's supplies. Royal walks behind the blindfolded doctor. He places his thick arm around his neck, squeezing it into the crook of his arm until the doctor passes out. Ella works to untie him from the chair. Royal tosses Doc over his shoulder just as Maddox comes back out of the room, and I start up the stairs.

When I get to the top, I head back the way we came and push through the door leading outside. Ella comes up beside me, opening the passenger door. I place Raena on the seat so I can speak with the boys about what to do about Doc before we leave. However, when I try to let go, she whimpers in my arms and clings tighter to me.

Ella notices, looking at me with sympathy. "Just get in with her, we will handle this. Turn on the heat."

She hands me the truck keys. It takes a minute for me to fold my large body holding hers into the truck. My knees are jammed into the dash, but I would endure worse discomfort to keep this little vixen wrapped around me like this a little longer.

Ella closes the passenger side door for me. I cradle her head with one hand, reaching over the small cab with the other to crank it over. The truck rumbles to life, and I let it warm up a few minutes before cranking the heat as high as it will go.

Raena's sobs have quieted, her breathing steadier than before. I gently adjust her head so I can look at her face, running my finger into her gorgeous red curls to push them back. She is so beautiful.

Her long lashes kiss her high cheekbones, her pouty, kissable lips make me ache to part them with my tongue to see what she tastes like. Will she taste like cherries, like Maddox calls her? Or something else?

She must feel my eyes drinking in her features, because her heavy eyelids open to look up at me. Her emerald green eyes, which were a sea of feral emotions earlier, are now calm as she reaches up and touches the tips of her fingers to my stubbled jaw, almost like she can't help herself.

"You're beautiful," she says with breathy reverence, almost like she doesn't realize she said that out loud. The smile that splits my face open must make her register her words, because a crimson blush tints her cheeks as she looks back down, withdrawing her hand like she did something wrong. "I'm sorry, I don't know what is wrong with me." Her timid whisper has me tilting her chin back up with my thumb under her jaw.

"You really think I'm beautiful, Baby Girl?" I ask, smirking playfully at her when her cheeks flame even brighter. "There is nothing wrong with you and nothing to apologize for. You can touch me anytime you'd like."

A slight smile comes to her lips as she lets out a tiny little chuckle, and we just stay like that for a moment, smiling and staring at each other. For the first time in my life, the world stands still, allowing me a moment to let everything else fade away.

I don't understand how someone can come into your life and instantly you know. You know you would do whatever it takes to keep a smile on their face. You know you would protect them no matter what. Kill for them. Die for them. I don't understand it, but I just know.

Looking into her eyes, I run my thumb along her plump bottom lip. "I can't explain to you what is happening right now, but you feel it as well. Don't you?"

"I can't explain it either, but yes, I do, I feel…" she says softly, her eyelids fluttering closed, exhaustion taking her. She relaxes even further into my body, burying her face back into my neck. I think she's fallen asleep until she whispers, "I feel safe." Her breathing evens out this time, her body finally giving in. I pull back enough to kiss the top of her head and hold her tighter to me.

"Sleep, baby. I'll keep you safe. I promise," I whisper into her hair as Ella opens the driver's door and climbs inside.

She looks at her sleeping friend in my arms, before looking up at me. "I am trusting you to keep that promise," she says confidently, but there is a silent plea in her tone. Her eyes search my face for a few moments as if searching for any hint of doubt before she puts the truck in drive, backing out of the alley.

I give her directions to our house, which sits on the other side of town, before looking back at my brothers who are sitting on either side of the truck bed, watching Raena sleep in my arms. It's crazy how there's no jealousy between us. It's clear this little vixen has reeled us all in. We're all very possessive men, but along with many other things tonight, I can't explain this either.

It feels like fate. Like our souls are puzzle pieces, and the three of us have been trying to get through life together while our missing piece was out there alone.

Chapter 16

The thick line of trees canopying our driveway passes by in a blur as Ella drives slowly up to the house. Before Ella even has the opportunity to put the truck in park, Maddox and I are jumping out of the bed of the pick-up seconds before it comes to a complete stop.

The two of us move in tandem to help Alek get Raena out of and into the house, as quickly and safely as possible.

She is still sleeping on Alek when we open the passenger door, and it's a sight to see. Alek is a big guy, almost six foot nine, stacked with muscles and broad shoulders. He looks like a giant compared to her tiny little body. It's almost comical.

"She's been out since we left," he whispers, his eyes on her as his hand cradles her head, moving through her hair absentmindedly and massaging her scalp.

"Why don't you take her in and get her settled, then meet us in the basement so we can talk? We'll get Doc set up down there." He nods, looking at her beautiful sleeping face before carefully unfolding himself out of the truck cab and carrying her inside.

I look at Ella standing at the back of the truck where Doc is still passed out in the bed. She is watching our exchange with amused curiosity. Her eyes meet mine, and she closes the distance between us.

"I am not going to pretend to understand what the fuck is going on with the three of you and my best friend," she starts again, and I get it. I don't understand what the fuck is happening either. "But... you can't let him get her. She hasn't told me everything that happened to her, but what she has told me is my worst fucking nightmare. She can't go back there. Protect her with your lives, and I will protect your secret. Hurt her, and I will fucking kill you and mount the heads of the Shadows above the bar at Twisted for all to see."

"Okay, easy there, killer," I raise my hands in defense. "We won't let anything happen to her."

"Good. Now, can you get Doc out of my truck? I need to get back home to check on Mom," she says, her sassy attitude is ever present.

Ella is a bad bitch. She kicks ass first and takes names later. I believe that if she ever thought we would hurt her friend, she wouldn't hesitate to put us in our place. *That's good.* Raena needs a friend like her who will look out for her no matter what.

Maddox walks to the tailgate of the truck, lowering it and dragging Doc out by his ankles. He's been extra quiet since we left Twisted. It sets me on edge that he is not being his normal self. I would bet anything it has to do with whatever information he got out of Doc, because while Raena said he didn't hurt her, it doesn't sound like he helped her either.

Stepping forward and grabbing the doctor's limp body from the open tailgate, I throw him over my shoulder, following Maddox into the garage.

"I'll be back tomorrow morning, so don't do anything stupid! Take care of her, or it'll be your asses I'm dragging out of my truck!" Ella yells to us as she pulls out of the driveway.

I don't know where exactly Alek is settling Raena in, but if she's awake, I don't want her to have to see or hear Doc when we bring him in. There is a hidden door that leads to the basement level without having to go through the house. This makes bringing back the occasional prisoner easier.

Maddox slides the storage shelf to the left and presses into the back wall to reveal the electronic panel. The red light flashes as it flares to life. You would never know it was there unless you knew where to press, but the storage shelf provides an extra layer of security for my peace of mind. The panel scans his palm print, turning the light green.

The door makes a hissing sound as it pops open to reveal a set of stairs leading down to the basement that houses our training area. But that's not all. We occasionally have to bring back prisoners to interrogate or deal with. We have a special place for those unfortunate souls– *The Playroom.*

Maddox named it that because it is basically his personal playground. While I handle the leadership and decision making of our group, Alek is the muscle, and Maddox, well, he is our resident psycho.

As we descend into the basement, a soft white light cascades along the walls, illuminating the path. Once we reach the bottom, there is a narrow hallway that splits off in two directions, one leading to the main training area straight ahead, while the other leads to the playroom.

Turning to the right into another short hallway, there are storage rooms down here on either side and it appears to be a dead end. However, just like in the garage, Maddox presses into the wall at the very end to open the access panel, the door pops open once he's scanned his palm. Another set of stairs takes us down one more level, so far down, no one could ever hear the screams while Maddox works.

The Playroom resembles what I imagine a serial killer's den would be like. The concrete room houses a variety of different toys and tools to make even the toughest of grown men beg for their mommy in a pool of their own blood, sweat, and piss.

There is a drain in the middle of the floor for easy clean up, with a slight downward slope from the walls to the center like a swimming pool.

The cells are down another hallway off the furthest wall, so we cross over the slanted floor and head to where we'll keep Doc until we figure out what to do with him.

I don't want him anywhere near Raena again, but with it being unclear what exactly he did or didn't do to her, I won't make a decision without her. She isn't in the right frame of mind tonight to deal with this, so it looks like this will be Doc's home for the foreseeable future.

"We'll put him in the last cell," Maddox says, making his way ahead and unlocking the steel door. These aren't your typical prisoner cells. These are solid concrete walls, a solid steel door with a large observation window in the middle that allows us to see in but not them to see out. The rooms are high quality cells; they get their own bed and bathroom, which consists of a thin pad on a metal frame bolted to the floor, a toilet and sink in the corner.

Following him into the room, I toss Doc on the bed and start to undo his restraints. His eyes are darting around behind his lids when I remove his blindfold, a groan escaping his lips when the ropes are no longer binding him.

I stand to my full height just as his heavy eyes open and try to adjust to the low light and unfamiliar surroundings. He's never been to our home, always meeting us in the field or at Twisted when the Shadows required him. Because he worked for King, too, we never trusted him enough to let him know who we truly were.

"Wha– what's going on? Where am I?" He asks, his voice groggy and confused.

I choose to ignore him and his questions. There is no point right now. I need to speak to my brothers and to Raena before we deal with him. I'm afraid if he says something sideways, Maddox is going to lose it. He is too quiet, too calm right now. That's never a good sign with him. He is chaos personified 24/7. When he gets like this, it usually means a bloodbath will ensue soon.

"Get some rest, Doc. You're going to be here for a while," I say, walking out of the cell and shutting the heavy door behind us.

The locks engage once the door latches. We stand at the observation window in the door and watch him get his bearings and realize just what shit he has gotten into tonight.

***

The house is quiet when we make our way into the kitchen after settling Doc into the basement cells. Maddox follows behind me, taking a seat on one of the island barstools. I grab two beers from the refrigerator, sliding one to him before leaning back against the counter.

"Maddox, are you okay? Talk to me," I say, uncapping my beer and lifting it to my lips with my eyes still on him.

"I don't know what I am right now." He runs his hands up his face and into his hair, pulling on the ends. "All I know is it took everything in me not to gut Doc without getting an explanation from him. I know he was involved in whatever happened to her, but the reaction she had to his voice-- it set me off. I wanted to cut his fucking tongue out so she never had to hear it again."

"I know, but we need to get more information first and we need her to be in the right mental state to tell us what happened. She is too

114

unstable tonight to think clearly and we don't kill innocents. This could all just be a misunderstanding. Did Doc tell you anything before you gagged him?" I ask, knowing Maddox would have tried to get something out of him first because that's just who he is.

"Not really. He kept insisting that he didn't remember her, that she was mistaken. There is a part of me that hopes that is the case, that we don't have to put down the only doctor in this town. But…there is another part of me, the part that went feral with bloodlust when she was cowering in that corner half-naked, that doesn't really give a fuck if he is innocent or not."

Nodding at him, I round the island to stand behind him and place my hand on his shoulder. "I know. I don't know what it is about this girl that makes you want to burn the entire world down for her, but I feel it too," I tell him honestly.

There is no point in lying about how we feel. We've lived so long in trepidation because everything we've ever loved has been ripped away from us. That changes now.

She changes everything.

He slowly turns in his seat to look up at me, understanding in his eyes, but also desire. I'm not blind. I know he has sexual feelings for me. I've never encouraged it because he's my brother first and I would never want to lose him over something as stupid as sex. But I can't deny the curiosity I feel when he looks at me like that or makes his comments and jokes. I'm curious.

Shaking my head, I try to bring my thoughts back to the topic at hand, and he finally responds.

"I've never felt anything like this, Royal. What if I completely fuck this up? I'm crazy. Between my past and King, I am a blood-crazed psycho. She has clearly endured trauma. What if she takes one look at how fucked up I am, and runs for the hills?" He puts his head on the island top and I rub his back.

115

"You're scared," I say, because it isn't a question. "Guess what? So am I. This is new to all of us. We've never had someone come into our lives like this and completely change the game. We will figure this out like we do everything else. Together. Now let's go see where Alek took her. I need to see her, and I think it'll make you feel better too."

"Look at us. We've only known her a few hours, and I can't fucking stand that she isn't in my line of sight. This is fucking insane, you know that right?" He laughs, his familiar playfulness seeming to return after he unburdened himself from his own fears.

He isn't wrong. This girl has no idea what kind of men she just went home with. While we would never hurt her, we are not your average vanilla men. Each of us have our own things we enjoy where women are concerned. She might not be ready for anything like that right now, but eventually, she will be.

When that time comes, I want her begging for it.

He pulls himself up from the barstool and we make our way through the house into the living room, past the solid glass wall overlooking the forest. This house is one of the newest to be built in Shadow Forest, and I designed it.

A wall of glass backlit with soft white lights rests within the lush greenery. Sleek, wooden black beams lay in perfect, clean lines. The modernized and classy exterior is a deep contrast to the whimsical and chaotic beauty of the overgrown forest resting outside the pristine fortress. The sun will be peaking through glass walls soon, reminding me that we haven't even gone to sleep yet. I'm so exhausted, but I need to speak to my brothers, so sleep will have to wait.

We climb the black metal-framed stairs past the living room. On this level, we each have our own bedrooms with adjoining bathroom suites, as well as a guest room that we currently use as an office. Another set of stairs takes you to the rooftop loft, an open space three stories high, overlooking Grimm River. On the rare occasion, we get to relax, that is where we go.

Coming to the first bedroom on the right, Maddox steps inside his room and turns back to me. "I'm going to get out of these soggy clothes before we find her. You should, too."

He continues on to his room and I head to mine across the hall. These clothes are heavy and stiff now, but my socks are soggy in my boots. I need a shower and some whiskey after the night we've had.

Making quick work of my boots and rain-soiled clothes, I step into my oversized walk-in shower, hitting the digital panel to turn on the shower heads. The water pours down my aching body from the overhead rainforest sprayer, reminding me that I literally jumped off a cliff tonight.

My muscles in my upper back and shoulders are burning from the hyperextension when I climbed down the tree roots, and my leg muscles are tight from chasing my dark Angel through the forest before that.

Dark Angel. I like that.

It seems fitting for the little shadow dressed in all-black who turned me and my brothers inside out tonight in a matter of hours.

This shower is fucking phenomenal. The scalding hot water sprays from every direction, giving me a full massage as it washes away the forest dirt and tension out of my body. I want nothing more than to just go find my girl and brothers, curl up for the rest of this morning, and sleep all day long in a cocoon of ignorant bliss. But that isn't going to happen anytime soon.

I've got to figure out what to do with Doc, then figure out how to find an untraceable hunter before they make their next kill, and King takes it out on Emma.

Finishing up in the shower, I shut the sprayers off and grab a towel from the warming rack. The warmth of the tile floors hit my bare wet feet as I step out of the shower and make my way into my room, drying my body as I go.

"Well, hello there, big boy," Maddox says from his spot in the middle of my bed, grinning like the Cheshire Cat.

He's reclined back on my pillows with his hands behind his head, his hair wet and messy from his own shower. His tattoos on full display, covering almost every inch of his body, disappearing down into his low slung gray sweats.

My favorite tattoo now stands out on his side. What was once a rose, dripping with blood, and *three* thorns, now has four. One thorn for each brother, and now the stab wound that our Angel created.

He must be enjoying the show because I can see the imprint of his pierced dick growing bigger by the second. Rolling my eyes, I grab my sweats from the dresser, adjusting my own cock as it decides it likes his playful attention. But like always, I ignore the fucker. We don't have time for this right now.

"Let's go find our girl," I tell him, walking out of the room and heading down the hall to Alek's room. I can hear Maddox quickly following behind me.

Alek's door is slightly open but dark inside. Pushing it open, I am surprised to see them both in bed. I figured he would have insisted on taking the couch because he is a fucking gentleman like that. But considering I know what it feels like when she pulls you in and doesn't seem to be able to let go, I guess it's not that surprising.

It was extremely hard for me to let her go earlier to get her injuries tended to. She might not know us yet, but she seems to subconsciously understand that she wants us close. She trusts us even if she doesn't realize it yet.

Alek is laying on his back with Raena almost on top of him. She is curled around his body like a little spider monkey, holding on for dear life. He opens his eyes when he hears the door hinge creaking, looking up at me as I move to stand next to his bed. He is still fully dressed except for his shoes and mask.

"How is she doing?" Maddox whispers as he comes up on the opposite side of the bed, both of us taking a seat on the edges and touching her. He plays with the ends of her flaming red curls, and I gently trail my finger up her arm on Alek's chest.

"She is doing okay, considering. She doesn't understand what's happening right now anymore than we do, but she told me she feels safe." Alek stares at her head as he speaks, a look of unconditional devotion on his face.

We all just stare at her for a few moments, taking in the weight of her words. She feels safe with us, even after everything she has been through. It makes my heartbeat erratically in my chest because on one hand, I'm terrified.

This is just another person I have to protect. But on the other hand, nothing has ever felt so right in my entire goddamn life.

I have lived my life putting everyone's needs above my own, pushing away my own desires so I can protect the people I love. I won't do that here. Even if I wanted to, I can't. My soul called out to hers and laid its claim on this girl the minute I laid eyes on her, down at the bottom of that rocky cliff. She doesn't even know it yet, but she is our whole world now.

We've never had a woman like this. Sure, we've had sex before, but there were no feelings involved, and definitely no one who would inspire three possessive alpha men to share them. I haven't been with anyone since Emma was taken from us. And, though I'm not positive, I don't think my brothers have either.

Finding Emma has been more important than chasing a temporary release for a few fleeting moments. Not to mention, anyone we bring into our fucked up world will have a target on their backs.

She might not like it very much, but she is going to have to stay hidden until we can deal with this hunter, find Em, and deal with King.

119

I won't lose her when we just found her. If I have to tie her to my bed, keeping her blissed out on orgasms, I will.

"Why don't you go grab a shower and then we can talk. We'll stay with her," I tell him.

He looks as if he wants to protest. If this Angel was clinging to me like she is him, I wouldn't want to move a single muscle either. After a few moments, he kisses the top of her head and nods. "Okay, help me lie her down, I don't want to wake her up."

We maneuver her off of his massive body as gently as we can. Rolling her back into Maddox, she twists her body and buries her face into his chest. She pulls him into her, leaving enough room for Alek to get up. She doesn't even wake up when Maddox lifts her onto his body so he can lie down completely.

Alek stares back at her for a heartbeat or two before heading to his bathroom. He doesn't bother shutting the door, and I know it's because he doesn't want to lose sight of his *Baby Girl* in his bed.

Chapter 17

Cold.

I'm so fucking cold. It seeps deep into my bones, chilling me to the core. My bruised knees dig into the concrete floor as blood runs down my wrists to the tips of my fingers, guiding the gruesome medium into the crevices.

I didn't even feel the shards of glass piercing through my knuckles when I shattered the mirror above the grimy sink. Nor the pain when I slit my wrists with the shattered remains. Only relief.

Pain is an unrelenting presence I can't escape. Like this cell. The only escape I can find in this musty cell is my art.

The bloody depiction emulates my desolate existence. A broken girl on her knees for an evil Monster that haunts her.

It wasn't always like this. Before him, I was a vibrant, happy girl. My life was filled with enchantment and wonder. I had my Grams, Ella and dreams of a future. Ella and I were going to go to college and figure out what we wanted to do with our lives.

I have no future now beyond the walls of this cell and what the Monster wants from me. All I have now is an endless cycle of pain and blood.

The torment never ceases.

The pain never ends.

The blood keeps spilling.

I'm so lost inside my mind, I don't realize I'm not alone anymore until I feel hands gripping my tangled curls in their fist, pulling me to my feet and away from my masterpiece.

"You stupid, stupid girl," the Monster snarls in my ear. "What have you done?"

"What I had to do to escape you," I mumble back.

My body feels like it's floating and my stomach churns, making bile rise in my throat. Darkness edges my vision, as images of my old life flicker like an old movie in my mind. Maybe this is it. My body is finally letting go of what I can't. Maybe I'll finally be free.

"You'll never escape me, Little Wolf. I own every inch of your goddamn soul," the Monster snarls, and it's the last thing I hear before my eyes flutter shut one last time.

***

White light burns my retinas when I try to pry my heavy eyelids apart.

Am I dead?

Will I see Grams again?

Hope blossoms in my chest for the first time at the possibility, giving me the strength to ignore the blinding light and open my eyes once more.

That hope is crushed to dust when the familiar ceiling of my concrete hell stares back at me. I want to scream and cry, but my tears only fuel the Monster's depravity, and I'll be damned if I give him anything more than he already takes.

I'll never escape.

I'll never know peace.

I will live and die at the Monsters mercy.

Trying to bring my hand to my face, resistance pulls them back down to the bed. Of course, he fucking restrained me. He thinks I was trying to kill myself. It wasn't my intention, but it would've been fucking nice.

Resignation floods my body as I close my eyes, sinking back into the thin mattress in defeat.

"Welcome back, Little Wolf," the man himself says. I hear the heavy door close behind him before his footsteps echo closer and closer to me.

Keeping my eyes shut, I try to ignore him, but I should've known he wouldn't allow me a single ounce of peace. His fingers dig into my now bandaged wrists, and I force my eyes open. I level him with a look of indifference— one I've almost perfected during my time here. I learned early on that he craves my reactions just as much as he craves hurting me.

"That was a stupid thing to do. If you wanted my attention, all you had to do was ask, Little Wolf."

"I want nothing from you, Monster," I state, detaching myself from the anger his presence induces.

I hear a sharp crack and my head snaps to the side, before the sting from his hand even registers. Hatred burns so hot inside me, fire could shoot out of my eyes if I'm not careful. I carefully reign in the rage, before turning my eyes back to the ceiling.

I would rather he beat me to death than give him another fucking piece of me.

His hands softly brush my hair out of my face, the gentleness a direct contradiction to how he just slapped the shit out of me.

"Okay, Little Wolf."

He moves away from me, and I hear his footsteps retreating back towards the door. I don't move an inch. If now is the time he decides to give me a goddamn break, I'll fucking take it. But of course, that's not the case at all.

"Bring it in." He says to someone once he opens the door.

My mind reels with all the possibilities of what fresh hell he could unleash on me as punishment, but I don't move my eyes from their fixed position on the ceiling.

"Put it in the corner."

I hear feet shuffling and something scraping against the floor, before the footsteps disappear out of the door again.

"Consider this a gesture of good faith." he says, stepping back towards the bed. Confusion blankets me, but I hold steadfast, refusing to give in to the urge to look. His hands tangle in my curls as he lowers his face to mine. His gentle demeanor glitches to the Monster, the falsity falling away like a broken mask.

"You only bleed for me, Little Wolf. At my hand and my command. Try that shit again. Anything I've done before now... will feel like simple child's play."

MADDOX

Chapter 18

Quiet.

For years, there has been a constant buzz beneath my skin, racing thoughts and mania fueling my body every single day. Cherry quiets that.

I don't know how, but my head is clear and my body is still. With her in my arms, I no longer feel the incessant need to climb out of my own skin or go downstairs to gut the doctor.

The moment her tiny little body clung to me when I lifted her to lie down, she made everything go still. The buzz beneath my skin is gone, and in its place, is peace. Well, peace and a little pain. Now that I'm not raging out in my own head, my body is realizing the alcohol has long worn off, and getting stabbed hurts like a bitch. I don't mind pain, though– it keeps me grounded.

Her shirt has ridden up her back, revealing her mangled scars that set my blood on fire.

Who the fuck would do something like that to her?

My hand absentmindedly runs along the raised flesh between her shirt and the top of her leggings. They will die for this. But not before I peel their skin from their flesh, inch by agonizing inch.

I'm going to teach my Cherry how to leave her marks on them before we bleed them dry. I will make damn sure she gets her wicked revenge.

Royal must see my thoughts playing out on my face, turning more murderous by the second because he grabs my hand that's on her back, gives it a light squeeze, and brings his eyes to my face.

"It was King," he whispers, his eyes darting to her exposed back so I know what he is referring to. My entire body tenses at the realization.

"What. The. Fuck?" I say, louder than I should. Raena starts to stir against my chest.

After a moment, she settles back into me, her sweet breath tickling across my bare skin. He must see the murderous rage amp up even more in my eyes.

"We can't do anything stupid. He will die for everything he has done to us. To Em. And now what he has done to her. Trust me. But Maddox, we have to find Em first. We have to deal with this hunter and find our sister," he pleads with me, begging me not to do anything that could get us killed.

With a heavy sigh, I bury my nose into my Cherry's hair, searching for the peace I had moments ago. Her beautiful curls tickle my face, her scent grounding me like the pain does.

"Whatever it takes, brother," I tell him, holding Raena a little bit tighter to my chest. I hope he knows whatever talk he wants to have is happening right here because now that she is in my arms, clinging to me for security, I can't let her go.

Alek walks out of the bathroom with a towel wrapped around his waist, steam billowing in behind him. "Let's talk. I'm exhausted. I just want to lay down next to her and sleep for a week."

He lets the towel at his waist drop to the floor, as he bends down to grab his sweats from the bottom drawer, giving us a full view of his decadent ass.

Fuck. This man is built like a brick-shit-house. My already rock-hard cock twitches beneath this red-haired beauty.

Down boy, read the fucking room.

"Me too," Royal sighs, rubbing his hands down his face before discreetly adjusting himself, but I saw it. Royal is curious too. I smirk at both of them, keeping my inner thoughts to myself for once. "What are we going to do about Doc?" he asks.

"I know she said he wasn't on her list, whatever the fuck that is supposed to mean, but I think he still needs to die. He obviously did something for her to react that way to him," Alek says, moving back to his side of the bed, pulling the covers from under me and Raena before climbing into the middle next to me. He sits with his back against the headboard and tucks the covers around both of us.

"I agree with Daddy," I smirk at him. "He needs to die. When I questioned him at Twisted, he insisted that he didn't recognize her, but I'm not willing to risk it. Also, as much as it pains me to say, I think we need to wait for her to wake up and ask her what she wants to do. This is her decision to make."

They both nod back at me. I can be wise. *Sometimes.* "Besides, we already know she isn't afraid to get a little stabby. I want to see my girl get her revenge. I think that starts with Doc. We can help her take her power back."

"I agree. We wait until she wakes up and she can tell us what she wants. But he is a threat regardless. If she chooses to spare him, he will stay locked up until King is dead. I won't risk him exposing her to King," Royal says.

"Agreed," Alek and I say in unison.

"Okay. Now, do we know why she was at Jackson's house tonight, dressed like us?" Royal asks, and I hadn't really thought about it until then.

"Well, she was dressed the same when I saw her at Twisted earlier tonight. Maybe she saw us going in there and followed us in? I don't fucking know." I'm confused as fuck. She is obviously terrified of King. Why would she be at one of his ranking guards' houses? Does she know him? "You don't think she was fucking him do you?" I ask, rage boiling in my veins at the thought of her with another man. Which is crazy, but I don't really give a fuck.

She is ours.

"No!" Royal says harshly, his bright blue eyes darkening to a shade that matches his name. "She isn't fucking him."

"Okay, well she's going to have to tell us when she wakes up then because I don't fucking know. Let's just get some sleep. It's already almost daylight. We have to be up in a few hours to deal with King's bullshit about this fucking hunter," I say, exhaustion weighing heavy on me.

Alek nods his head, scooting down in the bed and spooning the both of us. "Get in or get out, Royal. We need a few hours of sleep before the shit show starts again," he says, lifting the covers in invitation behind him.

Royal doesn't even hesitate, slipping in behind him. Royal is a big guy, but Alek is huge. Royal being the big spoon in this little love nest is hilarious.

"Hey Royal, try not to poke daddy in the ass tonight. I don't want him humping my leg in his sleep," I jab at him.

"Shut up, Maddie," Alek tells me.

Somehow, I earn a head slap from one of them, but it's too dark to tell now without the bathroom light illuminating the room.

"Ow, fucker. You're going to wake her up." Neither of them respond, choosing silence instead to torture me. "Sleep tight, assholes," I finally say, snuggling my Cherry tighter and inhaling her scent as I let the exhaustion and darkness take me under.

***

"No no no! Please, stop! Noooooo."

I'm jolted awake with a sharp pain to my abdomen, my stab wound is screaming. It takes me a few seconds to clear the sleep from my eyes to realize that it's Raena thrashing and screaming on top of me.

Alek and Royal remain dead to the world as I grip her waist tightly to my body, swing my legs over the side of the bed and take her into the bathroom. She's quiet, but she's still struggling in my grasp when I shut the door and turn the light on.

"Cherry, you're safe here. It's a nightmare," I tell her, sitting down on the floor with her straddling my legs. I pull back away from her to grip her face, rubbing my fingers into her hair as I speak to her. "Hey, it's okay. I've got you. It's just a dream."

The fight leaves her body as she sags against my hold, her tightly shut eyelids starting to open. When her emerald green eyes find mine, they widen, and her breath catches her throat.

"Who are you?" she asks, her voice hoarse, barely a whisper. *Oh shit!* I forgot she has never seen my face without the mask, unlike my brothers who came out of that exam room unmasked.

"I'm Maddox, baby. It's okay. Just breathe for me. I'm not going to hurt you." My brothers must have told her my name because she let's out a sigh she was holding in, and the tension leaves her body instantly.

I release her face and rest my hands at my sides to show her I'm not a threat. Her eyes slowly roam my face, trailing down my body before she reaches out and gently touches the bandage at my side, her face paling as she realizes that I'm the one she stabbed last night.

"Oh my God! I stabbed you." Her eyes widen in shock.

"You did. It's okay. It was crazy hot," I wink at her, grinning widely.

"What?" She asks, her cheeks pink up beautifully.

"Oh, Cherry. You're fucking adorable." Chuckling at her, I grab her hands in mine. "You'll learn I'm a different breed. Stabbing me is like foreplay."

"Ohhh…" Her pouty lips form the cutest little "O" as she realizes what I meant. "Well, still, I'm sorry. It was a reflex. You startled me. I wasn't expecting anyone to be there."

I might as well get this out of the way now since she brought it up. "What were you doing there?"

Her face turns pale again, all evidence of bashfulness gone in the blink of an eye. "It doesn't matter," she mumbles, turning to look around the bathroom and refusing to meet my eyes. "Can I take a shower?" Her almost whispered question stuns me for a second.

"Ye-yes," I stutter out, blinking the shock from my eyes at how quickly she retreated back into the quiet, shy girl she was in that exam room earlier.

What the fuck happened to her?

She moves to stand and I steady her with my hands on her waist. "Let me show you how to work the panel and I'll go find you some clothes."

Getting up off the floor, we walk over to the massive shower with sprayers in all directions. "Holy shit, this is the fanciest shower I've been in," she says in awe, taking in the bougie ass shower Royal insisted we needed in all our bathrooms.

"Yeah, Royal designed this entire fancy-ass house for us, and he insisted we needed these fancy showers in all of our bathrooms. It took me months to figure out how to work these fuckers."

I quickly show her how to turn it on and adjust which sprayers she wants and the temperature levels. "Can you just, um, turn them all on, scalding hot please?" She asks, looking sheepishly at the panel like she doesn't want to fuck it up.

"Yeah, I can do that, pretty girl," I say, chuckling at her again, turning the sprayers on and adjusting the temperature to nearly Satan's asshole for her. "I'll leave you to it. I'll grab you some clothes from my room."

"Thank you," she says, smiling shyly at me before looking toward the floor and melting me into a fucking puddle like a schoolboy.

"No need to thank me, Cherry," I say, gently lifting her chin to look into her eyes.

Her smile lights my soul on fire. Kissing her forehead, it takes every ounce of my strength not to lift her up and pin her to the fucking wall. I turn around and head out of the bathroom.

Royal and Alek are still sleeping like the dead, but Alek is now spooning him. Laughing to myself because I know without a doubt, Royal will be getting his monster morning wood soon, and I am here for it. I slip out of his bedroom and go to my own. We are all way bigger than Raena, but I'm the smallest of us all, so I grab her some boxers, sweats, and a t-shirt.

I will say, regardless of size, I really want to wrap her in my scent. I'm having this primal urge to see her in my clothes. I've never had this desire for anyone, so this feels foreign to me.

After grabbing what I need, I walk back down the hall, through Aleks bedroom and stop dead in my tracks when I peer through the crack in the door.

The scene in front of me sends a lightning bolt of desire straight to my cock. Raena is standing under the sprayers in the glass shower stall, one leg up on the bench. She has one hand on the wall, with the other one wrapped around the detachable shower head. The direct stream of water is aimed between her legs. Her red hair is in waist length ribbons shrouding her face from view with her head angled down.

Holy fucking shit.

A soft moan escapes her and hits me right in the cock. I slowly open the door to get a full view of the show she is putting on for me. She looks like a fucking goddess right now, pleasuring herself with absolutely no care in the world.

I will gladly worship at her feet every fucking day of my life. When I die, I'll worship her from the afterlife as well. There will be no escape for her.

Throwing her head back to the ceiling, her moans get louder and louder. I don't want to wake my brothers so I step inside the bathroom and close the door to muffle her delectable sounds. I want to keep them for myself for now.

The sound of the door latching catches her attention and she rolls her head to the side to look dead into my soul. But she doesn't stop. She locks eyes with me as she reaches the peak of her orgasm, and I'm a fucking goner. I don't think she understands the beast she just unleashed.

I'm a psychopath.

Certifiably insane.

I think I fucking love her.

Chapter 19

The flood of euphoria filling my body from my orgasm makes my knees weak. Dropping the shower head to hang from the wall, I put both hands on the wall to steady myself, my body still twitching as I suck in deep breaths.

I don't know what came over me. I have never felt desire like this before. The pulsing between my legs was too strong to ignore. These men. They make me feel things I don't understand. I barely know their names, yet when Maddox caught me getting off in the shower, I didn't stop.

His eyes on mine made my orgasm rush to the surface, and I shattered harder than I ever had. But it's not enough. I want more. Tell me why I want this man I don't even know to step into this shower with me and fuck me into this wall?

"Cherry," he says in a strained whisper, dropping the clothes in his hand to the floor and leans back, placing his palms flat on the door behind him.

His eyes roam over every inch of my scarred skin. I expect him to twist his face in disgust, but I can see his impressive cock imprint in his sweats. He isn't deterred by my ruined flesh.

"Maddox," I whisper to him, my eyes begging him to lose control and make me forget about the nightmare I just had, and how everything is so fucked up right now. "Please."

That one little word is all it takes for his control to snap. He is across the room with his hand lightly around my throat, my body pressed into the glass wall, his knee spreading my legs open. He didn't even bother undressing, his sweats must be getting soaked. His nose presses into the crook of my neck, and his deep inhale lets me know he is sniffing me. *Again.*

"What do you need?" He growls into my ear as he lightly nips it with his teeth, and I swear to fucking God, I nearly orgasm again just from this alone.

No one has ever touched me like this. The only sexual touch I've ever had was forced on me. It made me feel dirty, used, and damaged. When these men touch me, it feels like my entire body is being consumed. I just want to drown in their blazing touches, setting my entire body on fire.

"Make me forget. Please just make me forget." My words rush out in a broken whisper. Tears have built in my eyes from the emotions running through me rapidly.

"I got you, pretty girl," he says, pulling back enough to look at me. His thumb swipes the tears from my cheeks as he cradles my face in one hand. Closing my eyes for a moment, I lean into his touch, allowing myself to completely soak up his affection.

Looking back into his eyes, I see them dart down to my lips, and my breath catches in my throat at what I know he is going to do.

Out of everything King and his disgusting men did to me, I've never been kissed. My heart is pounding, my eyes roaming his face before fluttering closed as he slowly leans in and presses his lips to mine.

The kiss is slow at first, light pressure as his lips softly caress mine, but when his tongue licks at the seam of my lips, I fucking melt.

Opening my mouth to grant him access, his tongue roams over mine for a moment before it joins in, our tongues dancing as our hands roam. My hands slide up and down his slick body, over his tattooed abs, being careful not to touch his bandaged wound. I move up his chest, wrapping my arms around his neck and pulling him tighter into me.

Using his knee between my legs, he hoists me up with one hand under my bare ass until my throbbing pussy is settled high on his thigh. The delicious friction as he rocks my body back and forth on his thigh has desire shooting through my veins, bringing me closer to the release I need.

Breaking our kiss, he says, "That's it, Cherry. Ride my thigh like you want to ride my cock." His voice is strained and sexy as hell. Like he is holding himself back.

I can feel the energy vibrating through his body. A live wire being held back by a thread. I want to make his control shatter on the shower floor. I feel his cock pressing into my hip as my pussy throbs against his thigh. My hands travel down to grip him through his sweats, but he releases my throat and stops my hand before I can touch him.

"Trust me, you're not ready for that yet."

"Why not?" I ask.

I want him and he obviously wants me. It's just sex. Even though I've never been a willing participant, I know how sex works.

"Because when I fuck you, it won't be a quick fuck in the shower," he says as he grips both of my hands in his and places them above my head. He balances me on his thigh, moving his other hand to my breast, taking the weight in his hand and teasing my nipple with his thumb as he speaks. "I'll take my time."

His mouth descends on my pointed nipple before his teeth bite down painfully, causing a startled cry to fall from my lips. He immediately soothes the ache with his tongue, sucking and caressing it before doing the same with the other. He releases my sore nipple with an audible "pop."

His hand travels down my slick stomach, over my scar and I freeze. What if he notices? How do I tell him something like that? Or any of them? I let… *NO!* Fear and grief threaten to drown me again, but I refuse. I won't allow myself to fall into that pit of despair again. Pushing the thoughts down in my mind, I focus on Maddox. His hand stopped just below my belly button, he must have seen the internal battle on my face.

"Hey, where did you just go?" The concern in his voice almost breaks me.

"Somewhere I want to forget. Please. Just touch me."

I am begging this man. I still don't know him, but my soul does. He feels like home. They all do. But their touches are like a fire trying to consume me, and I'd willingly let myself burn for them.

"You will tell me soon, my little Cherry. All of your secrets will be mine."

His fingers dip lower, grazing my swollen clit. His touch is feather light, and I can feel the arousal flooding out of my pussy as my stomach clenches at the contact.

"This pussy is mine," he says, still slowly moving his thumb against me, agonizingly slow and so light he is barely touching me. "Your mouth," he says, leaning in to lick the seam of my mouth. "Every single inch of your body, mind, and soul, they're all mine. You are all of ours. Do you understand that?"

I'm stunned into silence.

They want... me? Like this? All of them? Why?

Everything is so crazy right now I don't know which way is up. All I know is this man has his hands on my naked body, and I would crawl on my knees to him and beg him to come back if he walked out of this bathroom right now.

I must take too long to answer him, even though I don't know what I would have said, because he slaps the top of my pussy quickly. "I asked you a question, Cherry?"

"Oh fuck." The sting sends shockwaves through my body, the pain morphing into intense pleasure that makes my eyes roll back in my head. "Do that again."

"Not until you answer me. Do you understand that you're ours now, pretty girl?" His hands stills, waiting for my answer.

I would think the question would scare me, or cause me to pause. But the only answer I have comes flying out of my mouth before I can even think about it.

"Yes, Sir."

Chapter 20

"Alek," I growl.

This motherfucker.

My eyes snap open when I can't roll over. His monster dick is pressing into my ass, and his big ass mammoth arm is thrown around my waist, pinning me to him.

"Alek!" I shove my ass back into his dick as hard as I can. "Let me go, you overgrown man-beast."

He only pulls me tighter against him, digging that monster into my ass harder.

Fucking hell.

"Get the fuck off me, man. I need to take a piss." I ram my foot back into his shin as hard as I can until he finally groans, rolling onto his back and releasing me from his tight hold to grip his shin.

"What the fuck, Royal?!"

I don't say anything. I just roll out of bed and stumble around towards the bathroom.

"Um, where the fuck are they?" Alek says, making me stop dead in my tracks. Turning around, I flip the light switch on to see him in bed alone. "You hear that?" He asks, and I turn towards the bathroom. I can hear the water running.

"Shower," I say as he jumps out of bed and follows me to the door. We stop and listen closely, I can hear my girl moaning through the door and Maddox's voice, but it's too low to make out what he is saying.

Slowly opening the bathroom door, the sight that greets us steals the breath straight from my lungs. Maddox has Raena pinned against the wall, balancing her on his thigh, with her hands pinned above her head.

"This pussy is mine. Your mouth, your ass. Every single inch of your body, mind, and soul, they're all mine. You are all of ours. Do you understand that?" He says, and we stand there with bated breath, awaiting her answer. She doesn't answer him immediately– the look on her face tells me she is in her head about it.

Fuck. What if she doesn't agree?

The sharp sound of wet skin being slapped jars me and my breath rushes out. He slapped her pussy.

Goddamn, that's hot as fuck.

My cock is hard as stone, tenting my sweats. I don't look at Alek to see if he is in a similar state, but I can assume so with the scene in front of us. I can't take my eyes off of them.

"Oh fuck. Do that again," she begs, and it sounds so beautiful coming from her lips. I want to hear her beg, on her hands and knees, as she crawls to me.

"Not until you answer me. Do you understand that you're ours now, pretty girl?" He asks. Her response is quick this time, nearly buckling my knees.

"Yes, Sir."

My tiny shred of restraint I've had these last few minutes snap like a fucking twig with her consent. I step fully into the bathroom, Alek right behind me.

"Angel," I whisper, stepping into the glass-walled shower with them, my sweats getting soaked immediately. Her gorgeous eyes lock on mine, heavy with desire, her pupils blown, making her emerald color appear a haunting forest green.

Closing the distance between us, I cradle her face in my hand. "Tell us what you need."

Alek steps to her other side, running his hand through her hair and angling her head back to look up at him. "Yes, Baby Girl, let us in."

"Make me forget. Please. I just want to forget everything before this moment." The pain in her voice shatters me. I don't know what she has been through, not the details anyway. I can piece together enough to understand she's been through hell at the hands of Kingston Wolfe.

"Maddox, bring her back to bed," Alek says, his tone deep and commanding, and fuck me if it doesn't do something for me.

He carries her through the bathroom and into the bedroom, a trail of water dripping off them both the whole way. I shut the water off before grabbing some towels off the rack.

I quickly slip my wet sweats off, wrapping one around my waist. Alek grabs one, doing the same before we walk out. Maddox lowers her to her feet at the foot of the bed before grabbing a towel and moving back into the bathroom to lose his dripping wet sweats, too.

"Here, let me dry you off," I say, bringing the towel to her head and squeezing out her flaming red curls before drying every inch of her body.

Maddox returns next to me. I notice he now has on a pair of boxer shorts. He hands me and Alek a pair, too.

"Lie back on the bed. Right in the middle," Alek tells her.

When she turns to do just that, we turn our backs to her and slip the boxers on before discarding the towels in a heap on the floor. She looks at us confused, and if I'm not mistaken, a little disappointed. She doesn't understand why we are covering ourselves when we just told her we would take care of her needs.

The three of us stand at the foot of the bed, staring at our girl like starving men stare at a feast before them. But this isn't about us.

This is about giving her what she needs. She wants us to make her forget everything before this moment right here.

Be careful what you wish for, Angel.

Chapter 21

Holy fucking shit on a cracker.

These three men stand before me, now only in black boxers, staring at my naked body laid out on the bed.

I had a flash of doubt that they weren't going to take this any further when I saw them putting boxers on, but their eyes bore into my body, caressing my skin with their intense gaze. The molten blaze of desire I see staring back at me, I know they want this just as much.

Alek stands in the middle, Maddox on the left, and Royal on the right. They look fucking delicious with their tattoos on display.

Alek is the biggest of the three and seems to have the least amount of tattoos on him. They cover his broad shoulders, running up his neck, down his chest and both arms to his hands. He is a stunningly beautiful man. His abs are sculpted all the way down to the delectable V.

My eyes travel down to his happy trail of thick black hair that disappears into his boxers. The imprint of his cock straining against the tight fitting fabric makes my eyes bulge out of my head. *Holy fuck.* He is huge. I haven't even seen him completely naked, and I can already tell that massive thing isn't going to fit anywhere in my tiny framed body. It will split me in two.

Maddox is the smallest, but they're all huge. He is a few inches shorter than the other two, but still tall and slender with tight, rigid muscles. Tattoos cover almost his entire body, starting at his neck and disappearing into the waistband of his boxers. He doesn't appear to have any hair on him, his body smooth and sculpted.

He is ridiculously hot, in that "bad boy who will ruin your life" kind of way. The frantic energy rolling off of him should scare me, but it doesn't. It makes me excited. Maddox is chaos incarnate. His cock is straining against his boxers as well. I can tell it's not as big as Alek's, but still, it scares me.

Royal is almost as tall as Alek, but he's not as broad. His body is also muscular and covered in tattoos, though they seem to be more spaced out than Maddox's. They also start at his neck and go down his tight, sculpted abs but stop just above his waistline.

I caught a glimpse of his back when I got onto the bed, and his biggest tattoo covers the whole thing. It's a large skull that starts at the top of his back and is shaded all the way down to his tight, round ass. It's hauntingly beautiful.

After a few moments of appraising each of their bodies, they finally move. Alek climbs onto the bed from the bottom while Maddox and Royal come around on either side. Alek is the first one to break the silence.

"Do you want this, Baby Girl? Do you want us to touch you?"

I'm a little stunned by his question. I thought that much was obvious. I nod my head eagerly before moving my hands to cover my face, embarrassment washing over me with how fast this is moving. We just fucking met a few hours ago, and now here I am, laying naked in bed willingly with all three of them, my pussy dripping onto the sheets with how much I want this.

I feel warm hands on my own, pulling them down from my face. "Don't you dare hide from us," Alek growls from his knees as he leans over me.

He lifts my chin to look into his golden-brown eyes. They have yellow and green specks floating in them. He has a way of making me feel safe with his warm, soul-piercing gaze.

"I need you to say the words." His voice is dark and commanding, making me want to comply just to feel the flutters it provokes.

"Yes, Daddy," I say, smirking at him, suddenly feeling more confident than I was a few moments ago.

I watch his pupils blow, making his eyes turn almost black. *Well fuck.*

"Careful, Cherry. Daddy likes that." Maddox snickers at me before Alek smacks him on the back of the head, making me smile at their playfulness.

"There she is," Royal says, smiling as he lightly grazes my thigh, trailing his fingers up and down, causing goosebumps to pop up on my pale skin.

"Eyes on me, Baby Girl." Alek gives me no warning before he grips my thighs under my knees and jerks me down the bed to him, spreading me open for him. The rush of arousal floods me, catching me by surprise.

"Oh shit," I gasp out as his tongue makes a full swipe up my slit.

The tip of his tongue moves lazily up and down, from my entrance to my clit. I can feel my wetness leaking out of me, running down my ass, and soaking the sheets beneath me. I want to be embarrassed, but I obey him and keep my eyes on him.

Maddox nuzzles his face into my neck, sniffing me again. His mouth sucks on the skin beneath my ear, before biting down lightly, sending tingles racing up and down my spine.

Royal runs his hand over my breast, lowering his head and sucking my pointed nipple into his mouth. He flicks his tongue back and forth over the bud before biting down, causing a strangled cry to fall from my lips. His tongue soothes the ache before he sucks hard and repeats his action again.

My eyes must have closed from the combination of their glorious torture because I feel a sharp sting on my other nipple before Maddox whispers into my ear. "Eyes on Daddy, Cherry."

He slapped my breast. "Holy fucking shit!" I cry out. It's too much and not nearly enough at the same time. "Please." I am begging, even though I don't know what I need. My emotions are running wild, flooding my system as tears run down my face.

"That's it, Angel. Let go. Give it all to us," Royal says, bringing his face to mine, stealing my fallen tears with his tongue.

His hand grips my throat, not tight enough to restrict my air, but enough to feel the power radiating off him in seductive waves. He presses his forehead into mine, grounding me, and the tears fall harder.

The release I'm chasing is close. Alek's tongue moves faster over my clit, flicking harder and harder. I'm a dripping, panting mess.

Maddox latches onto my nipple as Alek sucks my clit into his mouth, pressing two fingers into me and curling them, rubbing a spot inside me I didn't know was there. And I shatter.

His fingers start pumping into me faster and faster as my release threatens to drown me in orgasmic bliss.

"I think... I am..." I can't form any sentence as my body tenses and liquid sprays from my pussy, undoubtedly covering Alek's face.

"OH. MY. GOD." I pant out. "Did I just… pee on you?" I know my face is fifty shades of red with my mortification.

"Look at me," Alek commands, and Royal backs up so I can see his face. It's literally dripping down his chin. "You made a mess all over Daddy," He says, smirking at me. "But you didn't pee. You squirted. You've never done that before, Baby Girl?"

"Squirted?" My voice is shaky. "No… No, I've never been with anyone.. like that before," I admit, shame immediately weighing me down.

"Are you a virgin?" Royal asks kindly, his hand absentmindedly rubbing my hair back.

"No," I whisper, closing my eyes. I don't want to see the look on their faces when they understand what I'm telling them. "I've never been with anyone… willingly."

Each of their bodies are touching me somewhere, so I feel them tense at the realization of what I just said.

Chapter 22

That motherfucker.

"I will paint this town red with his goddamn blood!" I roar, jumping up from the bed and pacing the room.

I'm spiraling. My thoughts race with all the possible ways to kill King. I pull at my hair to the point of pain. I don't give a fuck.

He hurt my girl. He scarred her body. Forced her to do God knows what. I want to pull his intestines out through his ass. I want to peel the skin from his face and feed him his own eyeballs. Cut his disgusting rapist dick off, blend it up, and funnel it down his throat. I want to bathe my girl in his blood. I will paint the walls of my playroom with his screams.

"Maddox, calm down," I vaguely hear Royal say through the blood rushing in my ears.

I can hear my own erratic heart beating. I feel it pounding in my chest. My body is vibrating with unleashed rage. I need to bleed something. NOW!

"Come on, Maddie. You're scaring her," Alek says, grabbing me from behind and spinning me to face him. He grips the back of my neck and brings his forehead to mine. "Just breathe." I take a deep breath in, holding it to steady myself. I don't want to scare my Cherry. "That's it. Let it out." Blowing out the breath, I close my eyes and focus on controlling the manic energy coursing through me. "Good boy," Alek whispers, pulling me tighter against him.

Goddamn it! Fuck me if his daddy energy doesn't ground me enough to pull back and look at her.

She is sitting up against the headboard, her hands covering her face, resting on her knees that are pulled up to her chest.

"Cherry," I whisper, moving out of Alek's grip and climbing back onto the bed slowly. "I'm so sorry, pretty girl." Pulling her into my arms, she straddles my waist, burying her face into my neck. "I didn't mean to scare you. I will never hurt you." I hug her tightly against me, my face in her hair. I inhale as deeply as I can through my nose, and even though she smells like Alek from her shower, she still has that sweet cherry smell that calms me.

She isn't crying, just holding on to me. I don't know how long we stay like this, holding on to each other, calming each other down with our bodies clinging together. My breathing has slowed. My heart is beating a normal rhythm now.

Opening my eyes, I see Alek and Royal moved on either side of us in the bed. I didn't even feel them get up here. They each have a hand on one of her thighs, softly tracing patterns to soothe her.

"I'm sorry for upsetting you." Her timid voice is barely a whisper. I don't like it one bit.

"Look at me," I say, bringing her face into my hands when she lifts her head. "You are not responsible for this. Do you understand me? I'm the one who's sorry. I didn't mean to lose it. That man…" I trail off, giving myself a moment to breathe so I don't lose my shit again. "He will never hurt you again."

She nods back at me before burying her face back in my neck. The sun is already peaking through the windows. I feel like I haven't slept at all.

"Come on, Baby Girl. Try to get a few more hours of sleep. We'll talk more once you're rested." Alek assures her, and I lift her and lay down with her on top of me.

"Your head looks good. How do you feel? Any pain?" Alek asks, his daddy persona coming out strong right now, always needing to take care of everyone.

"It's not too bad," she mumbles into my neck, her voice exhausted from everything that has happened tonight. Her breathing has already evened out, and she's drifting off to sleep quickly.

"Lift her up," Alek says, bringing a new bandage for my wound and sealing it on. He tosses the towel he must have laid under her earlier from the bed before pulling up the covers around us both. "Get some rest with her, Maddie. Come down in a bit, and we'll talk more."

They both kiss the top of her head before heading out of the room. It doesn't take me long to drift off, her soft breath on my cheek and her sweet cherry scent consuming me, relaxing me more than anything ever has.

Chapter 23

Sitting on the floor of our gym, the sound of Royal wailing on the punching bag and grunting his frustrations out fills the space. He's feeling out of control. Raena's confession, even though we'd already suspected it was going to be bad, sent him into a rage.

I sit here with my arms draped over my bent knees, watching him to make sure he's okay. He gets like this sometimes. He hates feeling out of control.

When he was a little boy, he had to take care of his crack whore mother and baby sister before they both died. He was only eight years old when he was sent into foster care.

Maddox and I were placed in the group home within days of each other, but Royal had been there a year already. We were only eight at the time. Little kids who had already lost everything and were thrust into another bad situation.

He took care of us. He protected us from the bastards running the home, gave us his food when they would take ours away for 'breaking the rules'.

I remember the first time they put me and Maddox in the time-out box in the basement. We were there for three days, with no water or food, before he found us. I can still smell the piss and blood that coated the 'time-out box' on my bad days.

"Alek! Maddox!" he exclaims, shining the light in his hand in my eyes.

I am so tired. I refuse to fall asleep, scared they will come in and take Maddie out for 'punishment' again if I close my eyes. I don't know how long we've been in here, but it feels like forever.

I am so hungry and thirsty, I have even considered licking the pee from the disgusting metal floor.

"Royal?" I groan. I gently shake Maddox, who fell asleep in my lap some time ago. I'm careful not to move him too much since he is hurt. His sides turned a weird purple color when they brought him back last time, and he said it's hard to breathe. He has cuts all over him, coating his bare skin in blood. "Wake up, Maddie." He tries to sit up fast, grabbing his chest and crying out at the pain.

This isn't time-out; this is torture.

The time-out box is a metal box bolted to the floor. It's not tall enough to stand in, but we can get to our knees and crawl around. The door on the front has thick bars like a prison cell. They've taken Maddox out of this box twice since we've been down here.

I help Maddox get to the front of the box while Royal fumbles with the lock on the end, but he can't get us out. He doesn't have a key. The guard took them with him. He can't get us out, but at least he knows we're here, that we didn't abandon him.

"I can't get it open!" he yells, making my fear rise to new levels. I know if they find him down here, they won't hesitate to throw him in here with us. I'm scared for him.

"Shhhhhh. Don't let them hear you. We're okay. They can't keep us down here forever," I tell him. They will eventually let us out. We can survive if he can sneak us some things in. "Where are they? Can you get us some water down here? They haven't given us anything since we've been here."

"They left about an hour ago. I've been looking for you both since. This is the first time they've left since I woke up and I couldn't find either of you. I don't know how long they will be gone. They locked me in my room, but I climbed out the window on the roof and used the tree to climb down," he says, looking frantically around the basement for something. "If I can find something, I might be able to break the lock."

"No!" I whisper shout at him, grabbing Royal's fingers through the bars. Maddox crawls next to me, latching onto the bars as well. "They will just punish you too. We will be okay. We can take care of each other. I've got Maddie. Just bring some water back if you can, but don't get caught."

"What did they do to him?" he asks, a horrified look on his face when he gets a good look at Maddie's bruised and blood-coated body.

"Punishment," I say as rage fills my body like nothing I've ever felt.

He didn't do anything wrong. These are just bad, evil people. I've been around enough to know them when I see them. They have that look in their eyes. The same look I saw in my mother's eyes when she would take me to visit her 'friends'. They had the same look, too. Pure evil.

"We will get out of here soon. I'm working on a plan." I know what he's talking about and it makes my stomach hurt. It doesn't feel right. I don't trust them.

"Don't do anything stupid, Royal. We will figure this out together when they let us out. Promise me." I am begging him. I just have a bad feeling.

"I promise. Take care of each other. I'll be back."

Pulling myself from that memory, I see Royal still beating the shit out the bag. Enough is enough. He's going to hurt himself if he keeps on like this. He isn't even protecting his hands.

Pulling myself up from the floor, I walk up behind him and touch his shoulder. He immediately turns and swings on me. I barely miss his right-hook before I twist out of the way, grabbing him and flipping him to the mat.

"Fuck, man. You almost got me. Chill the fuck out," I growl at him, pinning him down beneath my massive body.

The struggle leaves his body almost instantly, and he shakes his head to clear the fog from his mind. He was completely lost inside his head.

"I'm sorry. I just reacted," he murmurs, rubbing his hands down his face before looking up at me. "I'm fine now. Get the fuck off me, man."

Rolling off him, I sit on my ass next to him as he sits up and hangs his head.

"We'll get him, Royal. I promise you that. He won't ever touch her again. We'll find Em, bring her home, and kill that evil bastard."

"I just don't know how to protect all of you. He has Em at his mercy. You fucking saw Raena's body. What has he done to Em?" Fear is rolling off him in waves as he speaks.

"It's not your job to protect us anymore, man. Don't you get that? I know you feel like you have to because it's all you know. But we aren't helpless little kids anymore," I remind him, turning my body to face him.

"Look at me." I wait for him to pick his head up and look me in the eyes, his own icy blue ones filled with so much worry that I know he's drowning. "You were just a little kid yourself. But we are all grown up. We take care of each other. Always. Brothers bound in blood."

I grab his bloody right hand, turning it up to trace the long scar on his palm from our childhood. We might not be blood related, but we bound ourselves with a blood oath when we got adopted together. All three of us have the same scar.

"Brothers bound in blood," he repeats the words of our past.

"Brothers bound in blood." The words startle me. Looking up, I see Maddox leaning against the door frame in a pair of black sweats now. Pushing off, he walks to the mat, all of our phones in his hand.

"I hate to interrupt this brother bonding session," he starts, molten rage in his still sleepy gray eyes as he hands them over. "But we've got a problem."

Motherfucker.

Chapter 24

The sound of a door shutting jolts me from my sleep. The warm bed cocoons my aching body. I feel like I've been hit by a truck, my muscles protesting when I stretch out like a cat.

Groaning, I open my eyes and immediately recognize I'm not in my cottage. I sit up, allowing the covers to fall down my body, pooling at my waist. I'm completely naked.

Where the fuck am I?

The memories come flooding back to me instantly. Jackson's house. Stabbing. Running. Hiding. Panicking. Falling. Then, them. They saved me.

Royal.

Alek.

Maddox.

The *Shadows.*

They must have pulled me from the bottom of Grimm River when I fell. I remember waking up with that old man and his voice triggering memories I've long since buried to protect myself.

The comfort I found in their arms surprises me. No one has ever made me feel like that before. Like I was *safe*. I've been wary of all men since escaping King's grasp. I wasn't scared of them though. I knew deep in my soul they wouldn't hurt me. Even with my time spent in Aspen's sanctuary with her guys, it took a long time for me to feel safe around them.

I don't feel that with these guys. My soul calls out to theirs. Their touch sets me ablaze, their kisses leave embers of fiery lust in their wake, tantalizing me with the desire to let their flames consume me.

Looking around the elegant, yet simplistic space, I wonder whose room this actually is. Taking the cover with me, I wrap it around myself as I get up. The open space is lined with sleek glass and wood. The masculine touch is evident with the neutral dark tones. Everything is black, dark wood stained, or clear glass. There is no color in this room.

Walking over, I pull the black-out shades open. The glass window-wall reveals the forest and Grimm River below me. I'm at least two stories up, maybe more, the rocky shores of the river just below.

Being saved wasn't the only thing they did to me last night. What happened in the shower and then the bedroom, just the memory of it causes my stomach to flip and my thighs to clench together. I've never been touched like that. For my pleasure.

I mean, I've touched myself, but it doesn't come close to the feelings they invoked in my body and mind. I was on a cloud of pure orgasmic bliss.

And that kiss.

Maddox kisses like he's drowning and has to steal the air from your lungs to survive. I can't believe the guy I stabbed last night ended up being my first real kiss. That will be a story of a lifetime.

Moving away from the window and dragging the blanket with me, I continue exploring the room. I need to find clothes. Finding a third door, which I assume is the closet, I open it up. It's a massive closet fit for a giant.

The masculine vibes extend in here as well. Lights line to top and bottom of the walls and illuminate the way inside as I move deeper within the closet. Clothes are color and style coordinated, hanging on both sides of the space. The back wall is divided by glass cube shelves on top with backlighting making them glow. The bottom portion is a black marble countertop with different size drawers below it. This is ridiculously organized and stunning.

Turning back to the hanging clothes, I find an entire row of extremely oversized black hoodies. Grabbing one off a hanger, I let the blanket pool at my feet. Holding the giant hoodie up to my body, it should fall well past my knees. This will be perfect to cover my naked body until I find some clothes or go home.

Slipping it on, I grab the discarded blanket from the floor and walk out of the closet, tossing it on the bed. The hoodie is so giant that it could almost be considered a dress. I make my way out of this room and down the hallway.

There is a door across the hall from this one, and I pass two more doors, pausing to listen for any movement coming from behind each of them before coming to a landing and set of metal stairs. The landing has glass panels and a metal railing that overlooks the massive open space downstairs.

This looks like something out of a magazine. Most of the exterior walls are made of glass, giving you the feel of sitting right in the middle of the enchantingly gorgeous Shadow Forest.

I know from the bedroom I just left that we're somewhere on Grimm River in the Forest, and it makes me wonder how close we are to my cottage. It can't be too close; I chose that cottage because there weren't any close neighbors, needing privacy when I snuck back into town.

Descending the staircase, I take in the massive living area that leads into an open kitchen. The entire house seems to have the same theme. It's ethereally beautiful.

Walking through to the kitchen, I see an open door with a set of stairs descending down. Stepping into the doorway leading down, I hear voices coming from below. Going down the stairs, the lights illuminate the further I go. This house is too fucking fancy.

"What the fuck did you just say?" The voice stops me in my tracks half way down. It's a voice I will never forget. It haunts my nightmares and I'm immediately frozen in place.

"No one showed up. We waited all night," I hear one of the guys respond. I'm not sure which one, but I think it was Royal.

"You know what's at stake here, don't you, son? Do you want little Em to pay for your failure? Again? I thought you cared about your sister. It seems to me like you need a little motivation."

"NO!" They shout in unison, and I realize they are talking on speakerphone. The realization he isn't actually here has me continuing to creep down the stairs.

"Find me that goddamn hunter, boy. Or poor little Emma is going to feel every ounce of my fucking wrath." Icy tendrils of fear shoot up my spine as the line goes dead. I know exactly how he likes to work out his anger on innocent little girls.

I have to do something. I have to save her.

If it means saving this child, I will give up my hunt and take her place. No child should ever have to endure the things I know him to be capable of. I won't let history repeat itself here.

"Call him back," I say, stepping off the steps and revealing myself.

"Angel," Royal closes the distance before drawing me into his arms. "I'm so sorry. I didn't know you were down here. You shouldn't have to hear his voice."

"Baby Girl, are you okay?" Alek asks, moving beside us and rubbing my back.

"I'm okay. I need you to call him back." I say with steely determination. It's the only choice. I need them to listen to me.

"Why, Cherry?" Maddox asks, stepping on our other side.

Pulling back out of Royal's grip, I look at each of these men. Our time will be cut short now, so I need to memorize their faces to help me through what I have to do next.

I'm sorry we didn't get more time.

"He wants the hunter. Call him and make a deal. The hunter for your sister."

"You know who the hunter is?" Royal asks. I look at each of them as they stare back at me with an equal mix of hope and confusion in their eyes.

"I do." I say simply, trying my best not to let my fear of what's to come consume me.

"Who?" They ask in unison.

With my voice breaking on a whisper, I shatter the illusion they have of me.

"*Me.*"

Chapter 25

"What the fuck do you mean, 'me'? *You're* the hunter?" I ask, disbelief that this tiny little thing could be the elusive hunter that has grown men running scared.

"I meant what the fuck I just said," she responds, clearly not appreciating the implication.

"I mean no offense. You're just so... small. You overpowered three grown men. Killed them?"

"I cut their shriveled-up dicks off, too," she deadpans back, putting her hands on her hips, making Alek's hoodie ride a little higher on her legs.

"Will you marry me?" Maddox asks, bouncing on his heels like an overexcited child. He drops to one knee in front of her, grabbing her hand with a shit-eating grin splitting his face wide open.

"Maddox! Knock it off." I slap the back of his head until he gets the hint that now is not the time to be fucking off.

"My offer stands, Cherry," he says, kissing her hand before getting to his feet.

"Thanks?" She responds, shaking her head to dispel his weird ass comments and get back on topic.

"Listen, you don't have to believe me. I don't really give a fuck if you do. But call him back!" She pleads with me, and the urgency in her voice sets my hair on end.

"I don't understand," Alek says.

"There is no fucking way, Ang..." I start but before I can even finish my words, I'm lying flat on my back, with her right forearm pinned against my throat and her left hand tightly squeezing my crown jewels through my sweats.

"*Fuck*, that's hot. Please fucking marry me," Maddox begs, but I don't pay him any attention, even if I'm thinking the same thing.

"You were saying?"

In this moment, I don't see the broken damsel in distress she was in the forest or the timid, scared girl she was in that room at Twisted. She is fucking glorious.

I'm so fucking confused and turned on. I can feel my dick twitching as it turns to stone in her hand. I know she feels it too because she gives it a hard squeeze before she lets go and gets up from straddling me. I barely suppress the moan threatening to spill out of my throat.

It takes me a few moments to get myself together enough to get up off the floor. I thrive on control, it grounds me. I never expected to get so turned on by having someone overpower me like this.

"Like I said, call him back. He wants the hunter, and we have to save your sister. He will make this trade. Me for her. I know he will," she says, adjusting the oversized hoodie to cover her ass again.

She has lost her goddamn mind if she thinks I'm going to let King get his hands on her again. She can brat all she wants. While I know we need to save Em, I will not trade one for the other. I will save them both.

I stalk toward her, and she backs up. Her face tells me she's on alert, but she isn't scared of me. I keep my pace steady. She steps back, and I step forward. Going step for step together until her back hits the wall by the doorway.

Caging her in with one arm beside her head, I press my body into hers, gripping her throat lightly. She naturally tilts her head back to look up at me, and I don't miss the desire that widens her pupils before she steels herself, and the brat wins out.

"Not fucking happening, Angel. If you think for one second we would let that happen, you haven't been paying attention. I will tie you to my fucking bed if I have to." I growl at her. Leaning down, my lips a hair's breadth away from hers. "You. Are. Ours. King will *never* touch you again. We will find another way."

"You don't understand. I *have* to do this." Tears well in her eyes, but I keep going.

"No, I don't understand. But I will once you've told us what the fuck is going on." She winces back at my tone, and I hate myself for losing my shit with her.

I feel out of control, and my tether is about to fucking snap. I will make good on my threat if she wants to test me. I will tie her to my bed and keep her a drooling, begging mess. She won't be able to even think about giving herself up when the only thing she can think about is reaching the orgasm I refuse to give her.

Alek steps up beside us, reminding me that we are not alone here. I'm so focused on Raena that I forget for a moment my brothers are in the room.

"We can continue this conversation later. Ella is at the gate," he says, holding up his phone with the security stream from the front gate.

"Let her in," I say. I completely forgot she said she was coming back today to check on Raena. Alek and Maddox head up the stairs, but I keep her pinned against the wall for a few moments. Leaning back into her, I kiss her forehead before pulling back to look into her eyes, hoping she can see the seriousness in mine. "This discussion isn't over, Angel."

I release my grip on her throat when she nods back at me, and I step back out of her space, even though it pains me to lose that connection. I just need her to be near me. I need to know she's safe. I'm not going to question what this is anymore. It doesn't matter. She is mine. She isn't leaving my fucking sight.

"Let's go," I say, grabbing her hand and leading her up the stairs, through the kitchen and into the living room where Ella and my brothers are waiting for us.

"Rae!" Ella exclaims, rushing over to us and hugging Raena tightly to her chest. "How do you feel? Are you okay? Do I need to kick one of their asses? I've got my curb-stomping boots on."

She laughs, and it sounds like warm honey. I could listen to her laugh everyday. "I'm fine, I promise. I can't breathe though," she wheezes out around the crushing hug from her friend.

"Sorry, sorry. I've just been so worried about you."

"What's all this?" Raena asks, gesturing to the bags Ella sat on the table in front of the couch.

"I brought you some clothes and had the kitchen make some food up at Twisted since you weren't home to eat what I had delivered there."

"You know we can feed her, right?" Alek asks, offense dripping from his voice.

"Have you? Because I'd bet my left tit she hasn't eaten anything since the last time I fed her." Ella steps up to him, challenging him.

Alek whips around to look at Raena. She has her eyes cast down, staring at her bare feet like they are the most interesting thing in the world right now. "Is that true, baby?"

She doesn't look up or respond, clearly embarrassed at being called out like this.

"Maddox, bring the bags to the kitchen," he says, closing the distance between us and stealing Raena from my grasp. He grabs her hand, leading the way into the kitchen, the rest of us following behind them.

Alek has this need to take care of everyone, especially feeding them. I'm pretty sure a therapist would say it's because he was starved of that attention growing up, having no one to take care of him. So we indulge him when he is feeling like this.

"Sit," he orders, pulling out a chair at the table and sitting down. Raena moves to sit next to him, but he pulls her back. "Not there. Here." He pulls her onto his lap, forcing her legs to rest over his, and kisses her temple. "That's better."

He starts opening the bags Maddox laid on the table. I walk around the table to grab some plates from the cabinet before laying two in front of him and laying the rest on the table. Maddox and I take a seat on each side of them, and I look back to see Ella at the other end of the table, just staring at us with a smirk on her face.

"Are you going to take a seat, Ella? Or just stand there and hope some food falls into your mouth?" Maddox says, not even looking at her, just continuing to unpack the bags on the table.

"I've already eaten, dipshit." She shoots back at him, before walking around to the opposite side of the table and sitting across from us. "It's just a sight to watch 'big daddy' here manhandle my best friend like a rag doll."

"Ella!" Raena exclaims, her cheeks flaming a flustered pink that makes me want to slip that hoodie off and see just how far that blush extends down her stunning little body.

"It's okay," Alek says, kissing her head and chuckling at the little blonde. "Here, take a bite." He holds a fork up to Raena's face, and she looks confused.

"You want to… feed me? How are you going to eat?" She asks, more pink flushing her cheekbones.

"Oh, I *am* feeding you, Baby Girl," he states, leaving no room for argument. "And you'll eat every bite I give you. Then, I'll eat."

"Okay then, Daddy." She gives the sass right back to him, smirking at him and causing Maddox to choke on his eggs.

Between her and Maddox, I think they are going to give him an aneurysm. She doesn't understand his need to do this, but she lets him anyway. She really is perfect for us. I love that she is getting comfortable enough around us to step out of her shyness and be herself.

"Come on, Raena. Tell these two asshats to fuck off and run away with me. I am begging you here." Maddox pleads with her, a shit-eating grin on his face and his hands covering his heart.

Raena just laughs, clearly already figuring out he has a couple screws loose in his head.

"Oh, you'd have to fight 'big daddy' *and* 'pretty boy' over there if you want her to yourself, 'little psycho'," Ella chimes in laughing. We all can't help but laugh, too.

Her nicknames for them are a little too accurate. Alek definitely has the whole 'big daddy' thing going for him, and Maddox is batshit crazy.

We settle into a comfortable silence as we watch Alek continue to feed Raena, whispering praise to her as she takes the food from him like a baby bird.

"That's it, Baby Girl. Just a little more."

It's different, watching him act like this. He has always been a natural caregiver, but I've never seen him hand feed a woman before.

There is absolutely no reason this exchange between them should be this erotic. I have to reach below the table to discreetly adjust so I don't pop a tent at the kitchen table with guests over.

Get your shit together! I mentally scold myself for acting like a prepubescent teenager who can't control his dick around the general public.

"Um, hi. If he's done force feeding you now, is there somewhere private we can go? I brought you some clothes, and I *need* to talk to you, Rae," Ella asks once Raena has had enough and pushes his hand away.

Raena looks around the table, silently asking where they can go. This is her house now. She can go wherever the fuck she wants, as long as she doesn't leave this house without one of us.

I don't say that though. I have a feeling she isn't ready to come to terms with the reality of what I meant when I said she was ours. That can wait until later, when I have her tied to my bed and she can't get away.

"You can use any room you'd like, Angel."

"Thank you." She pauses a moment to look at Alek before leaning down and kissing his cheek.

It's his turn to blush now, and it's outright comical to watch him getting flustered like a schoolgirl.

Before she gets up, she leans in next to his ear and whispers loud enough for me to hear, "Thanks for breakfast, Daddy." I watch as his face turns even darker.

Fuck. This girl is dangerous.

Chapter 26

"This house is fucking insane," Ella whispers, looping her arm through mine as we walk back into the living room.

She grabs the duffle bag off the table before we head up stairs. I know they said any room was fine, but I'm more comfortable in the room I slept in with them.

"I've never seen anything like it. It's gorgeous, isn't it? I haven't been outside but the view from the window up here is like a fairytale scene," I tell her, moving down the hall and into the bedroom I came from earlier.

I'm assuming it's Alek's room since he brought me in last night and the size of the hoodie I stole from the closet appears to be his size, which is fucking huge. He makes me feel so... small.

Ella walks around the room, taking in every sleek detail and feature before stepping into the bathroom.

"Holy fucking shit," she gasps, and I know the feeling. That bathroom is fancy as hell and I'm 90 percent positive I'm going to fuck something up in there.

"I know, ain't it ridiculous," I say laughing.

"Can I move in? I'll just live in this bathroom," she asks playfully.

"Right? That shower is huge. It fit all four of us in it last night," and as soon as the words leave my lips, I'm internally slapping myself for opening my mouth.

"Back. The. Fuck. Up." Her eyes are as big as saucers as she animates her words with her hands. "The four of you? In the shower? I need details. Right the fuck now."

"Ella!" I shout, "Stop it. Nothing happened. Not really."

"Come on. You gotta give me something. Big Daddy has got to be packing at least a foot long," she pleads, with puppy dog eyes and a big ass grin.

"I wouldn't know. Now, can we talk about something else."

"Listen, my kitty might be a virgin, but I have the soul of a slut. I need more than that." Her crass words and folded arms make me laugh.

"Wait, you're a virgin?"

"Like I'd fuck anything in this town. Except maybe the Shadows, but I think you've already claimed them for your harem," she says with a smirk. "Now, stop avoiding. Spill!"

"Fine. They… touched me. That's all. I didn't see anything they were packing. Is that enough for your slutty soul?"

"For now," she responds, bouncing on her heels excitedly, a dreamy look in her eyes.

"Okay, then. Now, you said you brought me clothes."

She opens the duffle bag, sitting on the counter. Pulling out what she brought, I notice everything is black. Leather leggings, corset style top with tiny criss-cross straps across the top of the chest attaching to the tiny shoulder straps. She also has a black leather jacket and knee-high black boots that lace up.

"Well, we haven't seen each other in years, yet you know my exact style. It's like no time has passed at all," I joke with her.

"I might have snooped in your closet the other morning before coming out. I was surprised to see all black. You really are their perfect little shadow." Her words seem to trigger something in me.

What the fuck am I doing?

There is a little girl out there who needs me to help her. I will not allow history to repeat itself. I have to figure out a way to get out and negotiate a deal with King without them knowing. Royal made it perfectly clear he wasn't going to arrange this for me.

"Raena, what's wrong?" Ella's voice switches from playful to serious in a matter of seconds. She can see the fear on my face.

"Ella, I need your help," I whisper, pulling her in front of me. "I need to save their sister. They don't understand, but I do. I know what King will do to her if I don't do this. He wants the hunter. I can negotiate a deal. Her for me. He won't be able to resist. You gotta help me." I am begging her. She is the only one who can help me. I know the guys won't even hear of it.

"Whoa. Calm down. You want to turn yourself over to King? The man who tortured you for three years?"

"It's the only way to save their sister before it's too late." She has to help me. She just has to.

"Raena," she whispers, and I can see the hesitation in her eyes. "I don't think that's…"

"NO! Listen to me. That little girl is going to die if I don't do this. Please just help me."

"Okay. I'll see what I can do. Just... take a shower and get dressed. I'll wait for you downstairs."

"Okay," I breathe out, relieved that she is at least going to try to help me. It's a start.

She steps back out of the bathroom, closing the door behind her. I make my way into the shower, trying to remember how to work the panel. After fumbling with it for a few minutes, the water sprays from every direction, steam billowing from the scalding temperature. Stepping under the sprayer, I let my mind run through everything I need to do to prepare for giving myself up to King.

I try to push the guys from my mind. They might be what breaks me. My soul feels connected to theirs on a level I didn't know existed, and now I will lose them because of King.

Yet again, he will steal whatever joy I manage to find in this fucked up world. And I'll allow it, if it means saving their sister and returning her to them.

It would be an honor to the memory of what I wasn't able to save.

***

I finished up my shower and got dressed as quickly as I could in the clothes Ella left on the counter. As much as I want to drag this out and spend this time with Royal, Alek, and Maddox, I know it's just going to make my decision that much harder.

They won't understand until they get their sister back in their arms. Then they'll get it. Until then, I want to memorize every little thing about them and this place. Maybe I'll be able to draw like last time and make physical representations of these memories to help me through when all I want to do is die.

I get my boots laced up and head back downstairs to find them all standing by the door waiting for me. The guys are dressed in their familiar blacks. The only things missing are their masks and gloves.

"Everything okay?" I ask, the looks on their faces are stoney and blank.

"Everything's fine, Rae," Ella says, but her eyes tell me she is holding something back. As much as I want to ask, we can talk about it once we're alone.

"Ella is going to give us a ride. We left our bikes out last night," Royal says, his jaw clenched and ticking, making me wonder what they were talking about.

"Oh, I need to stop by my cottage too," I tell them, remembering I left Nightshade parked in the forest. Maddox steps up next to me, grabbing my hand.

"We can do that," he says, as I feel something cold wrap around my wrist before hearing a metallic click that sets me on edge. "Wh-what are you doing?"

"Oh, this?" He asks, grinning at me as he picks up my hand and clicks the second handcuff around his own wrist. "I got us matching bracelets, pretty girl. Do you like them?"

Before I can even respond, Royal steps in front of me, his jaw still ticking as he stares down at me.

"It seems like you weren't listening earlier, so these are just a precaution. You can't get Ella to help you give yourself to King if you're handcuffed to Maddox, can you?"

"El, you told them?" I ask, hurt and pissed off at this entire situation.

Why won't they listen to me?

"I'm sorry Rae, I really am. But I just got you back. We will find another way. Together."

"Ella, can you go wait in the truck please?" Royal asks, his eyes never leaving mine. She waits for me to give her the okay with a simple nod of my head before walking out the front door. Restrained rage paints his face, but his eyes give him away.

Fear swirls through his icy blue eyes like a storm. He is scared for not only his sister but for me. I know I'm not the only one dealing with these strange new emotions between us, and even if I don't understand it completely, I understand his fear.

"I'm sorry." I whisper, "I'm just scared for your sister."

"I know, Angel," he whispers back, leaning forward to press his lips to my forehead before turning toward the door. "Be a good girl while we're out today, and maybe I won't tie you up when we get back home." He smirks as he walks out of the house. I can't decide if I want to slap that smirk off his face or kiss it off.

"You are not alone in this anymore," Alek says, kissing my cheek as he passes me, following Royal out the door.

I stand there with Maddox cuffed to me, trying to figure out how these men can play with my emotions the way they do.

They make me feel so many things at once. Maybe they're right. Maybe we can figure this out together. All I know is every second that passes that their sister is in King's hands is too long.

It's been a year, and they're still searching for her. What has King done to her in that time? Is she even still alive? I have all these questions running rampant at once, my mind racing to find answers I don't have.

"Hey, look at me." Maddox brings his hands to my face, turning me to face him, the cuff chain dangling between us. "Get out of your head, pretty girl."

"How do you do that?" I ask, staring into his smokey gray eyes.

"Do what?" He smiles his signature smile back at me, making my knees weak.

"How do you know when I'm lost inside my head? When my mind races?"

He brings me into his arms, tilting my chin to stare up at him. "I know what it feels like to be lost inside your own head. Your thoughts racing faster than you can latch onto one. That's my mind every day. I know what it looks like." His honesty brings tears to my eyes, his thumb swiping away the ones that escape down my cheek.

"Don't waste your tears on me, Cherry. For the first time since I was eight years old, the thoughts have begun to quiet. Do you want to know when that started happening?"

"When?" I ask, his eyes gazing into mine as he speaks.

"That night at Twisted. I didn't even see your face. When your body pressed against mine, I smelled your sweet cherry scent. When I touch you, when you're near me, my head is quiet." He presses his forehead to mine, closing his eyes and inhales deeply.

"You think I smell like cherries?" I whisper.

Is that why he calls me Cherry?

"You do," he laughs against my lips before kissing me hard. "Now come on, we got shit to do. And Royal really doesn't like waiting."

"Oh no, what's he going to do, threaten to tie me up again? I'm starting to think his threats are empty." Sarcasm colors my tone, causing us both to laugh.

"Maybe you're right. I've been trying to get him to tie me up for years," he says, winking at me before closing the door behind us.

"Wait, wh-what?" I stutter out. Is he implying what I think he's implying? Have they been together like that? Something about envisioning Royal and Maddox together makes my thighs clench. I would pay good money to see Maddox tied up at the mercy of Royal any day of the week.

"Oh, pretty girl, you have so much to learn." I'm tempted to ask more, but we make our way down the front steps where the others are waiting. I will definitely be revisiting this later.

"Let's go. I want to get back so we can deal with Doc," Royal says, and I realize I completely forgot about the old man from last night. Just bringing him up makes me freeze in place.

"Where is he?" They haven't mentioned him at all, but that's not surprising. A lot has gone down in the few hours I've been here. It's crazy to think I only just met these men last night.

"We put him in the playroom," Royal states plainly, like I'm supposed to know what that means. He must read the confusion on my face because he says, "We'll show you when we get back, Angel. Let's get going."

Maddox opens the front passenger door, helping me slide in the middle next to Ella before scooting beside me, closing the door. I feel the truck bed dip as Alek and Royal jump into the back, banging on the side to signal they are ready. Ella looks at me for a moment, an apology shining in her eyes.

"It's okay, Cinderella. I understand. I'm not mad," I whisper to her, squeezing her hand on the steering wheel.

I get why she told them. I probably would have done the same thing to protect her if the roles were reversed. I can't be mad at her. She smiles softly back at me before turning the key in the ignition and setting off to wherever the guys left their bikes.

I am itching to get back to Nightshade. I hate leaving her out in the elements, but I didn't really have a choice last night. I have no idea how I'm supposed to ride while handcuffed to this beautiful psycho, but I guess there is a first time for everything.

Ella takes the outskirts of the forest, avoiding driving through town. The last thing we need is to be spotted together by King or the Kingsmen. Maddox seems to be anxious, practically vibrating in his seat next to me. His knee is bouncing a mile a minute, his fingers rapidly tapping his leg. I give him a few more seconds before I can't take it anymore.

"What's wrong?" I lean over and whisper to him, grabbing his hand and squeezing it tightly. Before I know what's happening, he picks me up, maneuvering me to straddle his lap. He buries his face into my fiery curls and inhales deeply. His body finally relaxes as he holds me tightly to him.

"That's better," he breathes into my hair. "I don't like exposing you like this. You're out in the open where King could see you."

"Oh, well, I don't think he would recognize me just seeing me in a truck," I tell him, trying to ease his fears.

"I hate to tell you this, Cherry, but your hair is kind of memorable."

"Yeah, but the last time he saw me, my hair wasn't red. It was blonde, well, almost white, like Ella's. I changed it after I escaped."

His hand fingers my curls, inspecting them. "Red suits you," he says, bringing a smile to my face.

I miss my icy ringlets sometimes, but they only serve as a reminder of the girl who died in that cell. I'm not her anymore. I'll never be her again. I've spent the last two years burying her and rebuilding myself into *The Hunter*. Into someone who can protect herself and her loved ones. What happened back then will *never* happen again. I'm pulled from my thoughts when Maddox directs Ella to turn down a narrow dirt trail.

"Where are we going?" I ask. I've never noticed this trail before.

"The shadow trails," he answers, "My brothers and I made these so we could look out for the people in Shadow Forest without being seen. We left our bikes out here last night."

The truck bounces through the puddles of last night's storm, causing my body to bounce in Maddox's lap. He tightens his hold around my waist, pulling me down on him as he lifts his hips, grinding his cock into me.

I can feel his length digging into me as lightning licks my spine and desire floods my veins at our position. I close my eyes, pressing my lips together tightly to suppress the moan threatening to slip out.

"Fuck, pretty girl. Keep bouncing on my cock like that, and I'll blow in my pants like a fucking teenager," he whispers in my ear, desire dripping from his words.

I can't help but press my ass harder against him, twisting my hips slightly in his lap. I lean my head back against his shoulder, my body shuddering against him as he grinds up into me again.

"I bet if I slipped my hand into your panties right now, I'd find your pretty little pussy soaking wet for me, wouldn't I, Cherry?" His lips find my ear as he sucks the lobe of it into his mouth, piercing my flesh with his teeth.

My breath catches in my lungs, the sting of his bite turning into pleasure. I can feel my pussy dripping. I find his ear, licking the outer shell.

"What panties?"

He responds by driving his hips up harder against me, while shoving me down at the same time. The action makes me forget we are not alone in the cab of this truck until Ella clears her throat.

Immediately pulled from the moment, I can feel my cheeks burning as I'm sure they turn a flaming red that rivals my hair.

"I hate to interrupt whatever– *that was*," she says, motioning to both of us with a wave of her hand and failing to hide the smirk she's flaunting. "But we're here."

I didn't even realize we had stopped. She's already thrown the truck in park before climbing out of the cab and walking to the back where the others are getting out.

"Don't worry, pretty girl. You're riding with me."

Chapter 27

He opens the door, sitting me down on the ground before climbing out with me, shutting the door behind us.

I look around the trail, spotting their bikes up ahead. They remind me of Nightshade, just missing the red accents. Their bikes are sleek matte black, and I'd expect nothing less with their shadow personas.

"You know, some girls say the vibrations alone can give them an orgasm," Maddox says, walking to what I assume is his bike.

I don't know how they tell them apart. They all look identical to me. He runs his hand over the seat, grinning at me. I don't even comment. I don't think they know I'm not a newbie around bikes, but I keep that information to myself for now. I'll let them think what they want, then sit back and watch their faces when we pick up Nightshade.

"Well, I'm not like most girls," I tell him, looking out into the distance.

You really can see the whole town from up here. I missed this trail and their bikes last night when I was running through the woods, since I ran in the other direction towards the river. I can see the back of Jackson's property from here. Looking back at the truck, I see Royal reaching into the back, pulling out an extra helmet I didn't know he brought with us.

He walks over, gathering my curls like I normally do, before placing the helmet on my head. He makes sure to tuck all the red ringlets inside the back of the helmet before popping the visor so I can see him.

"We have communication linked in each helmet, so you'll be able to talk to us and vice versa when we're riding. It might be scary at first, just hold on to him, lean when he leans," he continues, and I just nod my head like I'm taking it all in. "I'm going to uncuff you so Maddox can have both hands. Are you going to be a good girl for me?"

"What's the fun in that, man? I was looking forward to riding while cuffed to our girl," Maddox chimes in, pouting like Royal just took away his favorite toy.

"Safety first, dumbass. I'm not having her first time on a bike end in a road rash," Royal whips back at him, slapping his helmet that's now on his head.

"I'll be fine. I trust Maddox knows how to drive this thing?"

"I'd prefer you ride with me, but Maddox won our little wager," he grumbles back at me.

"Yep, I sure did." The smirk Maddox sports just serves to piss Royal off even more. His jaw ticks with irritation, but I can tell it's not too serious.

"And what wager would that be?" I ask, my hands planting on my hips.

"Oh, I bet you'd try to run. Didn't even make me work for that one, did you?" Maddox laughs.

"I wasn't trying to run. I was trying to help."

"I know, pretty girl," he says, running his hands down my arms before grabbing onto my waist and planting my ass on the bike. "Up you go."

I lean forward, my hands gripping the seat in front of me to steady myself. Maddox takes this as his opportunity to smack my ass, the sharp sound echoing through the woods.

"Hey, what was that for?" I shout at him, even though I kind of want him to do it again.

I reach my hand back and rub the sting through my leather leggings. I might as well be wearing nothing, with how thin and tight they are. Not ideal for riding, but they'll have to do until I can get back to my cottage and get my own clothes and gear.

"Because your ass looks delicious on my bike."

I smirk at him, arching my back even further on purpose, giving my ass a little shake and he groans. "Keep doing that, Cherry. I have no problem laying you out on this bike and eating you like a goddamn Christmas buffet." His signature smirk hides behind his helmet, but I can see it in his eyes. Before we can continue with our racy banter, Alek and Ella walk over to us.

"Y'all going to be good from here? I gotta get back to Mom before my shift. She wants to try to come with me today. She thinks she's ready," Ella says, stepping up beside me.

"That's great, El. Maybe it will be good for her."

"Maybe."

The worry in her eyes is prominent. I can't imagine all she has been through since her dad died. My heart breaks for her. I think because she had to take over everything, she hasn't had the chance to properly grieve her father, like I didn't get a chance to grieve Grams how she deserved.

Maybe when all this is settled, we can begin to heal the hurt we've had to endure in silence. I envy her mom for taking as long as she needs to grieve.

"Are you going to be okay, Rae?" She asks, and I know she is still worried about her ratting me out to the guys.

"I'll be just fine. These guys won't let me do anything stupid. I might get leashed if I try," I joke, aiming to ease the tension. And leave it to Royal to take my words to heart.

"Oh I can definitely put a leash and collar on you, Angel. If that's what you want."

"No, *Sir.* Thank you, though," I sass back at him.

"Okay then. Well, call me, babe. They have my number," she says as she starts back towards her truck. I look back at Alek, and he gives me a reassuring smile and nod.

"I will," I say. "Be careful."

She responds with a wave of her hand, getting into the truck, and backing down the narrow trail.

"Where to now, baby?" Alek asks, his helmet already on as he double checks mine is in place correctly. They haven't even thought to ask me if I know anything. They just assume, and it makes me giddy. I can't wait to see their faces.

"It's fine, Daddy," I tell him when he tries to check it for the third time. "I need to go to my cottage to pick up a few things, and grab Nightshade."

"Is that your cat?" Maddox asks, his face looking excited at the idea of me bringing a kitty home with us.

"Nope," I say, popping the 'p' before snapping my visor shut and speaking into their helmets. "I'll direct you as we go. Just head back the way we came and take a right at the main road."

They mount their bikes, and the sound of the engines is barely heard throughout the forest. If it wasn't for the vibration I feel in my core, I wouldn't even know the bike was on. They must have made similar noise canceling adjustments like I did to mine.

Maddox is right about one thing. The combination of the bike's vibrations and my aching core pressed against his hard body feels delicious.

It doesn't take long to make it back to the main road, the guys sticking to the side of the trail to avoid the puddles. They take a right like I instructed, Royal riding in front, and Alek behind us.

Before long, we are turning down my driveway.

"How did you know about this place?" Suspicion colors Royal's tone, making me nervous.

How does he know about it?

Maybe they knew who lived here before me.

"A friend of mine found it for me. I purchased this with cash under a fake name he helped me set up. This place was owned by a corporation. I needed privacy while still being inside Shadow Forest." My voice shakes with uncertainty, and I know they can hear it through their helmets.

I don't know why his question makes me nervous. Maybe it's because I haven't told anyone about my time in White Harbor or my friends who helped me after I escaped. If I'm going to trust these guys, I will have to tell them everything. I just hope I'm strong enough to do it.

"This place should have never been sold," Royal growls into the speaker. He's angry. I don't understand what's going on.

We stop just in front of my cottage, Royal dismounting his bike first and throwing his helmet to the ground. "Fuck!" He charges at Maddox, who has barely had time to put the kickstand down to stabilize us and take his helmet off. He drags him off the bike and my hands immediately grab onto the seat to keep myself from falling off. "Explain, NOW!"

"What is going on?" My voice is barely a whisper, his outburst setting me on edge. I don't like the shouting and angry displays. It fucks with my PTSD in a way I can't control. He wasn't even this mad when he found out I tried to run this morning.

"Royal, chill. I didn't sell it. I don't know what the fuck happened," Maddox says, confusing me even more. *This was their house?*

"You know what the place means to me." Royal's voice breaks as he lets Maddox go. I feel like I'm suffocating. I can't breathe. My vision starts to dim, and I feel something cold against my ass. I can't see the guys with my eyes squeezed tightly shut. I think I'm going to pass out.

I can barely hear someone shouting my name through my muddled senses. Everything is distorted. Suddenly, like a pressure valve releasing, I'm able to suck in a deep breath. It takes me a few moments of sucking in life-saving oxygen to realize someone took off my helmet. I didn't even realize it was still on.

"Raena, take a deep breath for me. In. Good girl. Now out. That's it. Again." Alek kneels in front of me where I must have fallen to my ass in the wet grass. I feel a solid weight at my back and comforting pressure around my chest. I keep breathing as he instructed, and soon, the ringing in my ears quiets down, my vision returning slowly. It feels like I was in that state of panic for hours, but in reality, I know it was only a few minutes, maybe less. Maddox is behind me, his chest allowing me to rest my back against him, his arms bound tightly around me, pinning my arms across my chest.

"I-I'm sorry. I don't know what happened." My words stutter out on a slow exhale.

"No. I'm sorry. I shouldn't have done that." Royal squats down in front of me, next to Alek, raising his hand to my face and causing me to flinch back at the sudden movement. It was just a reflex. His hand stalls in the air, a look of anguish crosses his face before he falls onto his knees completely. "Oh, Angel…" He starts, but he drops his hand to cover his face as his voice breaks. I wiggle out of Maddox's hold, scrambling to my knees in front of Royal, grabbing his hand.

"I know you're not going to hurt me," I say, grabbing his hands and placing them on my cheeks to cradle my face. "I'm sorry. I didn't mean to flinch away from you." My eyes plead with him to understand that I'm not scared of him. He didn't hurt me. "I thought I was over the panic attacks before I came back, but this isn't your fault, Royal. I'm just broken."

He looks up into my eyes, his icy blues raging with so many emotions. "Don't you dare make excuses for me, Angel. You are not broken. This is my fault. I am a grown man. I shouldn't have acted like a hot-headed asshole." He raises himself on his knees, pulling me into him and tilting my face to look up at him. "I will never raise a hand to hurt you, Raena. I swear."

"I know. I'm not scared of you. I *am* fucking broken. He fucking broke me, Royal. I turned 18 the day King murdered my Grams and took me to that *place*, and I haven't felt safe or had a single day of peace since. Then I met you, all of you, and I *finally* feel safe. It's like my soul recognizes yours. When you look at me, my broken pieces don't feel so broken. I can't explain it, and I don't understand it. We don't even know each other. But for the first time since that day, I feel… *peace*. King stole everything from me. My innocence. My family. My peace. My…" My voice breaks on a sob with the heartbreak I can't bear to speak out loud. Tears pour down my face as Royal lifts me into his arms, holding me to his chest.

"Shhhh, I know, I know. King will suffer for everything he has done to you. Done to all of us. He will die, slowly and painfully. Begging for a mercy he wouldn't give. I swear on my life, we *will* make him pay."

"He has to pay." My voice cracks with pent up emotion from the memories of everything King has taken from me.

"He will, I promise," Royal says against my lips, before sealing his mouth over mine, stealing our first kiss. His kiss isn't like the one I shared with Maddox. Whereas Maddox steals my air, Royal kisses like he wants to crawl inside me. His tongue invades my mouth without permission, sliding against mine until he physically can't get any deeper into me.

His hands tangle in my hair at the base of my neck, gripping and manipulating my head to move with him. His kiss is fierce. Passionate. It's a good thing I'm already on my knees for him, because right now, I would crawl on my hands and knees if he commanded it. I want to beg for his dominant, possessive touch all over my body. Putting me in positions I've never dreamed of.

That thought really should enrage the inner feminist in me, 'I am woman, hear me roar' and all that shit. But I really can't find it in me to give a fuck. Not when this man has me a panting, dripping mess of wanton need. I *want* him to lay me out on this forest floor and ravish my body like he is my mind. I *need* him to invade my body like he's invading my mouth, without hesitation or permission. With dominance and unrestrained passion.

But that's not what happens. Instead, he pulls back. Our breath is labored, and my heart feels like it's trying to beat out of my chest. I can feel his erratic beat through his jacket into my hand, pressing against him, the beat matching mine. When his eyes finally open and lock on mine, I see the need I feel reflecting back at me. After a few moments, he finally speaks. "Come on, Angel. Let's grab what you need and go home."

***

"We can come back and pick up the groceries in the truck later," Royal says, walking out of the cottage so I can lock up.

I quickly grabbed some clothes and my gear, shoving everything into my riding backpack. I don't have much here anyway, just what I could carry on my bike for the journey here from White Harbor.

"Thank you." I walk around to Maddox's bike, strapping my pack onto my back before grabbing the extra helmet. "I just need to stop on the way out and pick up Nightshade."

Since my hands are no longer cuffed to Maddox, I gather my own hair up this time, and shove the helmet on my head, tucking my curls into it like I always do. Maddox places me back on the bike like he did before, and I allow it. I kind of like being manhandled by them. He swings his leg over, mounting the bike and grabbing my hands around his waist, molding my body to his.

"Hang on tight, pretty girl." He barely gets the words out before taking off down the long drive ahead of the others.

The thick green forest passes us by in a blur. I turn around to see if the guys are following us yet, but I can't see them. Looking back ahead, I see the spot where I hid my bike.

"Slow down, it's just up ahead," I say into the helmet, pointing to where I need him to stop. He doesn't respond, but he must have heard me because the bike slows down to a rolling stop beside the thick brush covering.

He shuts off the engine, getting off before gripping my waist and lifting me off his bike. He pops both of our visors open. "Are you going to tell me what we're doing here?" He looks around the empty trail and into the forest.

"I told you. I have to pick up Nightshade." My simple answer confuses him more.

"What is a Nightshade exactly?" He follows me over as I start removing the leafy green brush covering her. Royal and Alek pull up next to us, getting off their bikes and removing their helmets. I don't answer his question, but it doesn't take long for him to figure it out once the covering is off.

"Are you fucking serious?" He asks, removing his helmet that was hiding his wide grin, while bouncing on his heels, as I start to push her out of the bushes.

"This is Nightshade." Taking off the borrowed helmet, I can feel the smugness radiating off of me as I stare back at the three of them. Each of their eyes shine with a mixture of awe and desire. Maddox is still bouncing, something I've learned he does when he gets over excited. I think it's adorable. He's like a feral little kitten. You don't know if you're going to get mauled or suffocated with cuddles. "Dude, my dick is so hard right now, I could drill a fucking hole through a glass wall," Maddox breathes out to Alek, who nods without responding, both of them adjusting themselves openly.

Laughing, I swing my leg over the seat, mounting Nightshade. I try to hand the helmet back to Royal, wanting to wear my black and red one, but he stops my hand, pushing it back toward me. "Wear this one for now. Until I can have yours fitted for communication."

"Yes, Sir." My sarcasm and eye roll earn me a sharp slap on the ass. Royal leans in, gathering my hair at the base of my neck and twisting it with one hand for leverage as he angles my head, bringing his lips to my ear.

"Watch it, little shadow. I could gag you, if you'd prefer." Royal's whispered threat elicits a response deep inside me as liquid desire shoots straight to my pussy. I'm going to be in a puddle of my own making if he keeps threatening me like this. He doesn't give me time to respond, just shoves the helmet down on my head, tucking my curls into it once more.

I try to control my panting breaths, watching them as they put on their helmets and get on their bikes. I need to pull myself together. I'm so fucking wound up from their constant edging today, mixed with the panic attack from earlier. I start up my bike, the boys doing the same.

I rock my hips discreetly, trying to relieve the aching pressure, a small moan escaping my lips from the friction. I'm worried I might actually come from the vibrations between my legs.

"Goddamn that's hot." My eyes shoot open and dart to Maddox as his words flow into my ears through the helmet. I guess I wasn't as discreet as I thought I was.

"Don't you fucking dare come on that bike, Angel," Royal growls at me, and I hear Alek and Maddox both groan.

I wonder how he would punish me if I did.

My pulsating clit tells me to test him, but my brain wins out. I might not be ready for his brand of punishment yet, so I begrudgingly still my rocking hips.

"Good girl," he growls back at me, making a shiver slither down my spine.

Goddamn, he is trying to kill me.

MADDOX

Chapter 28

Fuck me sideways and twice on Sunday!

I can't believe she has a fucking bike. And I don't know which one of them is sexier.

Her or it?

Maybe her on it?

Fuck. I barely stopped myself from bending her over it and railing her until she couldn't walk. I am still walking around with a massive boner, and we've been home for about 10 minutes now.

After getting everyone's bikes parked in the garage, we moved to the living room to talk about what Raena wants to do about Doc. I hope she says kill him. I don't know yet if he physically hurt her, but he damn sure didn't help her.

Her reaction to him in that room last night is proof of that. I want to bleed him out, paint my sweet Bloody Cherry in his blood, then fuck her in my playroom next to his mutilated body. I'm getting harder by the second thinking about it.

As soon as we got home, Alek stole my girl. She's now straddling his lap, hanging on to him like a spider monkey again with her head tucked against his neck. She still looks so small against him, like a big gorilla cuddling a tiny human.

It reminds me of when he would hold Em. Her tiny little body would cling to him just like this. An ache stabs me directly in the heart thinking about her, effectively deflating the boner I've been sporting since this morning.

"Baby Girl," Alek starts once we are all seated. "We need to talk."

"Okay," she says wearily, sitting up in his lap. Royal sits next to him on the right, while I am on the left. Her eyes find each of ours before she speaks again. "Well, out with it. You're making me nervous," she says, fidgeting with her hands on his chest.

"We need to ask you about Doc and what you want to do with him." Alek's voice is soothing and calm, jumping right to the point. His hands continue their path up and down her back, trying to keep her calm. We don't want her freezing up or freaking out again.

"Oh…o-okay." Her voice is unsure.

She isn't freaking out, but she is definitely feeling some type of way about this. I can see the war she is waging within herself. Deciding if she is strong enough to face this. I know she is, but I let her get there on her own. I see the moment she stiffens her spine and finds that confidence I know she has buried deep inside.

"I want to speak with him." Her voice is now unwavering.

"We'll bring you down, but the second you want to leave, you say the word, and we'll get you out of there," Alek tells her.

"I can do this. I'm not a fragile little flower. I hate that you've seen me be weak, but that is not who I am anymore." She gets out of his lap and stands in front of us.

I understand what she means. I've been through some fucked up shit too. I was a weak little boy when my father killed my entire family before killing himself. He tried to kill me, too, but I was the pathetic coward who pretended to be dead while he killed my little brother and baby sister.

I might be a batshit crazy psycho, but I am not weak anymore. It doesn't mean I don't have situations that make me vulnerable. Anyone with PTSD, like we all have, is going to have times when they fall apart. There's no magic cure. She's allowed to have moments where she can be in her most vulnerable state, and I won't think any less of her. I know the guys won't either.

Alek sits up on the edge of the couch, bringing her between his spread thighs until her knees hit the cushion, his hands gripping her waist.

"I don't think you're weak. You've just been through some heavy shit. You are allowed to break with us. We'll be here to pick up your broken pieces and put you back together every time. You're not alone in this. We are with you and will do whatever you ask of us. If you want to stay, we stay. If you need to leave, we leave. You are in control here."

Raena cups her hands around his face, bringing her lips down to his. It doesn't go unnoticed that this is the first time she's made the first move with any of us.

Lucky bastard.

It isn't a passionate, long kiss. Just a quick one as if to say 'thank you'. But it's progress. The longer she spends around us, the more comfortable she becomes. It's like watching a flower blossom in the spring.

"Thank you, Daddy," she whispers against his lips, pulling back to look at each of us again. "Thank all of you." Tears have welled in her eyes, but she puts a smile on her face, stiffening her spine again and doesn't let them fall. She's ready. "Let's go see him then."

We all get up and lead her downstairs. I'm practically skipping as we enter the basement, taking her down the hidden hallway that leads to my playroom. I can't wait to see how she likes it. If my gut is correct, she's no stranger to getting messy with blood and gore.

I saw the photos of what she did to those three Kingsmen. She cut their throats and chopped off their dicks. My Bloody Cherry is a stabby little thing. I can't wait to see her in action.

Once we get down the second set of stairs and inside the room, her eyes widen as she walks into the middle of the room over the drain, spinning in a circle as she takes everything in. "What is this place?"

"Welcome to *The Playroom*." My voice is excited.

I can barely contain the intense feeling. This place is my own personal safe space. Royal had it built for me when we moved out of King's house. When shit gets too hard, I can come in here and make men scream. I don't torture and kill innocents.

We created the Shadows to protect the innocent from the deviant scum who prey on them. Those are the types of people I play with here. People like Kingston Wolfe and my father.

Raena walks across the room, running her hands over the various toys I have out on my table, over the different blades and devices. She picks up one that looks like a metal pear.

"What's this?" she asks, rolling it around in her hand, feeling the smooth, rounded edges of the device.

"This is called a Pear of Anguish. The original medieval design was used to widen an orifice. I added a little something extra to it for the real special degenerates that come through here." Taking it from her hand, I turn the stem portion, showing her how it opens. "The end here is a turn-key. It opens up the pear-shaped bottom. I added metal hooks inside, one large hook surrounded by several smaller ones. You insert this in someone's ass, and crank the turn-key to open them up." The pear opens up like flower petals, revealing the tip of the large hook. "Then you push down on the key, deploying the hooks into their insides. They won't feel the hooks just yet, just the sting of their ass stretching around the object. You can leave it in for as long as you want. When you're ready, you yank it out, pulling their intestines out through their ass. It's fucking glorious."

Glancing up to see her face, I check to see if she looks disgusted or horrified, but she doesn't. She looks up at me from the device in my hand, as a malicious grin slowly spreads across her face.

"I can think of a few men I'd like to try this on."

"Anytime, Cherry. Anytime." My own manic grin splits my face open, both of us looking like unhinged psychos.

Fuck. She's fucking perfect.

"Alright, you two can plot mass murders later. We need to deal with Doc," Royal says, his own smile painting his lips at our little bloody shadow.

Tossing the metal pear back on the table, I grab Raena's hand and follow Royal across the slanted floor, down the hallway that leads to the cells.

"So how do you want us to do this? He's unrestrained in his cell, but we won't let him touch you. Or we can restrain him and bring him out to the playroom. It's your choice," Alek asks, walking behind us.

"Let me talk to him first. I want to make sure my mind isn't playing tricks on me. I never saw his face, but his voice…" She trails off, and I feel a shudder run through her body and her hand shakes in mine. I give it a reassuring squeeze, and it takes her a couple of seconds to rein her emotions back in. "I need to be sure. I don't harm innocents."

"Neither do we, Baby Girl," Aleks responds, placing his hand on her shoulder as we come to the observation door of Doc's cell.

Doc is laying on the metal bed on his side, facing the door. "Can he see us?" Raena asks, stepping closer to the glass to look inside.

"No. He can't see or hear us. The cells are soundproof." She nods her head absently as she looks around the cell through the glass. She looks like she is a million miles away.

"Hey, we can handle it if you don't want to go in. You don't have to do anything you're not ready for," I tell her, rubbing my thumb along her hand in mine.

"He kept me in a cell like this." Her voice is distant, almost like she's in a tunnel at one end, and us at the other.

My blood is boiling with rage. How long did he keep her captive in a cell? A week? A month? *Longer?*

She turns around after a few moments, taking a deep breath before her confidence returns, and I watch as her face transforms from the soft and sweet Cherry she has been to what I assume is her hunter's persona. And fuck me if it doesn't make my cock twitch seeing her bright eyes darken, her face an impenetrable wall as she locks down the emotions she's been struggling with.

Even her voice sounds different when she finally speaks, as she turns around and faces the door again.

"I'm ready."

Chapter 29

My heart pounds in my chest as I stare into the cell. The concrete walls remind me of my nightmares, but I push the rising terror down, turning around to face my men.

My men.

That sounds weird considering I know almost nothing about them, but it doesn't make it any less true. *They are mine.* I know that from the depths of my soul.

I've never really believed in love or soulmates. I thought it was something people made up to get through their mundane lives and feel better about the choices they made. I didn't understand it. Not until my soul connected with these three men on a level so deep and so fast it scares me, but I'm choosing not to question it.

They stare back at me, their eyes roaming my face, making sure I'm not going to break because of this. They've really only seen me at my weakest, and I hate that more than anything. I am not the same weak little girl King wanted me to be.

They know I'm the hunter. Now it's time for them to meet her.

I gather all of my fear and weakness, shoving it down so far inside me, it won't make another appearance any time soon. I feel myself stand taller, my spine stiffening to prepare myself for what I'm about to face. Like a warm comforting blanket, the hunter's persona slides over my entire body.

I am The Hunter.

"I'm ready."

Turning to face the observation window again, I wait for them to unlock the door. Maddox walks up next to me, pulling his phone from his pocket, and soon, the latch on the door clicks. The sound makes Doc sit up straight on the bed, his hands resting on his knees as he waits for the door to open.

"We'll be right here with you, Angel," Royal assures me, placing his hand on my shoulder and giving it a reassuring squeeze.

Maddox pushes the door open, each of them entering before me. I hang back, wanting to hear his voice again before I go in.

"Royal," he says calmly. His voice triggers me like it did before, but I don't panic. I allow the onslaught of memories to wash over me, needing confirmation before making a decision about him. "I should have known you three were involved with the Shadows."

There is no malice in his tone. He's simply stating facts. But the memories continue to assault me. The blindfolded monthly visits. Kings beatings and torture afterward. Then the monthly checkups when it all stopped for a while. King stopped coming to hurt me. Instead, he would bring me gifts like the desk and art supplies.

It wasn't long before I figured out the reason why. The day my life changed. I've never known such agony and pain. I thought I was going to die at this man's hands. Bile rises in my throat as they keep coming like a movie playing in my head.

I've heard enough.

Stepping into the cell behind Alek, I take a deep breath of his calming scent, letting the memories slide out of me when I exhale. I press my hand into his back to steady myself more before moving around him and into the doctors view.

His eyes widen as big as saucers, an audible gulp sounds across the quiet cell. Fear drains the color from his face before he schools his features, sitting up straighter on the edge of the bed.

"Do you know who I am?" My question comes out calm and confident.

He studies me for a moment, narrowing his eyes as he takes me in, scanning my body head-to-toe.

"I've never seen you before last night."

His response sets me on edge. I'm not crazy. I know this is the same man. Quicker than anyone can blink, I have his hair gripped in one hand as his throat connects with the edge of my dagger. The pressure is hard enough to show I'm serious, but not hard enough to break the skin. Yet.

"Try that again, *Doc.*"

I can feel Maddox behind me, his excitement radiating off him in waves, but I ignore him and wait for the old man to catch up. He doesn't move a muscle as he gets a closer look at my face. I see the moment he remembers who I am.

"I-I remember y-you." His panicked eyes close as he stutters out his realization.

"Good." My tone is short and sharp as I release his hair, lowering my blade from his throat and putting it back in my sheath. He lets out a loud sigh of relief as I take a step back, Maddox moving with me. His relief is short-lived though. "Bring him to the playroom," I tell them, turning around and walking back out of the cell.

His pleading voice rings out as I continue down the hall, but I don't stop. I keep moving until I'm back into the playroom. I take the space in entirely now. It really is nothing like I imagined. I was expecting a dungeon-like room that smelled of blood and piss.

The space is so clean it's almost sterile, making me wonder if they've ever actually used this space or if tonight will be the first time blood is spilled on the slanted concrete floor.

When I came in here a few minutes ago, I spotted something in the far left corner of the room. It is perfect for the doctor. I make my way over, just as the guys emerge from the hall.

Doc struggles to stay on his feet as Alek pushes him forward. There is something stuffed in his mouth. Coming to a stop as they spot me, he grips the doctor's shoulder to stop him from moving forward.

"Where do you want him?"

"Maddox, help me with this?" I ask, and he comes to where I stand. We push the table into the middle of the room, directly above the drain in the floor.

"Remove his clothes and put him up here. Strap him down." The guys immediately obey my commands. Maddox grabs a blade from his table, cutting off his shirt and pants with ease.

They place the doctor on his back in just his tighty-whities as he struggles against them. They restrain his arms in the straps attached to the table first before moving to the leg straps and banding it across both legs on his upper thighs, then each individual ankle. Once he is fully immobilized, they stand back, waiting for me.

"Do you remember strapping me down like this Doc?" I ask, walking around to his head, his cries muffled by his makeshift gag. If he responds, I don't understand him, but I keep going.

"You weren't on my list, you know. Because I never saw your face. It was pure luck that you were the one they called last night." I run my fingertips over the straps at his arms, his eyes wide and struggling to follow me as I move around him.

"You strapped me to a table similar to this. Do you remember? I struggled against the restraints too, screaming for help that never came." I don't look at the guys while I keep moving around the table slowly, but I see them out of the corner of my eye, standing a few feet away.

They are watching my every move and listening to my story. *Good.* I don't think I can deal with telling it more than once.

Pulling my dagger back from my thigh sheath, I run the tip of the blade down his skin, starting at the top of his shoulder, going down his arms and legs as I keep making slow circles around the table. I stop once I reach his head again.

"You knew what he was doing to me in that cell. It took me a long time to figure out how you connected to his agenda. You might not have hurt me like he did, but you helped him."

I make my first shallow cut slanted across his chest, not too deep yet. Just deep enough to cause pain. He screams into his gag and bucks against the straps holding him down.

As his blood pools and drips down from the wound, I make another cut opposite of the first one, creating my signature mark in the center of his chest. I am mesmerized by the artistic beauty for a few moments at how the blood spills down his chest, the streaks running down his sides and pooling on the table below him.

I want his entire body painted red before I take his life. I want to see it running from the table and swirling down the drain below. I want to hear his screams as he begs for mercy like I did. I don't realize I'm lost inside my head until I feel hands run up my arms.

"Can I help?" Maddox breathes into my ear, his hand sliding around my middle, underneath my shirt, pulling me back into a solid chest. A delicious shiver racks my body. I nod my head against his chest, my eyes never leaving the "x" I carved into his chest.

"Good girl," he whispers into my ear before planting a kiss on my temple. "Do you need answers from him?"

"Yes." My voice comes out on a breathy moan. Between the blood I'm spilling and Maddox's hands on my body, making me feel like a live wire, ready to spark at the barest of touches.

His fingers slide into the waistband of my leggings but not going where I need him. He teases the tender flesh above my scar there, reminding me of what I'm doing right now.

I grab his hand, pushing it further down inside my leggings. "Do you feel that right there?" His fingers trace the jagged flesh, his body tensing.

"Yes, I feel it." His voice is dripping in anger. "Who did this to you?"

"He did," I say, my own voice lowering as the terror of that day floods my mind. Stepping out of his hold on me, I bring my dagger to the doctor's hip.

"He strapped me down like this. Took a scalpel to my skin and cut me open while I was awake, begging and pleading for him to stop, screaming for his help. He didn't stop though. I passed out from the excruciating pain. I thought I was dead." I feel the silent tears, my rage boiling over, making tracks down my cheeks. "Ask him why."

My eyes meet Maddox's darken ones, I've never seen him look so sexy. His jaw is clenched tight, twitching with his own rage for me. He moves slowly, like a predator stalking its prey, approaching the doctor's head.

He roughly rips off the tape holding the gag in place, yanking out the material before tossing it to the ground behind him. Royal and Alek have moved closer. Alek presses his front to my back, lending me his unwavering strength without speaking.

"Please! Please don't kill me."

"You heard her. Why?" Maddox asks, sneering at him with venom coloring his question, as he presses his own blade against Doc's throat.

"I-it was K-King. He m-made m-me." Doc rushes out, stuttering through his panic and fear. "I-I didn't h-have a choice."

"NO!" I scream, slamming my blade into his thigh to the hilt. His guttural scream echoes around the concrete room. "*I* had no choice. You, on the other hand, had plenty of choices. You just chose wrong."

His excuses turn my vision red. How dare he act like he is the victim here. He had choices. He was free to come and go as he pleased. He could have packed up and left town if he didn't want to do King's dirty work. I was the prisoner locked in a cell at the mercy of soulless, vile men. I had no control. No choice. I had no way out until I made a way for myself.

He could have helped me. He chose to walk out of that cell every time and go back to his day to day life.

Leaving my blade inside him, I walk over to the table where more blades are laid out. There are different sized scalpels there, but I choose the largest before walking back over to the table.

A pungent smell hits me as soon as I step beside him, my eyes darting to his waist. His underwear are now see-through, darkened and wet, as he lays in a puddle of his own making.

Now this playroom smells like I was expecting. Blood and piss.

"Now, now Doc," my sing-song voice sounding strangely deranged to my own ears as I pat his tear-soaked wrinkled cheeks. "That's not very becoming of you. Pissing yourself when I have barely started with you."

His whole body shakes with sobs as I move down, trailing the scalpel over his skin like I did my dagger. "Please don't do this," he begs.

"I asked the same of you, Doc. But you granted me no such mercy." Moving the scalpel on the inside of his hip, I dig it into his flesh, holding it still as I continue. "I cried and begged you to stop. I begged you to take me to the hospital. You ignored me, pretended you couldn't hear my screams. You listened to *him* instead."

"You have to understand. P-please. It was the only way to save both of you. K-king wouldn't let me take you anywhere," he pleads, but I'm done listening to his excuses. He had ample opportunity before that hellacious day to help me.

"What do you mean? Save both?" Royal asks, confusion on his perfect face.

My heart races so fast, I'm scared it's going to give out. This is it. My stomach bottoms out thinking about all the questions they are going to ask when we are done here. I can't avoid it any longer though. If I want them to understand why I'm so scared, they need to know this.

"He's talking about my baby." Just speaking about my precious angel causes my hand to white knuckle the blade I'm holding, digging it in a little deeper. "He cut my baby out of me while I screamed and begged him to stop. Just. Like. This."

I drag the blade across his flabby stomach, hip to hip. His entire body jerks against his restraints, shaking so hard the incision is jagged across his lower abdomen. Just like mine.

"The pain was so unbearable, I passed out before he was done. I thought I died strapped to that table. I was afraid I would never get to hear their first cry or hold them." My tears flow freely down my face as I drop the scalpel onto the floor.

I want to fall to my knees at the pain in my chest at the memory of what he did that day. I didn't die. I survived to live in captivity another year before I escaped. But the memory of the excruciating pain threatens to consume me.

Pulling myself together, I finally open my eyes to see the guys staring at me with a mix of sorrow, rage, and... Awe? Love, maybe? The emotion is hard to name.

This thing between us has moved at lightning speed, but I don't know if we are at *love* yet. But even as the thought enters my mind, I know. *I love them.* They give me strength when I am weak. They take my broken pieces and put me back together. I've never been in love, but I know I love each of them.

The realization gives me the strength to keep going. To finish this. My spine stiffens, making my stance strong and unwavering. My eyes find Maddox, his body radiating manic, psychotic energy.

"I *need* you."

He steps forward, closing the distance between us in one stride. His body is practically vibrating in front of me.

"Whatever you need," he states as he puts his hands on my hips. I can feel his energy transferring into my body.

"Do your worst, Maddie baby."

MADDOX

Chapter 30

The second the words leave her lips, adrenaline and endorphins rush through me like a junkie shooting up for the first time.

Fuck yes. Put me in, Coach!

"We do this together," I tell her, leaning down to whisper my next words. "By the time we're done with him, I'll have your entire body painted red with his blood."

A shiver runs through her at the image it invokes, and I know without a doubt my words turn her on.

My girl likes blood. Good thing, too, because I'm not fucking around.

"Blindfold him and get him up," I growl at my brothers, but I don't look back at them.

My eyes are firmly on my girl in front of me. Her pupils are blown wide-open. She is so much more than I realized.

She's a fucking queen.

Blood drips down her fingertips resting at her sides. I take each of her hands in mine, bringing them to my face, smearing the blood on like war paint. Bringing my eyes back to hers, locking on the deep evergreen color that has darkened with her own endorphins and desires running rampant through her.

My eyes stay on hers as I drop to my knees in front of my bloody queen, and begin unlacing her knee-high boots. She lifts it up, planting the tip of her boot in the center of my chest.

Her breath catches in her lungs when I trail my fingers up her thigh once I've undone her laces. I stop just before her delectable pussy, then move slowly back down to pull them off. She is so turned on I can smell her sweet essence through her pants.

I almost lost my shit when she informed me she didn't have any panties on earlier. Once the first boot is off, I repeat the same actions with the other.

Planting both feet back on the ground, I bring both of my hands through the apex of her thighs, gripping onto her ass and jerking her forward, bringing her pussy right to my face, taking in a deep breath.

I'm a slave to her sweet cherry smell. It drives me mad and my stone hard cock punches at the seam of my pants, trying to unleash itself on my bloody queen.

Not yet.

I trace my nose down her slit, invoking a gasp that turns into a soft moan on my way back up as I nudge her clit, rubbing my face into her pussy.

These goddamn pants are in my way. Inching my fingers up the curve of her ass, I dig them into her waistband, swiftly pulling them down to her knees in one motion.

Her glistening pussy is right in my face, and I waste no time burying my nose back into her slit, inhaling her into my lungs before my tongue darts out, licking a line straight to her clit.

"Oh God!"

Her entire body quakes, jolting from the shock of pleasure. Her hands grip onto my hair, trying to hold her pussy to my mouth.

"I'm no God, just a servant on his knees for his bloody queen."

I plant a soft kiss on her tight little mound, before helping her step out of her leggings and socks. Standing before her, I finger the bottom of her shirt, lifting it over her head. "No bra either huh? You're just begging me to ravish your tight little body, aren't you?"

She gives me a smirk, her lust-hazed eyes darker than I've ever seen, and I can't resist taking her plush lips, letting her taste her decadence from mine. I swipe my tongue through her mouth, pushing her taste inside. Pulling back, I watch as her tongue darts out, tasting the sweet cherry pie off her lips.

My eyes drink in every inch of her luscious body. My hands slide up her hips, caressing the curve of her waist up to her perky little breasts. Her nipples harden into pointed buds as I softly glide my thumb across them, her breath comes in harsh pants.

"Please," she begs.

"Not yet," I tell her, grabbing her throat, and turning her around so her back is pressed to my front.

I know she can feel my bulge digging in. I want her to know she is not the only one struggling here. My fingers flex on her throat as my other hand slides down her stomach to her scar as my lips go to her ear.

"You gave him the same scar he gave you. Now you'll watch me give him the rest. He will wear every single mark on your body."

She nods her head against my chest as I kiss her neck, tasting her skin because I am a fiend, and I will never get enough. I guide her over to Alek and Royal, who stand beside the table holding Doc under his arms to support his weight.

Her dagger is still in his thigh, the blood trickles down his leg all the way to his feet in small little lines. *Smart girl.* She left it in to keep him from bleeding out too quickly.

The cut on his lower belly is pouring out though. She didn't hit anything major, his fat stomach protecting his internal organs, preventing them from spilling out on the ground. We need to work fast. The blood loss isn't enough to kill him, but I don't want him passing out just yet.

I shove the table out of the way, grabbing my phone from my pocket to bring up my digital panel. Everything in this room that could be mechanically operated, I have linked to my phone. There is a stationary panel located on the wall by the entry, but sometimes you just need fingertip access.

I push a button and a large butcher's hook descends from the ceiling beams right above the drain, the loud wrench whining makes Doc perk up, jerking his head in all directions to figure out where it's coming from with the blindfold stealing his vision.

Once the chain is far enough down, Alek and Royal drag him over in front of it. This double butcher's hook has two curved hooks extending down from it.

Moving around behind them, I take the hook in one hand, placing my other on the doctor's shoulder. One hard shove, his flesh and muscle is pierced with the tips of each hook just under his shoulder blades.

With the push of a button on my phone, the wrench rewinds, pulling the chain taut and digging the hooks deeper beneath his skin and bones, hanging him from the ceiling. Blood pours from the new wounds, dripping down his body onto the floor.

Raena watches as the doctor screams and struggles against the hooks, but his movement just makes it worse for him. He's a big man, therefore his weight adds to the wounds, pulling at his skin as the blood flows from his body.

I walk over to my table, pulling a few things I think I'll need from it before placing them on my rolling metal cart and wheeling it back over to my brothers and my girl. I stop in front of Raena.

"Alek, get behind her," I tell him, and he steps behind her, pulling her back to rest on his chest with his hands splayed flat across her stomach.

"My queen, you're going to watch me and Royal. Alek is going to touch you, and you are going to tell us everything King did to you as we do it to him."

"Just King? Or what his men did too? Most of my scars aren't from King himself."

Her voice is quiet, almost timid again as my spine stiffens and rage fuels my blood. The more I learn about her past, the more my blood boils. It's starting to make sense though. That's why she went after his men first instead of him. I make eye contact with my brothers, both with the same rage in their eyes as I have.

That piece of shit motherfucking cock sucker.

"I want names," Royal says, his voice deeper than I've ever heard as he steps in beside me, cradling her cheek in his hand. "I want to know exactly who put each mark on your body. I want to know every single detail. Can you do that for me?"

"I don't know all the names. Just their faces." Her eyes are closed, and I can tell the memories of their faces and what they did are tormenting her.

This will be healing for her. She needs this more than we do. This trauma of hers is more than I'd imagined, and I'm an imaginative motherfucker.

"That's okay. We can work out names later. You just tell us what you remember." Royal leans down, kissing her forehead before moving to my cart and picking up one of the blades laid out there.

We both back up and stand on either side of Doc, waiting for her to begin. He's still whining, but he has figured it out: the less he moves, the less painful it will be. Too bad this isn't the worst he has coming to him.

She takes Alek's hands from her stomach, moving them up over the swell of her breasts to the scars that marr her skin. Short scars layered on top of each other like they were cut over and over in the same spots, about 2 inches long on each breast.

His fingers trace the scars gently, her eyes fluttering shut as she begins. Her voice is now monotone, as she tries to tell her story without losing it.

"One of his men cut me here. He liked to make me bleed for him when he would rape me. King wouldn't let them touch my pussy. That was only for him. So they would rape my ass or force themselves in my mouth. He put a lot of the smaller scars you see on me. Here," she says, holding Aleks hands against her chest, moving his hands around to her hips where the same type of scars are on each side, "and here."

"Open your eyes, my queen." I want her to see the cuts as we make them. She needs to see the blood as it paints his body and know that it was spilled in her honor.

She doesn't open her eyes, a small whimper escaping her lips.

"Alek." His eyes meet mine, and I give him a nod. The sharp sound of him slapping her pussy echoes across the room, her eyes snapping open immediately on a gasp.

"I said eyes on us, Raena. Alek is going to touch you now, and you are going to keep your eyes open. You close your eyes, you don't get to come. Understand?"

She nods her head, frantically, her mouth dropping open as Alek brings his hand down her stomach to her pretty little pussy. She moans loudly when he strokes his finger through her slit, finding her clit.

Her eyes struggle to watch as Royal and I make the first matching cuts on his chest with our blades. His screams drown out her moans as the blood pours down his body.

We move to his hips, slicing through his skin with ease as he struggles against the hooks suspending his body just barely off the ground.

"Where else?" Royal asks, her concentration broken as she drowns in the pleasure Alek is giving her.

One hand strums her clit while the other squeezes her throat, his lips on her neck, kissing and sucking marks into her creamy skin.

"M-my back. J-Jackson…he put the biggest scar there. The doc, h-he stitched it up after," she stutters breathlessly as her orgasm builds, but she can't shatter. Not yet.

"Turn her around," I command Alek, and she whines when he stops playing with her to do what I asked. "Don't worry, Cherry. You can come soon. Show me the scar."

I saw this scar at Twisted when she was cowering in the corner, but hearing who gave it to her sets my blood on fire.

Fucking Jackson.

His death will not be quick.

Her scar goes from the top of her left shoulder, to the bottom of her right hip. It's deep and jagged. Like he stopped and started as he cut her. I cannot fathom why someone would want to hurt her.

211

What could she have possibly done to King to make him do this to her? To unleash his depraved men on her. What was his motive?

I need answers.

I spin the doctor around so his back is now facing us, bringing the blade to his shoulder in the same place as hers. His back is bigger, so his scar will be too. I don't really give two shits about it.

He could have saved her many times over, but he chose the coward's way. Turned a blind eye to her torture and blindly followed King's commands. He might as well have made the cuts himself.

I dig the knife into his back, dragging it down at an angle while he screams. I have to stop before my knife hits the hook. I yank it out, blood spraying across my face and soaking into my clothes. I jab the blade back into his back below the hook this time, continuing my cut to his right hip.

His body goes slack, his screams stopping just before I rip the knife out again. He passed out from the pain. *Good.* I can hear my girl now.

Looking back at Raena, Alek has turned her back around, his hand back on her pussy, but her eyes are on me. I know I must look feral right now, my face covered in his blood, but she doesn't look disgusted. If anything, she looks even more turned on.

"C-can I please come now?" She pleads, her knees buckling under the weight of the pleasure. I can see his fingers now pumping into her pussy and she grinds her clit down on his palm. "P-please," she begs. "I need to c-come."

"You can come, Cherry. Come on his fingers." I stalk forward, dropping to my knees in front of her soaking wet core.

Her arousal is running down her thighs. I run the blade of my knife gently up her inner thigh, then down the other, smearing his blood onto her skin.

Alek pumps his fingers harder and faster, her knees completely giving out as he holds her up by her throat. Her body seizing as she screams out her release, just as he pulls his fingers from her, and starts rubbing her clit furiously. Her sweet pussy squirts and sprays her come all over my face.

The knife clatters to the ground as I bury my face into her cunt, licking and sucking everything she has to offer. Her entire body shakes while I clean up the mess she made.

"Please... it's too much," she begs, her orgasm still going with my attention. But I am not stopping.

"Not until I drink every last drop of your come. You taste so fucking good," I say, pulling back briefly before diving back in as she squirms in Alek's hold.

Once I've had my fill, I plant a soft kiss on her swollen pussy before standing and taking her in my arms. She wraps her arms around my neck and legs around my waist, letting me hold her tightly. I grip the back of her head with one hand, tangling my fingers in her hair at the base of her neck.

My other hand rubs her back slowly, helping her calm down from the rush of her orgasm and all the emotions she has endured tonight. But we aren't done yet.

MADDOX

Chapter 31

"You did so good, pretty girl. Take a minute to catch your breath, then we have to finish this. I'm going to explode if I don't get inside you soon."

My words make her perk up. It doesn't escape my attention that none of us have fucked her yet. She wasn't ready before. But she is now. I will fuck her on this playroom floor tonight if it's the last thing I do. I will be the first one inside her.

She takes a couple of deep breaths into my neck before pulling back to look at me. There is blood and come smeared on her face.

Good. Red is her color.

I want to see her whole body painted red tonight. She is going to be a mess before we leave this room.

"I'm ready." Her voice is coming out stronger now that she's coming down from her high.

I lower her to her feet before softly kissing her lips, letting her taste herself again. She swipes her tongue into my mouth this time, the kiss more confident than our first.

She pulls back first, looking into my eyes for a moment before leaning back in and licking my lips like she can't get enough of her own taste. I know she can taste the blood too, and my entire body shudders. My cock is currently trying to punch a hole through my pants. I don't know how much longer I can wait.

She turns to face Doc again with determination and rage once more. He is just starting to wake up from passing out. He groans as he tries to look around, but the blindfold prevents him from seeing anything but darkness.

"Welcome back, Doc," she says, stepping in front of him. He whimpers as she gives his chubby cheeks a couple of hard slaps.

"P-please. No more," he begs pitifully.

"Oh, it's almost over. I just have one more question for you."

"I'll tell y-you anything," he stutters out, sounding hopeful that he is going to get a break from this torture.

Idiot.

If he doesn't realize his only reprieve will be in his death, he is fucking delusional.

"Did you help him get rid of my baby? Did he bury her, or did he have you throw her away like trash?" Her voice breaks at her question, but she remains strong.

"What? No!" He yells back at her.

She yanks her dagger from his thigh, pressing it to his throat. "Don't you fucking lie to me, Doc. What did he do with her?" She says through gritted teeth, rage bleeding into her tone.

"Sh-she's alive," he blurts out quickly. "He didn't kill her."

"Yes, he did. He showed me. He killed my daughter." Her rage consumes her at his lies. Faster than I can blink, she slashes the dagger across his throat, the blood spraying from the severed artery, drenching her entire body. He's gone in seconds.

She stumbles back a few steps, turning around to face us. Her eyes are dazed and unfocused. His blood runs down her body in rivets. She looks like a fucking warrior painted with his death.

The bloody blade clatters against the concrete as she steps forward, walking towards us but not seeing. She needs to come back to us. To me. I close the distance between us, gripping her shoulders and giving her a little shake.

"Hey, look at me," I say as her eyes lift to meet mine. "Good girl. You're okay." I gather her into my arms, hugging her tightly to my chest.

"Please, Maddie. Make me forget again," she pleads with me.

"I got you. Let me help."

Taking her face in my hands, I swipe at the blood dripping from her face, smearing it down her neck, into her chest, and over her heaving, perky breasts. I focus on her nipples, coating them in his blood, pinching and pulling on them until they are taut little buds.

Her body is starting to respond now that she's focused on what I'm doing, getting out of her head a little more with every touch.

"You were perfect, Raena. You did so well." My praise has her sighing, melting into my touch. I trail my hand down her perfect little body, over her stomach and moving around to her hips before sliding back up to her ribs.

I continue smoothing out the blood, going up and down her arms until she is literally painted red. "I wish I had a mirror in here so I could show you just how much of a fucking goddess you are right now."

"I'd rather see you, Maddie." She reaches for my shirt, pulling at the hem.

She doesn't have to ask me twice. I literally might die if I don't get inside her soon. I can see Royal and Alek standing beside us, watching how this will go. They can watch, or they can join. I don't give a fuck, as long as I am the first one inside her.

I reach behind my head, pulling my shirt over as she works my pants down my hips frantically. She drops to her knees in front of me, unlacing my boots like I did for her earlier. When she gets them unlaced, I quickly kick them off.

My pants come next, I feel like a teenager, racing to get naked for the first time. My heart is pounding so hard, my cock straining against my boxers.

She reaches for my waistband, slipping her fingers under and pulling them down, my cock bobs in her face.

"Oh my god," she gasps, "you're… pierced."

Her hand slowly reaches up, stopping just before she touches me. I need her touch like I need my next breath.

"Does it hurt?" Her question comes out shyly, making me laugh.

"It only hurts because you're not touching it, pretty girl."

Her fingers trace the piercings there. I have eight bars running the length, from base to just under the head, making up a Jacob's Ladder. One curved bar, the Prince Albert, pierced through the head itself.

Her touch grows more confident as she wraps her hand around me, slowly sliding up and down my length. I grab her hand, squeezing it tightly, gliding her over the metal studs faster.

"You're not going to hurt me, Cherry. Even if you did, I like the pain."

217

"I want to taste you." She looks up at me, but she doesn't look confident at this moment. "I just... I've never... I don't know how to make you feel good."

"I'll show you," Royal says, shocking the shit out of me.

Holy fucking shit. I might not survive this.

He drops to his knees next to her, wrapping his hand around hers on my cock, giving it a tight squeeze, almost buckling my knees.

"Goddamn, Royal."

My breathless words are punching out of my lungs as I struggle to stay on my feet. I've imagined Royal on his knees for me many, many times, but I never thought it would actually happen. And to have him on his knees next to our girl...

Holy. Fucking. Shit.

"Is this okay?" His voice is barely above a harsh whisper, looking up into my eyes.

For once in my whole fucking life, I struggle to open my mouth to respond, so I just nod my head back at him.

"I've never done this before, but I know what I like," he tells Raena, both of their eyes back on my cock, making it jump in their hands with their combined attention.

"This part here," he says, tracing his finger on the underside of my head along the curved barbell, "is really sensitive. So start like this."

His tongue flattens as he swipes it slowly across the bottom ball, and the sensation of his tongue threatens to undo me. Raena leans forwards when he pulls back, copying his motion, her tongue warm and wet as it tastes my cock for the first time. Her timid eyes find his icy blue ones, waiting for the next instruction.

I'm teetering on the edge of explosion, I need to be buried in one of their throats right the fuck now. Royal leans forward again, running his tongue along the bar at the base to the bar at the very tip. Pre-come oozes out, and he laps it up.

"Fucking hell, that's hot," Raena says next to him, patiently waiting her turn. She isn't wrong.

Watching Royal taste me, I am not going to last much longer like this. I'm so fucking close from the edging I've put myself through since our shower this morning.

"Can I taste?" Raena asks, looking at Royal, and I think she's going to copy him again, but she surprises me.

She grabs the back of Royal's neck, bringing his mouth to her, licking his lips until he opens for her. She slides her tongue into his mouth, tasting my come as both of them moan into each other.

She pulls back, her eyes opening and looking up at me before taking the head of my cock into her mouth, sucking the remaining drops out of me. She doesn't pull back this time, she flattens her tongue, taking me to the back of her throat.

My piercings rub along her soft tongue and when she goes as far as she can, she fucking swallows around my cock. She doesn't pull back or gag.

She doesn't have a gag reflex. Fuck yes!

"Just like that. Swallow my cock down your throat," I groan loudly as she moans around me.

The vibration feels fucking amazing. I look down and see Alek is now laying flat on his back under her body, letting her ride his face as he licks and sucks her sweet pussy into his mouth. The sight is my undoing.

"Cherry," I moan out, and I can't even give her a warning before I grip the back of her head, burying my aching cock as deep as I can, stealing her breath as my come shoots straight down her contracting throat. She keeps swallowing and moaning around me until she has taken every drop I have.

I slowly pull back, giving her a chance to breathe, her entire body shakes as she drenches Alek's face in her release.

While she rides her high against Alek's mouth, Royal grabs her face. "Open your fucking mouth, Angel. Stick out your tongue." She immediately obeys, and he sucks her tongue into his mouth, taking my lingering come from her. I've never seen anything this hot in my goddamn life. I'm still hard as stone and I need to be inside my girl. Right. The. Fuck. Now.

"Lay back on Alek."

He lifts his knees to support her back, as I get down on mine above his face. I'm very aware that my balls are in his face, but if it bothers him, he doesn't let me know.

"You're going to take every inch of my pierced cock, pretty girl. Alek is going to watch and count each bar as they disappear into your dripping little cunt," I tell her, and she nods along with me.

"Please, Maddie. Fuck me. I need you," she begs, and fuck me if it's not the most beautiful sound I've ever heard. Hearing that nickname coming from her pleading lips again, I know I'd do whatever she asked of me. No questions asked.

"I've got you, baby," Alek says from beneath us, his hands gripping her thighs and spreading them wide open as I notch my cock at her dripping entrance. Royal is now standing beside us, his cock in his hand, stroking it slowly.

Without rushing, I push inside her– her tight pussy stretching around me. "Goddamn. You're so fucking tight," I breathe out through clenched teeth as her pussy strangles the first inch of my cock.

"One," Alek counts, his hands massaging her thighs as she pants harshly. I pull back before pushing in again, two more barbells disappearing into her perfect little cunt.

Fucking hell!

"Slow the fuck down, Maddox. You're going to rip her," Alek hisses before taking his fingers to her pussy, sliding them beside my cock, and gently massaging and stretching her around me. His fingers grazing my cock makes my hips jerk forward on their own, earning me another inch and another growl from him.

"I- I'm okay," Raena says, her words choppy and breathless. "I can take it. Keep going."

"You like pain, don't you?" Royal says from above us, his cock dripping as he strokes it harder from the scene he is watching.

"I- I…" she starts, but I thrust into her in one hard push, burying my entire length inside her. "Fuck!" She screams, digging her nails into Alek's sides as she throws her head back. "Yes, I like it."

I give her a minute to adjust. "You're okay," I say, gripping her hair at the back of her head, and pulling her back up to look at me. "Just breathe. I'll make it feel better."

"Please, I need you to move," she tells me.

She doesn't have to wait any longer. I pull almost completely out, before pushing back inside her. I keep the pace slow but hard, and I feel my balls rubbing against Alek's face. My pace stutters when I feel his warm tongue lick a line from my balls to her dripping pussy.

"Fuck, Alek," I grit out, my restraint about to snap like a goddamn twig.

He doesn't respond, just sucking my balls into his mouth, and I fucking lose it. I grip Raena's thighs, leaning forward, spreading her wider, then start pounding into her pussy like a madman. Her screams of pleasure bounce off of the concrete walls, her pussy squeezing around me, letting me know she is close to losing it, too.

"Don't you dare fucking come yet, Cherry. Hold it." I growl at her.

"I can't...I'm going to come," she pants out.

"You can, and you will," Royal growls at her as he steps over us, separating our faces as he angles her head up to look at him. "Open your fucking mouth, Angel."

I can't see past his ass, but I hear his moan and I know he has buried his cock down her throat. His ass rocks in my face as he fucks her mouth roughly.

Leaning forward as I keep my punishing pace on her pussy, I swipe my tongue swiftly up his ass, teasing his puckered hole.

"Motherfucker!" He shouts, his own pace stuttering now as he stills his thrusts, his ass flexing as I reach up and grip his balls in my hand, feeling them contract as he pours his seed down her throat. I can't take it anymore.

"Come now, Cherry. Come on my cock, right fucking now," I grit out, pounding into her harder, feeling her shatter around me, pushing me over the edge of bliss. I still my hips, burying myself as deep as I can as I fill her cunt full of my come.

My heart pounds in my chest, our labored breaths the only sound to be heard. Royal steps back over us, sitting back on his heels. I slowly pull out of her swollen pussy, watching as my come leaks out and drips down her slit and onto Alek's mouth. He licks his lips, tasting my seed.

"Fuck," he grunts, gripping her hips and angling her so he can lick my come as it drips from her well-used cunt.

"Please, no more," she whines, the sensation too much.

She is exhausted from the fucking she just got, but he doesn't stop. He licks up and drinks down every drop of me from her. I sit back, watching her squirm on his face until she collapses back against his knees, her head rolling to the side.

"She passed out," Royal states the obvious. Getting to his feet, he picks her up and cradles her bridal style. "Let's get her upstairs and clean her up, then we can come back down and take care of this mess."

Alek gets to his feet first, holding his hand out to help me up. My stitches pull, making me grunt and reminding me that I was stabbed yesterday.

Funny, I didn't even notice the pain until now.

"I'll take a look at it once we get you cleaned up," Alek says as we follow behind Royal and our girl.

As we make our way back upstairs, I can't help but ask the question burning in my mind. "Do we need to talk about what just happened down there? Between us?"

They both stop on the stairs, looking back down at me. "Nope," Royal says, followed immediately by Alek's "I'm good."

"Okay then." I laugh out loud. "Fine by me," I say as we start back up the stairs.

If they're good, I'm good. I've been wanting to explore things with them for as long as I can remember.

Who knew it would take this little firecracker to come into our lives for it to happen.

ALEK

Chapter 32

We make our way up the stairs, all of us leaving a trail of blood in our wake to clean up later. This night is definitely not going how I thought it would.

What the fuck just happened?

That was so fucking intense. Between listening to her story, watching them torture and kill Doc, to making her shatter multiple times before Maddox fucked her, and I ate his come from her pussy. I need to get somewhere alone so I can take care of the massive ache I am left with.

I want her so fucking bad, but I won't hurt her. She barely took Maddox, and he is nowhere near as big as I am. I'm not being cocky, it's just the hard truth. The few girls I've tried to be with took one look at my cock and said 'not happening buddy' before running off.

So I find pleasure in other ways. Giving, instead of receiving. Then I just take care of myself. It's never been a problem for me. Until now. I've never wanted anyone like I want her.

I expect Royal to take her to his room, but he passes it and goes to mine. I guess he realizes she is most comfortable there since it's the only one she has been in. He takes her straight into the bathroom.

"Start a bath for her, Alek. Maddox, use the shower."

My tub sits on the opposite side of the bathroom, black-marbled and sunken into the floor. I have the biggest one in the house thanks to my size.

It is easily as big as a full-size hot tub, complete with jets that make for an amazing massage when my muscles ache from my workouts or just our line of work in general.

I start the water, getting the temperature just right, before walking over to my sink and digging out my bath oils and salts. I might be a big motherfucker, but I enjoy a good bubble bath now and then. I walk back to the tub, pouring in the mixtures before sitting them down on the floor next to it. I strip out of my clothes and shoes, kicking them next to the hamper on the floor.

Royal is standing propped against the wall next to the tub, waiting for me. "Come on, Baby Girl. Let's get you cleaned up," I say, even though she is still out cold, taking her from Royals arms and into my own. This should bring her back to the land of the living.

Stepping down the built-in stairs on the tub, I sink us both into the warm sandalwood and jasmine-scented water and turn on the jets. Her eyes flutter open to look up at me with a blissed-out gaze.

"Hi," she whispers softly, giving me a smile.

"Hey," I say, my grin spreading wide across my face. I grab the detachable sprayer, setting the dial to the shower position as I tilt her head back slightly. "I've got you. Let me take care of you."

The water darkens her blood-drenched curls, tinting the water pink as it runs down her body into the tub. As I'm wetting her hair and rinsing off the blood staining her body, Maddox gets out of the shower, grabbing a towel.

My eyes track the water as it runs in rivets down his tattooed chest and defined abs, all the way down to his pierced cock. My cock is still rock hard, and I know Raena can feel it twitching against her closed thighs.

"I'm going to go get dressed, then Royal and I will take care of the mess downstairs while you take care of our girl." He dries his body off quickly before wrapping the towel around his waist. He walks over to the side of the tub. "We'll be back soon, pretty girl."

Royal steps up next. "We won't be long, Angel. Let Alek take care of you."

They both linger for a moment as she nods, her eyes falling closed again, and I can tell they don't want to leave her. But I also know they don't want her to have to see any evidence of what happened downstairs again. By the time we finish here, there will be no trace of blood or a body left behind. It will be as if it never happened.

They finally turn and exit the bathroom, leaving me alone with her at last. When she hears the door shut, she peaks her eyes up at me, a smirk curling at her plush pink lips.

"What's that look for?" I ask, but I already have a feeling I know what she is smirking at.

"So, Maddox, huh?"

Her smirk spreads into a full shit eating grin. There is no judgment in her eyes, only curiosity and what I think looks like excitement. I have no reason to lie to her.

"We've never been together like that if that's what you're asking. What happened in the playroom tonight was a first for all of us."

"I see the way you look at him." Her hand comes to my face, rubbing my cheek as her voice softens. "You look at me the same way."

226

"And how do I look at you, Baby Girl?" I ask, my own smirk shining down at her gorgeous face.

"Like... I don't..." She struggles to put into words what I know she is trying to say. "Like you love me," she rushes out, dropping her hand to hide her face. "But that's crazy, right? We just met. You don't know me. But..."

"Don't hide from me, Raena. But what?" I pull her hands away from her face, tipping her chin up to look at me. I don't ever want her to hide what she is feeling from me.

"But I am feeling things. For you, for each of you. Things I didn't think I could feel. It's just fast, and confusing. I don't know what's happening between us. It feels like I fell over that cliff, and this is all a dream. This isn't real life."

Her eyes squeeze shut as her breath comes in labored pants. She isn't full-blown panicking, but she is working herself towards that. I push her wet curls back that have plastered to her face. "I need you to breathe for me, Baby Girl. Look at me. In and out." She takes a few deep breaths with me, calming herself down. I lean down and kiss her forehead before pulling back to look into her bright emerald eyes again. "Good girl."

"I can't explain it to you because I don't understand it either. But I can tell you, I've never felt this way for anyone in my entire life. The way I want you... it's not just sexual. I want all of you."

Her eyes shimmer with unshed tears, staring deep into my soul. She smiles softly at me as I open myself up to her. My hands tangle in her fiery soaked curls, massaging her scalp.

"I want it all." My fingers tighten in her hair at the base of her skull, at the memory of what she shared with us down in that playroom.

"All of your pain. Your nightmares. Your deepest fears. I want to crush them to dust. I want your darkest fantasies, the ones you're too scared to say out loud. I want your pleasure dripping from my tongue

227

every morning and every night. I want it all. With you. With my brothers. If that's crazy or too fast, so be it. It doesn't need a label. I just want you to know that you're not alone with these feelings. They are intense, and I'm fucking terrified of what it means. But we will figure this out together, baby. I'm not going anywhere."

Her tears finally fall down her cheeks in streams as she gives me a watery smile. She doesn't say anything for a minute, both of us lost in each other's gaze.

She leans up, swinging her legs over me, straddling me, looking down at me as she kneels above me. "Can I... kiss you, Daddy?"

I'm so fucking gone for this little fireball. My hands tighten in her hair on a deep growl, smashing her lips into mine. I take her mouth like a starved man, my tongue sweeping against hers, and she moans into my mouth. I feel her press down, her hot pussy lips spreading over my massive length trapped between us as she rocks on me. I groan into her mouth, releasing her hair to grip her waist, digging my fingers into her tender flesh to still her rocking.

"Don't, Baby Girl. I can't," I growl out, trying to hold myself back. I can't fuck her. It is killing me but I would never live with myself if I hurt her.

"W-why? You didn't get to come earlier. I can feel how much you need this too," she whines breathlessly, lifting herself up, slipping her hand between us to free my aching cock.

Her tiny fist slides down my cock, and her fingers don't even go halfway around me. She gasps when she gets a good look and feel of how big I am, and I mentally prepare myself for the rejection coming my way. It's not her fault. It is what it is.

"Trust me, baby. I want to. I want you so goddamn bad it hurts. But I won't hurt you," I tell her, opening my eyes to look at her.

She isn't looking at me though. She has a look of determination on her face as she stares at my cock. Like she is trying to figure out how to ride a bull and stay on for the full eight seconds when the bull looks like a goddamn elephant.

"I'm okay," I chuckle. "Don't worry about me. Let me clean you up and take care of you."

"And just who is going to take care of you, Daddy?" She shoots back as I grab the black loofah and soap from the edge, squirting some on and lathering it up. I pull her hair over her shoulder, bringing the soapy loofah to the back of her neck. I run it down her spine slowly. She arches her back, mewling like a cat as her perky little peaks come close to my face. The move makes her slick pussy slide against me again.

Goddamn! She is trying to kill me.

Chapter 33

It's official. I have lost my fucking mind.

I went over that cliff and I must be stuck in a coma because there is no fucking way this is real. In real life, I would run scared at the sight of this beastly man and the monstrous cock he's packing. I would never have the desire to impale myself around its massive girth, sink down on it as it rips me apart, and give myself a *good girl's* death.

But I do. I want to climb this man like a goddamn tree.

His heavy hands run over my body with the soapy loofah, washing away the blood from our night in the playroom. My skin pebbles with goosebumps when he brings it to my front, ghosting over my hardened nipples.

"Please, Daddy," I beg, and I'm not even ashamed at how whiny it sounds.

I need him so fucking bad. You'd think the orgasms from earlier would be enough to satisfy me, but I'm still so fucking turned on, and it has everything to do with this man. I was so lost in the torture and pleasure in the playroom, I didn't realize until after that Alek is the only one who didn't get off when we did.

Now I have this unexplainable desire to make him shatter. I don't know him very well yet, but what I do know is, he takes care of everyone around him. His Daddy aura drips off him, but I want to take care of him.

He says he can't fuck me because he won't hurt me. It makes me wonder if he has hurt a girl in the past.

The thought immediately makes my green-eyed monster rise to the surface. I mean, it's clear each of these men has a past. They look like sex on a stick, for fucks sake. I know they've been with other women.

For reasons I don't care to look into at the moment, the thought of them with someone else makes me feel murderous.

I shove down the jealousy and unhinged stabby feelings for now, focusing on the way his hands feel as he soaps up my naked body. I no longer feel ashamed of my scars when these men look at me. It's an odd feeling, but one I embrace. The way their eyes drink me in, I've never felt so desired and wanted.

He slides the loofah over my stomach, down to my aching core, and I moan embarrassingly loud. "You're so sensitive," he chuckles as I lift my ass for him.

I can feel the heat creeping up my neck and rising to my cheeks. With his free hand, he slips his thumb between my slick lips, tracing my slit before circling my clit as he continues washing between my legs and inner thighs. My back arches, pushing my greedy pussy into his hand more.

"So needy. Do you need something? Hmm?" He's teasing me. I've thrown all pride and dignity out the window I guess because I am not above begging this man to fuck me with his monster cock in this ridiculously big bathtub.

"Please. I need you. Fuck me, Daddy."

My breathless plea earns me a growly groan that I feel all the way down to my clit. He needs this too. I don't understand why he's so scared to hurt me. As much as I don't want to think about it, I know he has fucked other women before. This man is too skilled to be a virgin. If they can take it, so can I.

"I can't fuck you, Raena," he groans as if it pains him.

"Why not? I'm sure you've fucked other women before. I know you won't hurt me. I need you, Alek. Please." I grind my pussy down against his hard cock, looking down between us to see his swollen head leaking pre-come from the tip.

Swiping my thumb across it, I bring it to my mouth, sucking his essence into my mouth and moaning around the digit at his taste. He's sweet and salty. My favorite combination. Like sea salt caramel. "Fuck. You taste so good, Daddy."

His cock jerks against my pussy at my praise, his restraint close to snapping if the deep rumbling growl in his chest is anything to go by.

"I-I've never... fuck," he groans out, dropping the loofah in the scented water as he grips my waist and drives his hips up, grinding against me. We both moan loudly at the delicious contact. "I've never fucked anyone, Baby Girl," he finally gets out around his panting breaths. "I would rip you apart."

His words cause my entire world to stop on its axis. Is he telling me... "You're a virgin?" I blurt out loudly, shocked to my core as my eyes snap to his. I never would have thought that is what he was going to say. This man walks around dripping daddy vibes and sex appeal.

I see the moment my shock registers as rejection, his face falling for a split second before he schools it. I take his face into my hands, my fingers trailing up his stubbled jaw.

"Hey, don't do that. Don't take my shock as rejection. My shock is from realizing I will be your first. You have no idea how happy that makes me. I was feeling really stabby just thinking about all the women you guys must have been with before me." My admission makes him chuckle. I lean down and capture his smiling lips with mine before pulling back to look into his eyes.

"I'm not scared of you, Daddy. I want you. *All of you*. But I understand now if you're not ready. My first time was stolen from me." My eyes scrunch up at the memory. I shake my head to clear it from my mind and bring me back to the present. "As much as I want to slide down over your cock right now and feel it stretching me, I won't steal that from you. When you're ready, I will be here."

My lips linger above his, my words ghosting over them as he looks at me like I'm the most important thing in the world to him. His hands twist at my scalp, manipulating my head to close the tiny distance between us as he slams his mouth on mine. He kisses me like I'll disappear in the next second if he doesn't consume me. His deliciously long tongue slides down my throat, making me moan into his mouth.

The way I want this man right now. I am fucking feral for him. He makes me feel like a dog in heat, rubbing my pussy all over him, trying to get fucked. I grind down against him again, driving us both mad with lust.

"Keep doing that, and I'm going to explode all over both of us," he growls, his fingers digging into my flesh.

"Do it then. I want to watch you come. Let me take care of *you*, Daddy." My lips trail up his neck to his ear as my whispered plea makes him shiver.

"Fuck," he growls at me, both of his hands moving to my waist to slide me back and forth over his massive cock.

His hands are so big that his fingers almost touch as he grips them around me, pulling me down harder against him. I love how big he is.

He makes me feel like a princess, sitting upon her 6'9 throne made of pure muscle and tattooed daddy.

The sounds coming from him make my pussy clench tight around nothing. I would literally fuck his voice if I could. His deep, rumbling timbre just does things to my lady bits.

Fuck.

He brings one hand down to touch my aching clit, and my orgasm creeps up on me as he grinds against me harder, his thumb circling faster and faster.

I need more.

I want it all. I want to slide over his throbbing cock, splitting me wide open and stretching me around him. But I meant what I said. I won't push him. When he is ready, I will ride this man like he deserves. He's right. He very well might rip me apart. I still don't give a fuck. I've never been one to back down from a challenge.

"Come for me. Right. Fucking. Now."

His speed on my clit increases with his grunted command as he drives his hips up harder and faster. He is losing his composure quickly as he chases his release. Then he slaps my pussy hard and I fucking shatter all over him.

My come squirts all over his cock and stomach, up his chest as he rubs my clit furiously. My mouth opens to scream but no sound comes out as my body seizes with the force of my release.

"That's my good fucking girl, coming all over Daddy's cock. FUCK!" His growl turns into a shout as his release shoots from him.

Goddamn, this man might actually kill me.

He grinds against me in staggered thrusts, milking his massive cock. Our releases cover his torso, and when he loosens his grip on me as we catch our breath, I slide down his body.

My tongue finds the groves of his sculpted abs, his blistering skin, and our mixed releases mingle, making me moan again. My tongue greedily laps up what the rolling water doesn't rinse away. Thankfully, with this bathtub being so big, the water hasn't come up high enough, because I want every single drop.

Sliding down further, his cock is still twitching and pumping come onto his stomach, so I lick up the mess, savoring his sweet and salty flavor on my tongue before taking his still-hard cock into my mouth. My mouth is open as wide as it can go, my lips stretched tight around him as I try to fit in as much as I can. He is so fucking big.

"Goddamn, Baby Girl. Just like that. Take every fucking drop."

I suck on his head, lapping my tongue over the oozing slit and drinking down everything he has to offer. Pulling back, I place a gentle kiss on the tip, before collapsing my head down against his warm torso.

"Such a good girl, Raena," he praises breathlessly as his hands smooth my unruly curls down before sliding under my arms and sliding my body up his. "Come here."

He cradles me against his chest, rubbing my back soothingly with his rough calloused hands. He continues to whisper praises in my ear as I gently drift in and out of sleep against him. I don't know how long we stay there like that, but I am vaguely aware of him washing my body again before he shampoos my hair and rinses it out. I feel like a lifeless doll as he manipulates my body out of the tub with him.

The air feels cool against my wet skin for a moment until I feel a warm towel blanketing me, and then I'm sinking into a soft cloud. This mattress is heaven, but the moment his body heat disappears, my eyes snap open.

Please don't leave me alone.

I find Alek standing next to the bed, drying his body off with a towel. "I'm not going anywhere, Baby Girl." His response causes heat to creep up my cheeks quickly. I cannot believe I said my insecurities out loud. I quickly grab the cover and bury my face into it, groaning at myself. "Hey, what did I tell you? Don't hide from me," he says, pulling the cover down as he climbs in next to me, pulling my body into his.

"I'm sorry. I'm not usually so needy and insecure," I whisper against his chest as his arms pull me closer.

"You've been through a lot in the last 48 hours, baby. Too many emotions. It's normal to feel like that afterward. I won't ever leave you alone. That's a promise. You're mine, Raena. It's my job to help you bring your emotions back down. That's what the bath was for, but we got a little carried away in there," he chuckles, making me smile against his chest. "There she is."

"I meant what I said in there, Daddy. I want to be your first," I whisper to him, closing my eyes again as his heartbeat lulls me deeper and deeper.

He is so warm and cuddly. Like a big fucking teddy bear. I don't think I've ever felt safer in my entire life. His hands trail up and down my spine, and as sleep takes hold of me, I hear him whisper into my hair.

"You'll be my only."

Chapter 34

The early morning sunlight is streaming through the curtains in Alek's room when I finally open my eyes. My body is cocooned in a sea of warmth.

Royal is wrapped around me from behind, his inked hand cupping my bare breast. My face is squished into Maddox's tattooed chest, and Alek has his massive arm thrown over both of us from behind him.

I have no idea how I ended up in the middle of this delicious man-meat sandwich, but I am not mad about it. Royal's massive erection is pressing into my ass as Maddox's piercings dig into my stomach.

My pussy clenches as the memories of last night flood back to me. The playroom. There is a slight ache between my thighs from Maddox fucking me like a madman. I've never been so turned on in my life.

The way these men touch me, talk to me, I know I've lost my mind. And when Royal dropped to his knees to show me how to take Maddox, I thought I would combust with need. It was so fucking hot. I want to see more. Feel more. Do more. I've never wanted anyone in my life the way I want these men.

With all the shit I've been through, I think I deserve a moment of pleasure. I'm not going to complain about mind-blowing orgasms from three sexy-as-sin tattooed men. My body has only ever been abused by disgusting men for their pleasure. Men who got off on raping a teenage girl. Beating her. Using her for their pleasure with no regard to consent or mutual pleasure.

I never willingly orgasmed when I was held captive. The only good ones I've ever had, I've given them to myself. They've never come close to the orgasms these men have pulled from me over the last few days. My body has done things it's never done before.

The ache I'm feeling is replaced by liquid desire as I feel myself getting wet the more I think about everything that has happened. The memory of Alek taking care of me in the bathtub has my thighs rubbing together to smother the building desire, but I freeze when Royal's hand on my boob squeezes.

"Keep that up, and I'll really give you something to make you squirm," he grumbles into my neck.

His voice is thick with sleep, and all it does is make me wetter. A whimper falls from my lips when his lips descend on the sensitive skin behind my ear.

"I'm trying to be a gentleman. I know you're sore this morning. But if you keep wiggling your tight little ass on my cock, I'm going to slide between your pretty pink lips and fuck you until you can't walk."

"I'm not sore," I lie, but he doesn't need to know that. I've had worse aches than this and was never given a chance to recover. I can handle more than he thinks.

His tongue traces the shell of my ear as his hand releases my breast. I almost whine at the loss of his touch, but his hand descends down my stomach to my bare pussy. He slowly slides a single finger up and down my slit, teasing me with his light touch.

I need more.

I spread my legs a little wider, as much as I can while being sandwiched between them. Suddenly, he plunges his finger into me, making me wince and moan at the same time.

"Not sore, huh?" He withdraws his finger, bringing it to my face, my arousal glistening in the sunlight. "Open your mouth," he growls.

His deep, commanding tone has me obeying immediately. With his eyes locked on mine, he slides the slick digit against my tongue, making me taste myself. My cheeks burn with embarrassment as my sweet, tangy essence floods my senses.

His pupils blow, and his jaw ticks with how hard he's clenching it, but he doesn't withdraw from my mouth. He keeps sliding all the way to the back of my throat. When I don't gag or pull back, a growl erupts from his chest.

Good. I want him to be as affected as I am.

Before he can pull back, I wrap my lips around it and suction them closed. My tongue swirls around the tip, cleaning off every drop of my arousal. With a force that makes the breath catch in my lungs, he pulls his finger free with a loud pop.

"I should spank your ass red for teasing me," he growls, even deeper than before, his hand dropping to my throat, and his thick cock grinds against my ass. "But I think I'll just edge you instead. Get you so close to the release you so desperately need, over and over. Would you like that?" His fingers flex against my throat as he whispers threats into my ear.

"I could wake up one of the others. Or I can take care of it my–" I bite back, but before I can finish that sentence, Royal has me flipped on my back, pinning me to the mattress as he hovers over me.

His knee is between my thighs, and his hand remains on my throat, not taking away my air completely, but with enough force to make me work for the oxygen I need.

"You don't get to touch *my* pretty little pussy without permission." His breath fans across my face as he struggles to maintain his composure.

His restraint is going to snap at any moment. That should scare me. I should run for the hills at the thought of any man laying claim to part of my body. To me. But I'm not scared. I *want* to be claimed by him. By them.

This is my choice. I'm choosing to give myself to these men. I know, without a doubt, if I demanded he get off me and let me leave, he would. He wouldn't hold me prisoner and take what he wanted from me like *he* did.

I can feel the panic sliding up my throat at the memories, squeezing tighter than Royal ever could.

In and out. Just breathe.

I close my eyes and take a deep, calming breath around his hand. I will not let King control me or my body ever again. The only way I can take back my power is to choose for myself. Blowing out a long breath, I shove the panic back down and open my eyes to see Royal watching my face with a look of pride.

"That's my good fucking girl," he whispers as he presses a kiss to my forehead before he brings his lips down to mine, almost touching, but not quite.

He doesn't comment on what just happened, but he knows. He let me work through it on my own. His eyes pierce into mine, saying everything his mouth doesn't.

"Thank you," my whisper ghosts against his lips, causing a shiver to run through his body. I need his kiss. His touch. Him. I need him like I need my next breath. He doesn't make me wait any longer. Royal steals my lips in a slow, burning kiss. It's a claiming and dominating kiss, but also a comforting caress of passion.

He owns my mouth with his, sliding deeper with each stroke of his tongue. He nips at my lip before pulling back completely. It takes me a minute to figure out how to breathe again. For a few stolen moments in time, we just stare at each other, existing in our little bubble. With one final kiss on my lips, Royal groans as he shifts his weight off me, rolls out of bed, and grabs my hand.

"Alright, Angel. Let's get out of this bed before I do something stupid...like fuck you into a coma." I allow him to pull me up. He is right. As much as I want him right now, I *am* sore.

"Should we let them sleep?" I ask him, looking back down at the bed. Alek is full-on naked spooning Maddox. Both of them look so peaceful and content in their current state, I'd hate to disturb them.

"Hey, fuckers! Wake up." Royal shouts, throwing a pillow at them, and I can't escape the giggle that slips out of me as he hands me his shirt to slip on. Maddox jolts awake but Alek curls around him tighter in a protective 'daddy' move.

"What the fuck?" Alek complains, his sleepy timbre rumbling straight through to my very core.

"Well, good morning, 'Big Daddy'. Someone's happy to see me this morning," Maddox says through his cheeky grin, wiggling his bare ass against Alek's cock.

"Maddox," Alek grumbles, releasing him from his hold and shoving him away. He yelps dramatically, when his ass hits the floor.

"If you want to throw me around like a rag doll, Daddy, all you have to do is ask," Maddox says as he sits up and peeks over the bed. A pillow flies at his face a second later.

"Come on, Raena. Let's leave them to their pillow fight," Royal chuckles as he finishes slipping on some sweatpants. He takes my hand and pulls me from the room as I hear both men scramble to get up, taunting each other more.

We descend the stairs into the living room. He continues to pull me along to the kitchen, only stopping when we reach the island. He turns to me, without speaking, and lifts my ass onto the barstool.

"I know I'm small, but I am capable of sitting on a barstool," I say, rolling my eyes at his antics. Truth be told, I love the way these men handle me. They don't need to know that though.

"Roll your eyes at me again, and you won't be able to sit down anywhere for a week," he growls into my ear.

A shiver runs up my spine at his threat. I suddenly have the mental image of him bending me over his knee like a naughty girl and him taking his belt to my bare ass. I'm pretty sure that shouldn't excite me like it does.

"So many empty threats. I'll believe it when I see some follow-through," I tease him, a smirk playing on my face as his eyes darken to a deeper blue than they just were.

I can tell I've surprised him when he doesn't respond immediately, but it doesn't take long for him to recover. Before I can even process what is happening, he has me up out of the seat and bent over the island.

I barely have time to register his shirt being lifted before the first sharp slap lands across my exposed ass. Both sets of cheeks heat immediately, one from the spanking and the other from the humiliation of being punished. But neither compare to the blazing heat that spreads through my pussy.

I've been punished before, but it's never been even remotely pleasurable. I will give him shit all day, every day, if it means he will bend me over like this.

"I've been going easy on you. I *will* spank your ass for being a brat." *Slap*. "I *will* tie you to my bed and edge you to the brink of madness." *Slap*. "Make no mistake, I will *always* follow through." His hand soothes the sting left behind on my cheeks, kneading and caressing the tender flesh.

My face flushes with more embarrassment when he slips his hand lower, sliding his fingers through my mess. There is no hiding what he does to me. He can feel the evidence of it dripping down my thighs.

"Fuck. You're soaked," he groans, twisting my hair in his fist and lifting my top half off the countertop.

He spins me around, bringing his glistening hand to his mouth, sucking his fingers clean. The second he pulls his fingers free, he lifts me up and sits my ass directly on top of the island.

He doesn't say anything as he pushes my back flat against the cool surface. His tongue licks a long, straight line, from ass to clit, tasting all of me. He growls against my sensitive flesh, and the vibrations have my ass lifting up, chasing his tongue. His hands spread me wider for him, holding me in place as he suctions his mouth over my clit with vigor.

"Oh my—yes. Right there," I half moan, half scream out. I can feel the quivering in my pussy, and just as I'm about to fall over the edge of orgasmic oblivion, his mouth is gone.

"No! Please," I beg breathlessly, bringing my hand to my face as I try to catch my breath and slow my heart down.

"This was a punishment, Angel. Not a reward," he says, and I can hear the smirk in his voice, even with my eyes closed.

I'm so pissed off, I can't even move my bare ass off his island. I can hear him moving around, pulling things out of the refrigerator, and sitting them next to me as I try to compose myself enough to move.

"Royal, why is Raena looking violent this morning?" Maddox says from somewhere near my head.

I'm not sure how long he has been here, but since he can tell I'm pissed, he couldn't have been here very long. I'm still kicking my own ass for falling right into his trap. He told me he would punish me, and I pushed his buttons anyway. I'm mad at myself more than him.

"She is just learning about actions and consequences. Isn't that right, Angel?" Royal asks calmly, and it's still a struggle to contain the sass that wants to spill out of my mouth.

I want to tell him to fuck off, then go and fuck his brother. I don't, though. I don't want to find out what other punishments he could have in store for me. I don't think I can take the edging again just yet. I might combust.

"Yes sir," I say softly.

He can have this one. I might be pissy, but I can see this for what it is. Royal thrives on control. Just from our brief interactions, I can already tell he needs to feel in control of most situations so he doesn't snap.

"Good girl," he praises, and my face flushes hotter from his praise.

Goddamn, all of these men are trying to kill me.

"Alright. Up you go," Maddox says, grabbing my hands from my face and pulling me up from the counter.

He picks me up, sitting me back down on the barstool. I keep my mouth shut this time about my ability to sit on my own.

"We'll make some breakfast. I'm starving and Royal already ate my breakfast," he says, winking at me before turning back to Royal, who is standing in front of the stove.

I allow myself to get lost in my head as I sit there, watching them move around each other in perfect synchronization, cooking eggs, bacon, and toast together. I don't know how much time passes, but I don't even register when Alek enters the kitchen until I feel his hot breath on my neck and his large hands sliding over my waist.

244

"Morning, Baby Girl," he whispers into my ear before trailing his lips over my shoulder. My eyes flutter closed, and I allow myself to melt back into his warm embrace. It surprises me how different it feels to be in each of their arms.

Maddox feels like chaos personified. His energy is infectious. Royal makes me feel strong, even when he's dominant and possessive. His need for control means he wants me to submit, but the choice is mine. Whereas Alek feels like home. Being in his arms makes me feel safe and cared for. Nothing can hurt me as long as he is holding me.

Honestly, I don't know much about these men yet. But, the emotions they arouse in me with their actions and how they have treated me… I can only hope I'm not wrong to trust in them.

"Morning," I reply, smiling but keeping my eyes closed as he picks me up.

He turns me around to wrap my legs around his waist as he carries me to the table in the dining room. I have no idea why he feels the need to feed me from his lap, but I like it. He takes a seat with me straddling his lap. We don't talk for a few moments. I just lay my head on his bare chest and trace his tattoos there with my fingers.

I love their tattoos. I'm sure there are stories behind each piece of art inked into their skin. I want to ask about them, but I don't. Not yet. I trace a large one that starts on his side and wraps around to his sculpted abs– it's an angel holding a small child. It is ethereal and so beautiful I can feel the tears welling up in my eyes.

It reminds me of my daughter. She is with the angels now. While I can find peace knowing that she doesn't have to endure the things I have, it doesn't hurt any less. *She was mine.* My flesh and blood. She was brought into this world in a depraved and vile situation, but she was mine. It was my job to protect her and I failed miserably.

"Hey. What's the matter?" Alek questions, bringing my face up with his fingers under my chin. My tears flow freely when I look into his concerned eyes.

"I'm okay," I tell him, giving him a watery smile as I swipe at the tears staining my cheeks and nodding to the angel and child on his side. "Your tattoo, it just reminded me of my daughter. I'm sorry."

"Don't apologize for expressing your feelings, Raena. You're allowed to feel sad about losing your child. You're allowed to be angry. You're allowed to feel however you want," he assures me, taking my hand and placing it on top of the angel. His other hand cradles the back of my head, holding me against his heartbeat. "I got this for our sister. I hope wherever she is, she is being watched over and protected until we find her."

His deep voice is thick with emotion and my heart aches for their loss as well as mine. Their sister is in the same hands that murdered my daughter. I can only hope someone else is protecting her until we can rescue her.

"We have to find her," I whisper into his chest, my voice cracking with pent up emotions. I've kept them buried for so long, it's hard for me to express myself when the floodgates open and they come rushing at me like the Grimm River.

"I know, baby. We will," he whispers soothingly into my hair, his fingers massaging my scalp. "We will figure it out after breakfast."

I nod my head in agreement, focusing on his heart beating against my cheek and the warmth of his bare skin. We stay like that until Maddox and Royal finish cooking. They bring piles of plates over, placing them in the middle of the table.

We eat in comfortable silence, Alek feeding me in his lap until I can't take another bite. Only then would he even take a bite of food.

After everyone is finished, Alek and I clear the table together, putting the dishes in the sink. It's wonderfully domestic. I could get used to this, and that scares me slightly.

"So," I say when we are all standing around the island, staring at each other. I'm getting more anxious with every minute that passes. "What's the plan?"

ROYAL

Chapter 35

"We are getting nowhere," Alek says for the third time since we've been down in the basement, trying and failing to come up with a solid plan of finding Em. His hands run down the length of his face, like he can wipe away the tension twisting his rugged features. We are all stressed.

Raena is sitting on the small lounge chair behind the table with her legs folded under her. She has been frantically chewing her bottom lip and picking at the non-existent lint on my shirt. Maddox is pacing in front of me, trying to contain the chaos inside.

As much as I don't want outsiders involved, especially someone we haven't worked with before, he's right. We can't do this on our own. We need help.

"Okay," I finally conceded. "We need help."

Alek looks at me with relief. He has been saying this for weeks now. I just find it hard to bring new people into our circle. I have trust issues, I can admit that. I blame myself for bringing King into our lives.

If I wouldn't have accepted his offer, Alek and Maddox would have never been exposed to him. We could have survived foster care together. I could have gotten them out when I turned 18. Our lives could have been completely different.

I'm so lost in my thoughts, I miss what my brothers are saying. Shaking the self-deprecating thoughts from my head, I try to focus on the suggestions they are throwing out there.

"I'll put some feelers out with our people. See who they know," Alek says, digging his phone from his pocket.

"Um, I think I can help," Raena says, bringing all of our attention to her. She must see the look on my face that says I'm not going to allow her to put herself in danger because she quickly adds, "I mean, I know someone who I think can help." She stands from the chair, walking over to the table where we are at.

"Who?" We all ask in unison.

"The people who helped me when I escaped King. Have you heard of the Huntsmen?" She asks, nervously chewing on her lip again. The name sounds familiar, but I can't place it.

"In White Harbor?" Alek asks, confusion furrowing his brow.

"Yes. I met them when I ran. They took me in. Helped me heal from my injuries, and when I was ready, they trained me to be a hunter. I worked for them until I was ready to come back here. I think they can help find your sister."

"Didn't they kidnap the daughter of a powerful man to take over his businesses?" Alek asks, jogging my memory of where I've heard the name before.

"Years ago, King told us about a group of men who kidnapped this man's 18-year-old daughter. No one has seen or heard from the man since. It was rumored that they killed him and his entire family," I tell them.

"Don't believe everything you hear. The daughter of that man, Aspen Snow, is the one who helped me. Those men saved her," Raena says, jumping to their defense. I can immediately tell these people mean a lot to her.

"Easy there, Cherry," Maddox says, coming behind her and rubbing her shoulders. "We know better than to believe anything that comes out of King's mouth. Even still, if they have the capabilities to overthrow a major criminal organization like the one run in White Harbor, maybe they are exactly who we need to help us."

"So, I'm curious. What's the *real* story on the Huntsmen?" Alek asks.

"It's kind of a long story, but before Snow and her guys took over White Harbor, her father was murdered. Her stepmother wasn't a good person. She married Snow's father for his money, but that wasn't enough. She wanted to run drugs out of her father's businesses. When he wouldn't allow it, she killed him. Snow was only 16 at the time. She lived with her stepmother until she turned 18. That's when things escalated," she sighs, walking back to the chair and folding herself back into it.

"At 18, all her father's businesses went to Snow. Her stepmother didn't like that, so she sent three of her Huntsmen to kill her. They saved her instead. Snow took over the businesses, and her stepmother fled White Harbor."

That makes much more sense than the lies King tried to spin. He wanted to expand his territory and was looking into White Harbor. He needed a story so he didn't look weak for not being able to follow through.

"Where did you fit in? What kind of work did you do for them?" I ask, curious as to what she is capable of. Considering the files I've seen of her handiwork, I'd say they trained her well.

"After the takeover, most of White Harbor was full of people her stepmother was involved with. Criminals, rapists, drug dealers, and the like. I hunted them, took them out to protect the sanctuary Snow was trying to build after her stepmother destroyed everything her father worked for," she says, her smile beaming with pride.

"We've seen what you can do. We saw pictures of three men you took out before we found you. And then with Doc. No doubt you're a badass, Cherry," Maddox says, rubbing his hands together in excitement.

"They deserved everything they got," she responds with a fierceness I've only witnessed down in the playroom. She is unapologetic about what she did, and that makes all three of us smile proudly at her.

"Damn right they did, Baby Girl," Alek says, and Maddox and I nod in agreement.

"So, how do we contact these Huntsmen?" I ask. The sooner we find Em, the sooner we can take out King. Then our lives with our sister and our girl can truly begin.

"They gave me a phone to contact them, it's in my bag upstairs. They are going to be mad. I haven't checked in with them since I got back, but they'll forgive me," Raena says, an excitement coming over her that I haven't seen before. It makes me smile.

"I'm sure they will. Go grab your bag," Maddox tells her. He pulls her up from her seat before planting a kiss on her pouty pink lips and slapping her ass to get her moving.

Her cheeks flush the cutest pink I've ever seen, and she's smiling as she walks away from us and heads upstairs. I want to see her smile like that every day for the rest of our lives.

All three of us are still staring at the empty doorway leading upstairs, smiling like a bunch of love-sick idiots when the sound of my phone ringing pulls us from our peaceful moment.

Digging it out of my pocket, our peace is severed the second we see who it is.

"Oh look, it's *Daddy* King," Maddox sneers.

Where are you hiding, Little Wolf?

I know you're still here.

Lurking in the shadows.

Your essence lingers in the air.

Invading my senses.

Enraging my beast.

Commanding me to reclaim what's mine.

Your time is up, Little Wolf.

I'll have you home soon,

On your knees in front of me.

Screaming until your voice gives out,

As I carve your betrayal into your tainted flesh.

A gruesome reminder, imprinted for eternity.

You'll beg for death, but even then, it will be my face you'll see.

Dragging your tormented soul back where it belongs.

An eternity with me.

Chapter 36

"Mr. Wolfe, please. I just got her to sleep, she had a rough–,"

She doesn't get to finish those foolish words when I slam her into the wall, my hand tightening around her delicate throat as I cut off her words and her oxygen. With her feet dangling a few inches above the floor, I lean in, relishing in the way her fear filled eyes screw shut.

"You remember what happened to the last nanny? Hmm? She tried to stand in my way. It didn't work out for her. Try to keep me from her again, I fucking dare you."

She slides down the wall when I drop her, sucking in gulps of air. Her pathetic cries fade as I storm down the hallway, throwing the door open. Em is curled in her bed, a soft pink blanket tucked around her, all the way up to her chin.

"Get up!" My voice booms through her room, startling her from her sleep. Her eyes shoot open, darting around the small space.

When her eyes land on me, she sits up, drawing her knees up to her chest, and scooting as far away as she can. Tears pool in her wide, terrified eyes, but not a single whimper escapes the child's lips as I move toward her. I grab her arm, jerking her from the bed and dragging her into the middle of the room.

"Don't move, Little Soldier."

Putting my knife to her throat, I quickly snap the picture and release her arm. A satisfied hum rumbles through my chest when she doesn't move from the spot I put her in, even as tears stream down her cheeks. She has learned far quicker than Royal ever did.

Of all the mistakes I made when choosing him as my heir, showing him compassion was the greatest. I should have broken him from the beginning. Made him watch as I slaughtered his family, instead of trying to play the savior. It got me nowhere.

I look over the picture, smiling as I walk in a slow circle around her. *It's perfect.* With her blonde curls plastered to her tear-streaked face and the knife at her throat. Royal is losing motivation it seems, and this will light a fire under his ass to find The Hunter.

Putting the phone and knife back into my pocket, I kneel in front of her. She doesn't cower away from me this time. Her haunted eyes stare back at me, reminding me so much of her mother. "Chin up, little soldier. I'll be back soon."

Walking out of the room, I don't even speak to the nanny when I pass her, her arms wrapped around herself as she hugs the wall I left her on. If she values her life, she won't try that shit again. I'll slit her throat as easily as the last one.

***

"Yeah?" Royal snaps through the phone.

My leg bounces impatiently before I force it still, shoving the anger from my obsession down.

"Well, hello to you too, son. Where are we at with the Hunter?" Masking the simmering madness, my voice reflects a facade of calm, pissing him off. Nothing, and I mean *nothing*, pisses him off more than me calling him son.

"We *are* working on it," he grits out, hatred spewing in every word. "Kind of hard when Jackson is hiding like a scared little bitch at your place."

"So you have nothing? *Tsk, Tsk.*" I click my tongue mockingly. "You know, I'm getting tired of making empty threats. I think it's time little Em finds out just how much her brothers have forgotten her."

"I want proof of life. How do I know she's even alive?"

Picking up my phone from the desk, I pull up the picture I took. Little Em looks terrified, and truth be told, she was. However, unlike her brothers, she's already learned not to fight back when I tell her to do something. Even at a young age, she knows to obey me.

Their muddled growls rattle through the speaker, reacting exactly as I'd hoped when I took that picture.

Good. Get pissed off.

Royal has always been a protective bastard. He's delusional, though. His loyalty will be the death of all of them. All of his weak spots are exposed, like low-hanging fruit, ripe for the plucking.

"You son of a bitch. If you touch a single hair on her head, I swear, I will slit your fucking throat."

"Oh, I'm going to touch more than the hair on her head if you don't bring me that Hunter. I'm going to slit her throat like I should have done to her mother." My facade slips at his ridiculous threats before I smooth it out once more. "Sooner rather than later, *son.*"

"We will bring you the hunter, *Dad.*" Venom drips like bitter poison from his tongue, and I end the call before I say too much. I might enjoy pissing him off, but he pisses me off even more.

I swipe Em's picture out of the way, pulling up my obsession again. It won't be long now until she is back where she belongs.

Chapter 37

Daddy King?

King is their fucking *father?*

That one word has me frozen midway down the stairs. What did I just walk into? I heard the phone ringing when I was coming down the stairs, and Maddox's words stopped me in my tracks.

I should have known not to trust them. They pulled me in under a spell of lust covered in tattoos, and I let myself feel something for the first time since I lost my daughter.

"Well hello to you too, son…"

Son? I'm so fucking stupid.

Icy tendrils of fear wrap around my spine at the sound of his voice filtering through the phone. The blood swooshes in my ears, and my vision starts to darken. I need to breathe, but I can't seem to force the needed oxygen into my lungs. I need to get out of here. Sucking in a deep breath, I force myself to move. I can't listen anymore. I can't bear it.

Turning back and silently climbing back up the stairs, I quietly shut the door to muffle any sounds. I know the playroom is soundproof, but I don't know about the basement area. I take off in a run for the garage. I already have my riding bag, I just need to get Nightshade and figure out my next move.

When I slip into the garage, I head straight for Maddox's bike. I saw him push a button to open the outer gate when we returned the other night. I find the magnetic fob attached.

Snatching it off, I push the button to open the garage, before sprinting to Nightshade. I drop my bag on the seat to dig out some pants and my boots.

Slipping on the leggings and half-ass lacing up my knee-high boots, I shove my helmet on my head. I'm thankful for the sound modifications when I start her up with a light rumble. Hoping they haven't come upstairs to find me yet, they shouldn't hear me leaving. I'm going to need at least a small headstart to outrun these Shadows.

Just a few moments later, I'm speeding down their driveway, approaching the gate. The stolen key fob does its job, the gate opening before I make it to it so I don't even slow down. The road is blurry from the tears I didn't know were building, but I blink them away. I can process how stupid I was later. Right now, I just need to put some distance between us.

Realizing I can't go to my cottage because it will probably be the first place they look, I head to the only place I know I'll be safe from both them and King.

The parking lot at Twisted is deserted. I see Ella's truck parked in the alley that runs beside it. I need to find a place to hide Nightshade. I didn't think this through with my mind running a million miles an hour trying to process the betrayal and pain consuming me. This is my first time driving into the middle of town on my bike. My hair isn't even tucked into my helmet.

Driving along the back side of the businesses that line the town square, I find an old loading dock that looks derelict. The back roll-up door is busted in several places and open enough that I should be able to slip my bike through.

Taking the concrete ramp that leads up to the door, I slip off of my bike to take a look inside. The building is abandoned, broken down boxes and busted furniture litter the space. This will work. Sliding the door up a little further, I go back to my bike and ease her inside.

Finding a dark corner away from the busted windows, I shut off the engine as I climb off. I dig through my bag once more, pulling out my black hooded jacket.

Tucking Royal's shirt into my leggings, I slip my jacket on and tuck my unruly red curls in the hood. When I am finally comfortable with my concealed identity, I slip back out the back door, making sure to close it all the way.

The walk back to Twisted gives me time to run back through every mistake I've made in the last few days. I allowed myself to be caught by King's sons. *Nothing was real.*

They lied to me about protecting me. About how they felt about me. I should have known it was too fast for it to be real. I should have listened to the voice in the back of my head that told me I was too broken, too damaged, for anyone to love.

Goddamn it! I'm so fucking stupid. They would have turned me over to King. He is their father. They owe me no loyalty. We just met. I am nothing to them, and *he* is their family. *Oh god, their poor sister.*

Was any of it real?

My mind races faster with questions I don't think I'll get answers to. I'm so caught up in my head that I walk right through a crosswalk, and in front of a blacked-out SUV. My hands slam down on the hood as they come to a screeching halt, barely stopping in time to avoid plastering me beneath them.

My heart pounds out of my chest as I look up to apologize to the driver, but the windshield is so dark, I can't make out anyone behind the wheel.

This vehicle looks similar to the Black SUV parked in the guys' garage, so I half expect them to jump out and grab me. But no one gets out. I stare into the window for a few moments, squinting my eyes as if that will help me see through the darkness. My hand presses into my chest, trying to calm my racing heart.

"I'm so sorry," I yell, but I get no response. The SUV slams it in reverse, backing up enough to swerve around me and speed off.

"Asshole," I mutter under my breath, moving out of the crosswalk and pressing my back to the cold, stone building. I've got to get it together. After my breathing has returned mostly to normal, and my heart doesn't feel like it's going to beat out of my chest, I continue the short walk to Twisted. I need to talk to Ella. She can help me figure out my next move.

***

"Rae?" Ella asks, throwing down the towel in her hands she was wiping down the bar with and rushing over to me. My face is streaked with tears that refuse to stay inside. Her face twists in rage when she sees me crying. "I will fucking gut them. What did they do? Did they hurt you?"

"Oh, El," I cry with a broken sob.

She engulfs me in a tight hug, allowing me to fall apart in her arms. It takes me a few minutes to control the waves of heartbreak and betrayal crashing within the confines of my chest and leaking out of my eyes.

"Let's go to the office. We will be open for lunch soon," she says, taking my hand and pulling me down the dark hallway.

This is where I first met Maddox. He pulled me into his alluring shadows, enchanting me with his feral touch and intoxicating smell. I was drawn to him before I ever saw his face.

My heart breaks just a little more, but I shove it down like I always do. There is no time to wallow in my self-pity. I was stupid and allowed myself to be put in a position to be hurt. Again. They might not have hurt me like King did, but the emotional pain somehow seems to hurt worse. I can heal broken skin and bruises. I don't know how to heal the wounds on an imaginary organ.

"Okay. You better tell me right now what the fuck happened. I know where they live now. I will drive over there and–" She says, but I cut her off.

"No. Don't. Please," I rush out, grabbing her hands in mine. "They didn't h-hurt me. Not like that."

"Okay…" she says, drawing out a breath, relaxing a little. "How *did* they hurt you?"

I blow out a breath, trying to will the storming emotions not to muddle my voice, and then I tell her everything I've learned.

"Motherfuckers. I thought they would have told you," she says, relief evident in her voice that I don't understand.

"You knew? You knew and *you* didn't say anything?" My voice is laced with accusation and hurt. How could no one tell me? How could they think I would be okay in the dark?

"Raena, he is *not* their father."

"What do you mean? I heard him call him *Dad* on the phone," I ask confused.

"King adopted those boys when they were teenagers. They hate him almost as much as you. They have no loyalty to him. That's why they created the Shadows. To overthrow him. But from what we recently learned, they can't kill him until their sister is located and rescued."

"They still should have told me." Some of my pain has eased with her words, but the sting of betrayal still burns in my chest. They know what King has done to me. They should have told me from the beginning so I wasn't blindsided.

"Yes, they should have. I should have. I knew who they were the night they unmasked themselves. I'm sorry. I should have made sure you knew before I left you with them." Regret laces her tone as her face pleads with me not to be mad at her. I recognize the look from our childhood. She couldn't stand it if I was upset with her.

"It wasn't your place, El. I'm not mad at you. I just thought they were lying to me about everything, and none of our time together was real. I thought they were going to deliver me to King." My voice breaks, emotions threatening to swallow me whole again.

So many emotions shoved down inside me. I'm terrified that when the dam finally breaks, my body is going to be in pieces on the floor.

"They wouldn't do that, Rae. I can see how those men look at you. They would burn the world down before they let anything happen to you. Speaking of, where do they think you are?"

She looks concerned for a moment, and I don't blame her. They are probably freaking out right now. I'm going to be in so much trouble. Royal is going to make good on his threat to tie me to his bed and not let me out for days for running from them.

"Uh, I kind of…ran? I overheard them on the phone with King, and I guess I *kind of* overreacted? Maybe? I just took off. They're going to be looking for me. They might actually burn down the town if they can't find me."

ALEK

Chapter 38

Papers rain down around us as Royal sends the wooden table crashing into the concrete wall of the basement before it lands on its side.

"Fuck!" He screams, his hands immediately lacing behind his head as he squats down to calm his rage.

His phone in my hand shows the image King sent. Liquid ice runs through my veins as I stare at the terrified little girl who stole our hearts two years ago. The look of absolute horror on her face enrages me like nothing else. She's innocent. She's just a child. Her life should be filled with joy and happiness, not death threats and terror.

Maddox paces behind me, his hands pulling at the dark strands of hair on his head. He looks more unhinged than he ever has.

I hit the lock button on the phone, putting it in my pocket. I meet Maddox halfway through his pacing loop, gripping his neck and pulling his forehead to mine.

"Stop, Maddie. Just breathe," I tell him, making a show of taking a deep breath, and he mimics me. His hot breath slowly fanning across my face as he exhales. "That's it. Again."

"He is going to kill her, Alek. If we don't give him Raena, he is going to kill her just to spite us. You know he doesn't love her. He just uses her as a pawn to control us like puppets," Maddox whispers, his eyes shut.

"I don't think he will. Think about it. There has got to be a reason he took her in. She is important to him. We just need to figure out why," I tell him.

It's been nagging at me for a while. What connection could this little girl possibly hold to a bastard like King? She has to be important enough to him to go through all this trouble. Important enough to take her in to start with.

King is not a kind man. He only took Maddox and me in because he wanted Royal to be his heir. He thought he could mold out the perfect little soldier to follow in his footsteps. He wouldn't have taken in this helpless little girl unless it benefited him in some way.

"I think you're right," Royal says, standing to his full height. "Did you catch what he said about her mother on the phone? Something about slitting her throat like he should have done to her mother's. He told us her mother was just some junkie who overdosed. Why would he have wanted to slit her throat? Who was she to King?"

"I caught that, too. Something isn't adding up. I think if we can figure it out, we might get a step ahead of him for once," I tell them. The tension in the room decreases slightly as we contemplate what to do next.

The sound of our phones pinging with a security alert pulls us from our thoughts. I dig out both mine and Royals phones from my pocket, but before I can see the alert, Maddox has his out.

"It's the front gate. Someone opened it," he says, going over to his computer with me hot on his heels to pull up the surveillance footage. It takes him a minute to log in, and while he is scanning the footage, I spin around in a circle.

"Um, where is Raena?" I ask, panic lacing my voice.

"She should have already been back down here. She was just grabbing her bag from your room," Royal calls over his shoulder as he jogs to the basement stairwell to go look for her. Before he even makes it to the doorway, Maddox's voice brings him to a dead stop.

"Found her. She left."

"What do you mean '*she left*?'" Royal growls, jogging back over to see the footage for himself. Maddox backs the feed up, showing the front gate closed and hits play. The gate opens fully a moment before Raena's black bike flies through it, her long red curls hanging out of her helmet, blowing in the wind behind her.

"What the fuck are you doing, Baby Girl?" I mutter to myself. I realize I still have Royal's phone in my hand when he snatches it, shoving it in his pocket, and turning back towards the door.

"Are you two assholes coming?" he yells over his shoulder at us.

Maddox jumps up, both of us pocketing our phones before jogging after him. My mind is reeling a mile a minute, running through all the possible scenarios that would have caused her to leave. She was smiling when she walked out of the basement. She wasn't upset. She knows she isn't safe from King out– *King.*

What if he got to her somehow? No. There is no way he could have contacted her while he was on the phone with us. Something else happened.

"Why would she run?" Maddox asks what we all want to know as we race up the stairs to throw some clothes on.

"She was fine when she walked out of the basement. It doesn't make sense," Royal responds, his face set in a mixture of concern and anger. "I'm going to turn her ass as red as her hair when we find her," he growls as he heads into his room.

Maddox slips into his clothes and I keep going down the hall into mine, flipping the light before going into my closet and grabbing my black hoodie, pants, and boots before going back out to the bedroom.

I quickly slip my sweats off and change before jogging back into the hallway. My brothers are both coming out of their rooms when I make it to their doors.

"Let's go find her before she does something stupid, and King finds her first," Royal says as we set off down the stairs.

We're in the garage in no time, piling into the blacked-out SUV. Royal gets in the driver seat, I take the passenger, and Maddox jumps into the back. We are backing out of the open garage door in a matter of minutes.

"Where would she have gone?" I ask as Royal flies through the gate, pressing the button on his sunvisor to close it once we are through. Gravel kicks up behind us as he takes the turn out of the driveway, heading into town.

"She wouldn't have gone home. She knows that's the first place we'd look. She only has one other person in this town that knows she is back. We start there," Royal says, his speed getting dangerously high.

He's right, Ella is the smartest choice. Unless she decided to flee back to White Harbor, but I just don't see her taking off without saying goodbye to her only friend.

The trip into town takes less than half the normal time with Royal driving like a madman. He's clenching his jaw tightly, and he's white-knuckling the steering wheel. He is close to snapping, too. I'm going to have to monitor how he handles her when we find her. I won't allow him to take it too far.

I know she wouldn't run without a real reason behind it. For the life of me, I can't figure out what that reason could be, but I know she has to have one. We've given her no reason to fear us.

He drives down the back alley that runs behind Twisted and the other businesses in the town square. He slows to an almost stop, and I see Ella's truck parked in the side alley. "Her bike isn't here," I state the obvious.

"She's smart, she probably hid it somewhere," Royal says, turning down the alley and parking behind her friend's truck.

He shuts off the engine, moving to open his door when I grab his arm. "If she is here, we need to hear her out. I'm angry she ran too, but I'm sure she had a reason why she thought she had to."

He responds with a growl, jerking out of my hold and slinging his door open. Heaving a heavy sigh, turning back to look at Maddox.

"She'll be fine. We won't let him actually hurt her," Maddox says, reaching up to squeeze my shoulder. With a nod of my head, we both climb out to follow Royal.

We have to jog to catch up with him before he jerks the back door open with another growl, sounding like a pissed-off grizzly bear. The door slams loudly against the stone wall outside, light flooding the dark hallway as we enter.

Chapter 39

I barely register the loud bang of the door slamming shut behind us, I'm so angry with Raena for running.

What the fuck was she thinking?

King could find her before us. My worry almost outweighs my anger, and I try to take a deep breath to calm down, but the boulder sitting on my chest won't allow it. She could already be back in King's hands. He could be hurting her right now.

Stalking down the narrow hall, I hear Ella's voice behind her closed office door. Without knocking, I shove the door open, relief flooding through my system when I see Raena sitting on the couch with her. Her eyes wide with shock, the rims puffy and red from crying.

I'm aware my brothers are behind me, anxious to get to our girl, but I can't make my feet move. Alek nudges me just as Ella stands, her expression hardened in anger. She strides toward me with determination, squaring her shoulders as she approaches my frozen body.

Before I can process what she's doing, she rears back, punching me square in the jaw, shocking me from my paralyzed state.

"*Ella!*" Raena shouts, her hand coming to cover her mouth in shock.

"I'm going to ice my hand," she grumbles, scowling at me as she shakes out her hand. I stand there stunned silent, rubbing my aching jaw. She moves around me and exits the room.

"That was epic," Maddox laughs from behind me.

Raena is still seated on the couch, her eyes still wide and her hand covering her mouth. My feet move on their own, stalking toward her like a predator to its prey.

"Royal," she whispers behind her hand, fresh tears welling up in her eyes when I kneel before her. Her tears are drowning the anger inside me just a little.

"What the fuck, Angel?" I ask, my voice a deep whisper.

Alek and Maddox kneel on each side of me when her hands move to cover her face as she breaks down in front of us.

"What happened, Baby Girl? Why did you leave?" Alek says, his hand moving to squeeze her leg in comfort.

I know he's itching to hold her, but I need to feel her in my arms right now. I grab her waist, standing up and lifting her before sitting back down, cradling her against my chest. She buries her face in my neck, her hands moving to grasp my shirt as she tries to calm herself. I hold her tight, her warmth seeping into my skin through our clothes, reminding me that we found her. King didn't get her.

While we give her time to compose herself, my brothers move to sit on each side of us. When her sobs subside, she lifts her head and meets my eyes. I expect to see remorse, but anger shines through as well.

"You should have told me." Her voice is barely a whisper, but there is no mistaking the hurt lacing her words.

"Told you what?" I ask her, looking at each of my brother's confused expressions that I know match my own.

"King is your father," she states as the ice-cold realization hits me, stiffening my body. "I overheard you call him 'dad' on the phone. I thought you were playing me."

"He is *not* our father, he—" I start but she cuts me off.

"I know that now, Ella explained it to me. King adopted you. You still should have told me. You all should have told me." Her voice breaks slightly, betrayal thick in her tone.

"We should have," I agree, and my brothers nod their agreement. "Honestly, it wasn't something we intentionally kept from you. It's just something we try to forget."

"I can understand why you would feel that way, baby. I promise we didn't mean to keep it from you," Alek adds, rubbing his hand down her back. "I'm sorry. We should have told you."

"I'm sorry too, pretty girl," Maddox says, leaning in to place a gentle kiss on her temple.

We sit like that for a few minutes, each of us with our hands on her, needing to feel her and know she is safe.

"We were so worried King would find you before we did, Angel," I sigh, breaking the silence of our little bubble.

"I'm sorry I ran. I just didn't know what to do," she says, sitting up in my lap again. "Then, when Ella explained everything to me, I was worried about how angry you would be at me."

"Oh, he was plenty angry. I thought Mr. Growly Pants was going to pop a vein in his pretty forehead," Maddox chuckles from my side, earning a glare from me. Raena stifles her giggle as best she can but fails miserably.

"Don't worry, Angel. I am still going to spank your ass and tie you to my bed when we get home for this little stunt," I say, raising her chin to look into her emerald pools. I don't miss the way her pupils dilate with desire at my words.

"You wouldn't!" She gasps out sarcastically.

"Oh, I would. I told you what would happen if you put yourself in danger. I don't make empty threats. I thought you learned that this morning," I growl into her ear, my hands coming up to tangle in her hair at the nape of her neck, angling her head back.

My tongue traces down her throat, moving to her collarbone before going up the side of her neck. She lets out a cry that goes straight to my cock when my teeth sink into the flesh there. It's not hard enough to break the tender skin there, but hard enough to leave my mark.

She squirms in my lap, a moan escaping her when I suction my lips around the bite, bruising the skin. Pulling back, I see the imprint of my teeth and the beginnings of the purple mark around it.

"Fuck. You look good wearing my mark," I tell her, soothing the sting with my tongue.

She lets out a louder moan, grinding down in my lap, making my cock twitch against the backside of her thigh, and a groan vibrates through my chest.

I need to be inside her.

I need to feel her dripping pussy clenching as she comes on my cock.

"Let's get our girl home," Maddox says, standing from the couch and grabbing Raena's riding bag from the floor. Alek follows him up, reaching for her, but my hold tightens. The resounding growl coming from my throat has him backing away with a smirk.

"Okay, Mr. Growly Pants, you can carry her out," he says, his smirk widening. I just can't let her go yet. If that makes me a growly pussy, so be it.

With her tiny body cradled to my chest, I stand from the couch and follow them out of the office and into the dark hallway.

"I need to tell Ella I'm leaving," Raena says, raising her head from my neck to look down the end of the hall that leads to the main dining room.

Turning that way, her friend steps into the hallway, pressing a bag of frozen vegetables to her injured hand. The ache in my jaw is long forgotten now that I have my Angel back in my arms.

"You good, Rae? I will deck the other two if you need me to," she asks, a cocky smile on her face.

If it would have been anyone else, I'd be pissed that she hit me. But as it stands, I'm proud of her for standing up for her friend. At least I know our girl has someone else in her corner.

"I think you should deck them just for good measure," I tell her, giving her a smirk of my own.

"I think they learned from just the one," Raena says laughing. "I'm good though. We're gonna go. Thank you for everything."

"I'm always here for you, you know that," Ella says. "Let me know if I need to knock some sense into them again."

Once they say their goodbyes, I press my lips to Raena's temple before turning around and heading back down the hallway. My brothers head out the door first, the bright sunlight flooding into the darkness before we emerge into the alley.

As we approach the truck, Raena perks her head up again. "I've got to get my bike."

"I'll drive it back. Where is it?" Maddox asks.

"I hid it in an abandoned building a little ways down."

She must be talking about the old furniture store that closed down a few years ago. "Come on, we'll drop you off," I tell him. "Angel, can you grab the keys from my left pocket?"

She reaches down, digging into the pocket of my pants to take the keys.

"Alek, you drive," I tell him, and he takes the keys from her hand before I climb into the backseat, keeping Raena in my lap.

Maddox and Alek climb into the front seats, and we are backing out of the alley a few moments later. When we come to the loading dock behind the old store, Alek pulls to a stop.

"Key?" Maddox asks.

"In the front pocket of my bag."

He opens her bag on his lap, pulling out the key, before opening his door.

"Don't you dare wreck my bike," Raena shouts at him as he climbs out of the car. He turns around, smirking at her.

"I'll treat her like a queen, pinky promise," he says, reaching back into the car, his pinky extended. She takes it, shaking his hand before he pulls back and closes the door.

We watch him climb the loading dock, pushing the busted door open wide enough to get her bike out, before disappearing into the building. He drives down the loading dock and turns out into the back alley in front of us as we follow behind him.

Raena watches him to make sure he is treating her baby right, but after a few minutes, she relaxes back into my hold, her head resting in the crook of my neck. Her sweet breath fans across my skin, causing a shiver to snake down my spine.

I want to slip my hand down her leggings and make her come on my fingers, but I know if I touch her right now, I will be buried inside of her before we even make it out of town. The first time I fuck her will not be in the backseat of the SUV.

With monumental restraint, I rest my head on top of hers and keep my hands out of her pants for the entire car ride.

Pulling into the garage behind Maddox, I look down at Raena to see she has fallen asleep. Good. Maybe she will stay asleep for what I have planned. I've had the whole ride here to think about how I wanted to do this, and I'm aching to get her in my bed.

Alek's knowing eyes find me in the rearview mirror.

"Come on. We'll help you get her upstairs," he says, a single nod of his head letting me know he understands what I need. He climbs out before opening the door for me to climb out with her.

He helps me maneuver her head so I don't bang it on the frame when I unfold out of the SUV. We make our way inside, climbing the stairs and going into my room.

She has never been inside here. Making my way to the bed, I look around and take stock of what she might see when she wakes up. My room is pretty much a mirrored carbon copy of Aleks in the decor and layout, with the bathroom and closet on the opposite side of the room. We have the same bed and furniture. Everything is either black, dark-stained wood, or glass.

When I designed this house, I wanted everything to match. The entire house, except one room, follows this scheme– Emma's room. I had it painted light pink with white accents, just for her.

I wanted her to have some color and light in her own space. It sits untouched except for the cleaners who dust in there weekly, just waiting for her to come home.

Alek pulls back my black comforter, allowing me to lay Raena on my black sheets. He starts unlacing her boots, which I notice are not laced correctly.

I guess she was in a rush when she left us and just half-ass put them on. I remove her black hoodie slowly, careful not to wake her. She must have exhausted herself because she doesn't even stir as I manipulate both the hoodie and my shirt off her pliant body.

A warmth spreads in my chest at the fact that she didn't remove my shirt when she left. She kept a piece of me with her, regardless of the betrayal she felt at the time.

Once he has her boots off, he places them neatly inside my closet. I peel her leggings down her body, revealing her naked body to us. She still doesn't wake up.

Maddox is bouncing on his heels, having watched us undress her from the foot of the bed without helping at all. I can tell he wants to wake her, but I need this time alone with her.

The three of us stand beside the bed for a few moments, just drinking in her beautiful body bared to us. Her scars don't make her any less gorgeous. I can tell she is self-conscious about them, but she hasn't fully seen the scars that mar each of our bodies under our tattoos.

They tell the same kind of stories as hers. Ones of trauma that tried its best to take us out of this world, but the scars are proof that we survived– that we were stronger than the people who put them there. Alek taps Maddox on the arm to catch his attention.

"Let's give him some time with her. Let's go burn off some energy in the gym." He pulls Maddox along, nodding at me before walking out of my bedroom door. Maddox pokes his bottom lip out at him, looking back at Raena like he just told him he can't play with his favorite toy. He slumps his shoulders and makes a show of shuffling his feet as he follows Alek out of the room.

As the door shuts behind them, I head to my closet to get what I need. The black wooden box sits on the floor of my closet. I bend down and pick it up before moving back into my room, placing the box on the foot of my bed. The brass latch makes a slight click when I pop it open. I take out everything I want to use on Raena, laying them next to her feet.

I haven't opened this box in a long time. Not since we moved into this house. The familiar textures slip through my fingers, excitement running through me at the idea of them imprinting on her skin.

Once everything is laid out, I close the box, moving it to the floor next to the bed. My girl is going to be in for a surprise when she wakes up. I can't wait to see the look on her face when she realizes my threats weren't so empty after all.

Chapter 40

A warm, tingling heat licks at my spine, making my heavy eyes flutter open. My head rolls to the side, finding the only light source to be a lamp sitting on the bedside table next to me.

Confusion blankets me as I try to piece together where I am. This room looks similar to Aleks, but something feels off. I feel like I fell asleep in the car and woke up in an alternate reality.

My hand moves to rub the sleep from my eyes but immediately meets resistance.

"What the fuck?" I crane my neck up to see both of my hands restrained above my head with a rope. Panic floods my body instantly, my breath coming out in labored pants. I try to pull my arms down, making the soft rope dig into my wrists. I try to twist my body, but I can't close my legs either.

"Easy, Angel. It's me," The sound of Royal's voice breaks through my panicked breathing, making my body sag in relief against the restraints. It's only when he places his hand on my stomach that I notice that his head is between my legs.

"Wh-what are you doing?" I ask, the question rushing out as I take deep pulls of oxygen into my lungs to calm my racing heart.

"Exactly what I said I would do if you put yourself in danger," he says, and his warm breath against my bare pussy lets me know just how wet I am for him.

He doesn't say anything else, just dives back in, giving me long, slow licks up and down my slit. He's not in a hurry. He takes his time like he just sat down to his favorite buffet and has all day to graze.

The delicious torture has me arching my back and driving my hips up to meet the strokes of his tongue, silently begging him to go faster. Harder. My hands ache to grip his hair and grind my pussy against his face to set the pace I need to come.

The sharp sting of his hand slapping my pussy pulls a desperate cry from my lips. "I'm going to enjoy *my* pussy, and you," he growls, bringing his hand down once more, "are going to stay still and take it."

The vibration of his dominating words against my sensitive flesh sends sparks of lightning straight to my clit. A drawn-out groan claws its way out of my throat, but I force my hips to stay planted on the bed, allowing him to go back to his torturous pleasure.

He continues taking his time, adding two fingers and curling them inside of me, slowly stroking the spot that makes my eyes roll into the back of my head and my toes curl, pulling the restraints on my ankles tighter.

My moans echo around the room. I might be embarrassed about how loud I am, but he is driving me out of my mind, and I don't have it in me to worry about that right now.

Then, with no warning, he suctions his devilish lips around my clit, sucking and nipping at the swollen bud. I can't keep my hips on the bed

281

this time, the action jolting my entire body. His fingers increase their pace, rubbing that spot faster. I can feel my orgasm right on the edge of my reach.

"Fuck. Yes. Please," I cry out, begging him to push me over the edge and into oblivion.

He has been teasing me since I woke up tied to his bed. He drives his fingers into me faster. Harder. He alternates between flicking my clit with his tongue and sucking it.

"I'm going to—," I cry out, and just before I shatter on his tongue, he withdraws his fingers and mouth, sending me crashing down into a puddle of disappointment.

Angry tears prick the insides of my eyelids, and my breath comes out in harsh pants. I should have expected this. He warned me earlier. This is the second time today he has edged me, but this time I'm so pissed off I can't form words.

The bed dips as he moves from between my thighs. The loss of his body heat sends cool air directly to my dripping pussy, making me shake with more than just pent-up frustration. I'm so embarrassingly wet that I can feel it on the sheets beneath my ass.

He doesn't say a word as he grabs one of my ankles, but I feel him undoing the rope that is restraining me. I want to kick him in his beautiful fucking face right now, but I know that won't do me any favors.

He moves to the other ankle and I feel the rope slipping off a few seconds later. When his hand leaves my skin, I snap my legs closed, drawing my knees up. I can hear him walking around the bed, but I keep my eyes screwed tightly shut, not willing to give him the satisfaction of seeing my tears of desperation still building.

I sigh in relief when I feel his warm hands pulling on the rope at my wrists. But he doesn't release me. My heart rate picks up when his touch disappears until I feel something soft on my stomach. It's light like a feather, ghosting over my skin causing goosebumps to pebble in its path.

"Do you have a safe word?"

His deep voice crackles through the air like he is holding onto his restraint by a very thin thread. A shiver runs through my body at the sound, so it takes me a second to process what he said.

"Safe word?" I ask, confused about what he means.

"Yes. If you want to stop at any time, if it becomes too much or pushes beyond the boundaries of what you are okay with, you say your safe word, and I will stop immediately," he explains.

I'm a little embarrassed that I didn't know what a safe word was, but I do appreciate him giving me the option.

"I don't have one," my whisper barely audible around the lump in my throat. Thankfully I've still got my eyes closed because I can feel the heat creeping up my neck and staining my cheeks. I've never had any kind of relationship. I don't have experience with consent.

His fingers grip my chin, tilting my head back. "Look at me, Angel."

My heavy eyelids flutter open, finding his icy blue eyes have darkened to almost black. His stubbled jaw is clenched tight, the muscle ticking like a time bomb waiting to go off. His shoulders rise and fall with each heavy breath he takes.

"Pick a word for me," he growls, and I'm beginning to forget what his voice sounds like when it isn't dripping with barely controlled restraint.

Without thinking too much about it, I blurt out the first word that pops into my brain.

"Apple."

His already darkened eyes transcend into the deepest obsidian I've ever seen. Without waiting another second, he drops my chin and steps away from me. My tense body sags into the mattress, my eyes fluttering shut to hide the disappointment I feel at the loss of his touch.

My knees are still bent and tucked close to my body, but like a jolt of lightning, his hands grab my ankles, pulling them straight out before flipping me over on my stomach. A startled gasp rushes out of me in surprise, my entire body burning like flames licking against my skin.

"Get on your knees," he grits out.

His hands are like vice grips on my ankles as he pushes them forward to assist me. His commanding tone has my pussy clenching around nothing, desperate for a release I don't know if he will give me.

His hands leave my ankles, but his fingers trail a feather-light touch up the backs of my legs and over my round ass before disappearing. I raise onto my elbows as my head drops forward, my fiery locks shrouding around my head for only a second before he gathers it up in his hands, sending sharp pricks of pain on my scalp as he lifts my head and tilts it back.

I'm staring at the ceiling, contemplating how I ended up here, when I feel his hands gathering my hair. He twists and weaves it together, forming a braid with my unruly locks.

The gentle action stuns me, so tender, yet his touch is just as dominating. I don't let myself read too much into it, though, because as soon as he finishes, he lays the thick braid on my back and moves away from me again.

He gives me whiplash with how he treats me. Like he sees me as a fragile little doll made of glass, like he has to protect me from the world, but at the same time, he wants to break me so he can pick up all the pieces and mold them back together himself.

He reappears at my side, startling me from my thoughts when he gently places his thumb and finger on my chin, turning my face to him.

"Do you trust me?" He asks, and the look in his dark, stormy eyes has my mouth speaking before I can even think about it.

"Yes."

It's a simple word. But one that holds the weight of all my fears. Trusting in someone other than myself hasn't been something I've allowed myself to do since I was taken. It's something I tried to work on when I was with Snow, but it took a long time for me to even start trusting them not to hurt me.

I barely know Royal and his brothers, but my soul seems to know them. Trust suddenly doesn't feel like such a scary thing. It feels as natural as breathing.

"Good girl," he growls out, cupping my face for a moment, searching for any sign of distress or fear.

When he doesn't find anything, his hand falls away for a moment before my vision goes dark and I feel him wrap something soft over my eyes before tying it off at the back of my head.

Giving him my absolute submission, I stay silent, steadying my breath that wants to punch out of me in anticipation of what he has planned. Even though I know this is my punishment for running, I don't expect the sharp pain when it slashes across my bare ass. My loud cry echoes around the almost silent room.

He didn't spank me with his hand. The welt I can feel blossoming on my skin tells me he is using a belt or something similar. Before I can catch my breath and speak, his words cut through the silence.

"Do you know why I am punishing you, Raena?"

His warm hand massages the ache he caused. My body jolts against the sting before it melts into his touch, spreading warmth down my ass and straight to my already dripping pussy.

"Yes sir," I reply breathlessly. "I ran and put myself in danger."

285

I don't think I could get any more turned on than I am right now. The hand that is massaging my ass tightens, digging his fingers into the tender flesh as a deep rumble shudders through his body.

I might be the one on my knees, getting my ass spanked for running, but I can feel the power my submission gives me. He is just as affected by me, as I am by him. His grip on me loosens as he composes himself once more.

"That's my good fucking girl," His voice sounds like he smokes a pack of cigarettes a day, coming out gritty and rough. His praise sends a shiver down my spine and warmth spreads through my chest for pleasing him. I am so fucked for this man. "I am going to spank your ass five more times. I want you to count each one."

"Okay," I whisper, anxiety and excitement swirling in my chest equally as I nod my head in obedience.

His belt is swift, the first swing striking my ass with enough force to leave a mark, but not break the skin. Tears prick the back of my eyelids as I cry out.

"One!"

He doesn't stop to speak or massage the bruised skin. He just swings again, hitting the opposite cheek this time. My breath catches at the impact, it feels harder than the one before. The first tears escape my eyes, trailing down my cheek.

"Two!" I cry out again, overwhelmed by an intense release of emotion.

I expect to feel angry like I felt earlier, but this almost feels cathartic. Purging. Like a heavy weight lifting off my chest. I definitely don't expect the flood of liquid heat to rush out of me, dripping down my inner thighs.

By the time the fifth strike lands on my skin, the levy holding my emotions at bay bursts wide open, and the broken sob that leaves my lips is barely audible.

"Fi-five."

The belt thuds against the floor seconds before my wrists are released from their restraints and I collapse face down into the pillows and cry. I feel Royal's fingers untying the blindfold from my eyes, then the bed drips under his weight. He rolls me to my back making me hiss out at the sting of the sheets on my abused ass.

"You did so good, Angel," he says, picking up each wrist and softly kissing where the rope dug into my skin, then placing them down on the bed. His gentle tone makes me cry harder as he wedges his knees between my thighs, making room for his massive body.

He is still fully clothed. The rough material of his pants rubs against my bare skin, sending electrical currents through my already hypersensitive body. He grabs onto my raised knees, pressing them into the bed before trailing his hands along my inner thighs, undoubtedly feeling the evidence of just how much my body enjoyed his punishment.

"Goddamn. You're fucking soaked," he growls.

I know my tear-stained face is flaming red enough to rival my hair right now. I'm not ashamed like I was the first time Alek made me squirt. I didn't even know my body could do... *that.*

I'm embarrassed that it happened without him even touching my pussy. That it happened as a response to the pain of him spanking my ass with his belt. Now he knows just how fucked up I am. I get turned on by pain.

Groaning, I bring my hands up and cover my burning face. My body shakes with sobs from emotions still releasing from me, as I try to hide my response from him.

"Don't hide from me," he growls, grabbing both of my hands and pinning them on each side of my head. "Let it out. You can cry, scream, kick… whatever you need to do. Give it all to me."

His words only serve to make me cry harder as I lay there beneath him, my soul purging all of the things I've locked down tight. Things I never wanted anyone to see because that would mean *I* would have to see them again.

"I'm sorry," I say once my tears have all but stopped, opening my eyes to find him staring down at me with darkness swirling in his icy eyes.

"You have nothing to be sorry for, Angel," he says hoarsely, as he leans down and presses a kiss to my forehead.

His fingers intertwine with mine, the action making his hips grind into me. I can feel his thick cock through his pants, rubbing my clit against the rough fabric, making us both moan. His body is shaking, his control is dangerously close to snapping.

It seems he needs to release his pent-up emotions as well.

Somehow, I don't think a spanking is what he needs, though. He needs to release that energy, and I need him to fuck me like I need my next breath.

He just needs a little push.

ROYAL

Chapter 41

My dark Angel writhes beneath me, driving me absolutely mad.

My entire body is coiled tight, shaking as I try to hold on to the last remnants of my restraint. I don't know what I was expecting from her punishment, but it definitely wasn't this.

The dam broke on her carefully concealed emotions, and she let it all out. You could feel the purge happening within her as she cried out her release. I didn't even have to touch her sweet pussy, and she squirted just from my spanking. That has to be the hottest thing I've ever seen in my life.

Her tears have stopped now, and all that remains are the flames of desire burning in her piercing emerald eyes. I've been edging her since she woke up this morning, but it's been a long day.

The release she had during her punishment wasn't nearly enough to douse the fire blazing inside her right now. I can tell by the way she squirms against me, rubbing herself as best she can to find the relief she needs. Her eyes beg me to give her what she needs.

I need her mouth begging, too.

"Royal," she moans softly when I grind against her again.

"Tell me what you need, Angel," I grit out as best I can through the overwhelming urge to fuck her through the mattress. It's been too long since I've been inside a woman, but even then, I don't ever remember feeling like this.

This is stronger than lust. The way my body is shaking, practically vibrating with how much I *need* to be inside her. To feel her silky heat wrap around me as I sink into her for the first time.

"I need…" she starts, a look of uncertainty crossing her face before she closes her eyes and inhales a deep breath. When her eyes flutter back open, sexy confidence shines back at me. "I need you to listen to your own advice."

"Excuse me?" I sputter out, stunned and confused as I stare back at her.

"You told me to let all my bottled-up emotions out, but you need to do the same. You're wound up so tight your body is literally trembling. You're holding back. Why?"

I have a snarky response poised on my tongue before she's even finished talking, but it quickly melts away when I take the time to think about it. If I peel back the layers of myself, it all boils down to one single thing. I don't like losing control.

I am man enough to admit I'm afraid of what will happen if I fully unleash myself. If I give in to the primal beast that is roaring just beneath the surface, clawing at my insides and begging to be set free. I'm scared I might hurt her. But even now, as I stare into her unguarded eyes, I know I would never hurt her. I couldn't.

Dropping my carefully constructed mask, I allow her to truly see me. I bring both of her hands together over her head, grasping them with one hand and latching my other one around her delicate little throat, eliciting a gasp from her pouty lips. I'm not cutting off her oxygen, but her breath hitches as I restrict the air I'm allowing her to take.

"I don't want to hurt you."

She doesn't recoil from my possessive touch as her eyes darken with desire and defiance. My eyes dart to her mouth when she runs her tongue along her bottom lip before nervously biting into the pink flesh before she speaks.

"Maybe that's what I want. What I *need*."

There is a vulnerability in her voice like she is ashamed of asking for something so depraved. The beast rages inside me at her request and my hand flexes around her throat as my hips grind into her again making her eyes roll back in her head.

"Is that what my little dark Angel needs? Pain and pleasure? Can you handle that?" My voice drops even deeper as the remaining threads of my control start snapping, one by one. She nods her head in response, earning a growl as I cut off her oxygen momentarily. "Words, Raena."

When I loosen my grip, she sucks in a mouth full of air. Her eyes search my face for a moment before she finds her voice that is dripping with arousal and confidence once more.

"Yes, Sir."

My responding growl echoes around the dimly lit room. But what she says next snaps the last remaining thread I've been holding on to.

"Let me in, Royal." Her gaze cuts through me as she speaks. "Let me see the real you. Don't hold back. Break me. Shatter me into a million pieces. Just don't forget to put me back together when you're done."

My lips slam into hers with the force of a freight train as I lay claim to my woman like a man possessed. I kiss her until our bodies are molded together, tethering us for all of eternity.

She kisses me back with the same intensity, and when I drop her hands so I can tangle my fingers in her hair, she threads her own into mine, pulling me closer and scratching her nails on my scalp.

When I finally pull back so we can breathe, her lust-hazed eyes flutter open, searing me to the core with the desire burning in them. I place a gentle kiss on her forehead before I pull away completely and climb off the bed.

Her eyes follow as I reach behind me, tugging my shirt from my body in one swift movement. My hands fall to my pants, and I don't waste another second relieving myself of them, my painfully hard cock bobbing in the air.

Climbing back onto the bed, I trail my hands up her creamy white thighs, spreading her wider for me. A cocky smirk tilts my lips as she swallows roughly while she eye fucks me in all my glory. I'm not as covered in tattoos as Maddox or as bulky as Alek, but the way her breath hitches and the way she's biting her lip lets me know she likes what she sees just as much.

Gripping my cock in my hand, I run it along the seam of her soaking wet pussy, coating myself in her arousal, making her squirm.

"Look at how wet you are for me. You're already dripping." My voice is strained as I torture us both with this slow teasing. "You're going to come all over my cock until it's running down my thighs and soaking into the sheets. You're going to scream my name for my brothers to hear. You're my good fucking girl, aren't you?"

"Yes, Sir," she whispers with her thick and raspy voice.

"Your safe word?"

"Apple," she says, her eyes fluttering shut as I continue slowly sliding up and down her slit until she is shaking beneath me.

"Good girl."

Without warning, I drive into her silky heat in one thrust, bottoming out as she screams at the intrusion. Her hands come up to my sides, digging her nails into my inked skin as her pussy flutters around my cock, adjusting to my size.

I might not be as big as Alek, but I'm bigger than Maddox and I saw how she struggled to take him last night. No doubt she will be walking around tomorrow with a reminder of who she belongs to.

"Fuck," I grit when she clenches around me, and I have to take a second to rein in my cock who wants to explode into the first pussy it's been inside in years.

Leaning back, I grab both of her legs and put them on my shoulder, before I surge forward and sink into her once again. The beast within claws at me, so I let it take control as I cage her body in and fuck her relentlessly.

I keep my brutal pace until she is clenching down on my cock and screaming out her release. My name echoes loud enough that I know my brothers can hear her, even if they are still down in the basement. It won't be long before they get sick of waiting and burst through the door.

Not wanting to be interrupted before I've had my fill, I pull out of her and flip her onto her stomach in one quick motion.

"On your hands and knees," I command, and she obeys without hesitation.

Her submission is almost as hot as her brattiness and has my balls drawing up when she presents her perfect ass and dripping cunt to me.

"Your ass is fucking perfection," I growl at her, grabbing the plush flesh in my hands and massaging the reddened cheeks before spreading her open for me.

I spit directly on her tight little hole, then swirl my finger, teasing it lightly before sinking my finger to the knuckle. Her body tenses at the invasion, but I stretch her until she relaxes enough that there is no resistance. I add a second finger, scissoring them to prepare her for what's coming.

"This is *mine*. I will be the first one to claim this tight little hole while one of my brothers fucks your needy cunt, and the other chokes you with his cock down your throat. Would you like that? All of your holes being filled at once like a good little slut?"

"Yes, Sir," she moans loudly, pushing back against my hand.

My fingers pressing against her pussy are instantly flooded with just how much she would enjoy that.

"Soon, Angel, real soon," I tell her, withdrawing my fingers and squeezing her ass again as I line my cock up with her dripping pussy. I watch with rapt attention as it disappears inside her once again.

There is nothing on this earth that even compares to the feeling of her taking me to the hilt. It feels like her body was made just for me, and the domineering bastard that I am revels in the realization that she is mine.

No one, and I mean no one, outside of my brothers, will ever touch her again. Not if they want to walk away with all of their limbs still attached to their bodies.

"You are *mine*, Angel," I growl possessively. "Your body. Your soul. Your heart. Your past, present, and future. All fucking mine. I'll share you with my brothers, but no one else will ever touch you again. And I will kill every motherfucker who has ever laid a hand on what's mine. We will level this entire fucking town to the ground if that's what it takes to keep you safe. And then we will fuck in their blood as it runs the streets red with your revenge. I promise you this with every fiber of my being."

Warmth engulfs my chest as I lay out everything to the little spitfire who showed up and turned my entire world upside down.

Without a doubt, I know.

I am in love with her.

I can't seem to get the words out, though. Emotion clogs my throat, so I show her with my body, letting it say everything my mouth can't.

Pulling back, I wrap her braided hair around my fist, making her arch her back as I pull her up to me. My other hand wraps around her throat as I fuck her with everything I have.

Every emotion I've kept behind my walls rises to the surface, bubbling out of me with every thrust into her perfect body, threatening to drown me.

Instead of shoving it back down like I normally would, I allow the overwhelming sensation to wash over me entirely. It feels foreign to me, and I wonder if she is feeling everything as intensely as I am right now.

"Royal," she screams when I deepen my angle, and I feel her pussy squeezing around my cock, close to falling over the edge of oblivion yet again.

"Open your fucking mouth," I grind out through clenched teeth.

My balls are tightly drawn up, ready to fill her to the brim with my seed, but I keep it at bay. I want her to come all over my cock one more time before I allow myself to come with her.

She immediately obeys my command.

Letting go of her throat, I plunge two fingers into her hot mouth, relishing in the lack of gag reflex as I push past her slick tongue, and hold her against me.

She licks and laps her tongue around my fingers. It only takes two more brutal thrusts to have her convulsing around me, falling over the cliff she has been teetering on.

"That's it. Squirt all over my cock like my good little slut, and I'll fill your greedy little cunt with my come."

Her cries are muffled by my fingers stuffing her mouth as her pussy milks my cock. Her release floods around me, doing exactly as I commanded before we started. It drips down my thighs and soaks the sheets beneath us.

The force of her orgasm is hard enough to push my cock out of her, but I quickly drive back inside her just as ropes of my come fill her up like I promised.

Pulling free of her mouth and releasing her hair, she sucks in a deep breath as I band my arm around her waist, lowering her gently to the bed. Rolling over to my back, I pull her into my arms, enjoying the way she clings to me as she shakes from the aftermath of her orgasms.

A soft sob escapes her lips, making me hold her tighter. She is experiencing the emotional crash that comes from intense sessions like the one we just had. My own body is trembling and the warmth that was filling my chest earlier has turned into a raging inferno.

"You're okay, Angel. I've got you," I whisper into her hair, placing a gentle kiss on her head.

"I've got you too," she whispers back, clinging to me tighter.

The emotional clog in my throat is back, but she doesn't seem to need a response from me. We cling to each other, feeding each other silent comfort as we try to process everything we just unleashed.

My hand glides along the curve of her spine. I can feel the raised edges of her scars against the pads of my fingers. I will never understand why someone would hurt another human like this, but the scars on *my* back tell their own gruesome story of King's wickedness.

It's a time I'd rather not think about, and the sole reason I have the skull tattoo covering every inch of my back. I can hide the scars he left on my body, but some scars run deeper than skin.

My Angel knows the depths of his perversions all too well. It's not a question of what trauma she endured but of how deep the scars go. They don't end on her skin.

Her soul will forever be stained with his vile depravity, but I will spend the rest of my life removing his tainted touch from every inch of her.

"Can I ask you a question?" She asks, not moving from her position on my chest.

"Anything, Angel."

"Why were you so angry about my cottage? Did you know who owned it before me?"

I knew she would ask eventually. My visceral reaction to the entire situation was bad. I'm ashamed of how easily I let my anger control me and I owe her an explanation.

"I own it. Well, I did. I don't know how it was listed for sale. It doesn't make sense."

Running my fingers through my hair and down my face, I struggle to gather the courage to continue. This trauma has been buried for so many years.

"That's the house I grew up in before I went into foster care. It's where I lived with my mom and baby sister until I was eight. She wasn't a good mother– drugs were more important than raising her kids. She spiraled out of control when my father died. When the money ran out, used her body for her next fix. When I was seven, my baby sister– Rose– was born from her addiction.

"She couldn't take care of herself, much less two kids. So, I did everything I could for Rose. But it wasn't enough. When she was barely a year old, I came home from school one day and found my mother dead on the kitchen floor. Rose wasn't with her. She had puked all over herself, with blood and the remnants of pills caked into her hair and on her skin. Her pupils were giant. I didn't know at the time that meant they were blown. It scared me at first because I thought she was just staring at me, but then she didn't follow me with her eyes or blink. When I realized she was dead, I knew I had to find Rose. I searched every room in a panic until I found her floating in the bathtub. My *mother* drowned my baby sister and then overdosed. Those images will forever be scarred in my mind, my baby sister and my mother.

"The next few weeks are kind of a blur, I don't remember much. I was placed in a foster home that was even worse than my mother's house, but that's where I met Maddox and Alek a year later.

"The house was transferred to me on my 18th birthday. I gutted and remodeled it to what it is now. I couldn't let it go, but I also couldn't walk through the door without seeing all the ways I failed Rose."

An unrestrained tear sneaks down my cheek, making me pause. I don't remember the last time I cried, but this feels different. It's cathartic– healing wounds I've kept buried for decades.

Raena pulls herself up, straddling my lap and taking my face into her hands. Tears stream down her own cheeks as she holds my gaze.

"You were a child, Royal. You didn't fail Rose any more than I failed Grams or my daughter. I know what this guilt feels like– I've carried it for years. I've asked myself the same questions over and over– Why couldn't my mom put me before the drugs? Why did King take me? Why couldn't I protect the ones I loved the most?

"Do you know what I learned? We can't control the actions of others. We just get to survive the consequences. We were just children, forced to play a game we weren't meant to win. This is why I became *The Hunter*. I refuse to stand back and allow this broken cycle to continue. Innocent people– children, forced to live and die at the mercy of a Monster. Sometimes, you need a bigger monster. So I became one," she declares.

I wipe away her stray tears the same way she did mine and grip the back of her head, pulling her to my face.

"You're no monster, Angel. You're a Queen. Destined to rule from the battlefield, wearing the blood of the wicked as armor, with the Shadows as your shield, and your soul as a sword."

***

Raena is sleeping peacefully in my arms when my brothers walk back through my bedroom door looking freshly showered after their workout downstairs. Their hungry eyes roam over our naked girl that's sprawled out across my chest.

"Did you work out your issues?" Alek asks.

His brown eyes almost look black in this dim light, but I know it's mostly due to the little vixen he can't pull his gaze from. My mental barriers are still down, and I almost want to slam them back into place but I haven't felt this light, *this free*, in my entire life.

"We did," I answer him honestly, holding Raena closer to me as both of them climb into the bed on either side of us. Their hands immediately move to touch her, needing to connect with her just as much as I do. I appreciate them giving me this time with her alone. "Thank you."

"I get it, man," Alek says, mindlessly tracing his fingers up and down the curve of her hip. "You needed this, and I know she did, too."

His hand stills when he sees the marks my leather belt left on her ass. His eyes dart to mine as a deep rumbling growl emits from his throat. "Royal."

"Relax, man. She enjoyed it."

"That's not the point. You have to take care of it after," he grumbles, getting off the bed and storming from the room.

He returns a minute later holding a tub of something in his hand. He leans down and kneels on the bed, opening the container and scooping out some white cream on his fingers.

The second his hand connects with her red ass, she hisses and clings to me tighter, fluttering her eyes open as she tries to scoot away from the offending pain.

"Stay still, Baby Girl. This will help," he tells her softly, as his other hand grips her hip, halting her movements.

Her eyes flutter open and lock on mine for a moment before she cranes her neck to look back at him. He soothes her with soft words as he slathers her ass in the cream until her body relaxes back into me and she lets out a deep sigh of relief.

"Thank you, Daddy," she says hoarsely, her voice strained from screaming as much as she did. He sits the container on my nightstand, then climbs back into the bed next to us, careful not to press against her ass.

"Yes, thank you, *Daddy*," I say, smirking at him, but my eyes tell him how grateful I am for easing the pain I caused. I was going to do it after we got up and showered, but I know she appreciates the relief now.

His eyes darken even more at my playful tone, and he not so subtly adjusts himself, keeping his eyes on mine. More of that unfamiliar warmth fills my chest, and my well-spent cock decides to stir to life. I'm still naked, with Raena's thigh slung over me so I know she feels it pressing into her.

Chancing a look down at her, I see her eyes open and a smirk playing on her lips as she stares at Maddox. My eyes dart to him. He's holding her hand next to her face, smirking back at her. Letting my head fall back into the headboard, we all fall into a comfortable silence for a while until Raena taps my arm.

"I need to go to the bathroom," she says softly, untangling herself from me and crawling off the end of the bed.

All three of our hungry eyes follow her until the door shuts behind her. After a few minutes, I hear my shower turn on, and as much as I want to storm in there and shower with her, I also know she probably needs a few minutes to herself.

"Hand me my phone from the nightstand," I tell Alek.

When he tosses it at me, I immediately open the message I got from King earlier and stare at it, hoping it will give me some insight into where he is keeping her.

It's a close-up of her upper body, though. There isn't much to discern from it. I can see sunlight peeking around her, so it doesn't appear she is being held in a basement. There is a tiny sliver of what appears to be a window behind her, but nothing of any detail that will help us.

I hear the water shut off as I toss the phone on the bed and climb out. I doubt she wants to walk around naked all day, so I grab one of my shirts and black boxers from my dresser before grabbing a pair of sweats for myself. I need a shower, but I am not ready to wash the scent of her off of me just yet.

I'm just pulling them up over my ass when she steps out of the bathroom, wrapped only in a towel. Her red curls are thrown over her shoulder as she leans forward, her head tilted to the side as she squeezes them out in another towel.

"Those for me?"

A cocky smirk plays on her lips, her eyes darting to the clothes I'm holding hostage. I stand frozen to the spot, enraptured by a single droplet of water that runs down the column of her throat before it disappears down the valley of her breasts.

Finally, snapping out of the daze her enticing body captured me in, I make my feet move to the end of the bed where she stands, tossing the clothes down on the bed. I still can't make my mouth form words as I catch a whiff of my body wash coming off her skin. It does strange things to my cock, smelling myself on her, and I just want to bury my face into her freshly showered skin.

I'm vaguely aware of the towel she was drying her hair with hitting the floor as a startled gasp has me snapping my attention to her face.

"What's wrong?" I ask, concern bleeding into my voice, my eyes darting around to find the cause.

"What the fuck is this?" She says, her voice sounding detached and cold, so unlike the woman who was screaming my name a little while ago. My heart rate picks up when I see where she is pointing.

My phone screen is lit up, lying next to the clothes I threw there. The image of my terrified sister with a knife to her throat is still on my screen. My heart breaks at the image, the same way it did this morning and again when I looked a minute ago.

"That's our sister. King sent it this morning after you went upstairs," I tell her, reaching towards her to pull her into my arms, wanting to give us both comfort, but she shrinks back away from me.

"Th-that's not your sister."

Her whispered words are broken by a heavy sob, and she clutches the towel at her chest as she slowly backs away. I'm so fucking confused by her words, I barely acknowledge my brothers when they get up from the bed and inch closer to her. My hand is still suspended in the air while I try to work out what she means.

"Of course, that's our sister," Alek says, moving towards her. Her back hits the wall with a soft thud as she slowly slides down, curling her body around her knees and shaking her head. He kneels down in front of her, reaching up to lift her chin so she is looking up at him. "What do you mean?"

"That's my daughter. That's Emera. But it can't be. She's dead. I saw her body covered in blood. I don't understand."

Her breath and words come out choppy as she lets go of the towel and runs her fingers through her hair, tugging on the roots. She is spiraling out of control, confused at what she is seeing versus what she believes.

Suddenly, as if everything the pieces of the puzzle we've been missing slide into place, it fucking clicks.

"No, no, no…" I roar out at the fucking realization of what this is.

He fucking lied.

My hands cover my face, all of the dots connecting– the truth of everything we've been missing. I close the distance between us, dropping to my knees and grasping her hands in mine. I wait until her wide, panicked eyes find mine.

"She's alive," I breathe out, my heart lurching at my chest, beating so hard I'm scared it might burst through my ribs at any moment.

"She's alive?" She asks, hope shining through as she scrambles to her knees, Alek steading her shaky movements.

"Yes, Angel. *He lied.* Manipulated you into seeing what he wanted you to believe. He. Fucking. Lied," I tell her, pulling her into me and cradling her face.

"She is *alive.*"

Chapter 42

I found her.

My little wolf.

I finally fucking found her! I wipe the blood from my hands on this fuck-up's shirt before pushing off of him to stand up completely. He saw her in town, almost ran her over. Had the good sense to take a picture of her, but he fucked up.

He fucking let her go. He didn't follow her. So now he is bound and gagged to a chair in my basement cell.

His gaping throat reminds me of the message my little wolf left with my men. I knew it was her as soon as I saw the calling card she placed on their mutilated bodies. I'd seen it before in her cell. When she was with me, I encouraged her *unique* art. It was wicked and dark. A darkness I inspired in her, drawing it from the depths of her soul.

Walking out of the piss and blood stained cell, Jackson stands just outside the bars, holding out a towel for me. "Get this cleaned up, I'll be in my office," I order him, taking the towel from him and cleaning the rest of the blood from my hands before heading up the stairs to my office.

"Yes, Sir."

He scurries off like a good little soldier. He knows I'm the only thing standing between him and the hunter. He's been trying to convince me to name him as my heir for years.

That will never happen.

Royal could have been the perfect heir. He had the potential. There was a darkness lurking beneath a facade of control– a beast so similar to my own, clawing at his insides, begging to be unleashed.

I thought killing his mother and sister would shred the last of his resolve, but those boys made him soft instead. Adopting all of them was a mistake that bit me in the ass. Royal is too blinded by his loyalty to them to ever be loyal to me.

If it wouldn't put my entire organization in an upheaval, they would have been dead a long time ago. However, I refuse to put everything I've built at risk over some defiant little boys trying to play men.

They will be handled just like their parents. But not yet.

Tossing the bloody towel into the trash, I sit down at my desk and pick up my phone. The bitch picks up on the first ring, like a pathetic dog begging for any scraps I'll toss her way.

"King, baby... I was hoping to hear-"

"Cut the shit, Ava. I'm letting you out of your kennel. A chance to renew the deal we made."

"I'll do whatever you want, King. I just want to see you."

Desperation bleeds through her lies. She doesn't want me. The only thing she has ever cared about was herself and her next hit. She made that clear when she made her deal.

"I'll have someone pick you up. Don't even think of trying anything stupid," I growl, irritated by the used up junkie already.

"What do I have to do?"

"Catch a little wolf." I end the call before I tell her guards to strangle her.

Pulling up the grainy picture on my phone, my cock grows hard at the fear swirling in her green eyes through the windshield. I've seen that look before. I've caused it.

Nothing gets me harder than listening to her beg and plead for me to stop, knowing I won't but still trying anyway. She's a fighter. She learned pretty quickly not to fight me, but that didn't stop her from fighting herself. She couldn't fight her body's response to me.

The way her body turns black and blue from my hands. Her unfiltered screams of agony echoing around her cell. She calls me a *monster*, but deep down, she craves the depravity only I can give her. It's clear from the carnage she's caused already– I turned her into a monster, too.

When she is back in my possession, I'm going to enjoy every second of rebreaking her. Of watching my men defile and degrade every inch of her. Until all the fight leaves her body, like shattered glass scattered on the floor. She will beg harder than she ever did before.

I grip my cock through my slacks at the thought. Tears will streak her creamy cheeks as I take away her ability to breathe with my cock buried deep in her throat. But I won't come in her mouth.

No.

My little wolf knows the only place my come goes is buried deep inside her tight cunt. And only *my* come. I might let my men use her, but they don't get that privilege. It's all mine.

Her cunt is *mine*.

She is mine.

Chapter 43

My daughter is alive.

She is alive.

And she is also their sister.

Royal's words repeat over and over in my head as I stare into his raging, icy blue eyes. His hands caress my face softly while Alek trails his up and down my back soothingly.

Their combined touches help calm my racing heart and erratic breathing. I can see Maddox pacing back and forth by the bed, his hands in his hair as he tries to process this new information.

"Doc was telling the truth. If I would have just listened to him…" I trail off, struggling to calm my racing thoughts as they whirl through my mind like a rampant tornado.

"You didn't know, baby. It doesn't matter now. All that matters is that your daughter is alive. Em… Emera, she is alive. We will save her," Alek says.

"How?" I ask once I'm sure my voice won't crack under the emotion threatening to pull me under. I don't have to elaborate. They seem to know I don't just mean how are we going to save her or how is my daughter alive. I want to know how my daughter is their sister.

"When King brought her home, he told us her mother was a junkie who died of an overdose. We didn't even question if it was the truth–we just took her in as our sister, no questions asked."

I guess when I think about it, she is their sister regardless. They share a father, even if they are adopted and she is King's blood child.

"Oh my god," I breathe out at the revelation. "She is his *heir.*"

Each of them tense at my statement. Everything makes much more sense now. The doctor's visits, the things he would say he needed from me.

I thought I ended up pregnant by mistake, but I should have realized sooner this was the entire reason he kept me locked up. He needed a blood heir. It doesn't answer the burning question I've asked myself a million times since he kidnapped me, though.

Why me?

Why did it have to be me? What importance do I hold to him? This raises a new question in my mind that I didn't even think about– Why didn't he kill me after I gave him what he wanted?

"Well, that explains the things that never added up," Maddox says when he finally stops pacing and moves to kneel in front of me, too.

He reaches out, twirling a stray curl in his finger. I can see the wheels turning in his head as he tries to piece together the puzzle with these new pieces we've uncovered.

"From what I have pieced together, your escape lines up with when we tried to take Em from King. He must have realized he needed to hide his *heir* and faked her death to explain why you couldn't see her anymore," he says, giving me an apologetic look as if they are the reason I lost my daughter.

"You are not to blame for any of this," I tell him, grabbing his hand and giving a reassuring squeeze. I don't blame them.

This is *his* fault.

King is the catalyst behind every ounce of my pain and suffering. My mind turns murderous when I think about the terror on my little girl's face in that picture.

"Can I see it again?"

My voice is stronger, and I know my newfound hope of seeing my daughter again is fueling me so I don't fall into a puddle of despair right now.

Maddox reaches behind him, picking the phone up from the bed before sliding it into my hand. The screen lights back up, showing the image to me once again.

She's older now– her face isn't as round without her baby cheeks, and her natural blonde curls that match my own have grown longer. Her emerald green eyes shine with tears as the bastard holds a knife to her throat.

I recognize the tattoos on his fingers. It's fucking King, terrorizing his own daughter for the sake of keeping his sons in line.

My vision tunnels, and all I see is red as I grip the phone hard enough to break it. My entire body is shaking with restrained rage when Royal's hand closes over his phone in my hand.

"Do you remember my promise?" He asks me, and even in the soft tone, I can hear the dominance bleeding through. The promise he made when he was buried inside me fills my mind instantly.

He promised to fight at my side for my revenge. Promised bloodshed and carnage for anyone who has ever laid a finger on me.

With a fire blazing hotter than a furnace in my eyes, I give him a sharp nod, not trusting my voice to remain steady enough for words.

"We will get her back. Then we will level this town until the streets run red," he growls with murderous intent.

I know it's not directed *at* me, but rather *for* me. It turns me on more than it should at this moment, and I'd love nothing more than to have a repeat session of what we did earlier.

I can still feel the delicious reminder of his special brand of punishment across my bare ass cheeks and the ache between my thighs when I press them together. But now is not the time.

"We need a plan. I won't rest until my daughter is safe in my arms, and I drive my blade through King's flesh," I tell them, taking a moment to look into each of their eyes when I get to my feet. "I stepped back from my plan to help you search for your sister. But that ends now. I will rain hell down on this town, until the streets are coated in their corrupt blood. Until everyone who played a part in this feels the full wrath of my wicked revenge. I *will* get my daughter back, and when I do, I will bathe in Kingston Wolfe's blood as I watch the light fade from his cold, dead eyes. Are you here for that?"

Each of them remain on their knees in front of me, staring back at me with a mix of awe and devotion as I slip into the mindset of *The Hunter.*

I allow them to see me as I slam down my mental barriers, locking away the weak and trembling girl behind bars of steel in my mind and bringing forth the ruthless hunter who stalks and kills degenerates who get off on hurting little girls– those weaker than them. But even with my mask firmly in place, I don't shut down my feelings for these men.

I let them see every ounce of the strength they are pouring into me reflect back at them.

"Whatever you need, Cherry. You are my *queen,*" Maddox says, his cocky smirk in place, but behind it, I can see absolute chaos and promises of mayhem brewing in his stormy eyes. With a sharp nod of my head, my eyes fall to Alek next.

"Where you go, I go, Baby Girl. I'm with you," he says in that deep sexy timbre that has my knees weak and thighs clenching as he brings my hand to his lips and places a gentle kiss there. His words and gentle touch have a smile lifting my lips as I nod and move my eyes to the last man on his knees for me.

"Angel," Royal breathes out in his deep gravelly voice. His eyes say everything his mouth can't, but I'm learning that's just how he is. It doesn't matter. I can see the utter devotion and allegiance flaring to life in his icy eyes. His hands encase my waist as he stares up at me. "I will be by your side every step of the way. Your fight is mine. Your revenge is mine. You. Are. Mine. I bind myself to you."

Maddox gets to his feet, walking into the closet before returning in front of me, getting back on his knees as he hands something to Royal. My eyes dart to the object in his hand, seeing a dagger similar to mine.

"When we were young, we already knew we were brothers in every way but blood. So we made it official, binding ourselves as 'blood brothers'." Royal says, taking the blade in his hand and stabbing the point into his other palm.

Blood pools beneath the tip, but not enough to spill over the sides of his hand before he passes it to Alek. I watch with bated breath while he and then Maddox do the same.

After each of them has sliced into their palms, Royal takes the blade back. He waits until I look into his eyes before speaking.

"This is us, binding ourselves to you in blood. Vowing to stand at your side, fight your fight, and bring Em back to you. Your blood is my blood. Our blood."

Tears fill my eyes as I take in everything he is saying. They may have seen Em as their little sister, but she is my blood– therefore, she is their blood, too.

Once we kill her *father*, they will be there to step into that role beside me. They will protect her and love her, just as a father should.

Giving him my hand, he gently digs the blade into my palm, but I don't feel the pain of it over the beating of my heart, thumping wildly in my chest like a war drum. This moment feels every bit as big as it is.

Overwhelming love washes over me, crashing into me like strong waves washing onto shore during a turbulent storm. Much like our relationship as a whole, crazy and unpredictable. The blade clatters to the floor before he presses our palms together, mixing our blood for all eternity.

Alek presses his palm into mine next, his eyes holding mine as he proudly says, "My blood."

Maddox sports his typical manic smile when he takes my blood-coated hand in his, grinning like he just won the fucking lottery as he mixes his blood with ours. Bringing my palm to his face.

"My blood," he repeats, his tongue darting out to lick a line through the crimson mixture as heat uncoils deep inside me. He keeps licking the blood from my palm, and he doesn't stop until my hand is completely clean.

My knees threaten to buckle, and my body feels like it's on fire under the intensity of his depravity, the way his eyes never leave mine as he stakes his claim.

"My Bloody Queen."

The flames consuming my body turn into a raging inferno at his declaration. At all of theirs combined, really. I expect my body to combust at any moment.

I know I'm fucked up when Maddox licking our blood from my hand has my thighs slick and my clit throbbing. I push down the desire for fucking my delicious men to the back burner, for now.

"I need to call Snow. I know they can help us," I tell them as they get to their feet and surround me like a pack of wolves, ready to solidify what we are all feeling at the moment.

Their eyes stare into mine, hunger radiating off of them like starved men, but they shove it down the same way I did, with a silent promise that we will resume this soon.

Very soon.

Spotting my bag on the floor by the door, I step around them, walking over and tossing it up on the side of the bed beside the clothes Royal had tossed there earlier.

Instead of putting them on, I pull out my own leggings and a thin black tank top from the big pocket, slipping into them quickly before unzipping the small front pocket and grabbing the burner phone. I haven't even turned it on since I left White Harbor.

Anxiety churns in my stomach as I crawl onto the bed and sit cross-legged in the middle against the headboard. I know I should have called and checked in with them, but I didn't want to allow the sadness of them not being here distract me from my plans. I needed to do this on my own, though I have no doubt Snow will understand.

All three of my men surround me on the bed, offering me silent strength with their subtle touches as I blow out a slow breath and power the phone on.

As the screen comes to life, I bring up the only four contacts in the phone. Clicking on Snow's name, I place the phone on speaker and sit it on the bed. We wait anxiously as the trill ringing sounds out in the otherwise quiet room.

"Red? Are you okay?" Snow's soft voice filters through the speaker, panic bleeding into her voice that immediately makes me regret not calling sooner.

"I'm okay," I rush out, trying to ease her fears. "Listen, I can't explain everything over the phone but I need your help."

"Name it and consider it done," she responds immediately. I knew I could count on her.

"My daughter is alive," I whisper, my words breaking under the crushing of my vocal cords, making it hard to speak past the lump of emotion in my throat. "King has her. But we don't know where. I need you to come to Shadow Forest and help us get her back."

"We're on the way," she says, her own voice thick with emotion.

She knows everything about my time as King's prisoner and the loss of my daughter. She saw me at my lowest point and was there to help me pick up the pieces of my shattered life.

There is some rustling filtering through the speaker before I hear a man's sleepy voice in the background. "What's wrong?"

She must pull the phone away from her face because I can barely make out the words as she fills him in on the very few details I've told her.

"Red," Ronan says, his voice clearer now. "We're getting ready now. We'll drive all night and be there tomorrow afternoon. Are you at the cottage?"

My eyes dart up to Royal questioningly, knowing they don't allow just anyone to come into their space. "We'll text you the address," he says loud enough for Ronan to hear, squeezing my thigh reassuringly.

"Who is that?" Snow asks suspiciously, sounding like she is further away from the phone.

My eyes widen comically when I realize I don't know what to call him— or any of them for that matter. Friends? My boyfriends? Neither of which sounds right. They are so much more than that.

I know she would understand, considering her own relationship with three men, but I don't know how to explain that in our limited conversation over the phone while all three are listening intently.

"I'll explain when you get here," I say simply, choosing the coward's way out.

"Yes, you certainly will." Her voice is still serious, but I can hear the smirk through the phone that I know is painting her lips right now. She knows how I usually act around men, so she definitely can tell something is up.

"Thank you, Snow."

Emotion crawls back up my throat at the gratitude I feel for her willingness to help me. I'm not surprised, though. That's just who she is. She has built her entire empire around helping others, trying to restore the legacy her father had.

She took me in when I was a broken, beaten mess. Tears well in my eyes at her compassion and how she unconditionally loves her people. I am just fortunate enough to be one of those people.

"I will always be there when you need me. All you have to do is ask. We're getting our stuff together now. I'll see you soon, Red. Stay safe."

The line goes dead, and I take a second to gather myself, wiping the tears welled up in my eyes before they have a chance to fall. Alek pulls me into his lap, pressing my back to his chest and nuzzling my neck. I lean into his warmth, allowing it to seep into my skin and soak all the way to my bones.

He makes me feel cherished– they all do. Not like a possession to be owned, but like it's a privilege to even touch me at all.

It's such a deep contrast from the way King treated me, like a piece of property he could loan out to all his scumbag friends. I had no control. He could pass me around and let them all take a turn, and I was just expected to lay down and take it.

I pick the phone up from the bed, staring at it for a moment. "I need to tell Ella what's going on, too, but I don't have her number in here," I say mindlessly. I'm still trying to wrap my head around what is happening.

I can't slow the thoughts down as my mind races with every possible worst-case scenario I could find my daughter in. My breath comes in short, labored bursts, all of the oxygen seems to have been sucked from my lungs, and I can't refill them fast enough.

"Breathe for me, Raena," Alek says, tilting my chin up and lightly squeezing my throat. I expect the move to worsen my panicked breathing, but it grounds me instead. His hand contracts on every breath I take, making it easier for me to feel the air as it goes in and out of me. After a few moments of controlling my breath, his hand loosens to rest against my throat. "That's it, keep it steady. I'll text Ella and ask her to stop by in the morning."

"Thank you," I tell him, allowing myself to fall deeper into his embrace. I'm so exhausted, but still on edge.

"Anytime, baby. Tell us what you need right now."

"Usually, when I'm feeling like this, I take Nightshade out for a ride or go hunting. Neither of those things seem like an option right now," I say with an exhausted sigh, closing my eyes.

Maddox leans forward, his fingers dancing up my thighs.

"We have other ways of distracting you."

Chapter 44

She squeals when I climb off the bed, gripping onto her thighs and jerking her body down to the edge.

Her wet curls fan out around her like a halo dipped in blood and her legs spreading wide to accommodate my imposing frame.

Goddamn.

The sight has my cock trying to punch straight out of my sweats. Biting my lip, I peer down at her, watching her eyes dart to my tented sweats. She mimics the move, her teeth biting into the tender flesh of her bottom lip when I give my raging cock a tight squeeze.

"Soon," I promise, gritting my teeth from the tight grip on my aching cock. "I want you begging first. You will beg for our touch. Our mouths. Our cocks. Only then will we fuck you like the true queen you are."

Her eyes dilate and darken to shades I've never seen before at the promise of what's to come. I trail my finger up the inside of her thigh over the seam of her leggings, slowly inching my way to her thinly covered pussy.

The fact that I know she isn't wearing any panties right now sends a shock of desire straight to my throbbing cock.

"Would you like that, Cherry? Does that make your tight little cunt slick?" I ask her, continuing my feather-light touch up and down the seam covering her slit, making her legs shake with wanton need. "If I slide my hand inside here, will I find you dripping like my needy little slut?"

A shiver of pure ecstasy trembles through her, her eyes rolling back as she fists the sheets beneath her. "Y-yes."

She's right here, laid out in front of me, exactly where I've longed to see her for days, panting to catch her breath. I stand there for a few moments, watching the way her chest rises and falls with every inhale and exhale, silently battling in my head.

I want to reach inside her leggings and see just how wet she is, but if I touch her, I won't be able to drag this out. As much as I want to bury myself eight inches inside her right this second, she needs to get out of her head first.

With every ounce of my restraint, I pull back, giving her pussy a hard slap that has a shocked, gasping moan escaping her lips before I stand to my full height. Her hands reach behind her head, searching for Alek.

"Daddy, please touch me," she begs, grabbing his hand and pulling it to her chest.

"Not yet, Baby Girl," he says, moving his hand from her breast to under her arms, pulling her back up to sit against his chest again. "Let's get these clothes off of you."

He runs his hands slowly down her sides before reaching for the hem of her black tank top and pulling it over her head gently.

Gathering her hair on one side as his mouth descends down her neck, and she leans her head over to give him more access as he kisses down her throat and over her shoulder.

Royal moves in front of her. Without warning, rips her leggings right down the middle, eliciting a moan from her that has my cock pulsating inside my sweats, begging to be unleashed on her. He pulls them down her legs and tosses them to the floor.

"Look at this pretty pink pussy, dripping and begging for our cocks," he says, dragging his finger over her slit, barely touching her. She grips Alek's hands, moaning as a rush of arousal gushes out, running down the seam of her ass and pooling on the sheets beneath her.

"Royal, please. I *need* you," she cries breathlessly. "I need all of you. Please."

He slaps her pussy, earning another gush of liquid and a sharp cry from her. "You think you can take all of us, Angel? All three of our cocks, stuffing your tiny body until you feel like you might split in two?"

"Yes, Sir," she moans as he continues lightly stroking over her slit. "I can take it. Please."

"That's my good little slut," he says, giving her pussy another slap before pulling back and climbing off the bed. He reaches down on the floor, picking up a box and placing it on the end of the bed.

"We're going to need to prepare you for that." He pulls out several items from his box, laying them on the bed.

Fuck yes!

A smile splits across my face when I see what he has in mind for us tonight.

"You remember your safe word?" He asks her, closing the box and putting it back on the floor. He walks around to the end of the bed and waits for her response.

"Yes, Sir."

"Tell my brothers what it is, so they know it too."

"Apple," she breathes out in a moan, as Alek continues teasing her with his lips on her. I smile at her choice of safe word. It's weird, but somehow fitting for her.

"Good girl. Come here," Royal commands, his tone giving no room for argument, and damn if it doesn't have my cock twitching again.

She pulls herself out of Alek's hold, swaying her ass provocatively as she crawls on all fours to the end of the bed. When she gets there, she sits back on her knees, her hands laying in her lap as she waits for his next instruction.

Her submission and obedience is sexy as fuck. At this rate, I'm going to blow my first load in my pants like a fucking teenager.

"Turn around and rest your shoulders on the bed. Keep that ass up," he says gruffly, and she complies immediately.

When her ass is facing him, he runs his hand down her spine before picking up a bottle of lube. He pops the top and dribbles it over her ass. I watch with rapt attention as it slides from the top of her crack down to her already-soaked slit. His fingers immediately follow, probing at her puckered entrance, getting it nice and lubed up.

She hisses and her entire body tenses as he pushes against her resistance.

"Relax, Baby Girl," Alek says, leaning over to stroke her hair and push it out of her face where she has it smushed into the mattress. "Let him in."

I can see the moment her body releases that tension. She melts into the bed, allowing Royal to push past her barriers with one finger. He works it in and out while she takes deep breaths, inhaling and exhaling in the same pattern I've seen her do to calm herself when she gets overwhelmed.

After a few moments, when she is moaning louder and pushing back against his hand, he adds a second finger, probing and scissoring them inside her asshole, stretching her until she has no more resistance.

Reaching down, he picks up the smallest of the graduated plugs laid out. It's a shiny silver, with a red jewel on the end in the shape of a heart.

"You're doing so good, Angel. I'm going to pull out my fingers now, and replace them with a plug. When you feel me pushing in, bare down and push back against it. Don't fight it," he instructs, and she just nods her head, her mind already too overcome with desire to form words.

"Spread lube over this," Royal says, handing me the plug.

"Yes, Sir," I moan dramatically, smirking as I grab the lube and slather the bigger end until it drips onto the bed, before handing it back to him.

His eyes darken with lust at my smart mouth. "Keep it up, Maddie. Unless you want me to plug your ass, too."

"Oh don't tease me... *sir*. If you want to boss me around and play with my ass, just say so," I say, winking at him and wagging my eyebrows as he growls at me.

He goes back to the task at hand, pulling his fingers gently out of her ass and immediately pushing the plug in.

"Just like that," he tells her when she pushes against him, rolling her head and moaning into the mattress. "Just a little more, Raena. You've almost got it."

The plug snaps into place with a squelch, and she lets out a sigh of relief, her upper body melting into the mattress. He runs his hand soothingly over her ass cheeks, the welts from earlier looking faded but still there.

"Such a good fucking girl. You did great. Would you like your reward now?"

That perks her right up, her head lifting off the mattress as she nods her head frantically. "Please, Sir."

"Maddox, lie down with your head next to the headboard," he commands, and any sarcastic comment I would've had fizzles out when I hear the strain in his voice. Following his order, I lay down on my back.

"Now, sit your pretty little pussy right on his face, Angel. You're going to ride his tongue until you come in his mouth. He will drink every drop you give him like a good fucking boy. Won't you, Maddie?"

Holy. Fucking. Shit.

If my cock wasn't aching before, it sure as fuck is now.

"Yes, Sir."

I will submit to him like this any fucking day. I don't know where this Royal has been hiding, but it seems a certain little firecracker has unlocked all sorts of fuckery in us.

Raena crawls up my body, positioning her perfect pussy right over my face.

She grabs onto the headboard for leverage as she hovers over my waiting mouth. I can see the red jewel glistening with the combination of her arousal and the lube.

"*Fuck.* Your tight little ass stretching around this jewel is a fucking sight to see. But I need you to sit the fuck down. Don't hover. Drench me. Suffocate me with your needy little cunt, my queen. Ride my fucking face," I demand, grabbing on to her hips and jerking her down to my waiting mouth.

Her essence explodes on my tongue immediately, making my hips jerk upward on their own. She tastes like cherry pie, sweet with a tangy twist that has you coming back for more with every decadent bite.

My hands move to her waist as she picks up pace, rocking her hips faster on my face. She fills the room with her moans. My sweatpants being slid down my body have my own moans muffling against her.

A warm, wet tongue swipes across my pierced tip, making my hips lift off the bed again, chasing the contact when it disappears. I growl against Raena's pussy, the vibrations making her bare down harder.

A sharp sting impacts my cock, sending delicious pain ricocheting through my piercings.

Did I just get slapped in the dick?

"Don't fucking move. You'll take what I give you and you'll thank me when I'm done, Maddie. Or I'll edge you all night long with no release. Raena can tell you. I don't make empty threats."

Fuck.

I might bust all over myself before he even touches me again. I don't know if I've ever been this turned on in my goddamn life. I've got the girl of my dreams, that I'm fucking in love with, riding my tongue like a fucking pornstar.

And Royal, with his dominating 'big dick energy', about to suck my cock. All I need now is Alek to join the party, and I might literally combust. Right here on this bed. It'll be messy, but a death worth dying if you ask me.

Suddenly, my racing thoughts are silenced when Royal grabs my cock. He swallows me in one go, my piercing hitting the back of his throat, constricting around me. He holds steady, relaxing his throat until he pulls back and goes even deeper on the second try.

It's a real struggle to stay still with flames licking up my spine, threatening to make me come before I'm ready. If that happens, I won't even be able to warn him because my mouth is full of pussy at the moment.

He finds a steady pace, working my dick like a pro, and I use all of my willpower to hold off my impending orgasm. Raena is close, too. Her thighs are shaking against my head, her screams amping up in volume. I look up to see her face twisted in beautiful bliss as Alek kneels beside us, twisting her nipples between his fingers.

"That's it. Let go. Come in his mouth," he encourages her, now alternating between her breasts and twisting her nipples in quick succession.

Her mouth drops open in a silent scream when her body seizes to the pleasure coursing through her. Her pussy floods my mouth so much that it spills out, drenching my whole head. And she just keeps coming.

Wave after wave of her release hits my face, making the sexiest mess I've ever had the pleasure of witnessing all over me and the bed beneath us.

Her release triggers my own. With my cock buried in Royal's throat, I fill his mouth. He doesn't release me, though. His mouth suctions to my cock, and I feel him swallow every spurt of my come as it hits the back of his throat.

He doesn't waste a *single* drop.

Raena releases the headboard, and collapses into Alek's arms. He pulls her off my face just as Royal finally releases my cock with a pop. I'm still so damn hard I could cut glass right now. Which is good, considering we are not nearly done for the night.

No, this night is just getting started.

ALEK

Chapter 45

Pulling Raena's spent body into mine, I lift her off Maddox's face, cradling her to my chest.

My cock is a giant stone in my sweats right now, but I ignore it. Even with the hot-as-fuck scene Royal had going on, my eyes didn't leave her the whole time.

I watched her struggle to chase her orgasm as she battled with herself inside her head. It took some work, but she finally let go and allowed herself to shatter.

It was the most beautiful thing I've ever seen.

"You did so good, baby. Just rest for a minute," I whisper to her, my hands tangling in her curls as I massage her scalp. Her eyes are closed, but she nods her head against my chest.

"He's right, Angel. Catch your breath for a minute. You're going to need to conserve your strength for this next part," Royal says breathlessly, sitting up on his knees and wiping his mouth on the back of his hand.

"Maybe she's had enough for tonight," I say, but her eyes pop open, her head already shaking back and forth.

"No. I said I want all of you and that's what I meant," she says as confidently as she can, still struggling to catch her breath. "I *need* all of you. Please, Daddy?"

I know what she is asking, but I don't think she is ready for that. Honestly, I don't know if she will ever be ready. She's just so tiny, and I'm so big. I refuse to hurt her like that. She's been through enough trauma in her life. I'll be damned if I add to it.

"Baby Girl, we don't have to stop, but I still can't. You're not ready for that. Not yet," I whisper to her. Royal and Maddox know I'm a virgin, but it's just not something I like to openly discuss.

"Then I will get ready, Daddy. It might not happen tonight, I know that. But it *is* happening," she whispers back, her sass bleeding through even her gentle tone, making me smile.

Her confidence is something I love about her.

She isn't afraid to put us in our place when needed. She knows what she wants, and isn't afraid to go after it. She might have shown us her vulnerable side, but that just makes her strength even more prominent.

"Okay, baby," I conceded, knowing that if push comes to shove, I will give her whatever she asks of me.

"Thank you, Daddy," she says, closing her eyes and resting her head back on my chest for a few moments.

Maddox rolls off the bed, heading into the bathroom, returning a moment later, rubbing a towel on his head.

"You know, Raena, I know you marked your territory tonight, but later, you can help me find an empty spot of my body for your name," he says, climbing back in the bed next to us and kissing her cheek with a smirk.

"You do *not* want to tattoo my name on your body. That's bad luck for new relationships," she says smiling, hiding her face in my chest again.

"I hate to break it to you, my queen, but even if I doom our relationship by tattooing your whole face on my body, you still won't be able to get rid of us. You're stuck with us, Raena. Get used to it," he says, flipping the soaked pillow over and flopping over onto his back.

Raena pats my chest for me to release her and climbs out of my lap, moving to straddle Maddox's waist. "Well in that case Maddie baby, let me pick out where I want my *mark* to be."

His entire face lights up when he looks up at her, his lips widening into a shit-eating grin. "Yes! Anywhere you want, Cherry. My body is your canvas."

Her eyes and fingers trace over all of his tattoos, taking them in and searching for a blank spot. He already has pretty much every inch of skin from his thighs and up inked. It isn't easy to find clean, virgin skin.

He relaxes back against the pillow, closing his eyes and letting her explore his naked body. I can see his still-hard cock, trapped between their bodies. Every touch of her skin on his has it twitching, desperate for more.

"How about right here?" She says, finding an empty space between his belly button and his cock.

"I think that's perfect," he says grinning, grabbing her hand and tracing over the spot together. "That's your spot."

"Yes, it is," she says, rocking her hips and grinding down onto his cock. She reaches between them, lifting herself up to line him up with her entrance before sinking down slowly.

"*Oh shit,*" he groans, moving his hands to her hips to guide her.

"Fuck," she moans. "I feel so full."

Royal moves to her, straddling Maddox's legs as he kneels behind her. He places his hand on her back, gently pushing her forward.

"Lay down on him. Relax your body for me," he says softly, one hand rubbing her back soothingly so she stays relaxed. "This is going to hurt if you don't stay relaxed for me. Let me and Maddox do all the work. We need to do this if you want to take Alek's cock without tearing."

She nods her head, pressing her body into Maddox's. She buries her face in his neck. I move around, getting closer so I can see exactly what he is doing.

"Just breathe for me," he says, lining himself up with her pussy, right above where Maddox is buried inside her.

He pushes inside slowly, gritting his teeth and cursing with every inch that disappears. I imagine that between Maddox's ladder piercings rubbing him and the tight fit, he won't last very long.

"Oh my..." she says through a moan that transcends into a scream. Both of them instantly freeze, allowing her time to stretch and adjust. Her entire body shakes, and her breath punches out in short bursts. "Royal, take the plug out. It's too much. Please."

She didn't use her safe word, though, so I already know the answer before he ever speaks.

"No. You can take it. Keep breathing."

She sucks in a deep gulp of air, whimpering into Maddox's neck and nodding at them to continue.

Royal pushes forward again, sinking a couple more inches into her, but still not fully seated inside her yet.

"Good girl. You can't take both of us fully yet, but we will get there. For tonight, this is your limit," he tells her. "We are going to stretch you a little more like this, then I'm going to pull this plug out. Just like I promised you earlier, I'm going to fuck your tight little ass while Maddox fucks your pussy. And Alek is going to stuff your throat full of his cock."

"Goddamn it," Maddox curses, "I'd say she likes the sound of that. Her pussy is strangling me right now."

"I fucking know," Royal grits out, his hand moving to circle the gemstone plug she has in. Getting leverage on it, he twists it around for a second. "Okay, Raena. When you feel me start pulling this out, do the same thing we did putting it in. Bear down for me."

"Yes, Sir," she groans, her words slightly muffled against Maddox's neck.

Royal pulls on the gem and she bears down. All three of them curse before they breathe out a sign of relief when it pops free from her ass.

Royal slowly slides out of her, too, replacing the plug with his cock.

"Please. I need you both to move," she begs, rocking back and forth on their cocks. She lifts her head, her wide, desperate eyes finding mine.

"Fuck my throat, Daddy," she says in the sexiest voice I've ever heard.

She drops her mouth open and sticks out her tongue. I sit up on my knees, sliding my sweats down. My cock bobs in front of her face. Before I can even touch her perfect little mouth, Royal wraps his hand around her throat from behind, tilting her head all the way back to look up at him.

"Keep your fucking mouth open," he says before leaning his face over hers. He spits into her open mouth. The filthy action has a surge of pre-come oozing from my tip. "Don't you dare swallow, Angel. Let him fuck my spit into your throat."

He lowers her back down slowly, releasing her throat. She keeps her mouth wide open for me.

Leaning forward, I slide the tip of my cock onto her waiting tongue, mixing my pre-come with his spit before sliding past her lips. It's a tight fit, her lips stretching around my size, but once I hit the back of her throat, I pause, giving her a second to catch her breath.

Everything happens in a blur.

Maddox and Royal both move, thrusting in and out of her in tandem. The movement rocks her mouth on my cock, so I grab the back of her head to keep her steady, thrusting my cock down her throat in time with them.

With her moans vibrating around me, I know it won't be long until we all fall over the edge. I can already feel the tingling racing up my spine.

"Oh fuck..." I growl, and start to pull out of her mouth, but she reaches for me, grabbing the backs of my thighs and pulls me back into her.

She buries my cock as far as it will go into her throat. I roar as my release hits me like a freight train. My fingers tighten in her hair and she swallows every drop of come that I give her before I loosen my grip, and she releases my cock.

"Goddamn, Baby Girl," I say, grabbing her face and leaning down to take her mouth with mine. I can taste myself on her tongue, but I don't care. Pulling back, I look into her lust hazed eyes. "You're amazing."

"So are you," she moans, as her release gets closer. Her entire body starts to tremble and her moans turn to screams. "I'm gonna..." she cries. But it's too late.

Royal and Maddox's thrust start to fumble, their own releases have curses and growls sounding out around the room.

"That's it. Come on our cocks like our good little slut. Squirt for us," Royal grits out.

Raena's orgasm hits her full force, her body shakes and I can hear her release squirting out around their cocks. They follow her over the edge, roaring out their own releases before they all collapse into the bed.

"Holy fucking shit. That was..." Maddox says, out of breath as he pulls Raena next to him, kissing her forehead. She curls up next to him, her head on his chest and closes her eyes.

I get off the bed and go into the bathroom to get a warm washcloth to clean her up. She is exhausted. I doubt she could even stand to make it to the shower. So this will have to do for now. She is already sleeping when I return.

"Help me get her cleaned up, and we can move to my room for the night," I tell my brothers. This bed is soaked, there is no way we can sleep comfortably in here.

Once we are all cleaned up, I pick Raena up and carry her to my bed. Maddox and Royal head into the bathroom to get cleaned up and it doesn't take them long before they are piling in the bed with us.

"Tonight was unlike anything I've ever experienced before," I tell them in the quiet darkness.

"Same. She is special," Royal says, snuggling closer to Raena and kissing her hair.

"She brings out things in each of us I never expected. We're going to have to talk about everything soon, you know," Maddox says.

"We will, I promise," Royal replies, reaching behind him and grabbing Maddox's arm. He wraps it around his waist before closing his eyes. "For now, let's just get some sleep. I think we're going to have a crazy few days ahead of us."

Chapter 46

"You have ten seconds to wake her up before I knock the shit out of you again, Royal."

Ella's panicked voice wakes me from some of the deepest sleep I've ever had. Last night was mind blowing. I can still feel the delicious reminder of how well Maddox and Royal stretched me until I thought I was going to split in two.

"Make it stop," Maddox groans against my chest, his face nuzzled perfectly between my breasts before he rolls over and covers his head with a pillow.

Alek's giant hand flexes against my bare pussy as he growls in my ear and holds me tighter against him. "Who is yelling?"

"That's just Ella. She's worried. Go back to sleep. I'll go talk to her," I tell him, wiggling my body between them so I can get up.

He growls even deeper, tightening his hold on my pussy and grinding his massive morning wood against my ass.

"Baby Girl. Keep that up and no one is leaving this bed today."

"Oh. I'm sorry," I say, a quiet giggle bubbling out of my throat as I still myself, waiting for him to release me. He gives me one last snuggle, kissing my temple before letting me go. I scoot down the bed and climb off the end over the rail.

Grabbing Royal's shirt off the floor, I slip it over my head quickly and head out to see my oldest and dearest friend. On the way down the stairs, I realize there's this feeling in my chest that is hard to explain. It feels light. Free. Happy.

I know I won't truly be happy until my daughter is back in my arms, but there is no guilt for how much these men mean to me. I didn't think it was possible to feel this way about anyone, let alone three men at the same time.

I can't explain it, and it might sound batshit crazy to most people, but I know in my bones that my soul belongs to them. Their souls picked up the shattered pieces of mine, entwined them together, and made the pieces whole once again.

A smile ghosts over my lips by the time I step down into the living room, where Ella is standing toe to toe with a pissed-off, half-naked Royal.

He looks absolutely edible this morning, with his tattoos and muscles on display. If Ella wasn't looking at him like she's two seconds away from beating his ass, I might demand he put a shirt on.

"Finally. What the fuck, Rae? Are you okay? I get a message from 'Big Daddy' saying to be here this morning that it's an emergency, and then this constipated asshat won't let me speak to you," she rushes out, stepping around Royal and making a beeline for me.

"First, I'm sorry. It is an emergency, but I'm okay. I need to talk to you," I tell her, hugging her tight against me.

"I'll go start some coffee and breakfast. You can talk in the library," Royal grumbles, rubbing his hands over his face.

Both Ella and I whip around comically and gape at him. "You have a library?" We say in unison.

"Yes, some of us are evolved and like to read," he smirks back at us before his features soften just for me. "It's the first door on the left, just past the stairs. I'll give you a full tour later, Angel. This is your home now."

His words make butterflies erupt in my stomach and tears sting the backs of my eyes. I don't know what to say to that so I just nod my head. I haven't had a place to call home since before King happened.

I know Snow says I will always have a place in her home, but this is different. It feels like my life is finally starting to move again. I've been running in place for years– now, this feels like progress.

Taking Ella's hand, we head down a hallway I didn't even know existed beyond the stairs. A beautiful set of French doors sits just where he said, the sleek black frame with distorted glass panels preventing us from seeing inside.

"I guess you have a library now for all your dirty books," Ella snickers as I turn the handles and push both doors open. We gasp in awe as we take in the sight before us.

The space opens into a semi-circle, with an open glass wall that looks like the forest and Grimm River are inside the room with us. Curved shelves scale up two stories, with metal frame spiral stairs and sliding ladders sporadically placed to assist in reaching the upper levels of shelves. On the second story, in front of the glass window, is a reading nook. It looks like something out of a fairytale.

"Holy. Fucking. Shit," She says, as we step inside, both of us spin in a slow circle trying to take in the enchanting space in its entirety. There are books on some of the shelves, but for the most part, they are waiting to be filled.

"I could get lost here for hours on end. Days, even," I say breathlessly, coming around to face Ella again.

"So could I," she says, finally returning her eyes back to me. "But I've been worried sick all night. What is going on, Rae? What's the emergency?"

Grabbing her hand, I walk us over to a couch positioned next to the glass wall and take a seat. I take both of her hands in mine between us, closing my eyes and taking a deep breath to prepare for everything I'm about to tell her.

"Oh, Ella… I should have told you sooner– I just didn't know how," I say when I finally open my eyes.

"You're scaring me, Rae. Tell me what?"

"Okay. Don't freak out. Please just let me get it all out first," I tell her. She nods back at me eagerly.

"I have a daughter…" I start, still unable to fully process that she is alive after all this time believing she was dead. "King let me believe he killed her, but after all this time, she is alive. He didn't kill her, Ella. He took her, and she is the sister the Shadows have been looking for."

"What in the actual fuck?" Ella whispers in shock, her eyes as wide as saucers, before she pulls out of her trance with renewed vigor. "Holy shit, Rae. You have a daughter? King is her father? She's their sister? I'm not going to freak out, but I'm going to need the full story behind this."

So that's exactly what I tell her.

I start at the very beginning– the doctor's monthly visits, the brutal attacks that followed, and then how they stopped when he figured out I was pregnant.

I tell her the horror story of Emera's birth, the time I got to spend with her, and how I finally snapped the day King told me she was dead.

I explain what happened yesterday with the guys, how we figured out Em is Emera, and that she is very much alive and in danger.

She sits there and listens intently, asking questions and squeezing my hands in support when my voice starts to break. I feel better now that she knows everything. She is my best friend in the entire world, and I needed to share this with her.

"So what do we do? How do we find her?" She asks when we've both had a minute to process my massive trauma dump.

"I've called in some friends. You remember the people who helped me in White Harbor?" I ask, and she nods her head back at me. "They are coming to help us locate her. They are really good at what they do. I know they can help."

"Good. That's really good, Rae. We will find her. Don't worry," she reassures me, hugging me tightly. I cling to her support as memories of everything King has done play like movie clips in my head, turning my thoughts dark.

"I'm going to enjoy every second of his death. He turned me into a monster. Now, he's going to know what it feels like when the monster he created rips his world apart."

"Death is a mercy he doesn't deserve. Don't make it too quick. Make it hurt," she says with fire in her eyes.

"Oh, it won't be quick. And it's definitely going to hurt," Maddox startles both of us out of our little bubble from the library doorway.

He pushes off the frame, stalking towards us wearing only a pair of sweats, something I am learning all the guys wear around the house and look absolutely delectable in.

"Come on, ladies. Breakfast is ready," he says, picking me up from the couch and cradling me bridal style. I don't even protest this time. It's pointless, anyway.

"Oh, goodie. Do I get to watch 'Big Daddy' feed her again?" Ella snickers, following us out of the library.

"I fucking hope so," Maddox laughs as we enter the dining room.

Royal and Alek are already at the table, but at least they have shirts on now. Being in a room with all three of them without melting into a goddamn puddle is nearly impossible as it is without the extra eye candy of their defined muscles and dark ink on display.

Besides, Ella is here and Snow will be here soon. I'd hate for them all to see my jealousy on display as well.

"Delivery for 'Big Daddy'. One very hungry, very insatiable Baby Girl, sans panties," Maddox says, smirking in that adorable feral kitten kind of way, as he sits me onto Alek's waiting lap.

Alek looks down at me, like I'm his entire world wrapped in his brother's shirt, before leaning his mouth down to my ear.

"No panties, huh?"

***

The library has been a good distraction since breakfast. I couldn't just sit around and wait for Snow to arrive anymore, so I showered and got dressed, then wandered back in here.

Ella and Alek followed me— now the books have been sorted by genre and organized alphabetically. I was surprised to find a lot of children's books but even more surprised to find out that all three men have books in this library.

It is hard to imagine any of them sitting down to read anything, especially some of the dark romance books I found that belong to Alek.

El even assured me that she has looked after Grams' cottage all these years, and all of my books are still there. Once we got everything settled, she offered to help me bring them over. I have a lot of work to do if I want to fill these shelves up in my lifetime.

Alek brought me up to the reading nook a little bit ago when Ella found her a book and curled up on the couch. He plopped down in the middle of a giant bean bag, pulling me into his lap and cocooning us both in the fluff.

"You know, we originally built this library for Em," he tells me, stroking my hair with soothing, gentle touches. "We wanted her to have her own little escape. She loves fairy tales. Even at her young age, she would drag out books the nanny would bring her, crawl into our laps, and sit for hours while we read them over and over again."

Tears well in my eyes, but I don't speak. I never got to read her a story, but warmth spreads throughout my chest knowing that these incredible men were able to give her that time. At the very least, she has known unconditional love for at least some of the time she has been away from me. It wasn't all fear.

"We love that little girl, more than life itself. I want you to know that. We will do whatever it takes to bring her back to you. We will kill for her. We will die for her. She might not be our sister, but your blood is our blood. She is ours, Baby Girl," he tells me, swiping at my tears as they streak down my cheeks.

He leans over me, pressing his lips to mine in a sweet kiss that has me melting even further into the softness beneath us. Before we can take it any further, his phone dings in his pocket.

Pulling it out, he looks up at me with a smile so bright it's almost blinding.

"They're here, baby," he says, still grinning as he uses his unnatural strength to get us both out of the beanbag with me still attached to him. He carries me down the stairs and starts to head out of the library.

Ella's head snaps up from her book when she sees us pass her.

"Come on, El. I want you to meet my friends," I yell as Alek's long legs eat up the distance to the French doors. She jumps up, chasing after us as we stride into the living room and into the foyer.

Royal and Maddox are already there opening the door, both of them freshly showered and dressed since they spent their time in the basement gym after breakfast.

My heart pounds in my chest when Snow, Ronan, Jasper, and Dax step inside. Their eyes widen comically when they land on me, still clinging to Alek. .

"Red, blink twice if this big hunk of man-muscle is holding you against your will," Jasper says, winking at me as his lips twitch into a smirk.

"For fucks sake. Put her down, 'Big Daddy'. Let her hug her friends," Ella says, rolling her eyes, but I see the smile creeping up.

My feet barely have time to hit the floor before I'm immediately pulled into a group hug from all four of them.

"You should have called us sooner, Red. I've been worried sick about you, and you weren't answering the phone," Snow says as she squeezes me tightly.

"I know, I'm sorry. Everything happened so quickly and I thought I could do this on my own," I tell her, feeling slightly defeated as I pull back to look at her.

"I know you *can* do this on your own. The point is, you don't have to. We are your family, Red. Family means we come together when one of us needs help. There is no shame in leaning on the people you love," she tells me, squeezing my shoulders in reassurance.

I nod back at her, unable to put into words what that means to me. I swallow past the lump of emotion clogging my throat before attempting to speak.

341

"Thank you for coming all this way," I say, shimmying out of the middle of them. "Come in. I'd like you to meet some friends."

"This is Ella, my childhood best friend," I say. Ella steps up beside me, immediately embraced by Snow.

"Sorry, I'm a big hugger. It's nice to meet you. I'm Aspen Snow, but my friends call me Snow. Any friend of Red's is a friend of ours," Snow says, smiling warmly at her.

"It's nice to meet you, too," Ella smiles back at her. "Thank you for taking care of her when she needed you. I thought I'd lost her forever."

"Okay. Stop before you make me cry," I say, my throat still bogged down with emotions.

"This is Royal, Alek, and Maddox," I say, gesturing to each of them. They step up beside me, nodding to them respectfully. "Guys, this is Ronan, Jasper, and Dax. Huntsman– meet the Shadows."

Ronan's eyes look like they're going to pop out of his head while the other two just smirk at each other. Snow steps up to them first. "I've heard about you. I respect what you're trying to do in Shadow Forest. King needs to be put down. He has ruled this territory with fear and control for too long. Anything we can do to help, just ask."

"Thank you, we appreciate that," Royal says, as he joins the guys in brief handshakes.

It's not a bad first meeting– even if it is awkward as hell.

"Well, now that everyone has been introduced, can we go downstairs and bring everyone up to speed together?" I ask, turning to Royal for permission to invade their private space. I don't expect an issue, but out of respect, I don't want to just bulldoze over his hospitality.

Royal pulls me into him, leaning down to whisper into my ear. "I told you this morning, this is your home now. You don't need my permission."

I can feel heat creeping up my neck and staining my cheeks at his words. He knows just what to say to melt me into a puddle at his feet.

Chapter 47

"Can I see your phone?" Ronan asks Royal, as he pulls out his laptop and sets it up on the table.

We've been down in the basement for a little while now. We have all gone over every painful detail we can possibly think of that could help us.

"Sure, you can have access to anything that you think will be helpful," Royal tells him, handing his phone over. He is sitting in the chair I was in earlier, his legs spread wide, with his elbows on his knees. I know he feels defeated.

Em has been missing almost a year and they've made no progress to find her. I don't blame them, though. With everything on the table like it is now, they've had nothing to go on. No solid leads. Not even any half-baked leads. King has done everything in his power to make Em a ghost.

Walking over to him, I step between his knees. "Can I sit with you?"

"Of course, you can," he tells me, leaning back so I can climb onto his lap, and I run my fingers through his hair gently.

"Get out of your head, Royal. Everyone here knows you have all done everything in your power to find Em. King is the only one to blame here. He kidnapped and kept me hidden away for three years, and no one found me. The best way to hide someone is if no one knows they still exist. No one even knew to look for me."

"King is an evil bastard, but he's smart. He's good at what he does. We've been trying to tiptoe around him. Maybe we just have to be smarter if we want to get ahead of him," I tell him, pulling his head into my chest and stroking his neck.

"And I think we just got him," Ronan says from his computer. "He got cocky and fucked up."

"What do you mean?" I ask as Royal stands with me still against him, carrying me to the table where Ronan and the everyone else is.

"The picture he sent of Em has no geographical landmarks in the image, but he missed one very important thing. This picture is geotagged."

"Ronan, I swear to fucking God. You know I don't speak 'techie'. Tell me in words I can understand. What does that mean?" I grit out at him impatiently.

"It means, Little Red, I can pull the GPS coordinates and tell you the exact location this picture was taken," he says, excitement and self-assurance radiating off him as his fingers fly over his keyboard at lightning speed. "It means we will know exactly where your daughter is, or at least where she was as of yesterday."

"When?" Royal and I rush out in unison, disbelief and hope at war inside my aching heart.

"How long until we have her location?" Alek questions as Maddox paces the floor in excitement.

345

"Right now," He pushes out of his chair and hands Royal his phone back. "This photo was taken right here in Shadow Forest. The time stamp was yesterday morning, so he took this photo while you were on the phone with him. I sent you the coordinates."

"She's here? Close?" I cry, scrambling down out of Royals arms. "Let's go."

"Not so fast. This was easy. Maybe even too easy. I know I'm not the only one not willing to put your safety at risk if this is a trap. Let us check it out first, Little Red." Ronan says, and all three of my men nod with him.

"Fuck that, Ro. That's my daughter. You're telling me you want me to sit here and twiddle my fucking thumbs like a damsel-in-distress when it's my daughter. You've lost your goddamn mind."

"No, I'm telling you, this child has been missing for a year. Now suddenly, we show up and find her in the first few hours of searching–something smells fishy. I'm not willing to put Snow's life at risk, either. I'm only asking you to let us do some scouting first, at least. Just to get an idea of what we are dealing with. Then we will regroup and make the decision together, as a family."

"He's right, Rae," Ella says, taking my hands in hers. "I'm not saying don't get your hopes up, but let them check it out first. I just got you back. I'm not willing to lose you again because King pulled one over on us. I can't lose you again. Snow and I will stay with you."

Looking around the room, my head spins with every possible emotion I've ever felt. Anger, pain, soul-crushing grief, but most of all, fear. I'm scared of what will happen if I go with them and she isn't there. Or worse, if they find her dead. I'm also scared of what will happen if I don't go and she is there.

I haven't seen my daughter in two years. She was barely a year old when I lost her. She won't remember who I am. She isn't going to run into my arms and cry for the mother she lost that day, too. She will have to get to know me, just as I will have to get to know her again.

I've lost so much time with her. Staying behind seems like wasting even more of the precious time I've missed with her. But I also know that King could very well have laid a trap for us. I could put everyone in jeopardy if I go.

"I taught you everything you know, Red. You know this is the right call," Dax's gruff voice breaks me out of my spiraling thoughts.

"I know it is," I say quietly, spinning in a circle to face them all. "I'll stay behind, but I want you to call me as soon as you have an update. I'm going to continue to spiral until I hear from you. Don't make me wait until you get back here."

"Actually, I think I have a better idea," Royal says. "Ella, can you take the girls to Twisted? They can stay downstairs or in your office. That way you're closer to us, and I'll send some of our men just in case anything happens."

"Of course. Whatever you need. Should I close today?"

"No, we don't want to raise any suspicions. Business as usual. Raena and Snow can just stay out of sight," Royal tells her, pulling me into his arms and kissing my forehead. "I will keep you updated. I promise. We will get all the information and make a decision together."

"I trust you, Royal. I trust all of you. With my life and my daughters'. Just promise me one thing. If you see a safe opening, get her out of there."

Royal picks me up, crading me to his rock-hard body before whispering into my hair.

"I promise, Angel."

***

"Oh my God! Raena LeRoux. I thought I'd never see you again," Ella's mom says as she closes the office door behind her, tears filling her crystal-blue eyes that match her daughters.

"Mrs. Stone! It's so good to see you," I tell her, letting her pull me into a crushing hug that rivals both Ella and Snow in intensity.

"Ella just told me you were back. I'm so sorry about your Grams. She was a beautiful soul," she says when she pulls back to smooth my hair down like she has done many times in my childhood.

Mrs. Stone was more of a mother figure than mine ever was. Growing up, I had both her and my Grams to give me the motherly guidance I was lacking from my own mom.

"She definitely was. Thank you. Ella told me about Mr. Stone, I'm so sorry. He was an amazing man," I tell her, hoping my eyes show how sincerely I mean that. Ella has been telling me how much of a hard time her mom has had grieving the past year.

"He was," she says, a look of guilt flashing across her face so quickly I could have imagined it before she shakes her head. "Two amazing people, gone before their time. It's heartbreaking…" Her voice trails off as she gathers herself. "But enough with the sadness for now. Let me make you two some food. Is the special still your favorite?"

"Thank you. The special is perfect," I tell her, my voice breaking a bit. Snow nods, smiling at Mrs. Stone as she leaves the office.

Blowing out a breath, I take a seat on the couch once again, gripping the phone with my life and willing it to ring. The guys dropped us off here about an hour ago.

The GPS coordinates said the location was about 20 minutes outside of town. My leg bounces with anxious energy while my mind races with every possible bad outcome that could happen.

"Red," Snow says, sitting next to me, her hand stills my furious bouncing. "You're going to make yourself sick with worry. You know the guys will update us as soon as they have something. Why don't you tell me about those gorgeous Shadow men you've been hiding out with?"

I'm thankful for the distraction, even if this subject is a hard one, also. Blowing out a nervous breath, I tell her everything.

"I don't even know where to begin, Snow. I've never felt like this for anyone. I've never even been in a relationship with one man, let alone three at the same time. But it's like I have this pull to each of them. Picking one of them isn't even an option. The connection I feel with them, it feels like... like fate. Like our souls are tethered to each other. I know it sounds crazy. I sound crazy. We haven't even known each other very long..." I trail off, unable to explain this weird connection I have with them. "I know I sound batshit crazy."

"Actually," she says, giving me a warm smile, "it sounds like how I feel about my Huntsmen. I could never choose between them. What I share with each of them, the connections we have individually and as a family, it transcends love. It's special– not everyone will get it or even understand it, but I do. I am happy for you, Red. After everything you've suffered, everything you survived, you deserve a love that sets your soul on fire. A love that consumes you. And if you've found that, don't question it. Embrace it. Even if it scares you."

Tears prick the backs of my eyes as I listen to her. If anyone could relate, it's Snow.

"Thank you. I thought I would be alone for the rest of my life. Now I have a family I never knew I needed. I just want to get my daughter back and start our lives together. I want King to die for what he has done, and then I never want to look back. He has stolen so much from me. I won't allow him to steal another minute of my future with my family."

"Then, that's what we'll make happen, Red. You're not alone in this anymore. You have people to lean on, to fight this fight with you," she tells me, patting my leg as she stands to her feet.

"We aren't nearly done talking about this, I want all the juicy details of what you've been up to, but first, I really need to find the bathroom," she says, holding her stomach.

"Are you okay?" I ask, concerned.

"Well, this isn't how I wanted to tell you, but I'm pregnant. And this little one is not being very kind to my bladder," she says, pointing to her stomach.

"Oh my God. Snow! I'm so happy for you. You're going to be a wonderful mother," I tell her as I stand up and pull her into a hug. She is really going to be an amazing mom. She just has this nurturing aura about her. "Are the guys excited? Wait, which one is the father?"

"Thank you. Yes, they are all over the moon. And overprotective. And overbearing. This is one of the main reasons Ro was so concerned about me staying behind with you."

"I mean, I can't really blame him, though," I tell her, smirking at her complaints.

"I know. That's why I didn't protest. I wouldn't forgive myself if something happened," she says, walking to the door. She stops short just before opening it. "And as far as who the father is, we've decided we don't want to know. Any children we have will know that they have three amazing fathers in their life, and they will probably hate that at one point or another."

"If this baby is a girl, bless her little heart. She will probably never have a boyfriend," I laugh.

"Just wait. You already have a little girl, and those men of yours will be just as bad as mine— I can already tell," she laughs right back at me before slipping out of the room and closing the door behind her.

A goofy grin spreads across my face when I think about Emera being a teenager. Any boy who dares approach her when she's old enough to date will need balls of steel to face off with my Shadow men.

I turn around, walking back to the couch when I hear the door opening and close again.

"Well that was quick. You didn't find it?" I ask, finally turning around to sit back down.

The phone I've been clutching for the last hour clatters to the floor as I gasp in shock. It's not Snow standing just inside the door. It's the last person I ever expected to see again.

"Hello Raena."

She moves towards me with her head tilted to the side, looking me up and down with disgust. My entire body is rooted to the floor, frozen in place. "I'm sorry it came to this."

"Come to what? What are you doing here? I thought you were dead?" My words are rushed and barely above a whisper. My throat feels like it's clogged with a strange emotion as she stops in front of me.

Her emerald green eyes, so similar to mine, stare coldly into me like she is looking straight through me. Her pupils are blown wide open, her entire body shaking with whatever drugs she took.

The shock of seeing her after all this time begins to wear off, and I try to step back, but her hand darts out faster than I thought she'd be capable of in her inebriated state.

"I'm sorry, Raena," is all she says as something sharp pricks my neck.

My hand shoots up to grasp whatever she stuck in me, pulling out a syringe. It clatters to the floor as I stumble back, my balance unsteady. She grabs onto my arms, pulling me into her. The edges of my vision darken as her blurry face comes to mine.

"Take her."

Her voice echoes around in my skull, fading in and out as I struggle to stay conscious. I barely have time to acknowledge that we are no longer alone when a man's strong arms grab me, throwing me over their shoulder.

My eyes find hers once again as he carries me towards the door. My vision is swimming in almost all black now, making me sick as I try and fail to push off the man.

With the last ounce of strength in my body, I call out to her, but it's barely a whisper as I fade into darkness.

"Mom."

Do you need a ride to therapy?

Are you okay? Do you need a hug? Or an emotional support tittie?

Hopefully, that cliffy didn't leave you too traumatized. If it did, and you want to yell at me for it, or rant to others who feel the same, you can find me hanging out in our Good Girls Discord. Raena and her Shadow's aren't done with you yet!

! Book 2 in this duet is underway !

Follow Me on social media for updates! Scan the code!

If you loved this story as much as me, you should consider joining my Street or ARC Team for the next one! Sign-ups will be posted on my socials when they open, and spots are limited for early access!!

As I said at the beginning of this book, this duet is just the beginning. I have BIG PLANS for the future of the Grimm River Series. There are more fairytales and most importantly… more deliciously dark men to ruin your panties. *I told you not to wear them!*

I hope you enjoyed this story. If you did, ***please consider leaving a review*** on Amazon, Goodreads, TikTok, etc… or wherever you prefer to review! Indie Authors, especially baby ones such as myself, rely on word of mouth recommendation in the bookish community to spread the word about their work. Your support means the world to us!

If you share on social media, please tag me! I enjoy connecting with my readers and hearing your thoughts! I'll even let you yell at me about the cliffhanger on it if you want!

So listen… I am a BABY Indie Author. There will probably be mistakes in this book that were missed along the way. If that's the case, please email me at agoodgirlsbookclub@gmail.com and I will fix any issues!

About the Author

Heather Beal lives in a small town in Mississippi with her husband, three children and nine dogs. Yes! You read that correctly, she has seven Yorkies, a Labradoodle, and a rescue Pit Bull. Her passion for reading started early in life, reading 'Fabio' spicy books way too young. She started writing in middle school, filling up spiral bound notebooks with romance stories that were way too detailed for an adolescent. In high school, she went through a traumatic experience that no woman should ever have to endure and used writing to cope. The story of her trauma was published by Mississippi Gulf Coast Community College and she decided it was time to get back to her own dreams.

Her writing embodies her favorite aspects of the books she enjoys. So you'll find dark romance with lots of trigger warnings inside her books. Be sure to follow her on social media to stay up to date on what she's writing and reading!

–XOXO

Made in the USA
Columbia, SC
02 July 2024